WARM BLOOD

WARM BLOOD

BOOK ONE

written by JOSH TIERNEY
cover art & penny design by AFU CHAN
logo design by GIANNIS MILONOGIANNIS
book design by SHANNA MATUSZAK

— illustrators listed in order of appearance —

CHAPTER ONE: FIGURES
Saskia Gutekunst, Joysuke, Winston Young,
Naomi Franquiz, Marina Julia, Atelier Sentô

CHAPTER TWO: VISITOR
Jane Bak, Vlad Gusev, e jackson,
Leiana Nitura, Blakely Inberg, Eva Eskelinen

CHAPTER THREE: SLUMBER
Cleonique Hilsaca, Thomas Rouzière, F. Choo,
Sandrine Han Jin Kuang, Mathilde Kitteh, Shanen Pae

CHAPTER FOUR: ALLOWANCES
Stephen Rodgers, Sara DuVall, Cat Sukiman,
Xulia Vicente, Nuno Plati, Heikala

CHAPTER FIVE: ANSWERS
Crista Castro, Irma Kniivila, Stephanie Son,
Cristina Rose Chua, María Ponce Esparcia, Kat Lyons

PENNY'S ROOM SHORTS
Gaby Epstein, nims, Atelier Sentô

PINUPS
Afu Chan, Marina Julia, Joysuke, Ken Niimura

Buño Publishing, LLC.
Storme Smith: Publisher
Ulises Farinas: Chief Creative Officer
Melody Often: Vice President of Marketing
BUNOBOOKS.COM

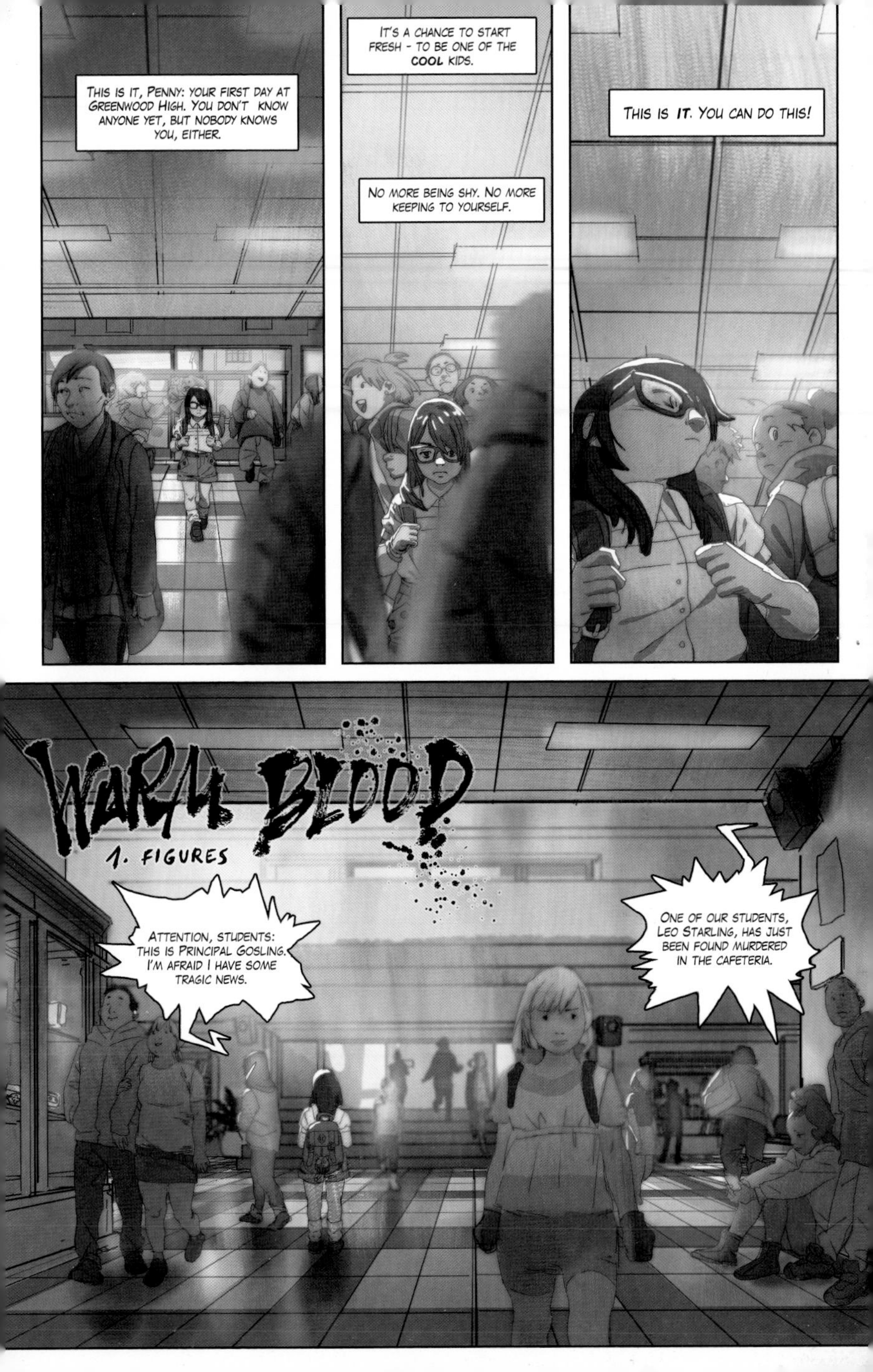
This is it, Penny: your first day at Greenwood High. You don't know anyone yet, but nobody knows you, either.
It's a chance to start fresh - to be one of the **cool** kids.
No more being shy. No more keeping to yourself.
This is **it**. You can do this!
Warm Blood
1. Figures
Attention, students: this is Principal Gosling. I'm afraid I have some tragic news.
One of our students, Leo Starling, has just been found murdered in the cafeteria.

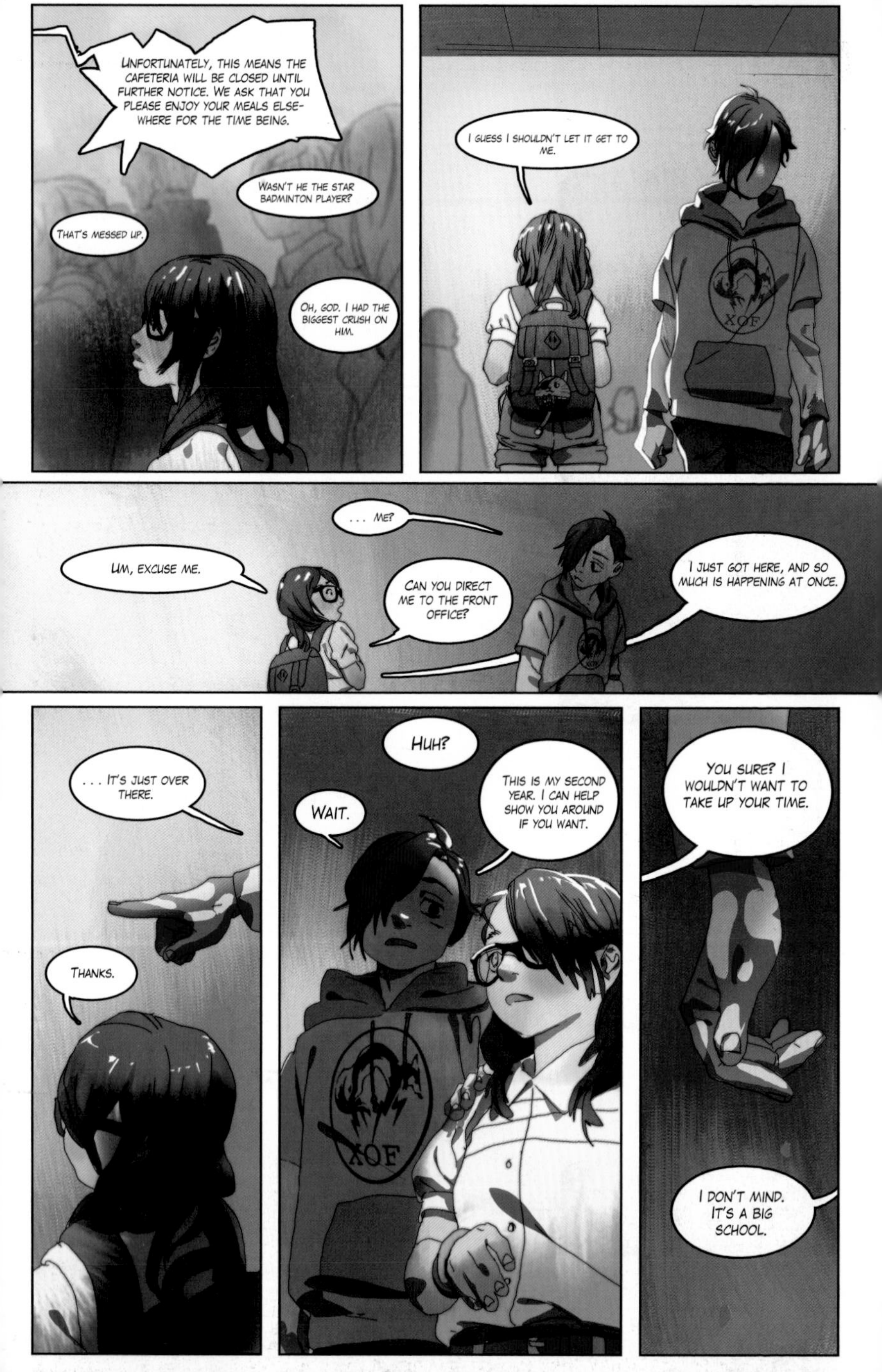
UNFORTUNATELY, THIS MEANS THE CAFETERIA WILL BE CLOSED UNTIL FURTHER NOTICE. WE ASK THAT YOU PLEASE ENJOY YOUR MEALS ELSE-WHERE FOR THE TIME BEING.
WASN'T HE THE STAR BADMINTON PLAYER?
THAT'S MESSED UP.
OH, GOD. I HAD THE BIGGEST CRUSH ON HIM.
I GUESS I SHOULDN'T LET IT GET TO ME.
UM, EXCUSE ME.
. . . ME?
CAN YOU DIRECT ME TO THE FRONT OFFICE?
I JUST GOT HERE, AND SO MUCH IS HAPPENING AT ONCE.
. . . IT'S JUST OVER THERE.
THANKS.
WAIT.
HUH?
THIS IS MY SECOND YEAR. I CAN HELP SHOW YOU AROUND IF YOU WANT.
YOU SURE? I WOULDN'T WANT TO TAKE UP YOUR TIME.
I DON'T MIND. IT'S A BIG SCHOOL.

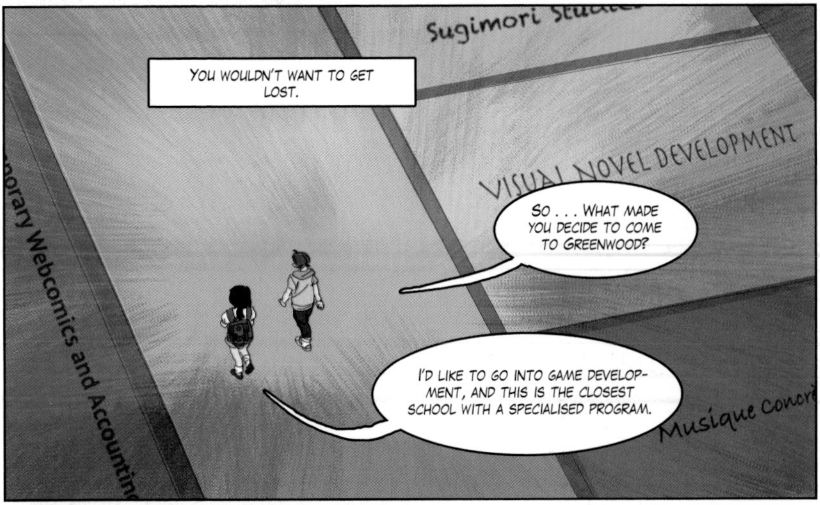
YOU WOULDN'T WANT TO GET LOST.
VISUAL NOVEL DEVELOPMENT
SO . . . WHAT MADE YOU DECIDE TO COME TO GREENWOOD?
I'D LIKE TO GO INTO GAME DEVELOPMENT, AND THIS IS THE CLOSEST SCHOOL WITH A SPECIALISED PROGRAM.

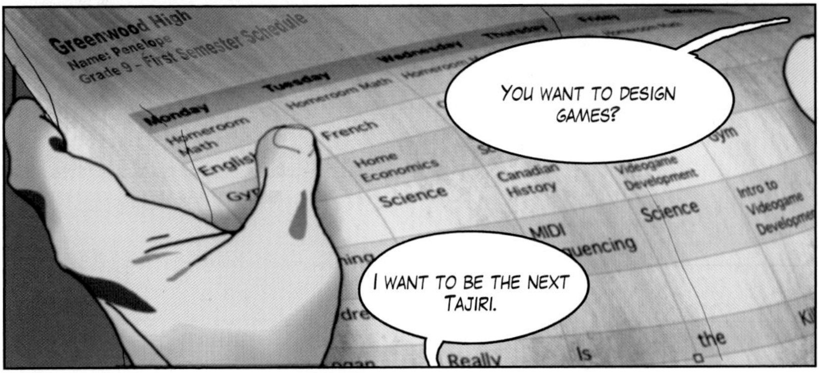
Greenwood High
Name: Penelope
Grade 9 - First Semester Schedule
YOU WANT TO DESIGN GAMES?
I WANT TO BE THE NEXT TAJIRI.

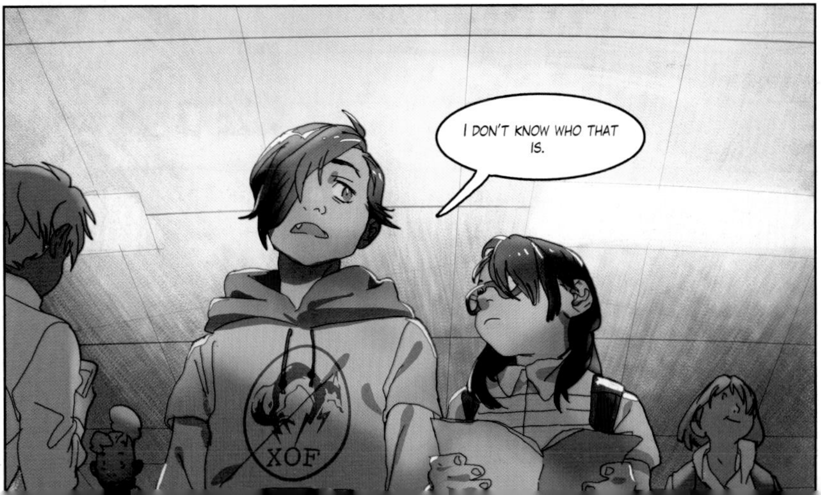
I DON'T KNOW WHO THAT IS.
XOF

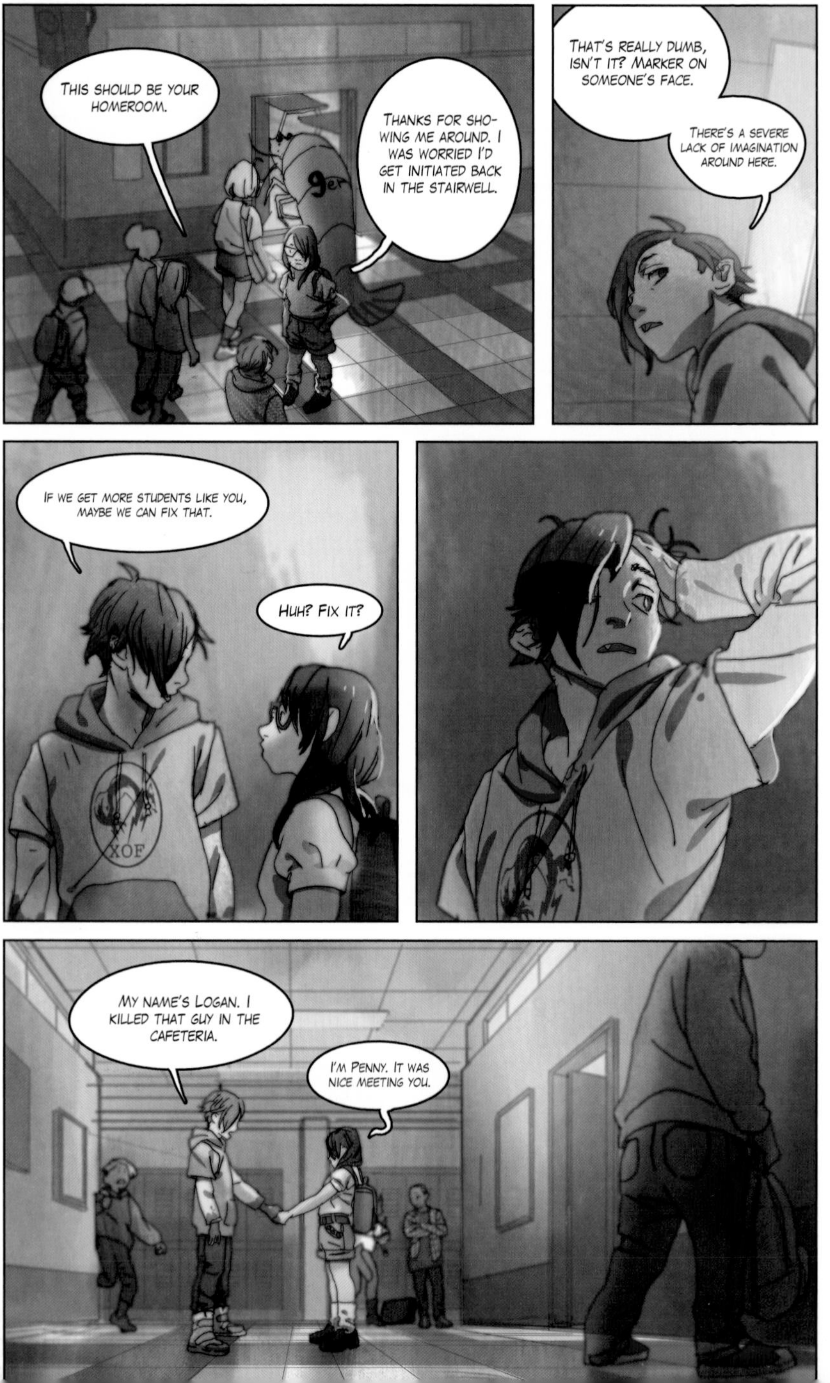
This should be your homeroom.
Thanks for showing me around. I was worried I'd get initiated back in the stairwell.
That's really dumb, isn't it? Marker on someone's face.
There's a severe lack of imagination around here.
If we get more students like you, maybe we can fix that.
XOF
Huh? Fix it?
My name's Logan. I killed that guy in the cafeteria.
I'm Penny. It was nice meeting you.

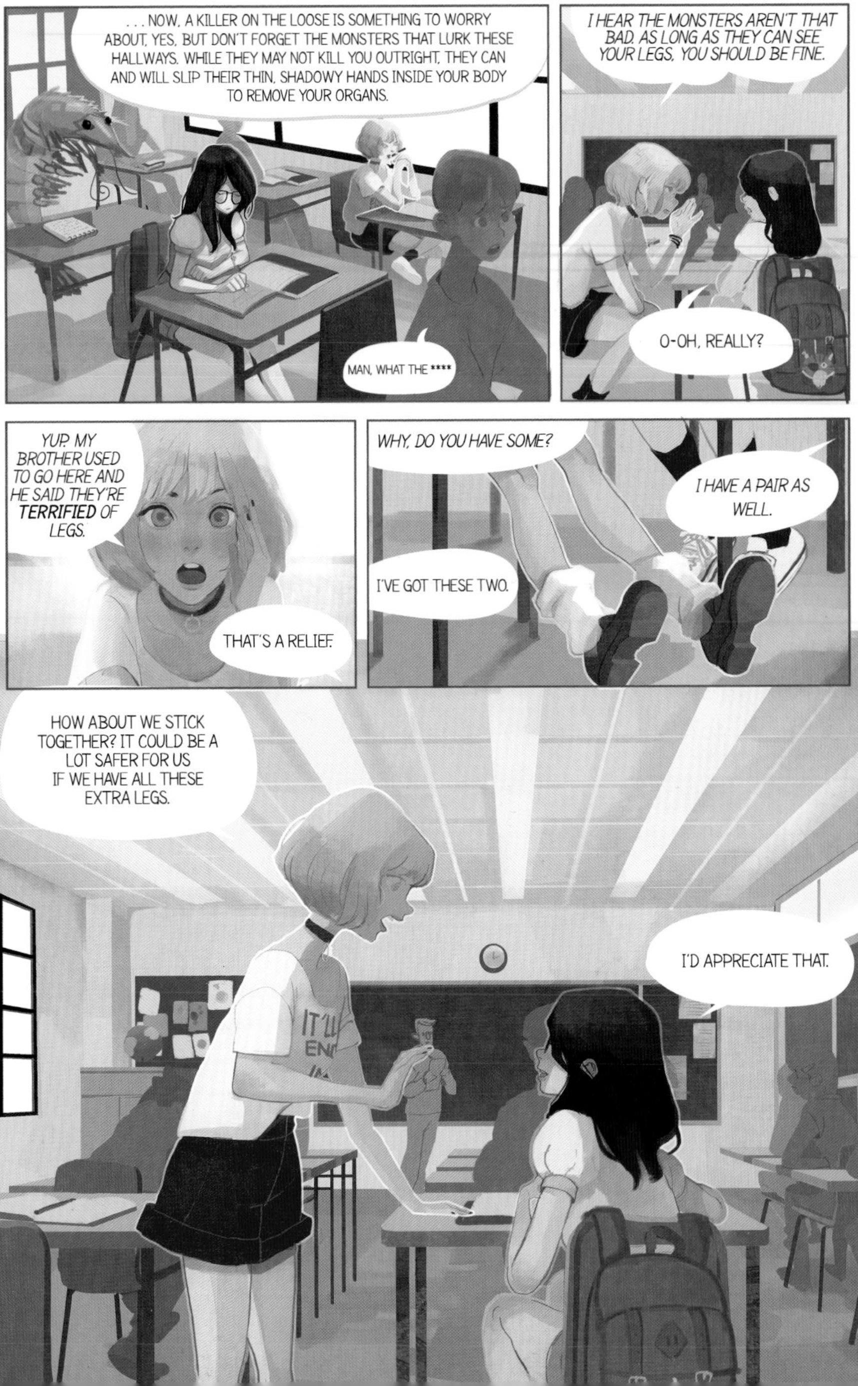
. . . NOW, A KILLER ON THE LOOSE IS SOMETHING TO WORRY ABOUT, YES, BUT DON'T FORGET THE MONSTERS THAT LURK THESE HALLWAYS. WHILE THEY MAY NOT KILL YOU OUTRIGHT, THEY CAN AND WILL SLIP THEIR THIN, SHADOWY HANDS INSIDE YOUR BODY TO REMOVE YOUR ORGANS.
MAN, WHAT THE ****
I HEAR THE MONSTERS AREN'T THAT BAD. AS LONG AS THEY CAN SEE YOUR LEGS, YOU SHOULD BE FINE.
O-OH, REALLY?
YUP. MY BROTHER USED TO GO HERE AND HE SAID THEY'RE **TERRIFIED** OF LEGS.
THAT'S A RELIEF.
WHY, DO YOU HAVE SOME?
I HAVE A PAIR AS WELL.
I'VE GOT THESE TWO.
HOW ABOUT WE STICK TOGETHER? IT COULD BE A LOT SAFER FOR US IF WE HAVE ALL THESE EXTRA LEGS.
I'D APPRECIATE THAT.

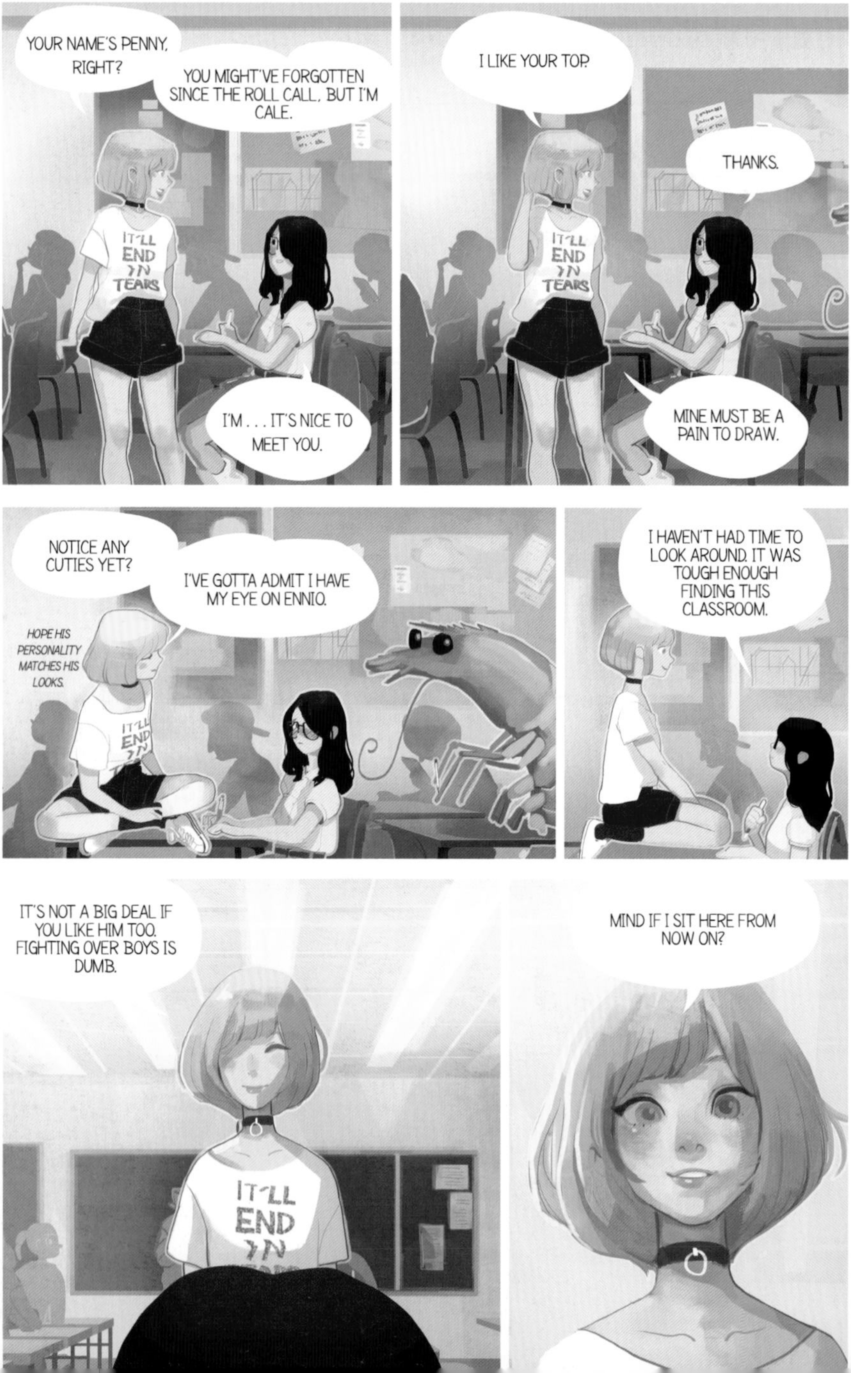
YOUR NAME'S PENNY, RIGHT?
YOU MIGHT'VE FORGOTTEN SINCE THE ROLL CALL, BUT I'M CALE.
IT'LL END IN TEARS
I'M . . . IT'S NICE TO MEET YOU.
I LIKE YOUR TOP.
THANKS.
IT'LL END IN TEARS
MINE MUST BE A PAIN TO DRAW.
NOTICE ANY CUTIES YET?
I'VE GOTTA ADMIT I HAVE MY EYE ON ENNIO.
HOPE HIS PERSONALITY MATCHES HIS LOOKS.
I HAVEN'T HAD TIME TO LOOK AROUND. IT WAS TOUGH ENOUGH FINDING THIS CLASSROOM.
IT'S NOT A BIG DEAL IF YOU LIKE HIM TOO. FIGHTING OVER BOYS IS DUMB.
MIND IF I SIT HERE FROM NOW ON?

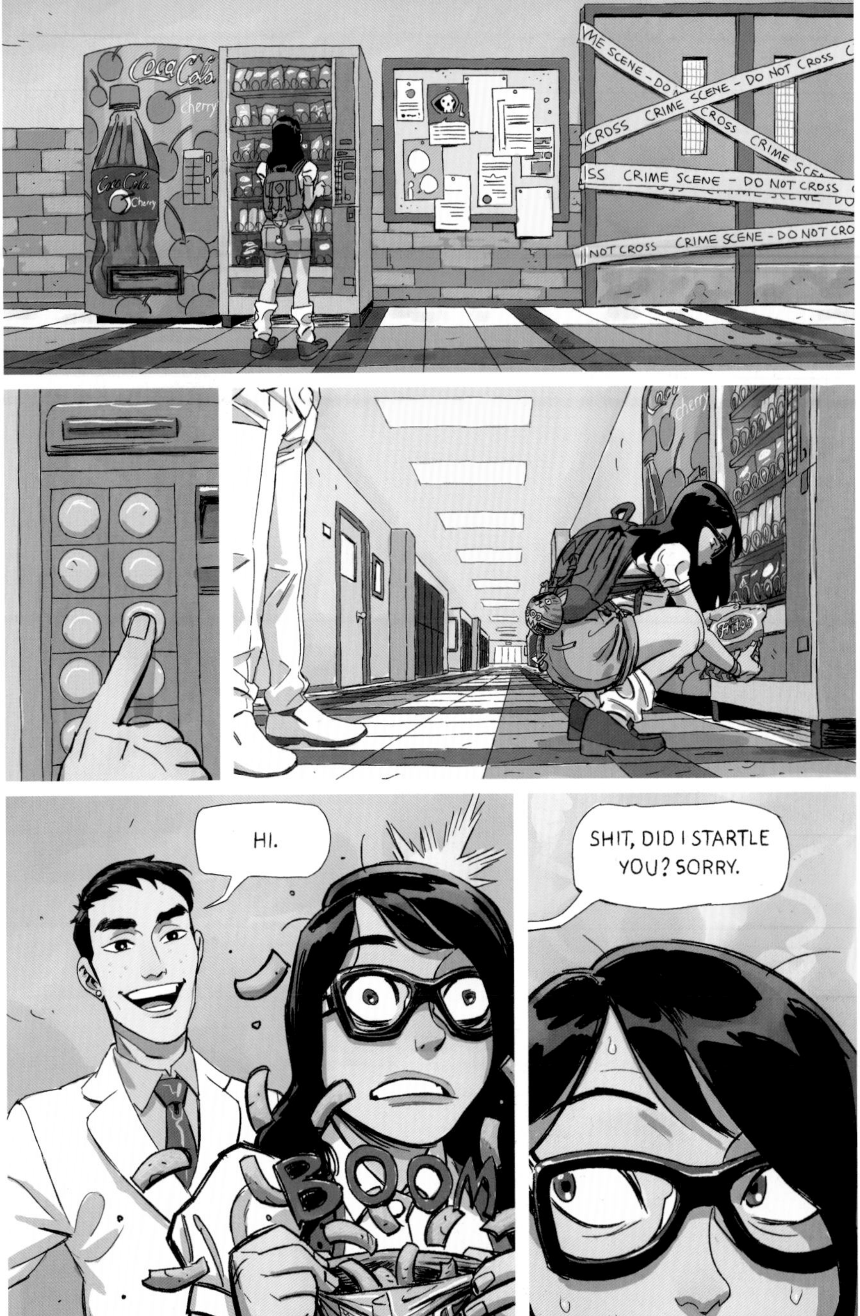
Coca-Cola cherry
Coca-Cola Cherry
CRIME SCENE - DO NOT CROSS
CRIME SCENE - DO NOT CROSS
CRIME SCENE - DO NOT CROSS
NOT CROSS CRIME SCENE - DO NOT CROSS
Fritos
HI.
BOOM
SHIT, DID I STARTLE YOU? SORRY.

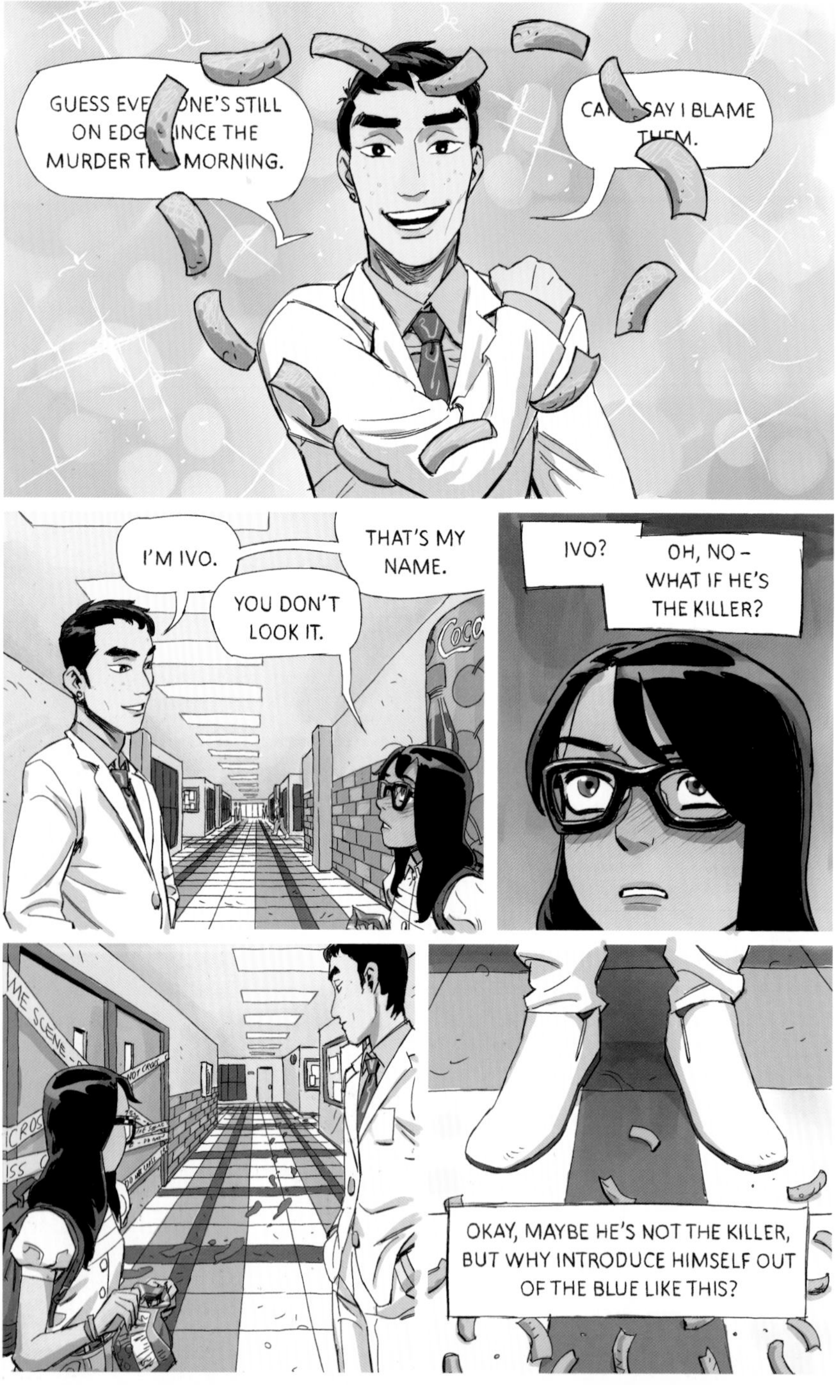
GUESS EVE ONE'S STILL ON EDG INCE THE MURDER T MORNING.
CA SAY I BLAME THEM.
I'M IVO.
THAT'S MY NAME.
YOU DON'T LOOK IT.
IVO?
OH, NO – WHAT IF HE'S THE KILLER?
OKAY, MAYBE HE'S NOT THE KILLER, BUT WHY INTRODUCE HIMSELF OUT OF THE BLUE LIKE THIS?

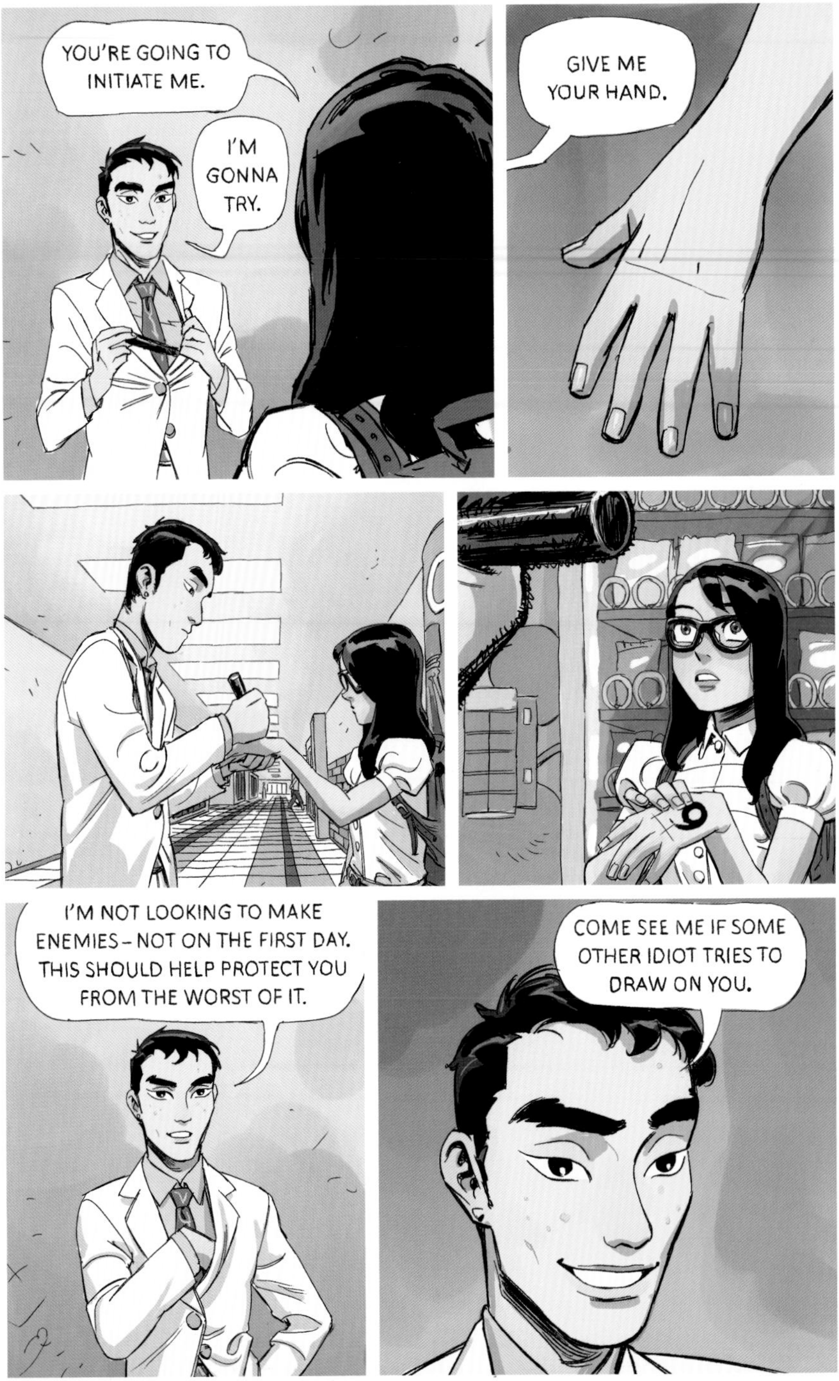
YOU'RE GOING TO INITIATE ME.
I'M GONNA TRY.
GIVE ME YOUR HAND.
I'M NOT LOOKING TO MAKE ENEMIES – NOT ON THE FIRST DAY. THIS SHOULD HELP PROTECT YOU FROM THE WORST OF IT.
COME SEE ME IF SOME OTHER IDIOT TRIES TO DRAW ON YOU.

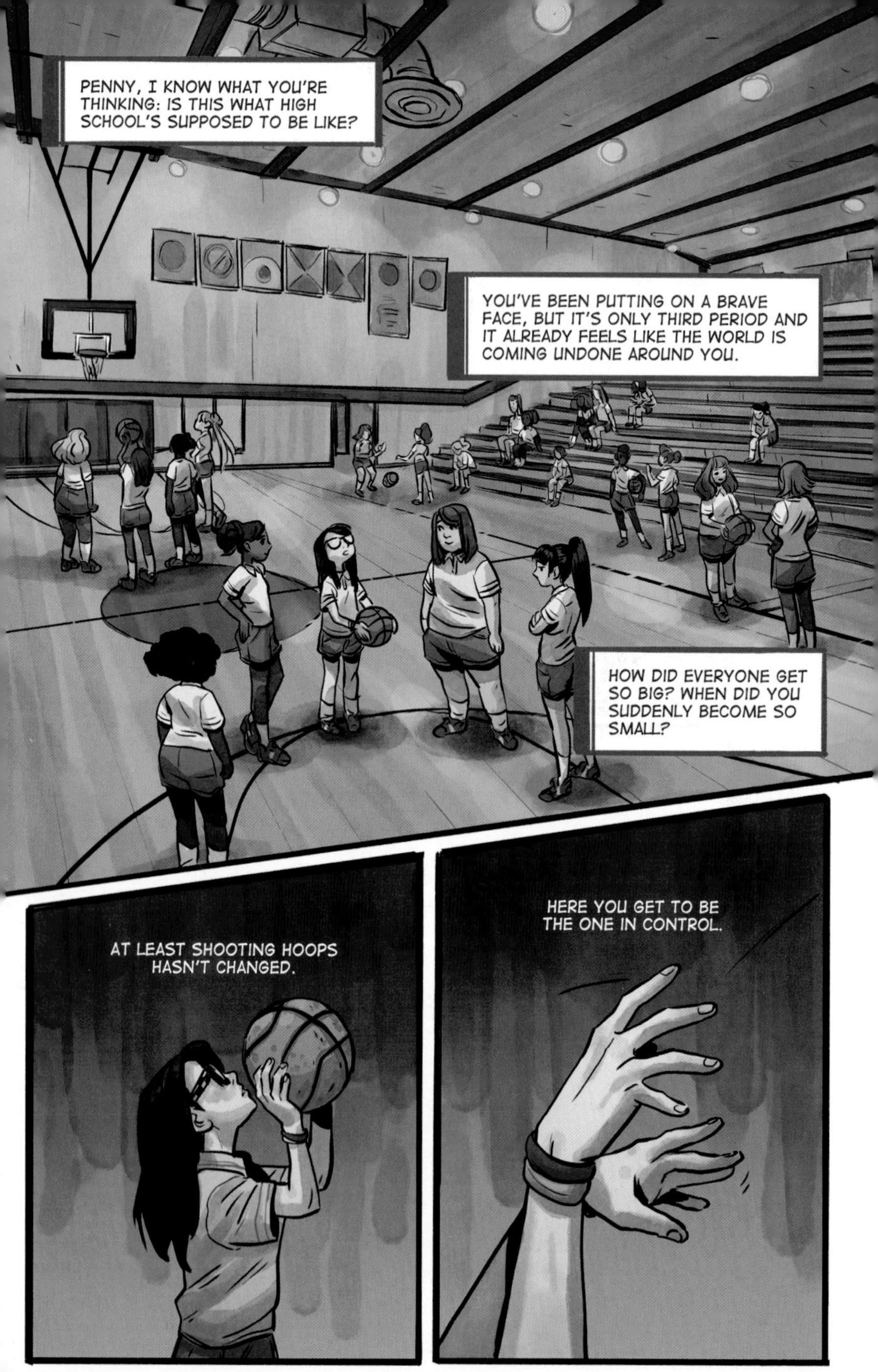
PENNY, I KNOW WHAT YOU'RE THINKING: IS THIS WHAT HIGH SCHOOL'S SUPPOSED TO BE LIKE?
YOU'VE BEEN PUTTING ON A BRAVE FACE, BUT IT'S ONLY THIRD PERIOD AND IT ALREADY FEELS LIKE THE WORLD IS COMING UNDONE AROUND YOU.
HOW DID EVERYONE GET SO BIG? WHEN DID YOU SUDDENLY BECOME SO SMALL?
AT LEAST SHOOTING HOOPS HASN'T CHANGED.
HERE YOU GET TO BE THE ONE IN CONTROL.

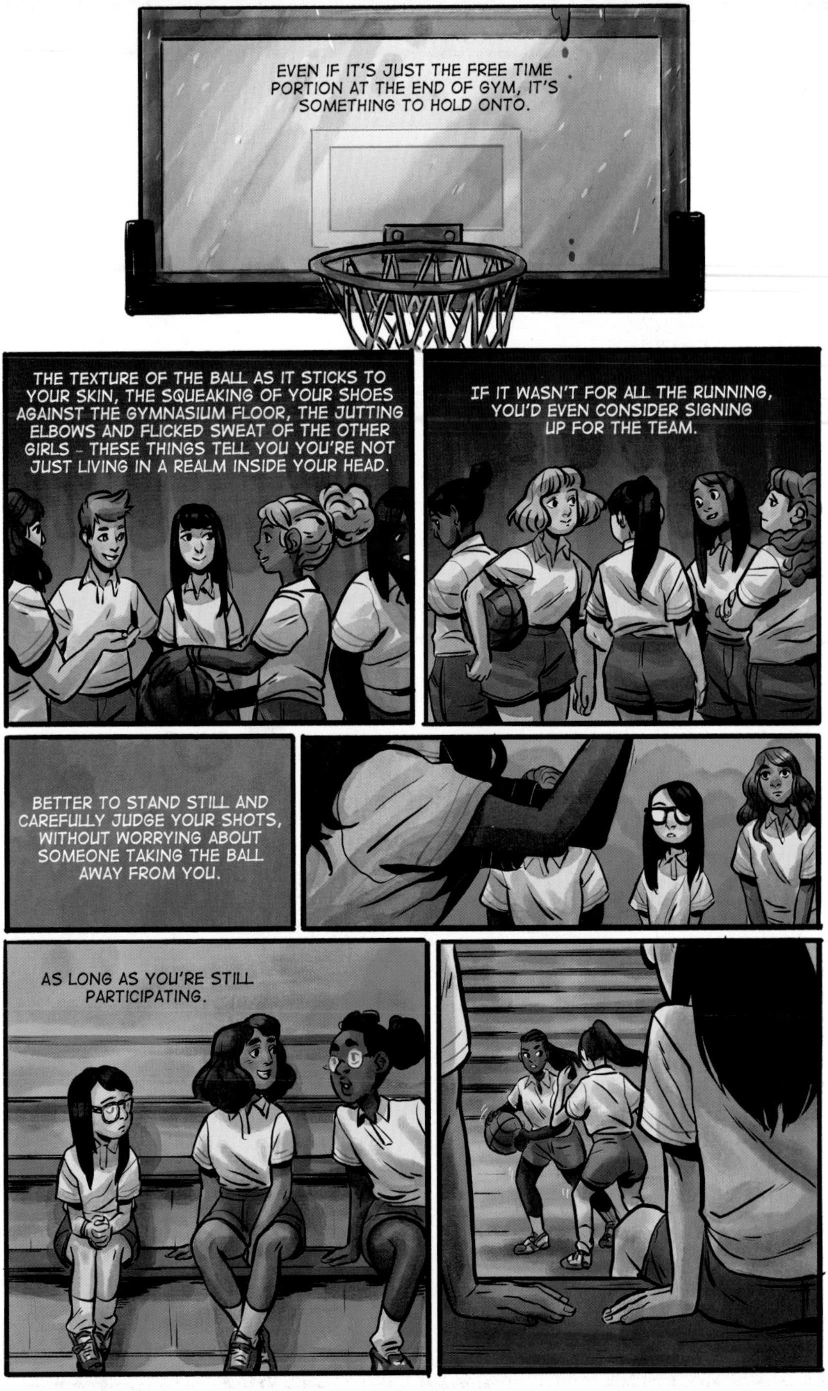
EVEN IF IT'S JUST THE FREE TIME PORTION AT THE END OF GYM, IT'S SOMETHING TO HOLD ONTO.
THE TEXTURE OF THE BALL AS IT STICKS TO YOUR SKIN, THE SQUEAKING OF YOUR SHOES AGAINST THE GYMNASIUM FLOOR, THE JUTTING ELBOWS AND FLICKED SWEAT OF THE OTHER GIRLS - THESE THINGS TELL YOU YOU'RE NOT JUST LIVING IN A REALM INSIDE YOUR HEAD.
IF IT WASN'T FOR ALL THE RUNNING, YOU'D EVEN CONSIDER SIGNING UP FOR THE TEAM.
BETTER TO STAND STILL AND CAREFULLY JUDGE YOUR SHOTS, WITHOUT WORRYING ABOUT SOMEONE TAKING THE BALL AWAY FROM YOU.
AS LONG AS YOU'RE STILL PARTICIPATING.

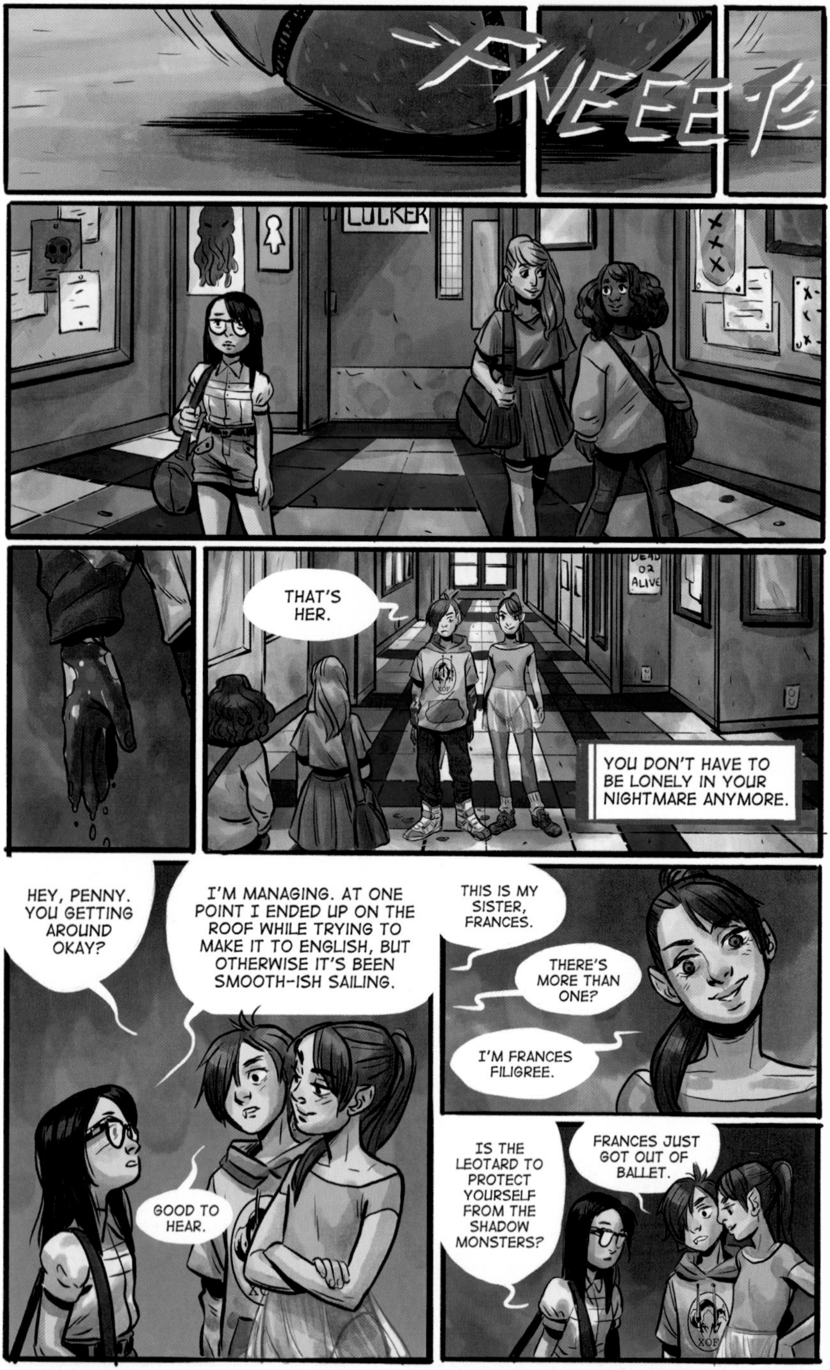
FWEEET
LOCKER
DEAD OR ALIVE
THAT'S HER.
YOU DON'T HAVE TO BE LONELY IN YOUR NIGHTMARE ANYMORE.
HEY, PENNY. YOU GETTING AROUND OKAY?
I'M MANAGING. AT ONE POINT I ENDED UP ON THE ROOF WHILE TRYING TO MAKE IT TO ENGLISH, BUT OTHERWISE IT'S BEEN SMOOTH-ISH SAILING.
GOOD TO HEAR.
THIS IS MY SISTER, FRANCES.
THERE'S MORE THAN ONE?
I'M FRANCES FILIGREE.
IS THE LEOTARD TO PROTECT YOURSELF FROM THE SHADOW MONSTERS?
FRANCES JUST GOT OUT OF BALLET.

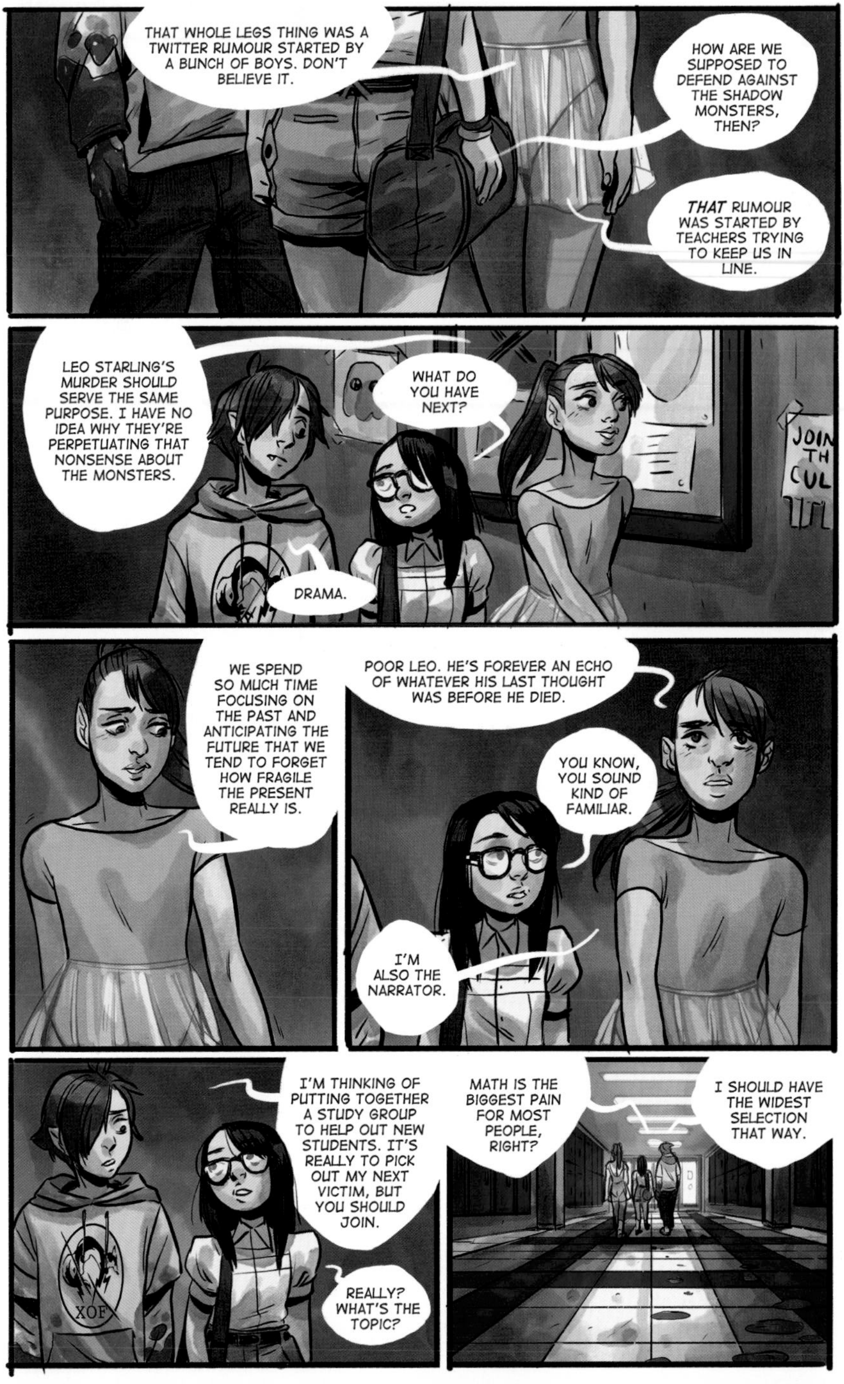
THAT WHOLE LEGS THING WAS A TWITTER RUMOUR STARTED BY A BUNCH OF BOYS. DON'T BELIEVE IT.
HOW ARE WE SUPPOSED TO DEFEND AGAINST THE SHADOW MONSTERS, THEN?
THAT RUMOUR WAS STARTED BY TEACHERS TRYING TO KEEP US IN LINE.
LEO STARLING'S MURDER SHOULD SERVE THE SAME PURPOSE. I HAVE NO IDEA WHY THEY'RE PERPETUATING THAT NONSENSE ABOUT THE MONSTERS.
WHAT DO YOU HAVE NEXT?
DRAMA.
JOIN TH CUL
WE SPEND SO MUCH TIME FOCUSING ON THE PAST AND ANTICIPATING THE FUTURE THAT WE TEND TO FORGET HOW FRAGILE THE PRESENT REALLY IS.
POOR LEO. HE'S FOREVER AN ECHO OF WHATEVER HIS LAST THOUGHT WAS BEFORE HE DIED.
YOU KNOW, YOU SOUND KIND OF FAMILIAR.
I'M ALSO THE NARRATOR.
I'M THINKING OF PUTTING TOGETHER A STUDY GROUP TO HELP OUT NEW STUDENTS. IT'S REALLY TO PICK OUT MY NEXT VICTIM, BUT YOU SHOULD JOIN.
REALLY? WHAT'S THE TOPIC?
XOF
MATH IS THE BIGGEST PAIN FOR MOST PEOPLE, RIGHT?
I SHOULD HAVE THE WIDEST SELECTION THAT WAY.

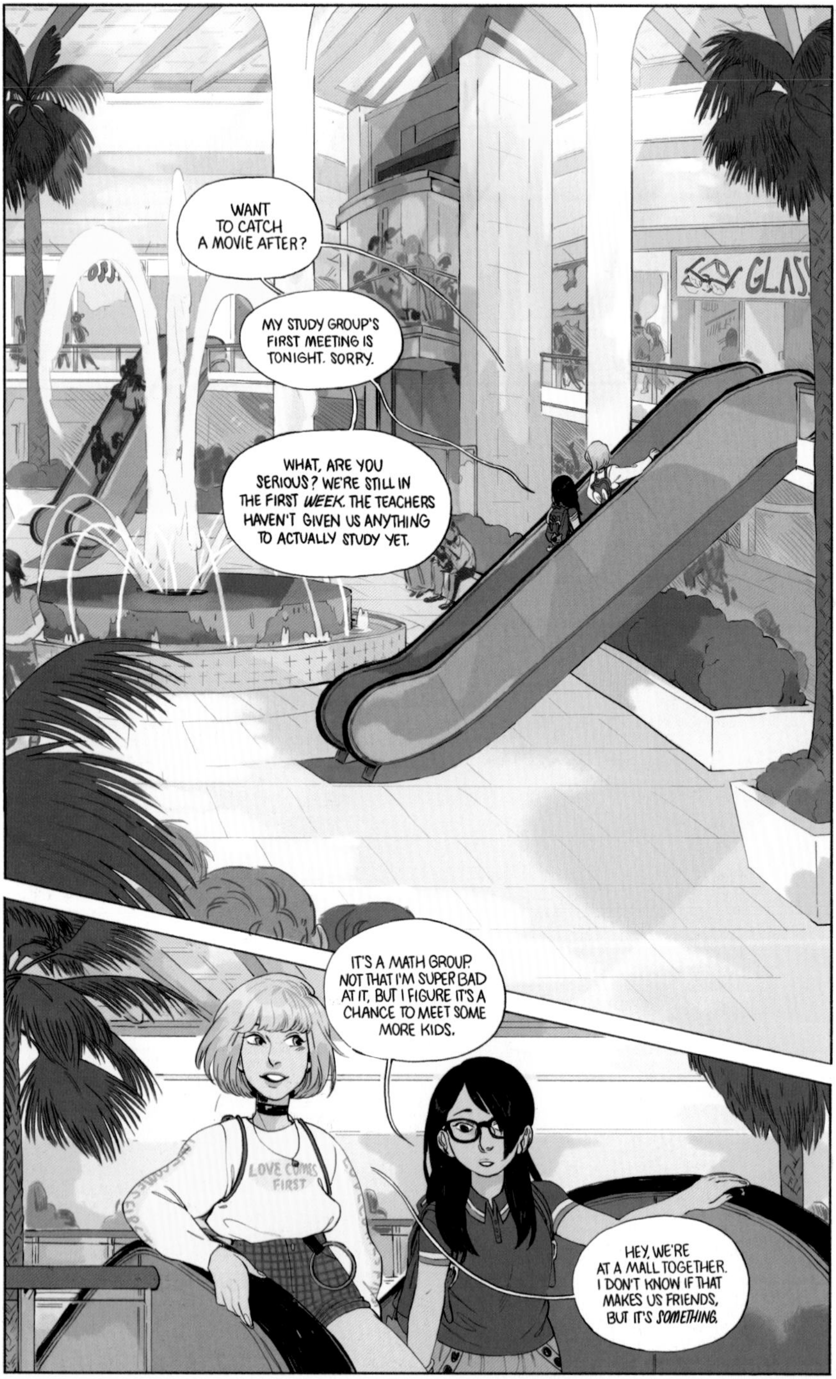
WANT TO CATCH A MOVIE AFTER?
GLASS
MY STUDY GROUP'S FIRST MEETING IS TONIGHT. SORRY.
WHAT, ARE YOU SERIOUS? WE'RE STILL IN THE FIRST *WEEK*. THE TEACHERS HAVEN'T GIVEN US ANYTHING TO ACTUALLY STUDY YET.
IT'S A MATH GROUP. NOT THAT I'M SUPER BAD AT IT, BUT I FIGURE IT'S A CHANCE TO MEET SOME MORE KIDS.
LOVE COMES FIRST
HEY, WE'RE AT A MALL TOGETHER. I DON'T KNOW IF THAT MAKES US FRIENDS, BUT IT'S *SOMETHING*.

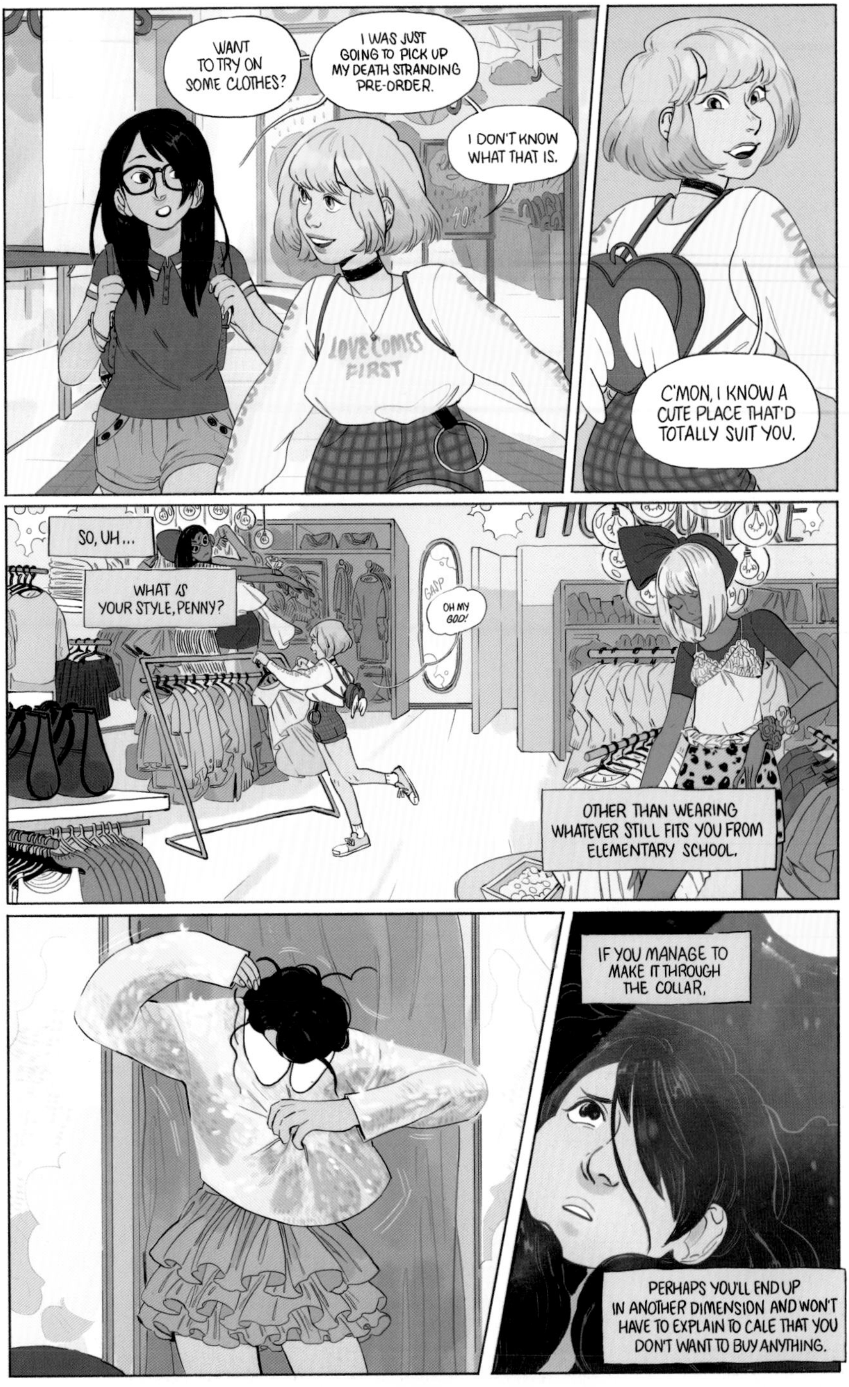
WANT TO TRY ON SOME CLOTHES?
I WAS JUST GOING TO PICK UP MY DEATH STRANDING PRE-ORDER.
I DON'T KNOW WHAT THAT IS.
LOVE COMES FIRST
C'MON, I KNOW A CUTE PLACE THAT'D TOTALLY SUIT YOU.
SO, UH...
WHAT IS YOUR STYLE, PENNY?
GASP
OH MY GOD!
OTHER THAN WEARING WHATEVER STILL FITS YOU FROM ELEMENTARY SCHOOL.
IF YOU MANAGE TO MAKE IT THROUGH THE COLLAR,
PERHAPS YOU'LL END UP IN ANOTHER DIMENSION AND WON'T HAVE TO EXPLAIN TO CALE THAT YOU DON'T WANT TO BUY ANYTHING.

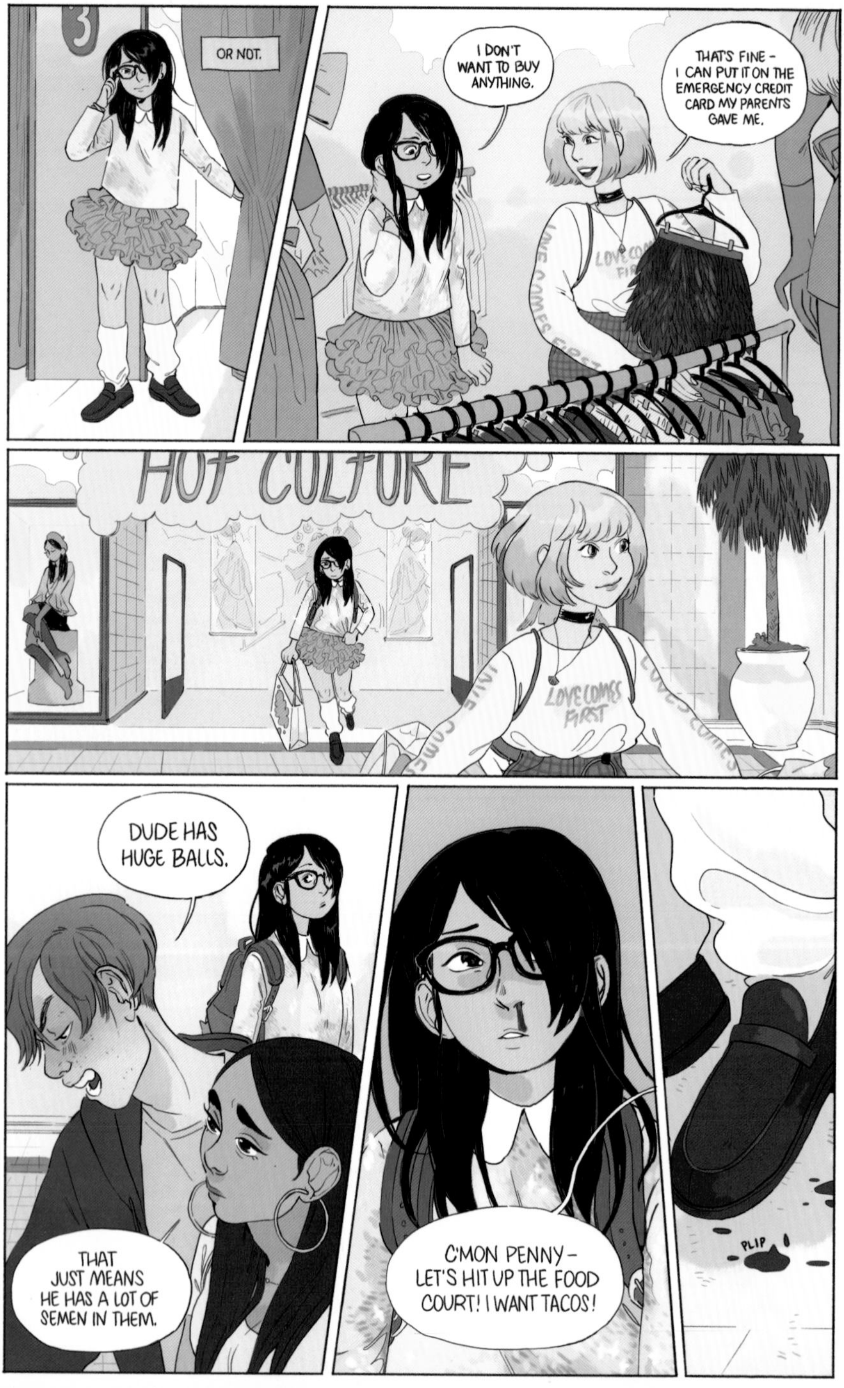
OR NOT.
I DON'T WANT TO BUY ANYTHING.
THAT'S FINE - I CAN PUT IT ON THE EMERGENCY CREDIT CARD MY PARENTS GAVE ME.
LOVE COMES FIRST
HOT CULTURE
LOVE COMES FIRST
DUDE HAS HUGE BALLS.
THAT JUST MEANS HE HAS A LOT OF SEMEN IN THEM.
C'MON PENNY - LET'S HIT UP THE FOOD COURT! I WANT TACOS!
PLIP

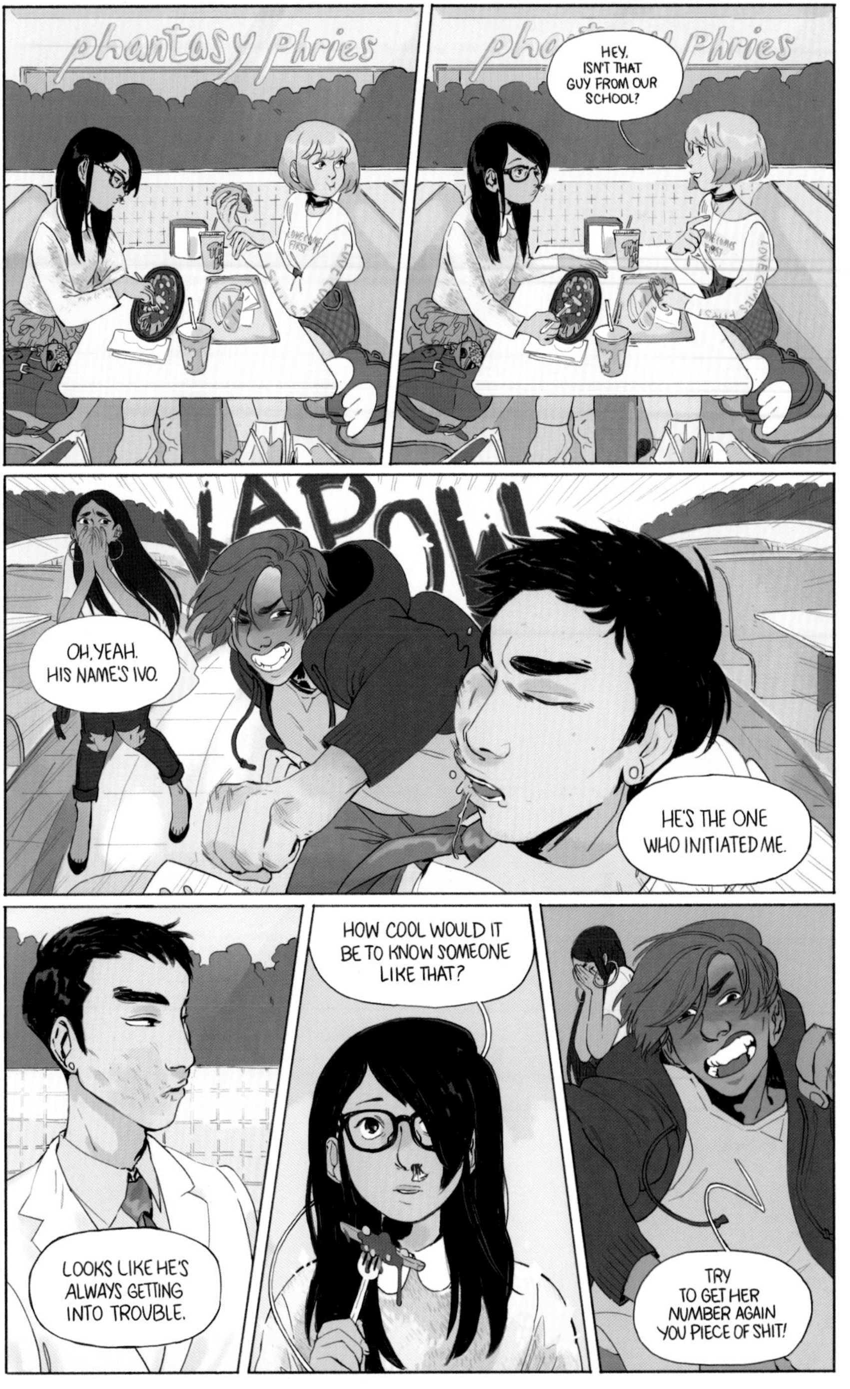
phantasy phries
phantasy phries
HEY, ISN'T THAT GUY FROM OUR SCHOOL?
KAPOW
OH, YEAH. HIS NAME'S IVO.
HE'S THE ONE WHO INITIATED ME.
LOOKS LIKE HE'S ALWAYS GETTING INTO TROUBLE.
HOW COOL WOULD IT BE TO KNOW SOMEONE LIKE THAT?
TRY TO GET HER NUMBER AGAIN YOU PIECE OF SHIT!

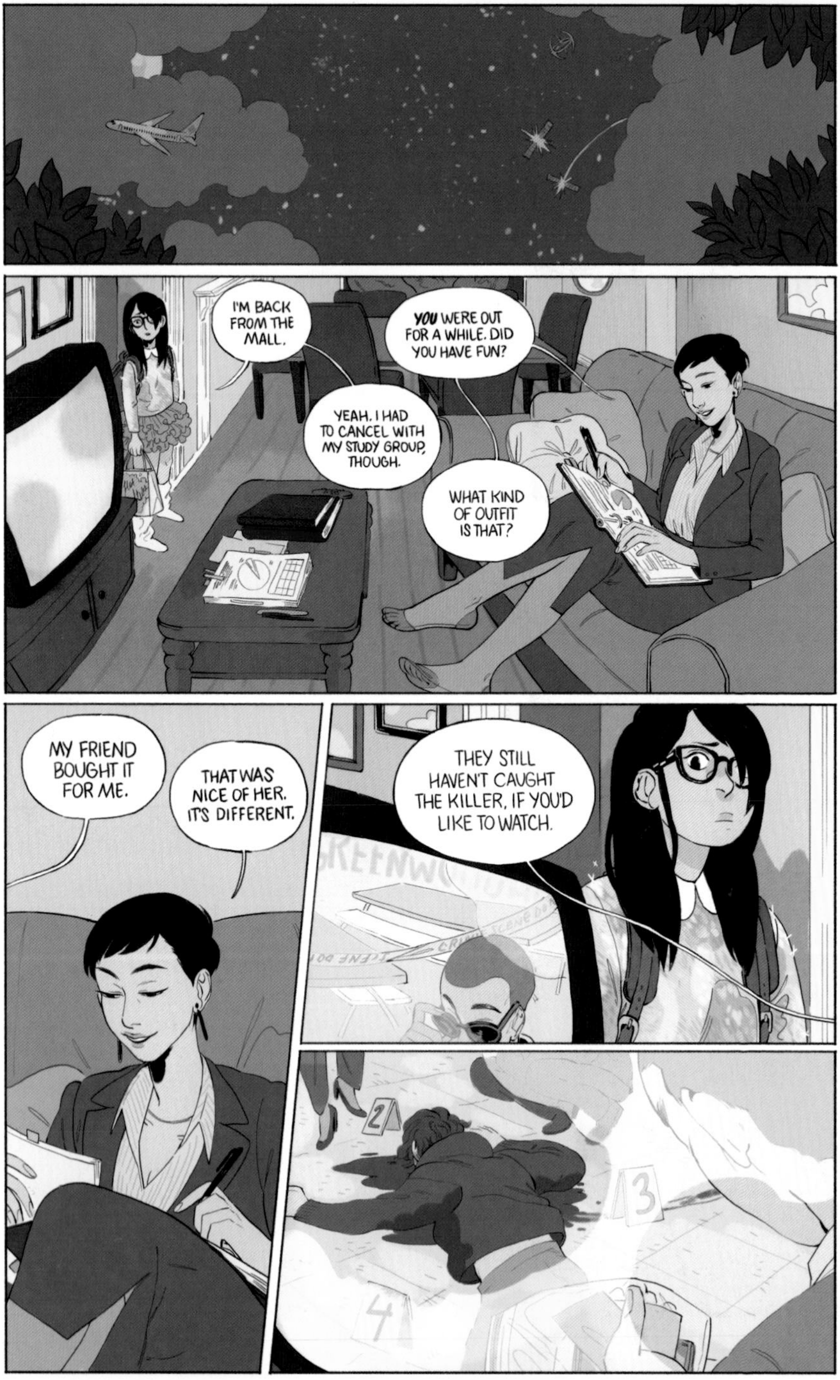
I'M BACK FROM THE MALL.
YOU WERE OUT FOR A WHILE. DID YOU HAVE FUN?
YEAH. I HAD TO CANCEL WITH MY STUDY GROUP, THOUGH.
WHAT KIND OF OUTFIT IS THAT?
MY FRIEND BOUGHT IT FOR ME.
THAT WAS NICE OF HER. IT'S DIFFERENT.
THEY STILL HAVEN'T CAUGHT THE KILLER, IF YOU'D LIKE TO WATCH.
2
3
4

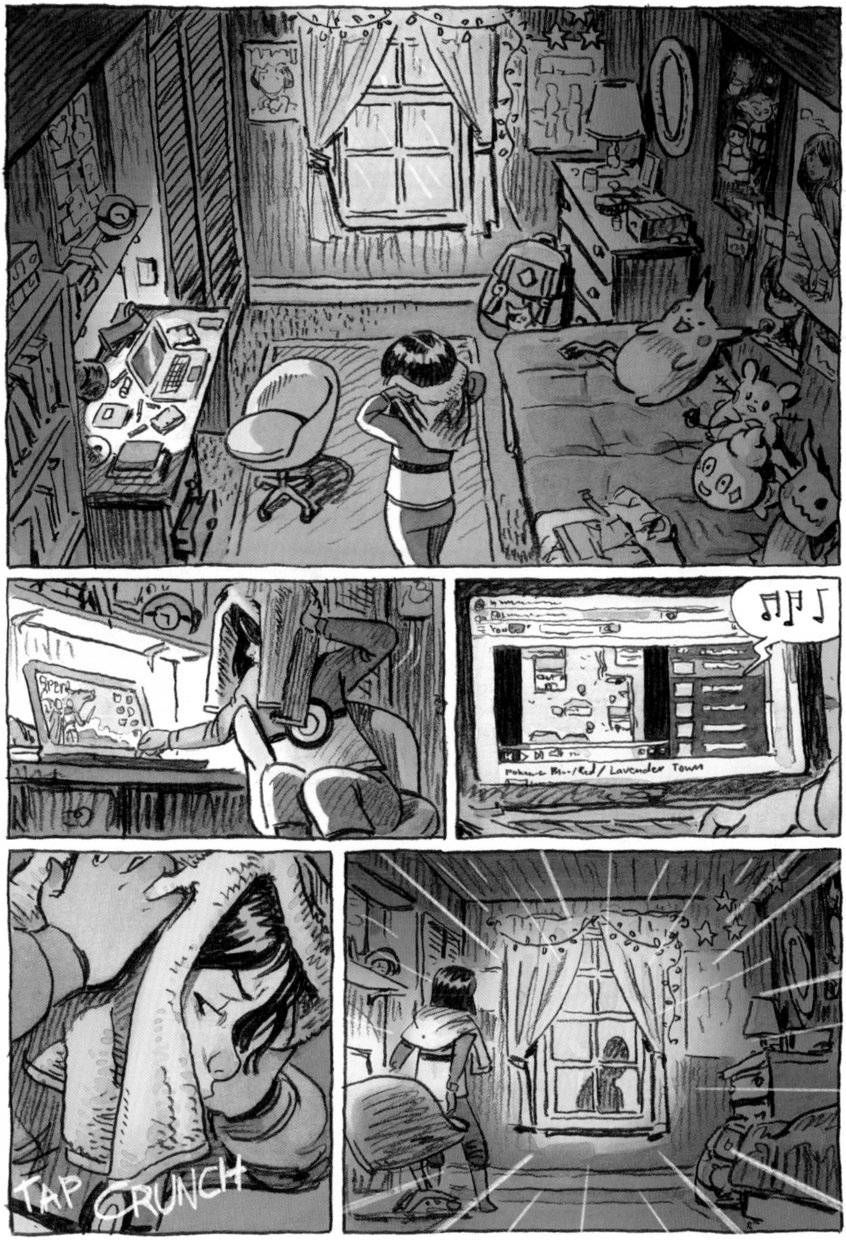
Lavender Town
TAP
CRUNCH

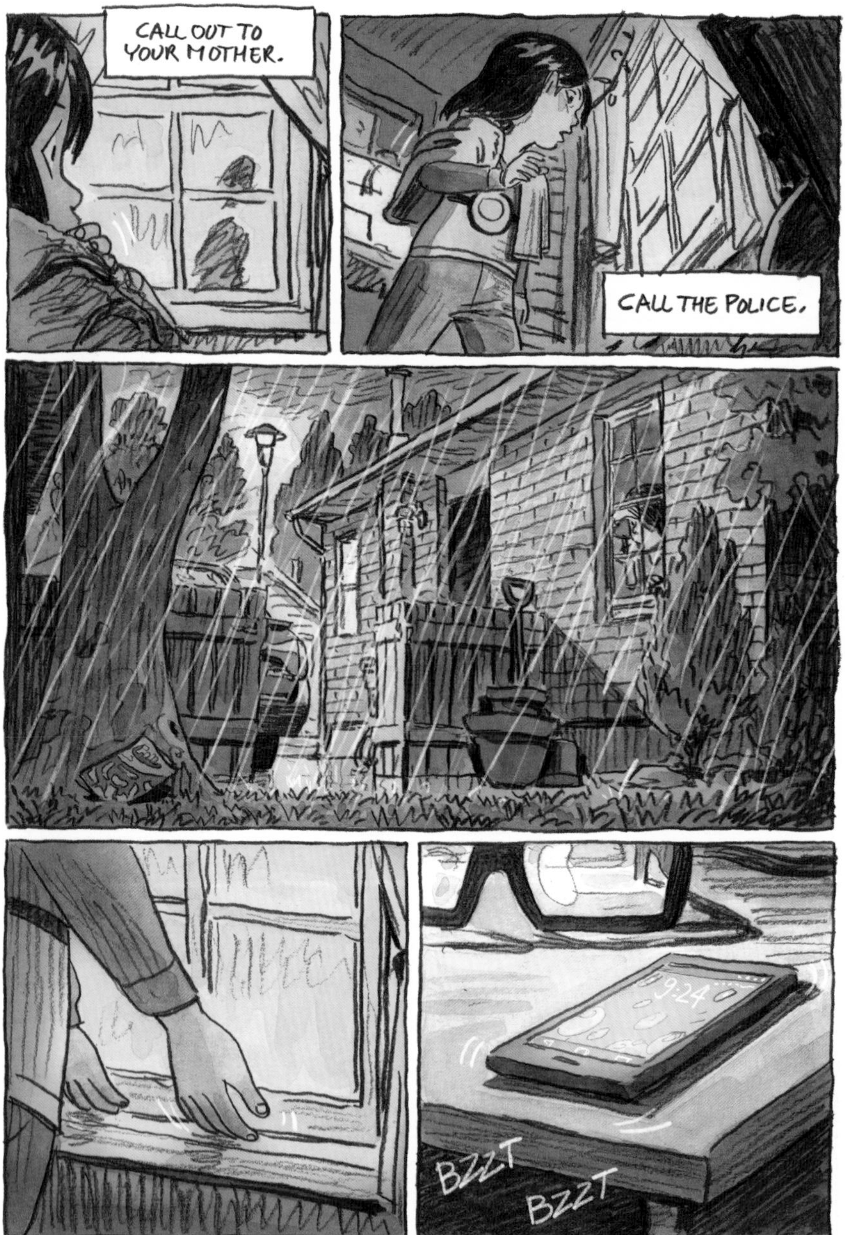
CALL OUT TO YOUR MOTHER.
CALL THE POLICE.
9:24
BZZT
BZZT

CALE

Penny! Have you heard?

It's been going around everywhere. Ivo's been

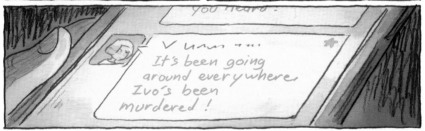

It's been going around everywhere. Ivo's been murdered!

T·CHAC

MOM!

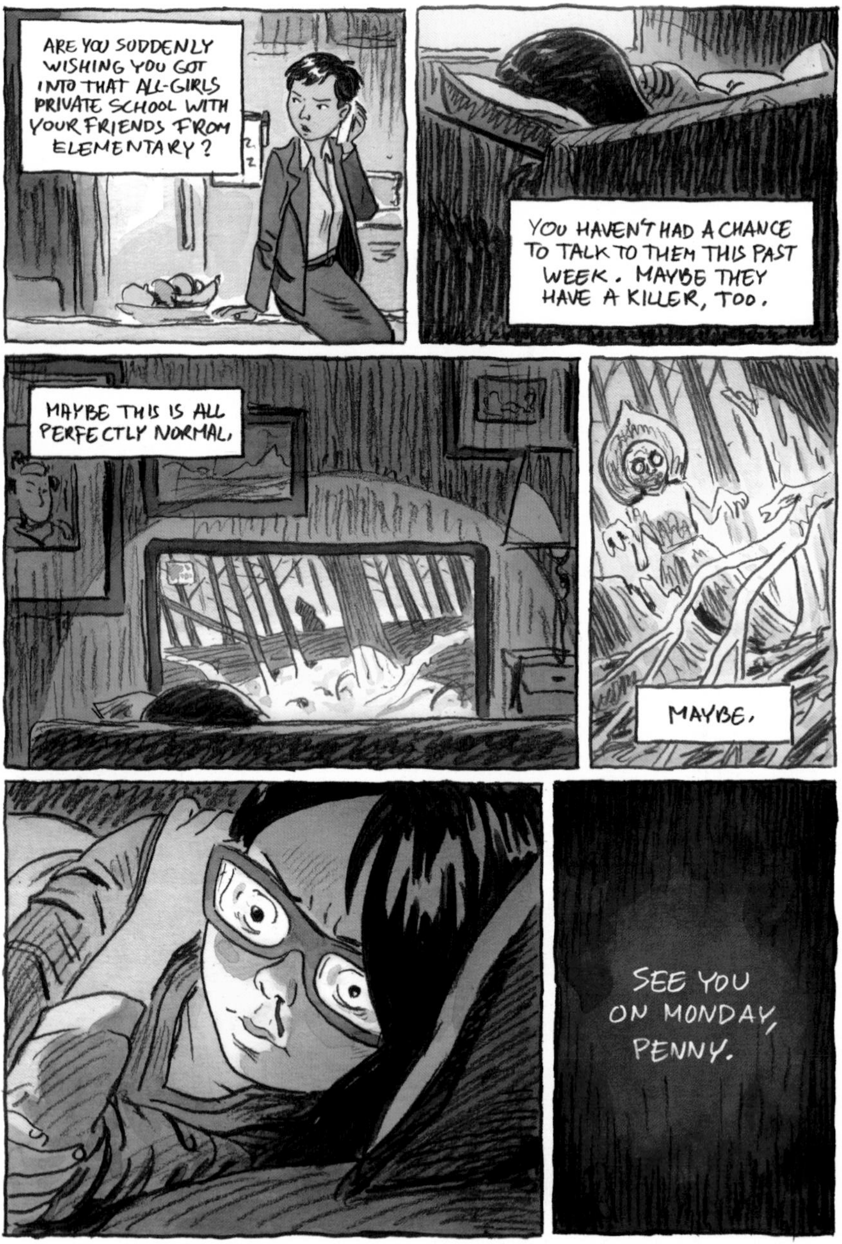
ARE YOU SUDDENLY WISHING YOU GOT INTO THAT ALL-GIRLS PRIVATE SCHOOL WITH YOUR FRIENDS FROM ELEMENTARY?
YOU HAVEN'T HAD A CHANCE TO TALK TO THEM THIS PAST WEEK. MAYBE THEY HAVE A KILLER, TOO.
MAYBE THIS IS ALL PERFECTLY NORMAL.
MAYBE.
SEE YOU ON MONDAY, PENNY.

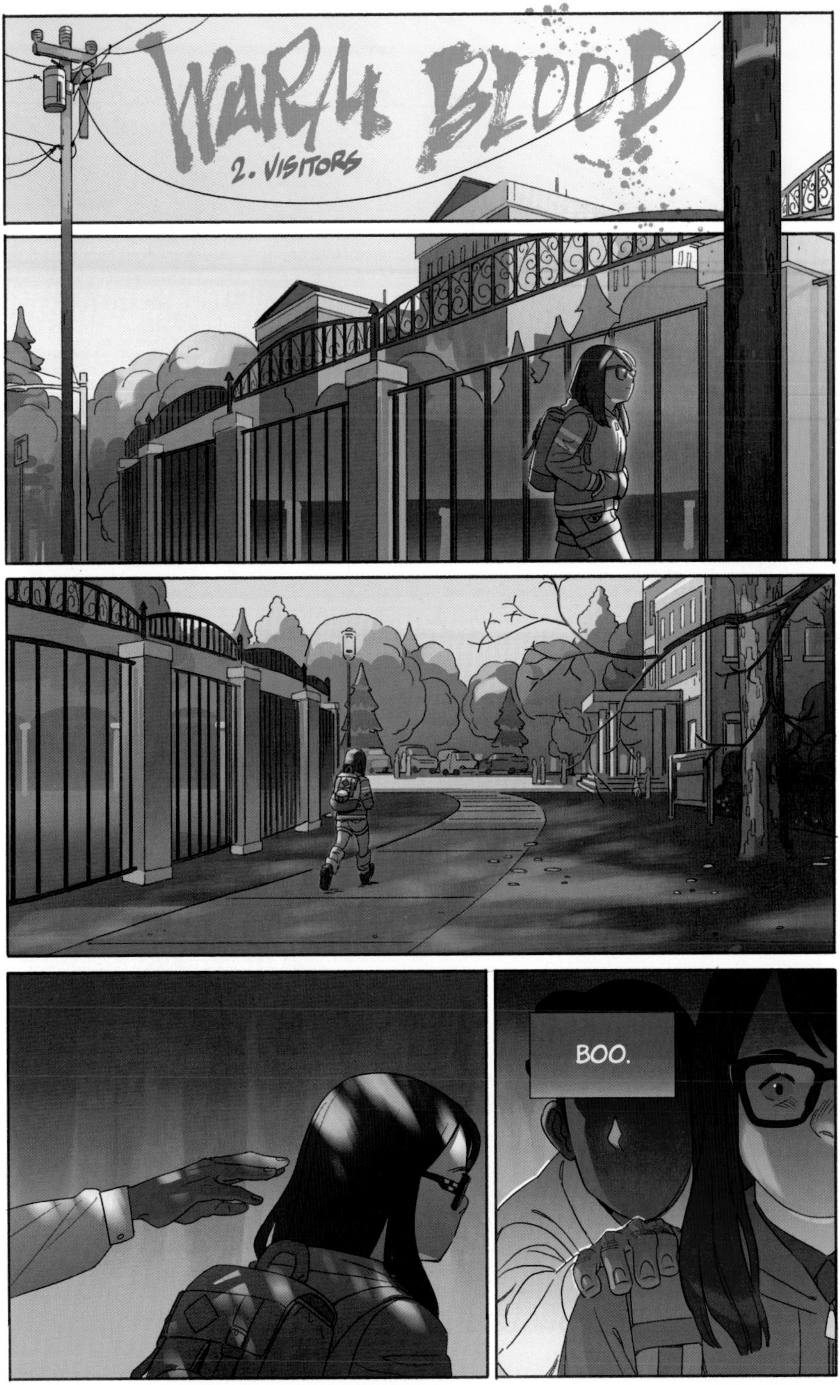
WARM BLOOD
2. VISITORS
BOO.

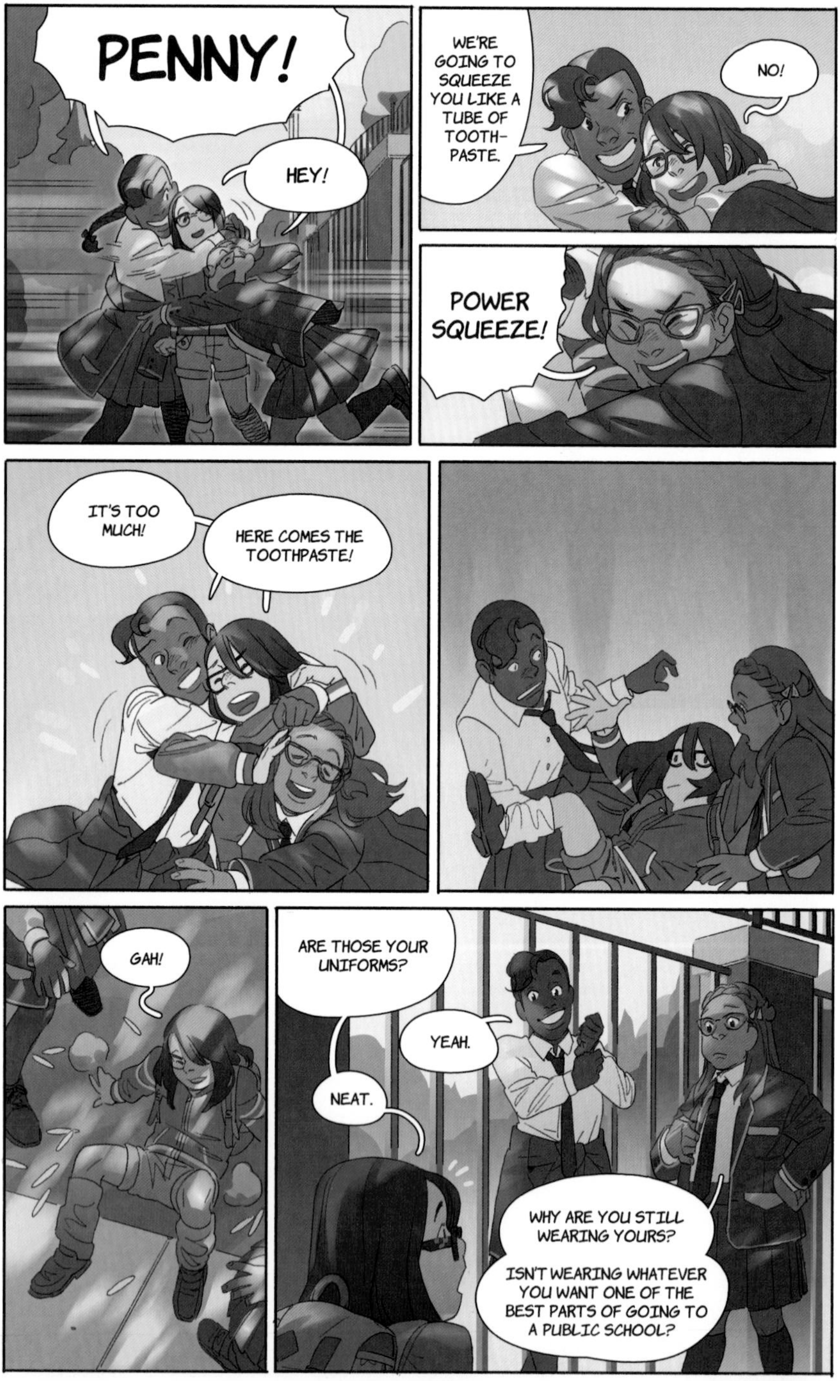
PENNY!
HEY!
WE'RE GOING TO SQUEEZE YOU LIKE A TUBE OF TOOTH-PASTE.
NO!
POWER SQUEEZE!
IT'S TOO MUCH!
HERE COMES THE TOOTHPASTE!
GAH!
ARE THOSE YOUR UNIFORMS?
YEAH.
NEAT.
WHY ARE YOU STILL WEARING YOURS?
ISN'T WEARING WHATEVER YOU WANT ONE OF THE BEST PARTS OF GOING TO A PUBLIC SCHOOL?

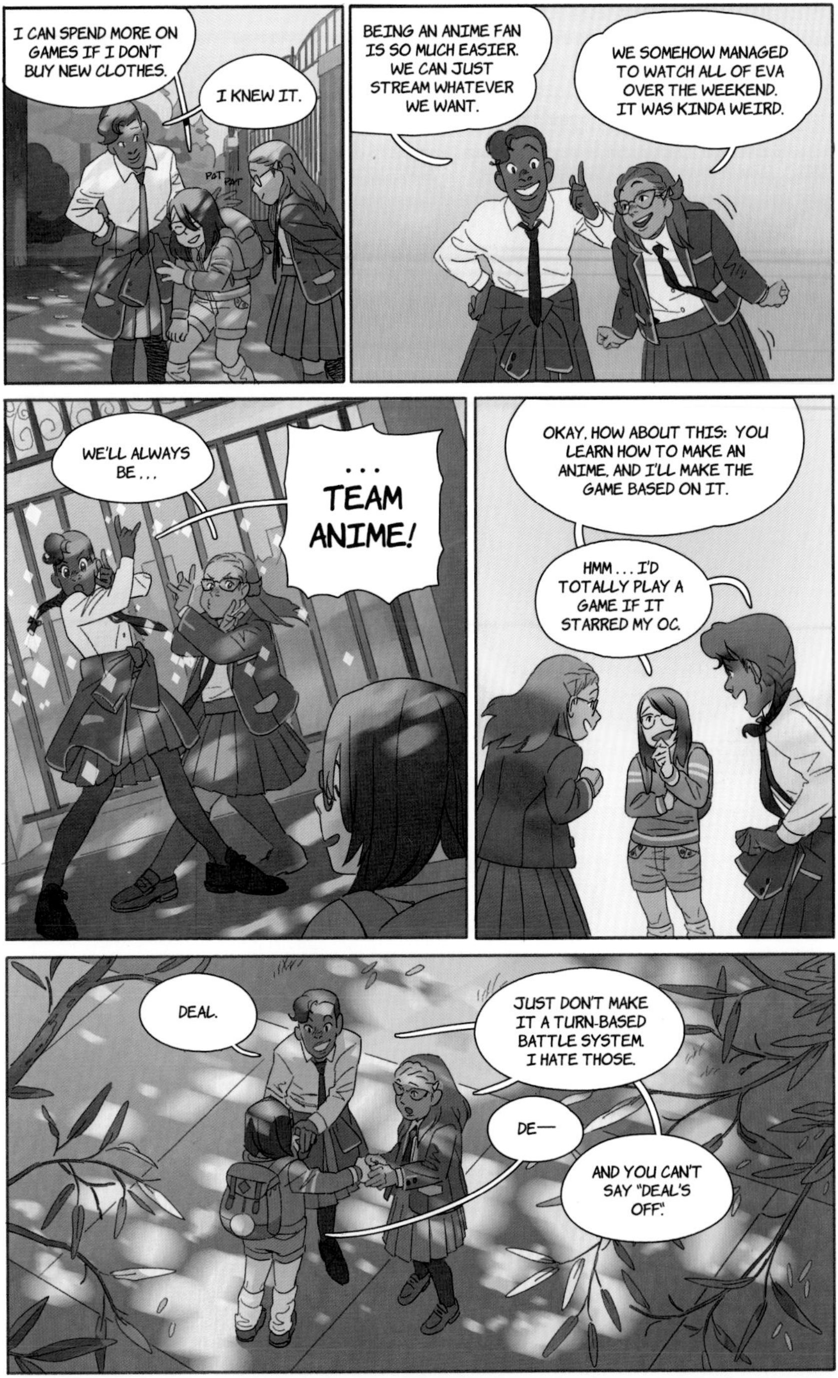
I CAN SPEND MORE ON GAMES IF I DON'T BUY NEW CLOTHES.
I KNEW IT.
PAT PAT
BEING AN ANIME FAN IS SO MUCH EASIER. WE CAN JUST STREAM WHATEVER WE WANT.
WE SOMEHOW MANAGED TO WATCH ALL OF EVA OVER THE WEEKEND. IT WAS KINDA WEIRD.
WE'LL ALWAYS BE . . .
. . . TEAM ANIME!
OKAY. HOW ABOUT THIS: YOU LEARN HOW TO MAKE AN ANIME, AND I'LL MAKE THE GAME BASED ON IT.
HMM . . . I'D TOTALLY PLAY A GAME IF IT STARRED MY OC.
DEAL.
JUST DON'T MAKE IT A TURN-BASED BATTLE SYSTEM. I HATE THOSE.
DE—
AND YOU CAN'T SAY "DEAL'S OFF."

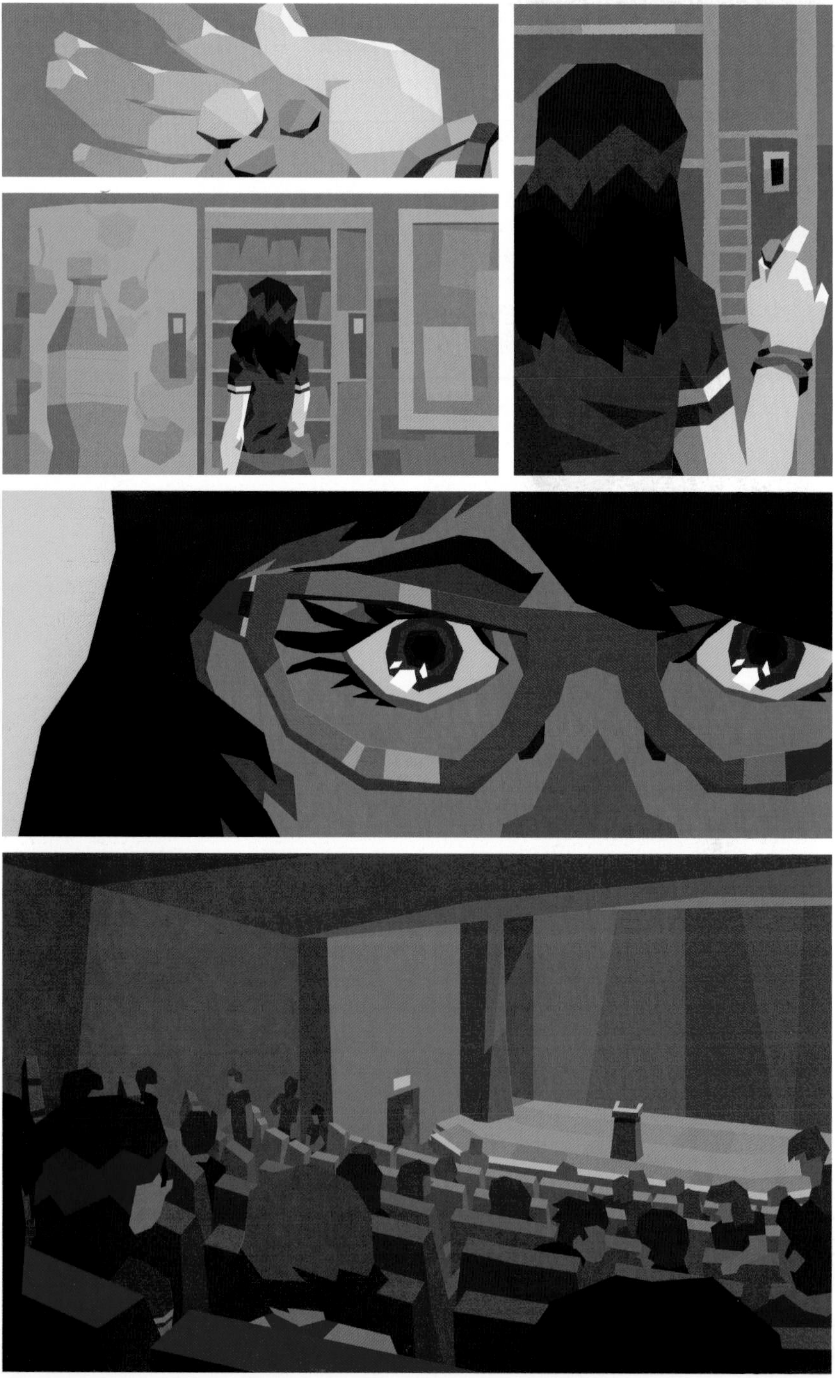

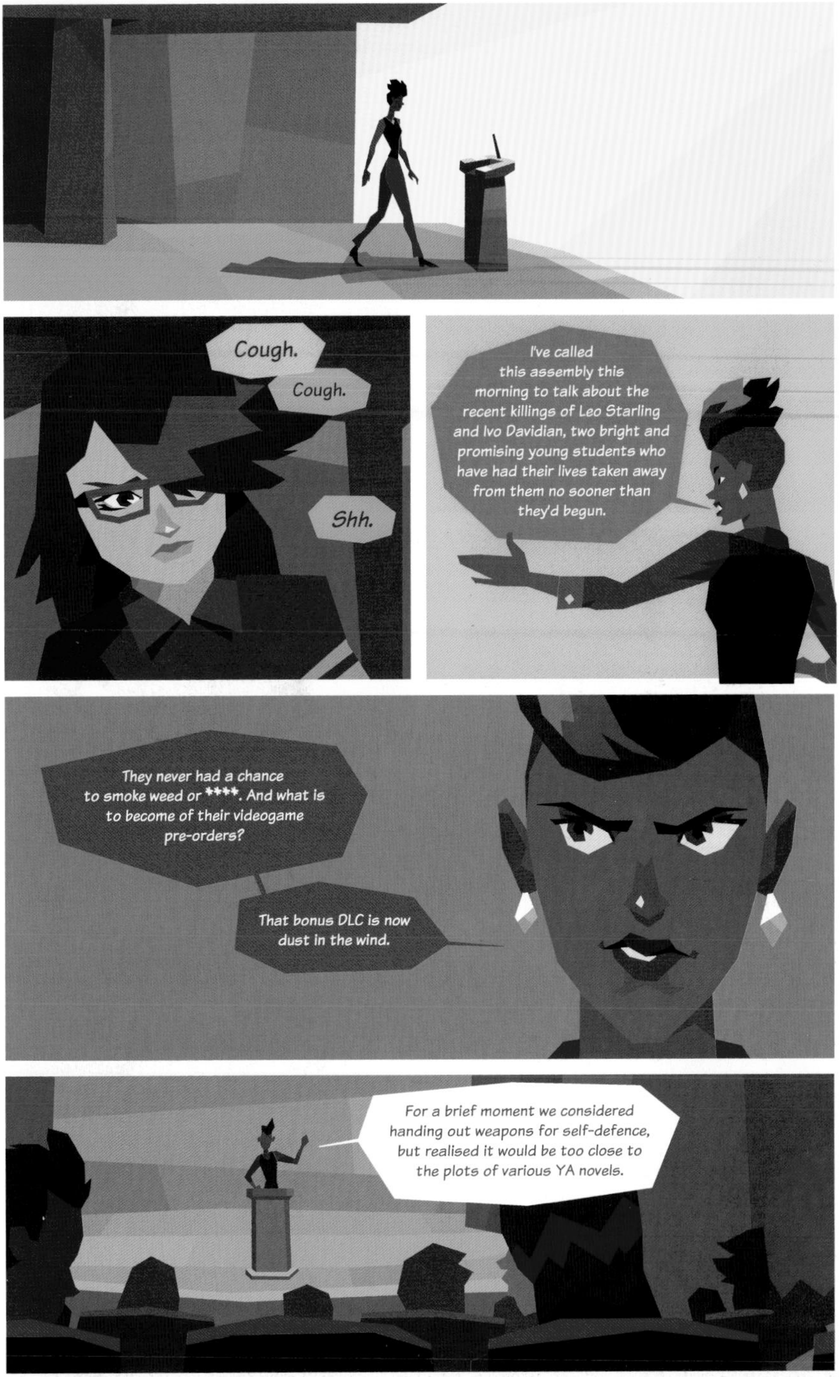
Cough.
Cough.
Shh.
I've called this assembly this morning to talk about the recent killings of Leo Starling and Ivo Davidian, two bright and promising young students who have had their lives taken away from them no sooner than they'd begun.
They never had a chance to smoke weed or ****. And what is to become of their videogame pre-orders?
That bonus DLC is now dust in the wind.
For a brief moment we considered handing out weapons for self-defence, but realised it would be too close to the plots of various YA novels.

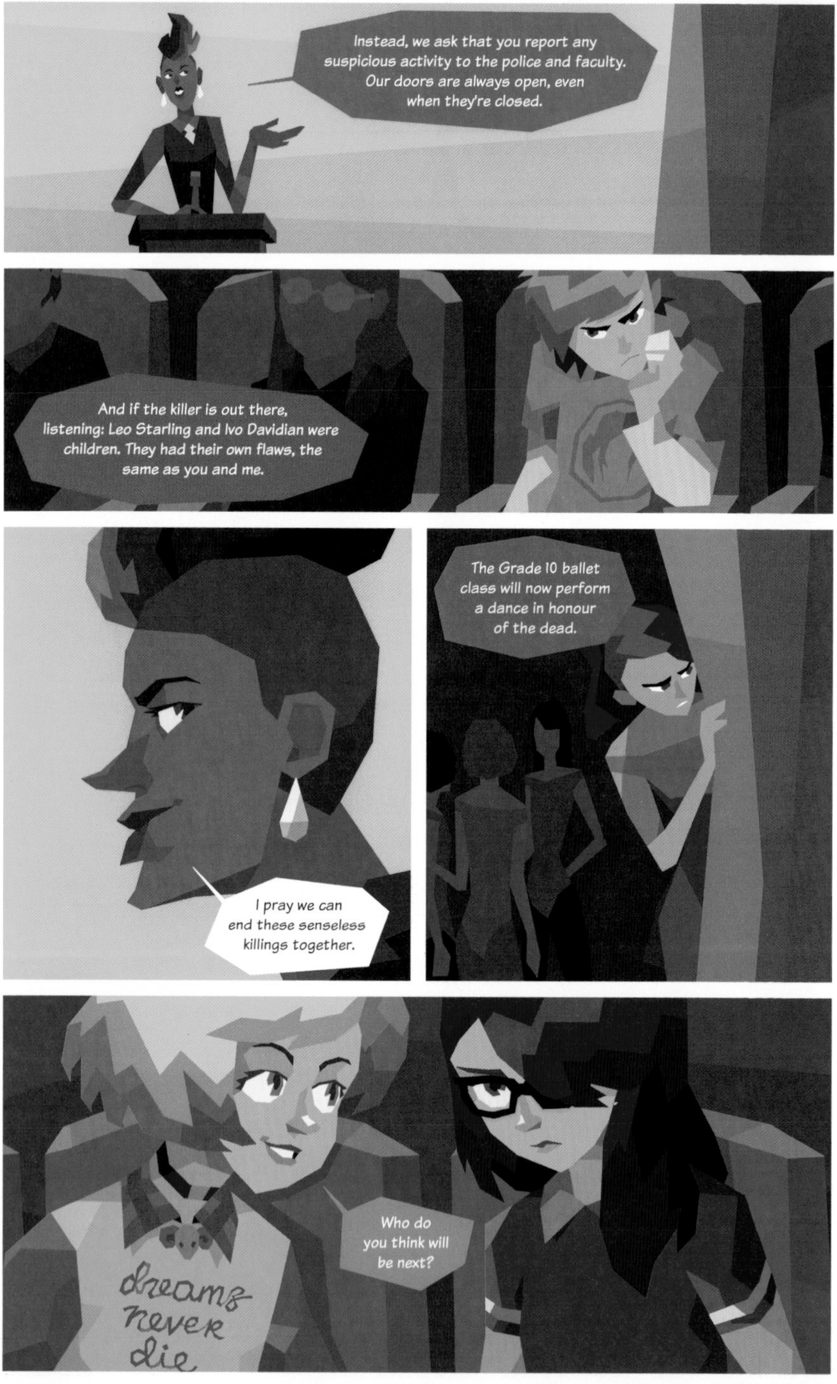
Instead, we ask that you report any suspicious activity to the police and faculty. Our doors are always open, even when they're closed.
And if the killer is out there, listening: Leo Starling and Ivo Davidian were children. They had their own flaws, the same as you and me.
I pray we can end these senseless killings together.
The Grade 10 ballet class will now perform a dance in honour of the dead.
Who do you think will be next?
dreams never die

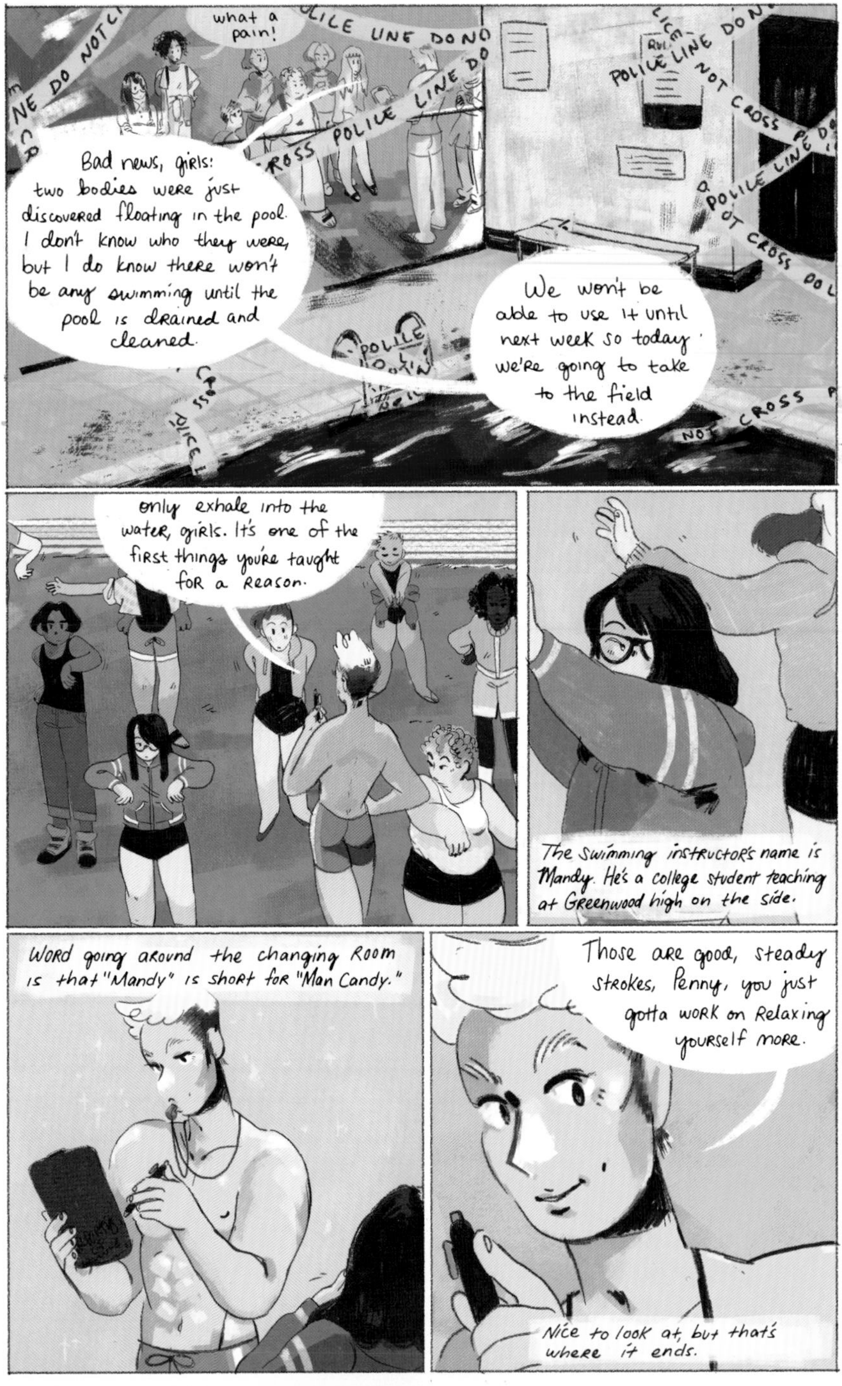
what a pain!
Bad news, girls: two bodies were just discovered floating in the pool. I don't know who they were, but I do know there won't be any swimming until the pool is drained and cleaned.
We won't be able to use it until next week so today we're going to take to the field instead.
only exhale into the water, girls. It's one of the first things you're taught for a reason.
The swimming instructor's name is Mandy. He's a college student teaching at Greenwood high on the side.
Word going around the changing room is that "Mandy" is short for "Man Candy."
Those are good, steady strokes, Penny, you just gotta work on relaxing yourself more.
Nice to look at, but that's where it ends.

FWEEE

Time's up— everyone out of the water!

Cale likes Ennio. You liked Ivo.

Logan was the first person you talked to and... he's weird and distracted, like someone who won't take school seriously enough in the end.

Wait, why does this even matter?

What happens when blood is brought to a boil?

what happens when you try to smoke it?

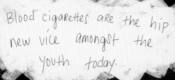

Blood cigarettes are the hip new vice amongst the youth today.

If you asked them why, they wouldn't be able to tell you, or at least not in a coherent fashion.

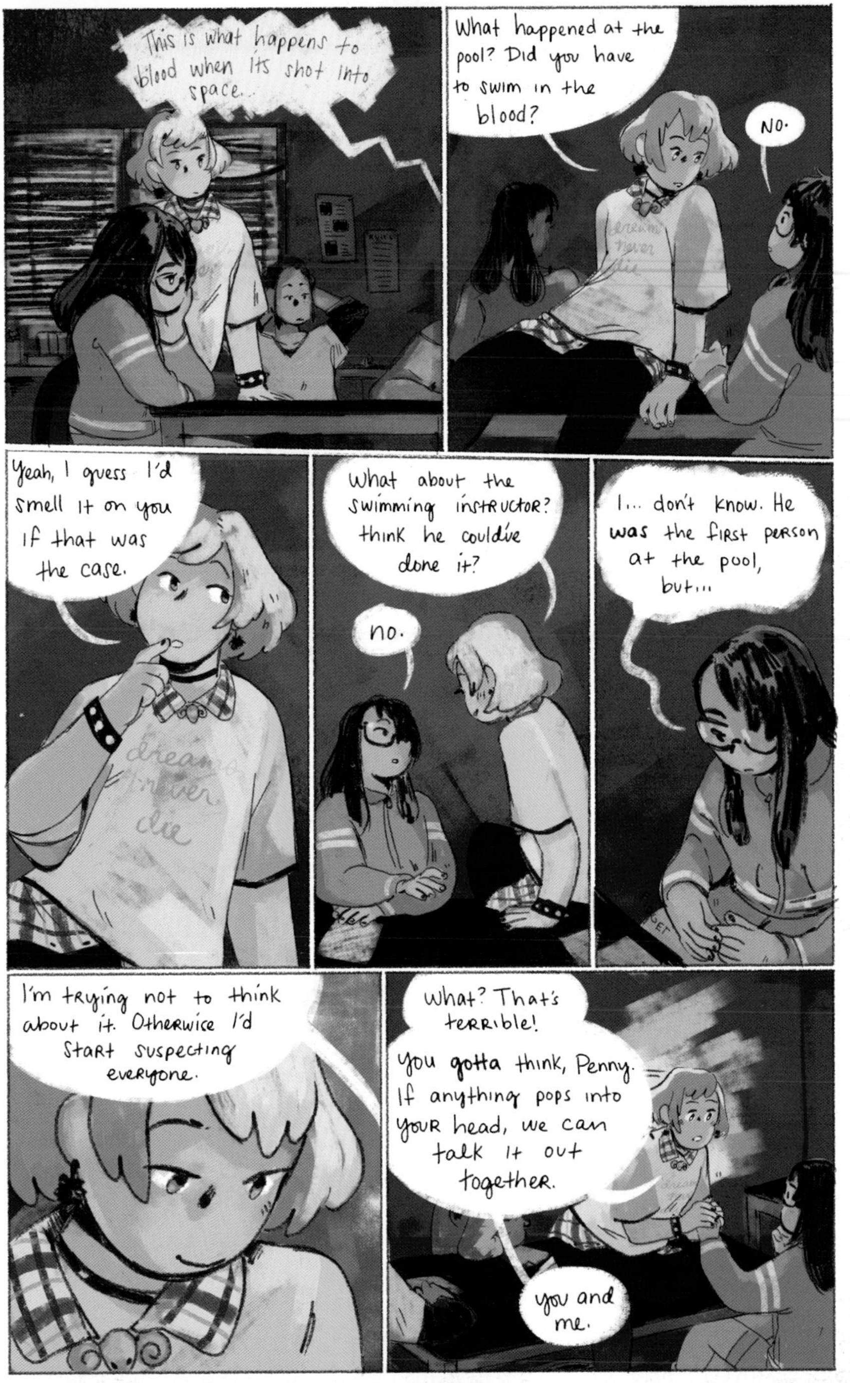
This is what happens to blood when its shot into space...
What happened at the pool? Did you have to swim in the blood?
No.
Yeah, I guess I'd smell it on you if that was the case.
What about the swimming instructor? think he could've done it?
no.
I... don't know. He was the first person at the pool, but...
I'm trying not to think about it. Otherwise I'd start suspecting everyone.
What? That's terrible!
You gotta think, Penny. If anything pops into your head, we can talk it out together.
you and me.

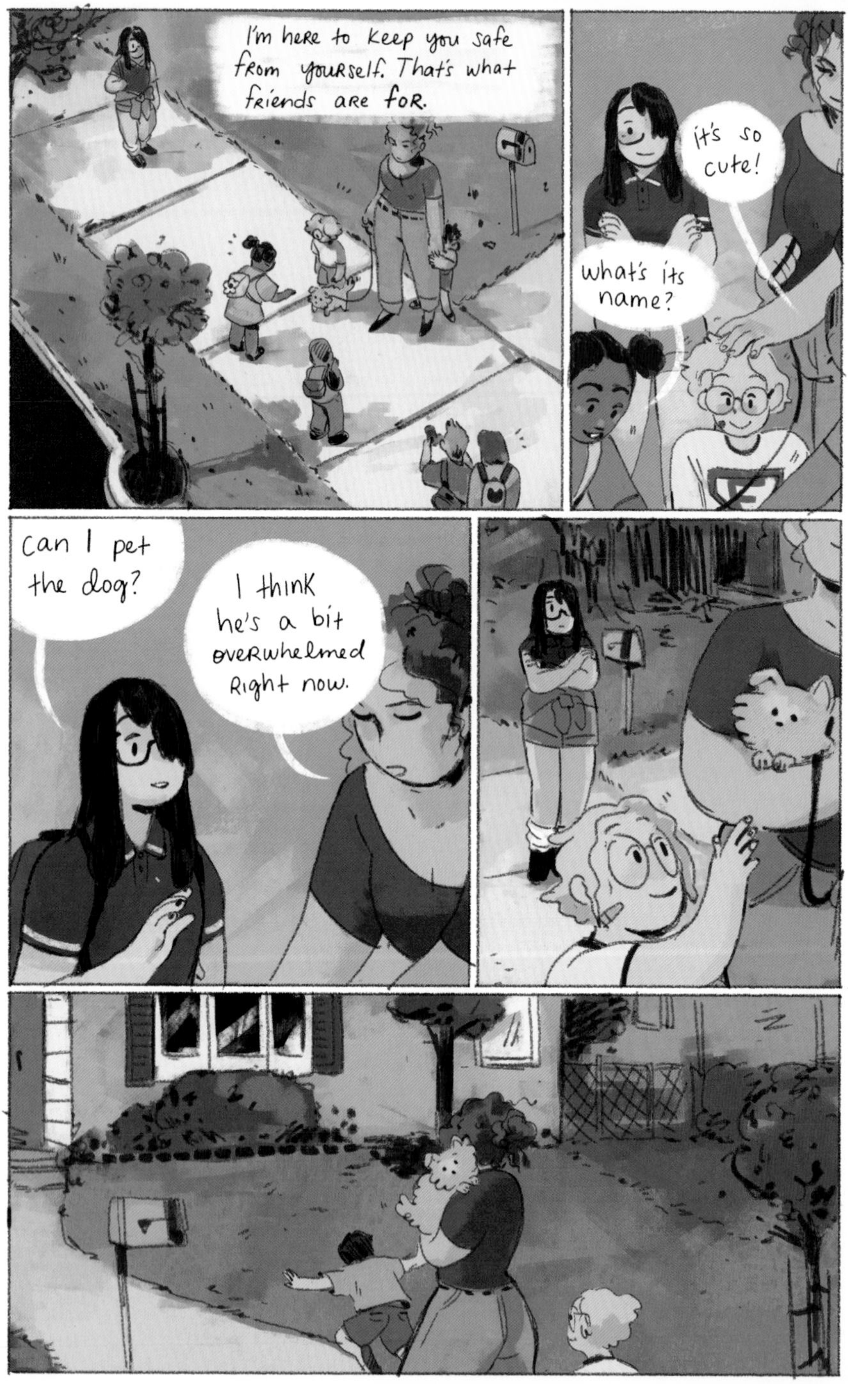
I'm here to keep you safe from yourself. That's what friends are for.
it's so cute!
what's its name?
can I pet the dog?
I think he's a bit overwhelmed right now.

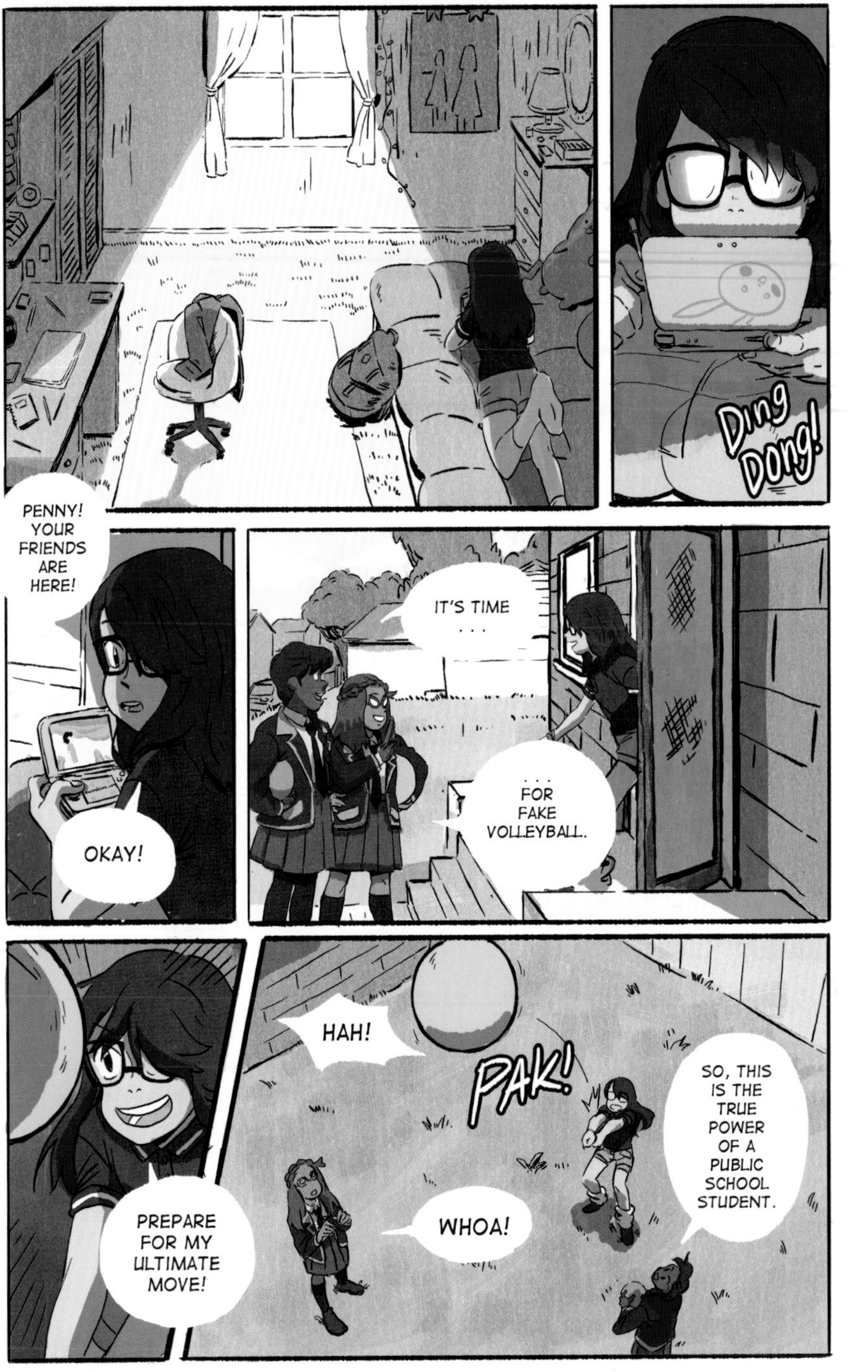
Ding Dong!
PENNY! YOUR FRIENDS ARE HERE!
OKAY!
IT'S TIME . . .
. . . FOR FAKE VOLLEYBALL.
PREPARE FOR MY ULTIMATE MOVE!
HAH!
PAK!
WHOA!
SO, THIS IS THE TRUE POWER OF A PUBLIC SCHOOL STUDENT.

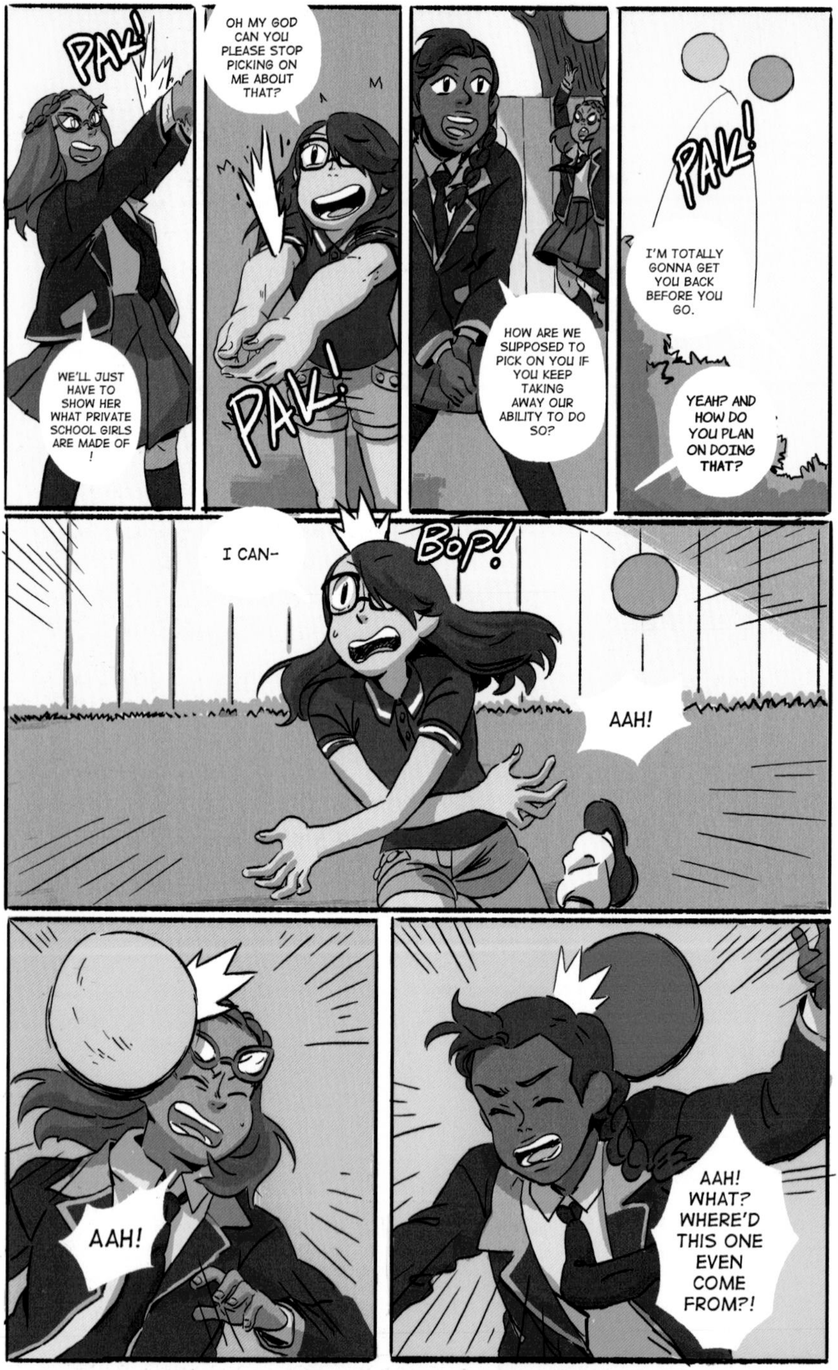
PAK!
WE'LL JUST HAVE TO SHOW HER WHAT PRIVATE SCHOOL GIRLS ARE MADE OF !
OH MY GOD CAN YOU PLEASE STOP PICKING ON ME ABOUT THAT?
PAK!
HOW ARE WE SUPPOSED TO PICK ON YOU IF YOU KEEP TAKING AWAY OUR ABILITY TO DO SO?
PAK!
I'M TOTALLY GONNA GET YOU BACK BEFORE YOU GO.
YEAH? AND HOW DO YOU PLAN ON DOING THAT?
I CAN-
BOP!
AAH!
AAH!
AAH! WHAT? WHERE'D THIS ONE EVEN COME FROM?!

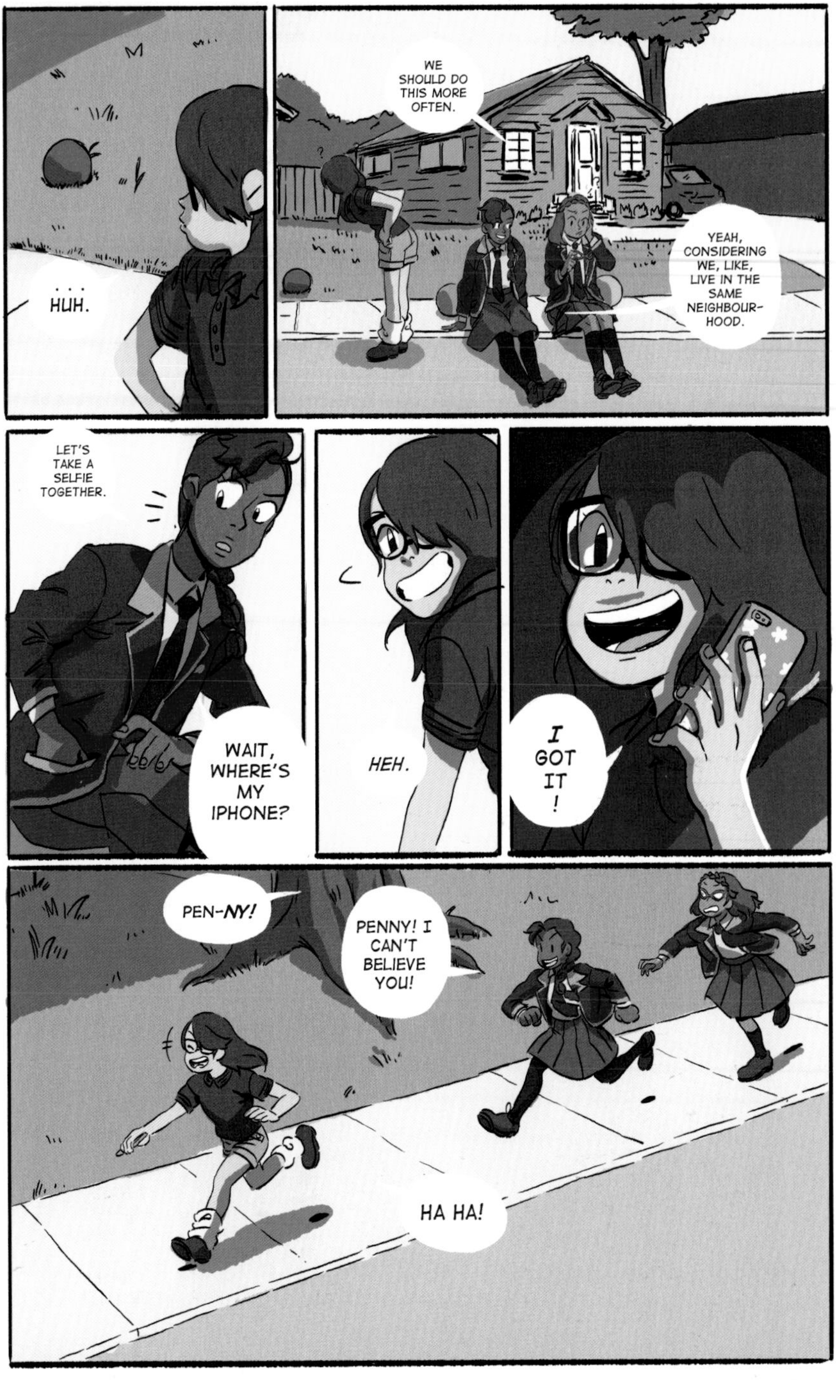
. . . HUH.
WE SHOULD DO THIS MORE OFTEN.
YEAH, CONSIDERING WE, LIKE, LIVE IN THE SAME NEIGHBOURHOOD.
LET'S TAKE A SELFIE TOGETHER.
WAIT, WHERE'S MY IPHONE?
HEH.
I GOT IT!
PEN-NY!
PENNY! I CAN'T BELIEVE YOU!
HA HA!

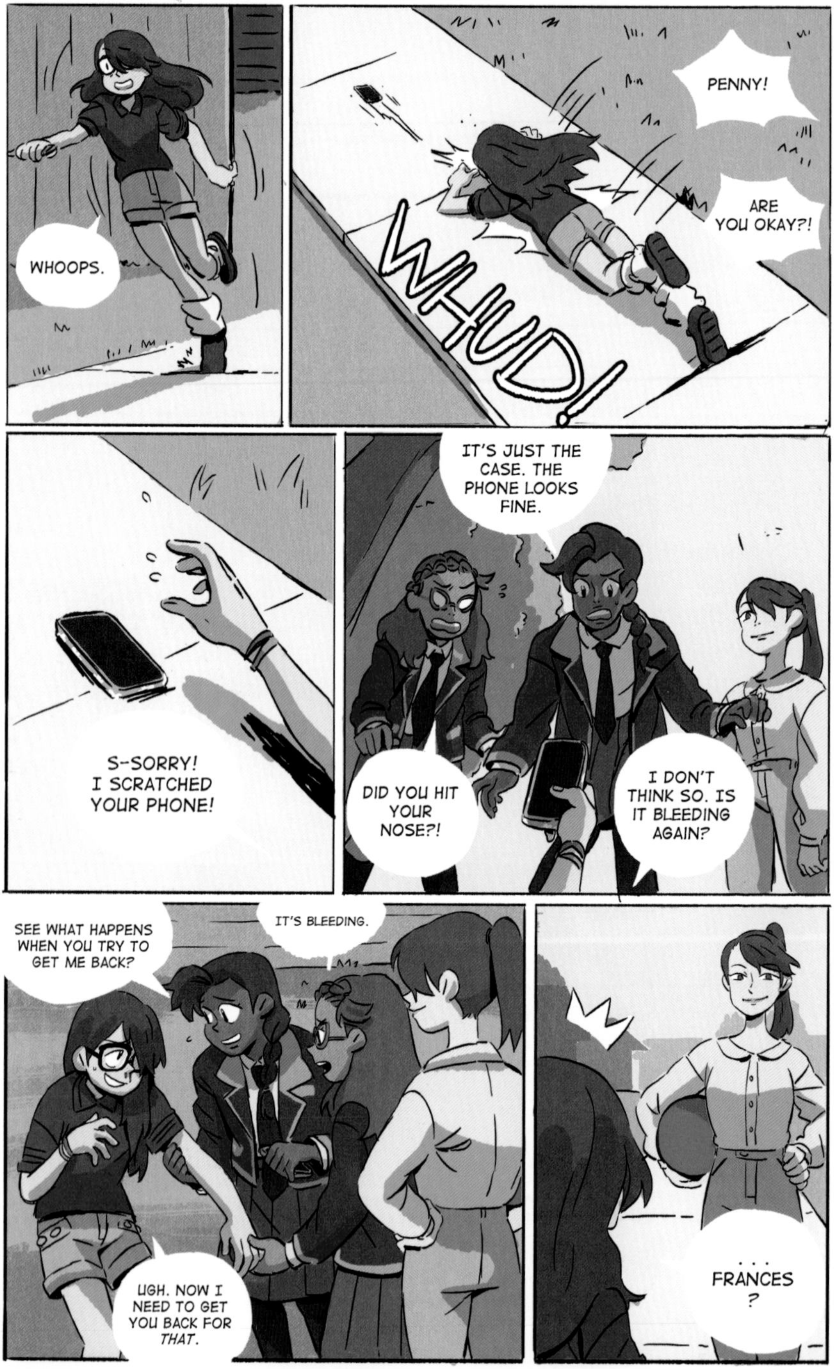
WHOOPS.
WHUD!
PENNY!
ARE YOU OKAY?!
S-SORRY! I SCRATCHED YOUR PHONE!
IT'S JUST THE CASE. THE PHONE LOOKS FINE.
DID YOU HIT YOUR NOSE?!
I DON'T THINK SO. IS IT BLEEDING AGAIN?
SEE WHAT HAPPENS WHEN YOU TRY TO GET ME BACK?
IT'S BLEEDING.
UGH. NOW I NEED TO GET YOU BACK FOR *THAT*.
. . . FRANCES ?

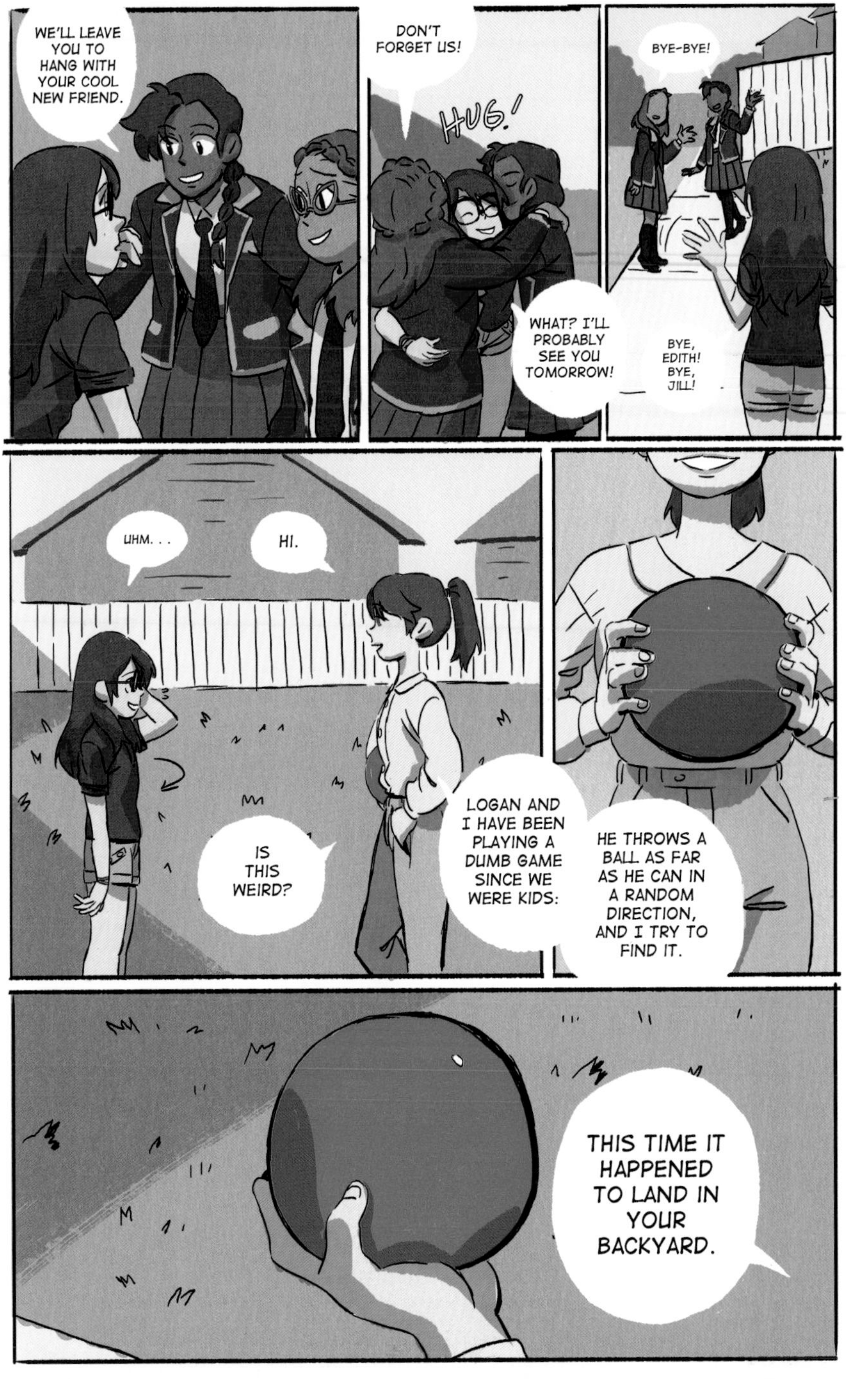
WE'LL LEAVE YOU TO HANG WITH YOUR COOL NEW FRIEND.
DON'T FORGET US!
HUG!
WHAT? I'LL PROBABLY SEE YOU TOMORROW!
BYE-BYE!
BYE, EDITH! BYE, JILL!
UHM. . .
HI.
IS THIS WEIRD?
LOGAN AND I HAVE BEEN PLAYING A DUMB GAME SINCE WE WERE KIDS:
HE THROWS A BALL AS FAR AS HE CAN IN A RANDOM DIRECTION, AND I TRY TO FIND IT.
THIS TIME IT HAPPENED TO LAND IN YOUR BACKYARD.

YOU CERTAINLY HAVE A THING FOR VIDEOGAMES.

YEAH.

I MEAN, I'M PRETTY PICKY. I MOSTLY PLAY POKÉMON AND SOME GAMES ON OUR SWITCH.

DO YOU PLAY POKÉMON?

I DON'T BATTLE MUCH BUT I LIKE TRADING. I HAVE ABOUT 300 MONSTERS RIGHT NOW, INCLUDING SOME MYTHICALS LIKE MELOETTA.

HER PIROUETTE FORME MAKES HER LOOK LIKE A BALLERINA.

OH, IS THAT A GAME SYSTEM?

I DON'T HAVE ANY MONSTERS, UNLESS YOU COUNT LOGAN

DO YOU LIVE CLOSE TO THE SCHOOL?

WE'RE ON THE OPPOSITE SIDE OF THE FIELD.

IF YOU TOOK A PIECE OF PAPER, FOLDED IT AND POKED A HOLE HALFWAY THROUGH WITH A PEN, YOUR HOUSE WOULD BE ONE HOLE AND WE'D BE THE OTHER WHEN YOU UNFOLDED IT.

LOGAN MUST'VE THROWN THE BALL FAR, THEN.

SOMETIMES I WONDER IF IT'S THE ONE THING HE'S GOOD AT.

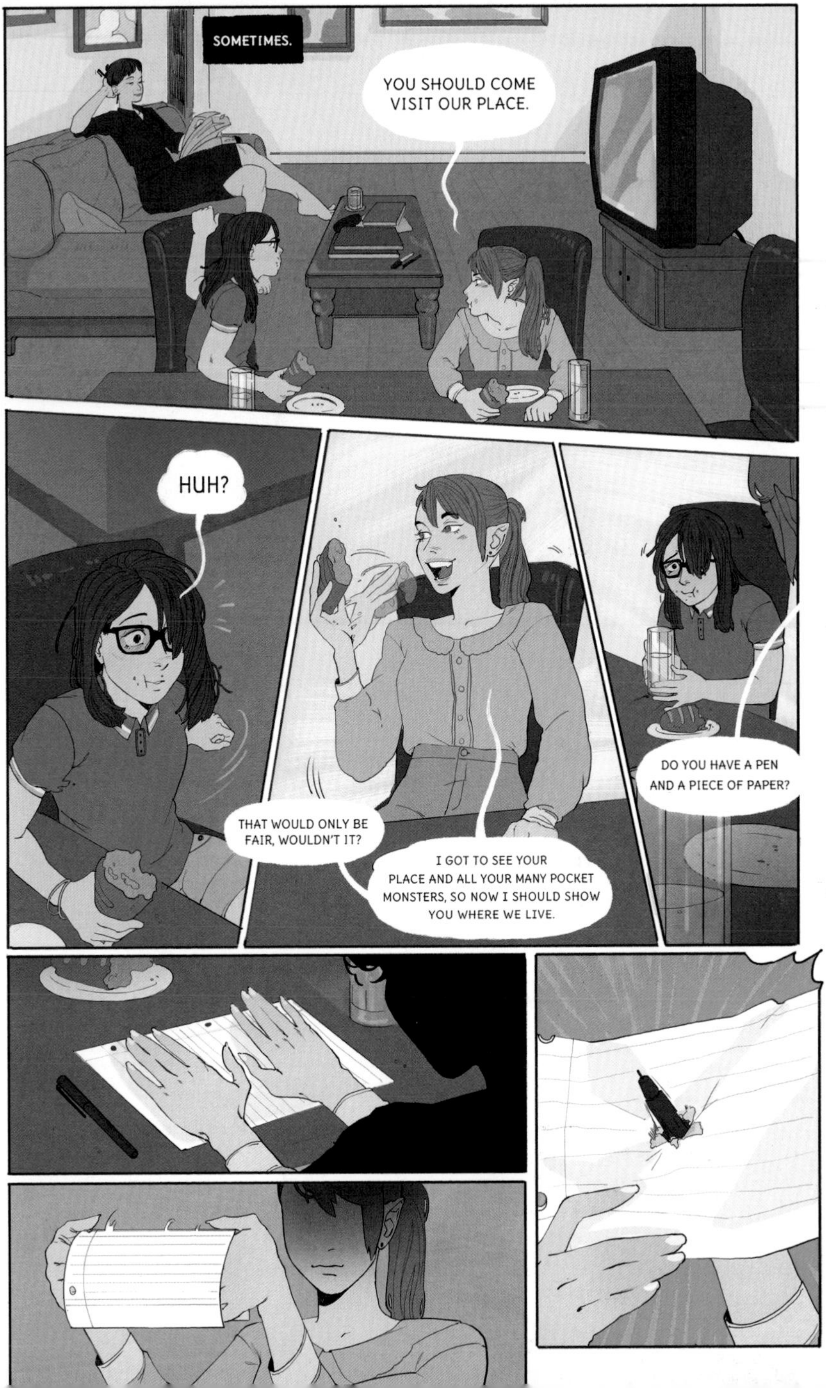
SOMETIMES.
YOU SHOULD COME VISIT OUR PLACE.
HUH?
THAT WOULD ONLY BE FAIR, WOULDN'T IT?
I GOT TO SEE YOUR PLACE AND ALL YOUR MANY POCKET MONSTERS, SO NOW I SHOULD SHOW YOU WHERE WE LIVE.
DO YOU HAVE A PEN AND A PIECE OF PAPER?

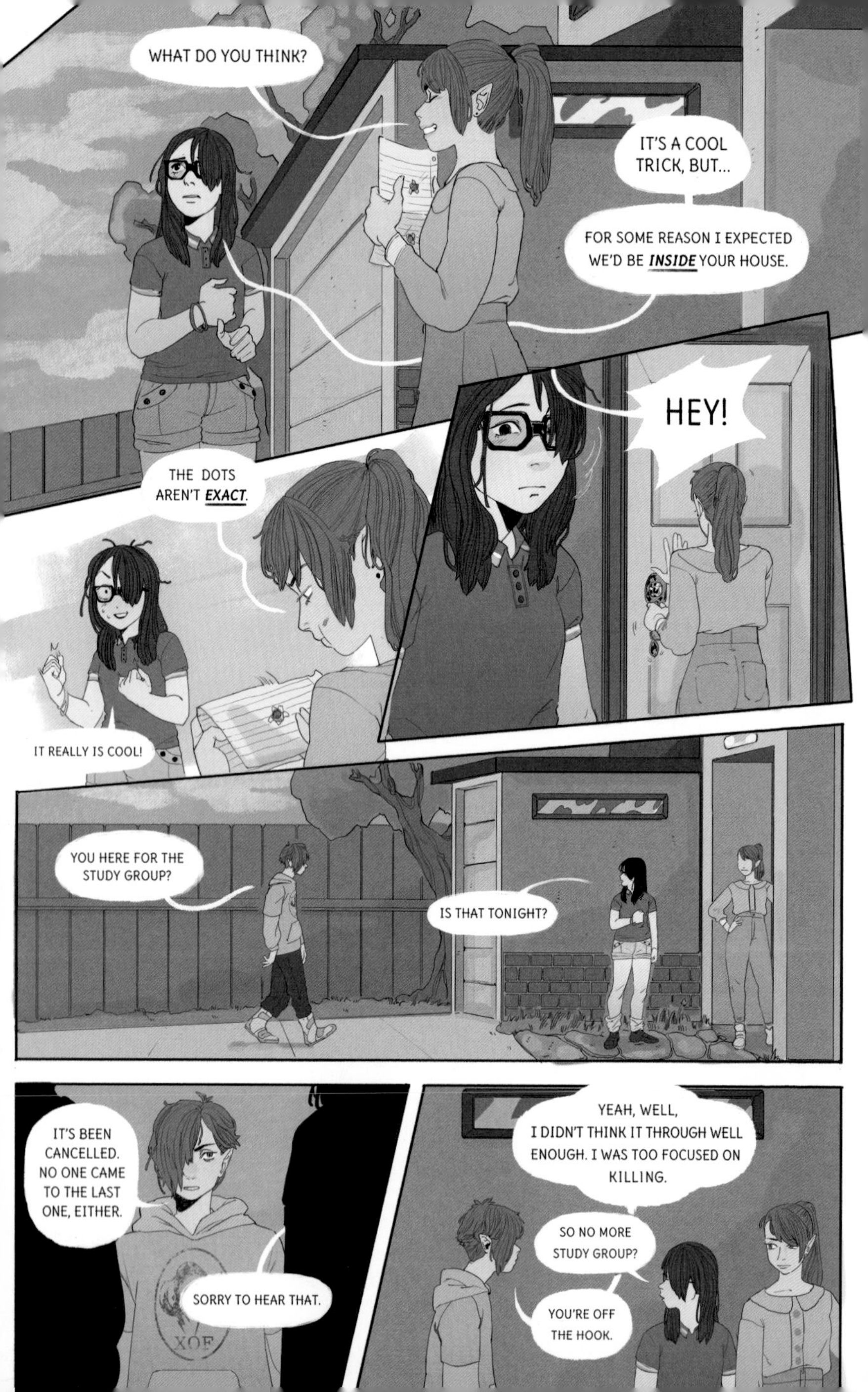
WHAT DO YOU THINK?
IT'S A COOL TRICK, BUT...
FOR SOME REASON I EXPECTED WE'D BE INSIDE YOUR HOUSE.
THE DOTS AREN'T EXACT.
IT REALLY IS COOL!
HEY!
YOU HERE FOR THE STUDY GROUP?
IS THAT TONIGHT?
IT'S BEEN CANCELLED. NO ONE CAME TO THE LAST ONE, EITHER.
SORRY TO HEAR THAT.
XOF
YEAH, WELL, I DIDN'T THINK IT THROUGH WELL ENOUGH. I WAS TOO FOCUSED ON KILLING.
SO NO MORE STUDY GROUP?
YOU'RE OFF THE HOOK.

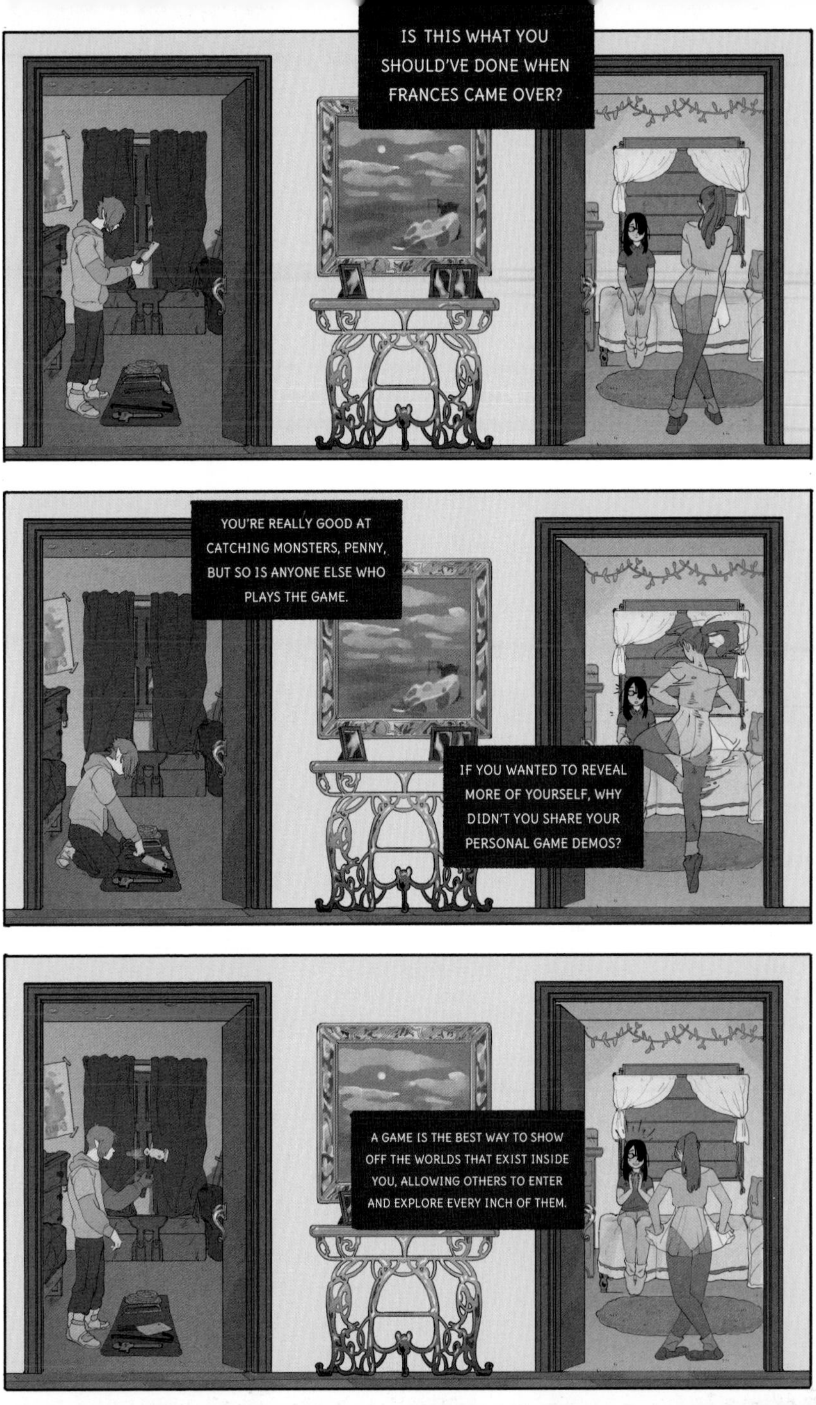
IS THIS WHAT YOU SHOULD'VE DONE WHEN FRANCES CAME OVER?
YOU'RE REALLY GOOD AT CATCHING MONSTERS, PENNY, BUT SO IS ANYONE ELSE WHO PLAYS THE GAME.
IF YOU WANTED TO REVEAL MORE OF YOURSELF, WHY DIDN'T YOU SHARE YOUR PERSONAL GAME DEMOS?
A GAME IS THE BEST WAY TO SHOW OFF THE WORLDS THAT EXIST INSIDE YOU, ALLOWING OTHERS TO ENTER AND EXPLORE EVERY INCH OF THEM.

MY FAMILY OWNS A CROWN THAT ONCE BELONGED TO A REAL-LIFE
PRINCESS. I CAN SHOW IT TO YOU, BUT YOU CAN'T TOUCH IT.

ISN'T IT PRETTY?

Y-YEAH.

I'LL BRING YOUR BALL BACK TOMORROW.

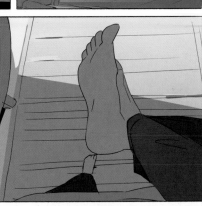

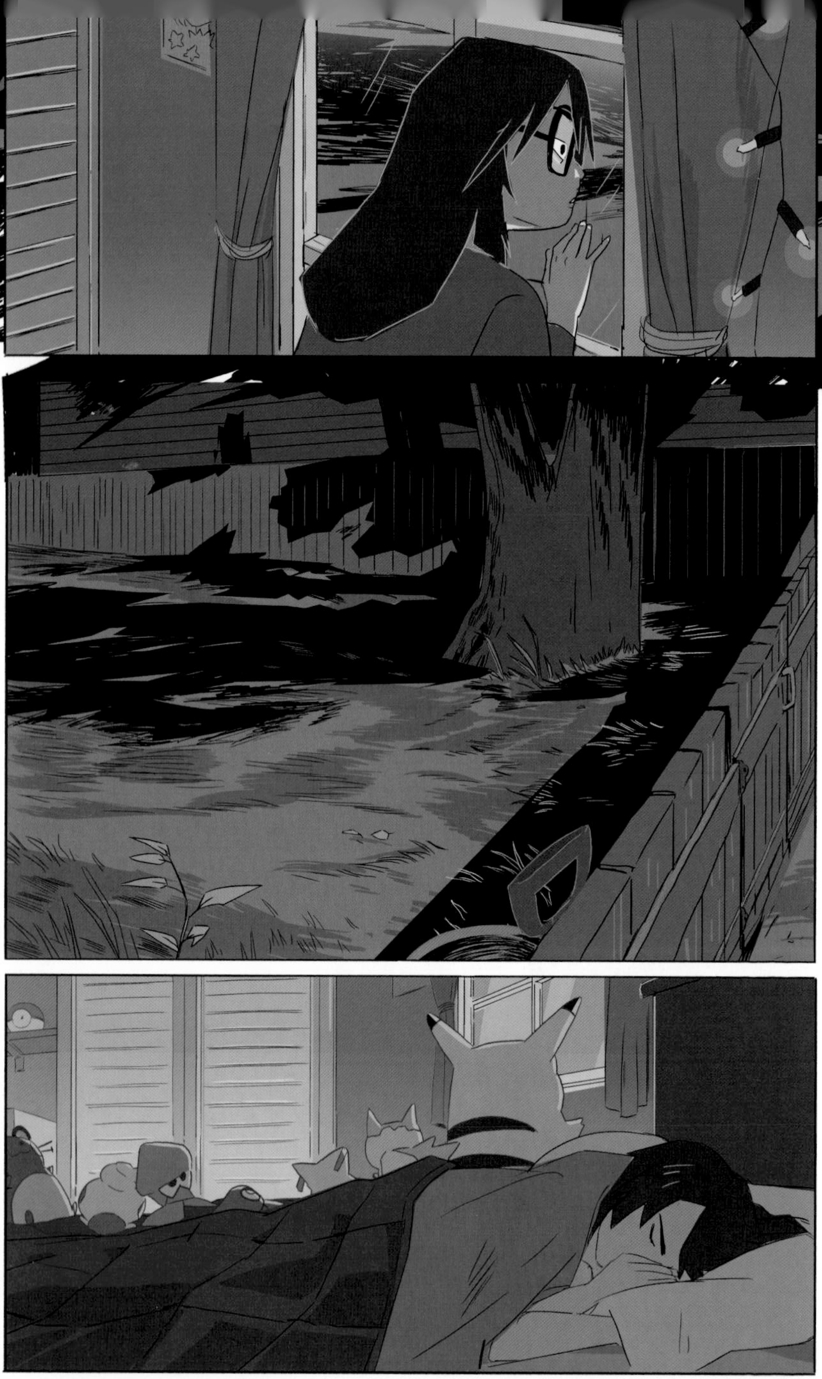

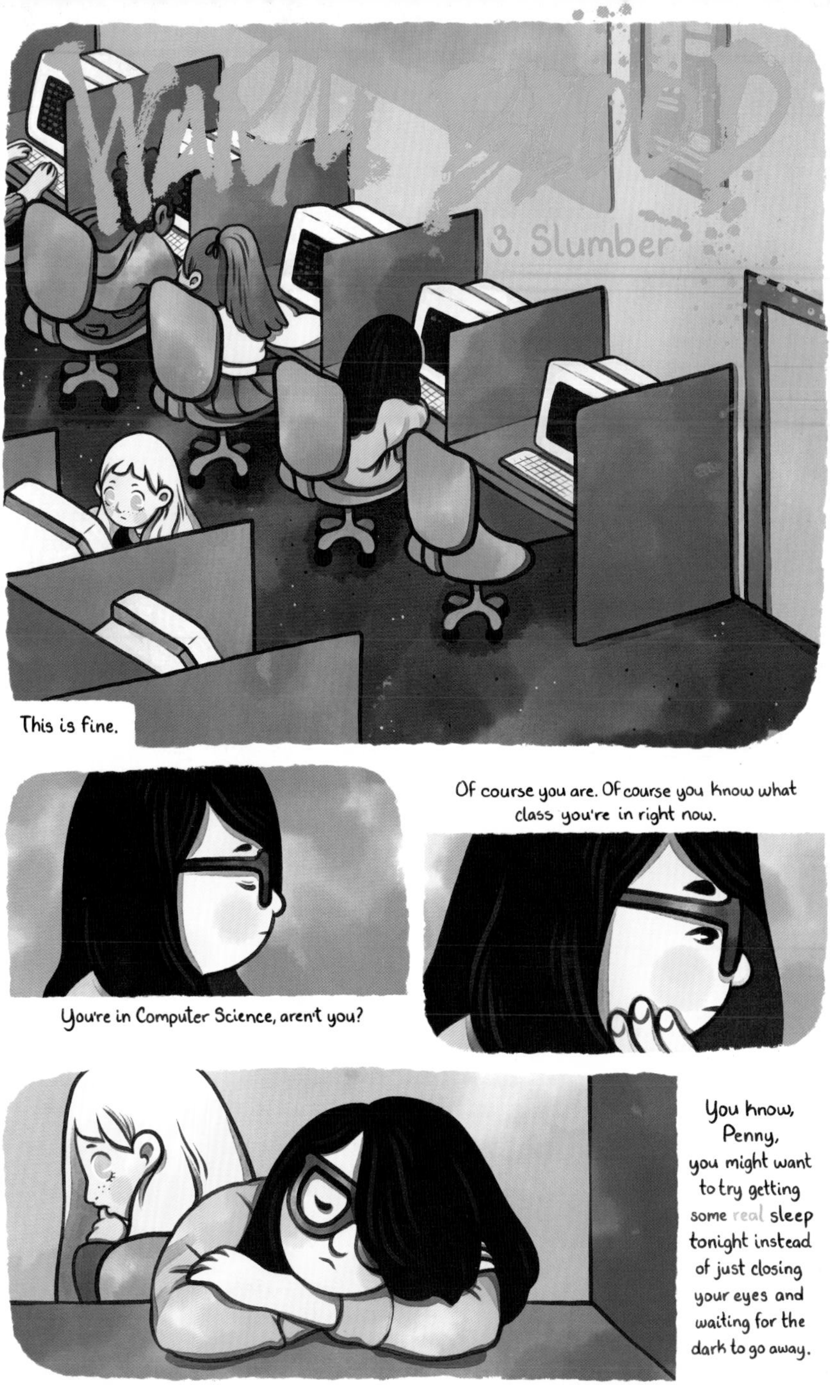
3. Slumber
This is fine.
You're in Computer Science, aren't you?
Of course you are. Of course you know what class you're in right now.
You know, Penny, you might want to try getting some real sleep tonight instead of just closing your eyes and waiting for the dark to go away.

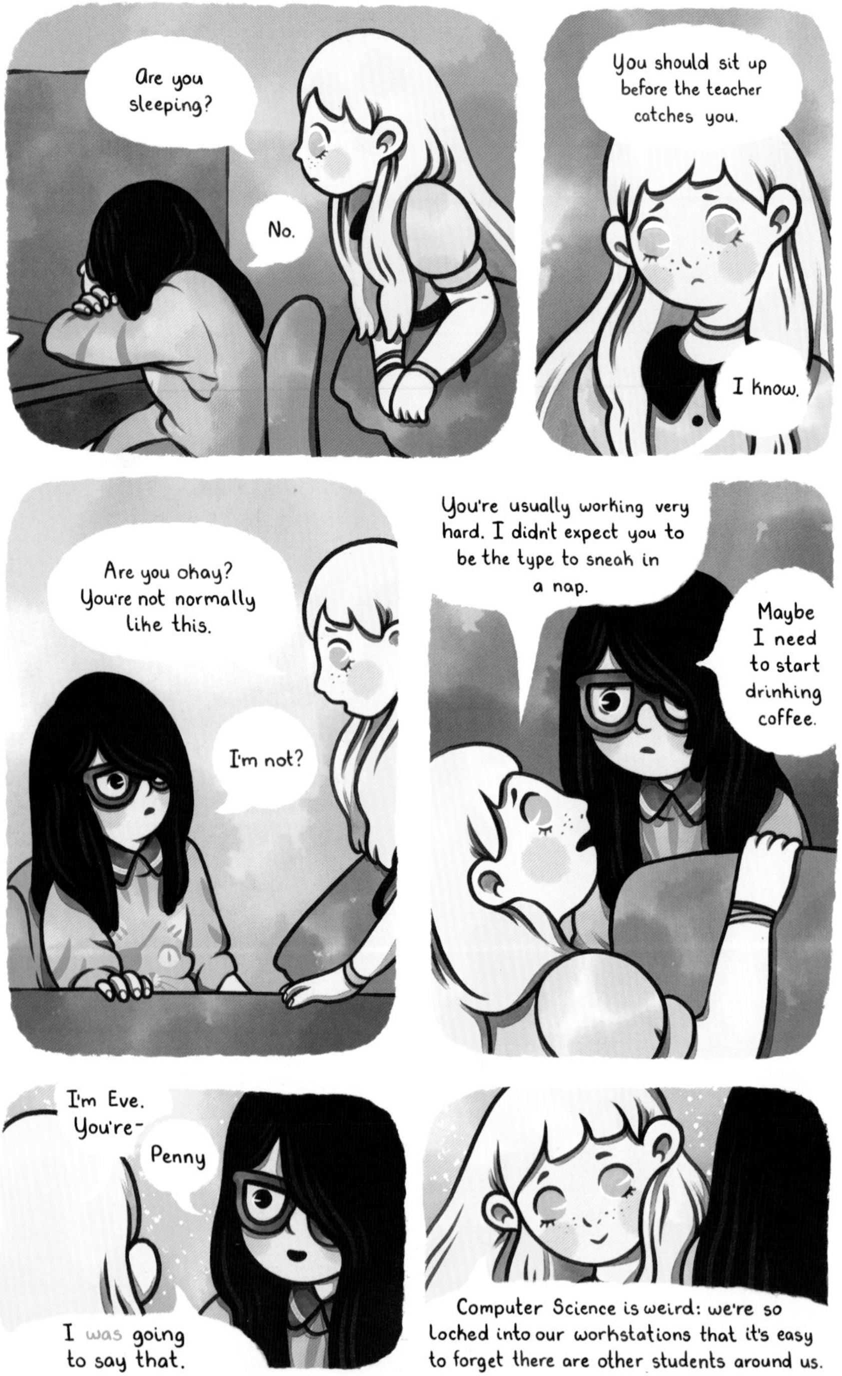
Are you sleeping?
No.
You should sit up before the teacher catches you.
I know.
Are you okay? You're not normally like this.
I'm not?
You're usually working very hard. I didn't expect you to be the type to sneak in a nap.
Maybe I need to start drinking coffee.
I'm Eve. You're-
Penny
I was going to say that.
Computer Science is weird: we're so locked into our workstations that it's easy to forget there are other students around us.

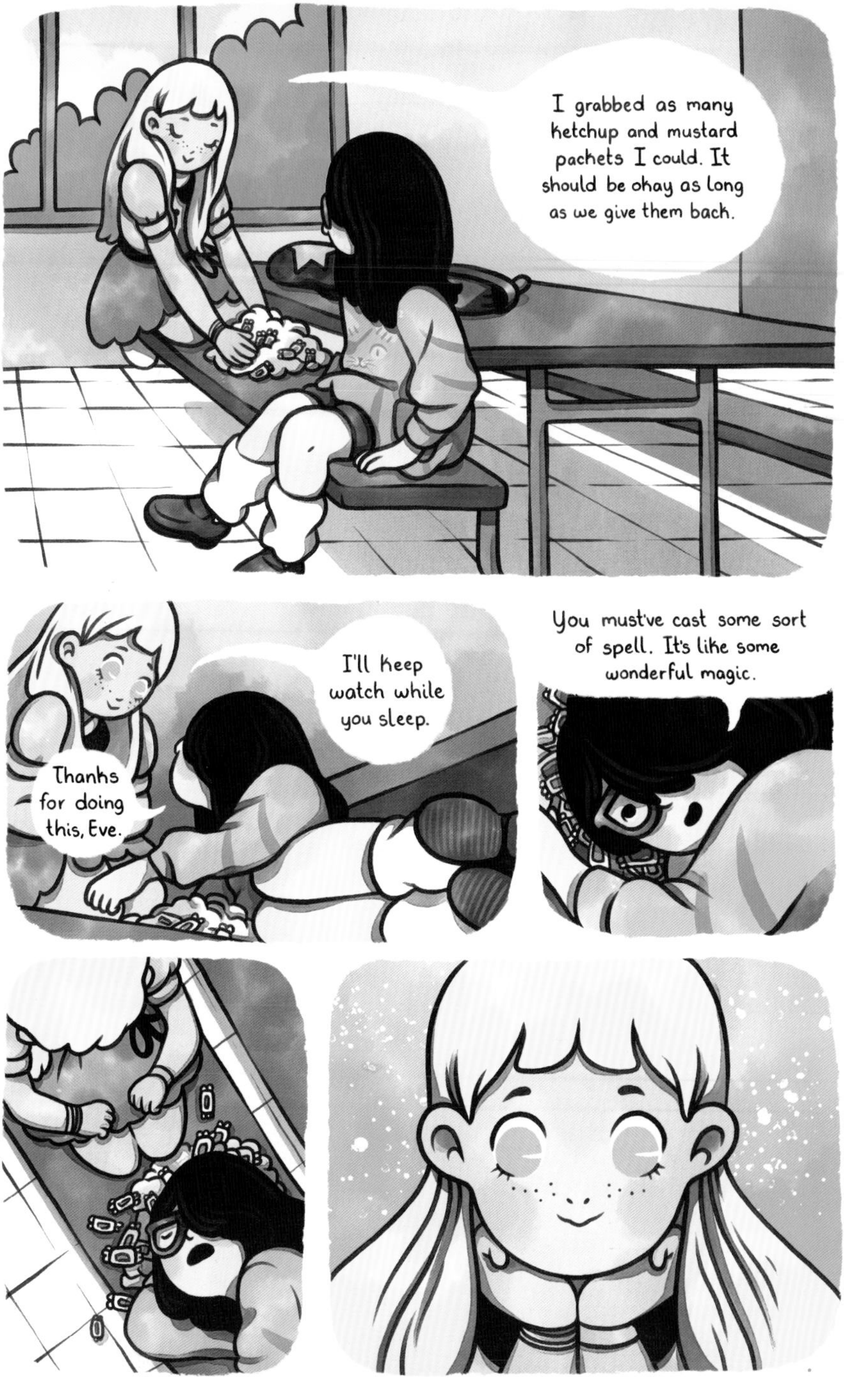
I grabbed as many ketchup and mustard packets I could. It should be okay as long as we give them back.
I'll keep watch while you sleep.
Thanks for doing this, Eve.
You must've cast some sort of spell. It's like some wonderful magic.

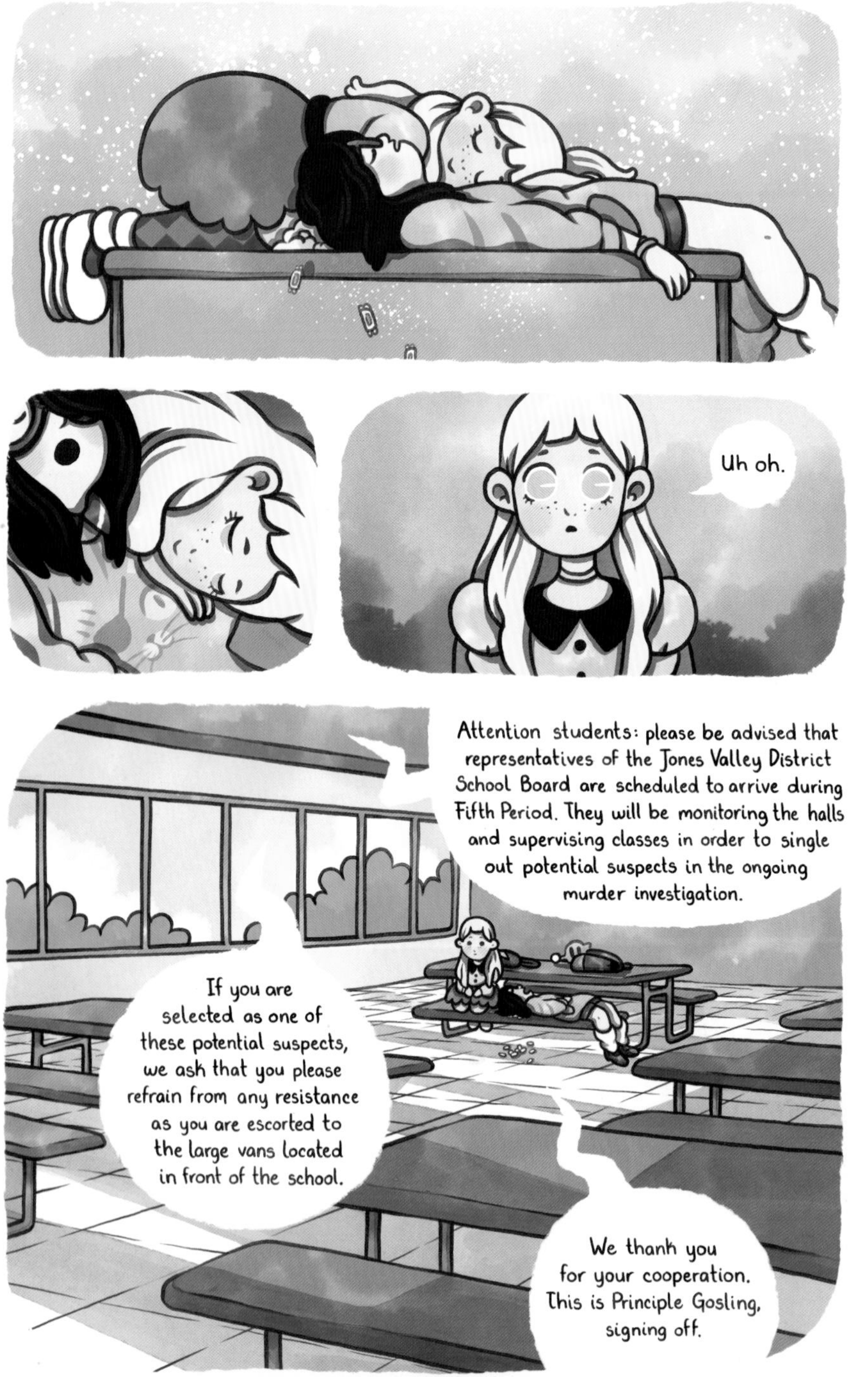
Uh oh.
Attention students: please be advised that representatives of the Jones Valley District School Board are scheduled to arrive during Fifth Period. They will be monitoring the halls and supervising classes in order to single out potential suspects in the ongoing murder investigation.
If you are selected as one of these potential suspects, we ask that you please refrain from any resistance as you are escorted to the large vans located in front of the school.
We thank you for your cooperation. This is Principle Gosling, signing off.

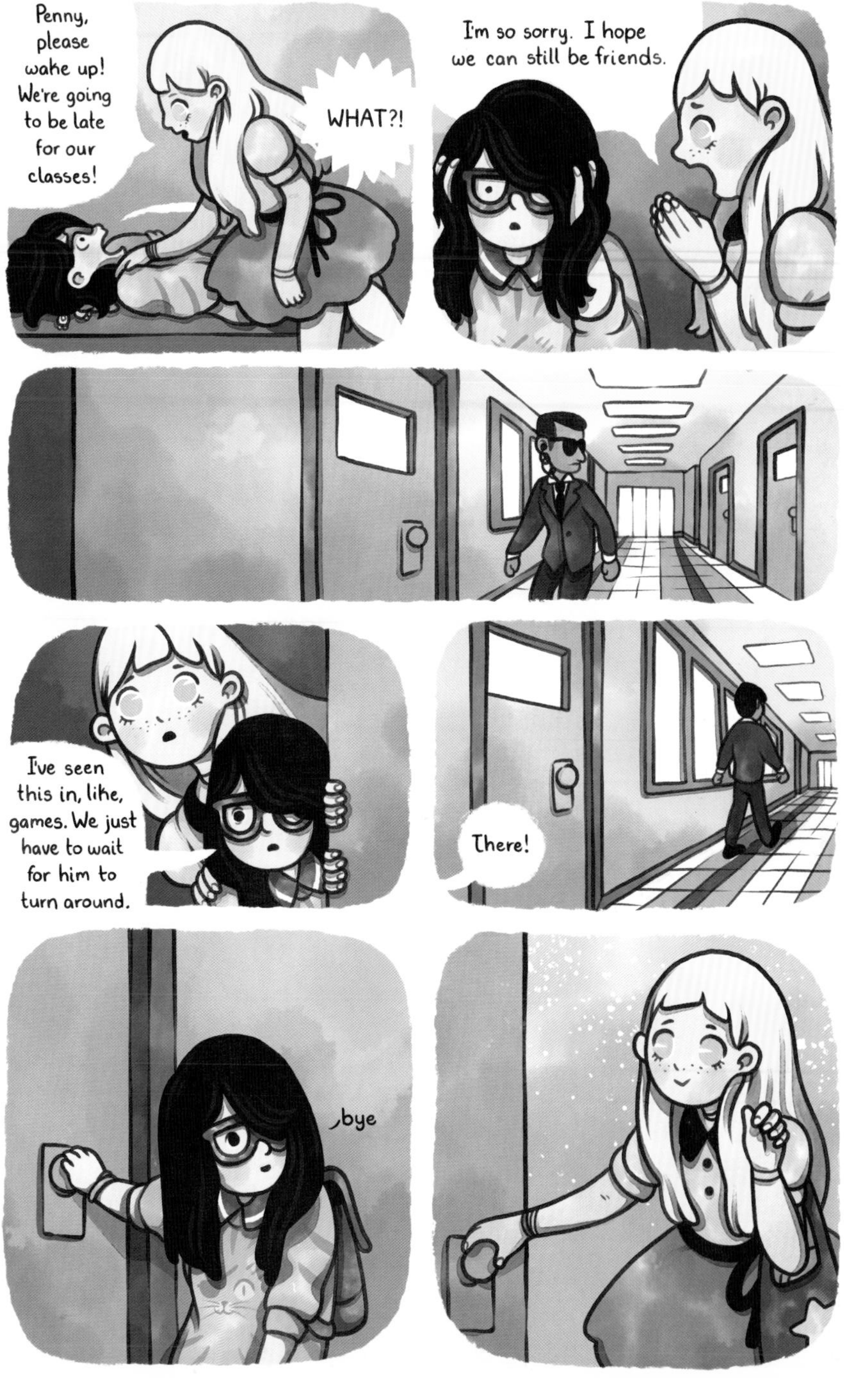
Penny, please wake up! We're going to be late for our classes!
WHAT?!
I'm so sorry. I hope we can still be friends.
I've seen this in, like, games. We just have to wait for him to turn around.
There!
,bye

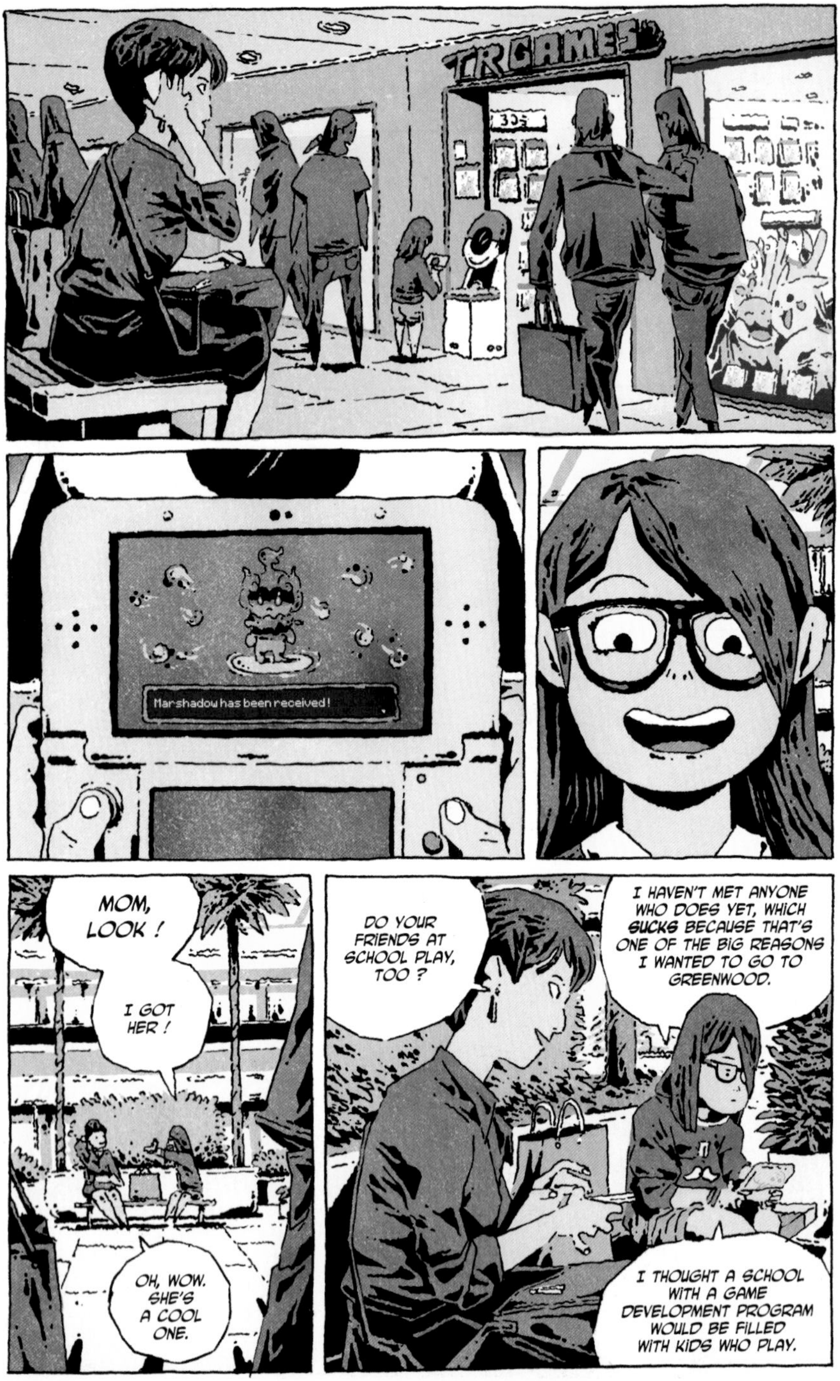
TRGAMES
Marshadow has been received!
MOM, LOOK !
I GOT HER !
OH, WOW. SHE'S A COOL ONE.
DO YOUR FRIENDS AT SCHOOL PLAY, TOO ?
I HAVEN'T MET ANYONE WHO DOES YET, WHICH SUCKS BECAUSE THAT'S ONE OF THE BIG REASONS I WANTED TO GO TO GREENWOOD.
I THOUGHT A SCHOOL WITH A GAME DEVELOPMENT PROGRAM WOULD BE FILLED WITH KIDS WHO PLAY.

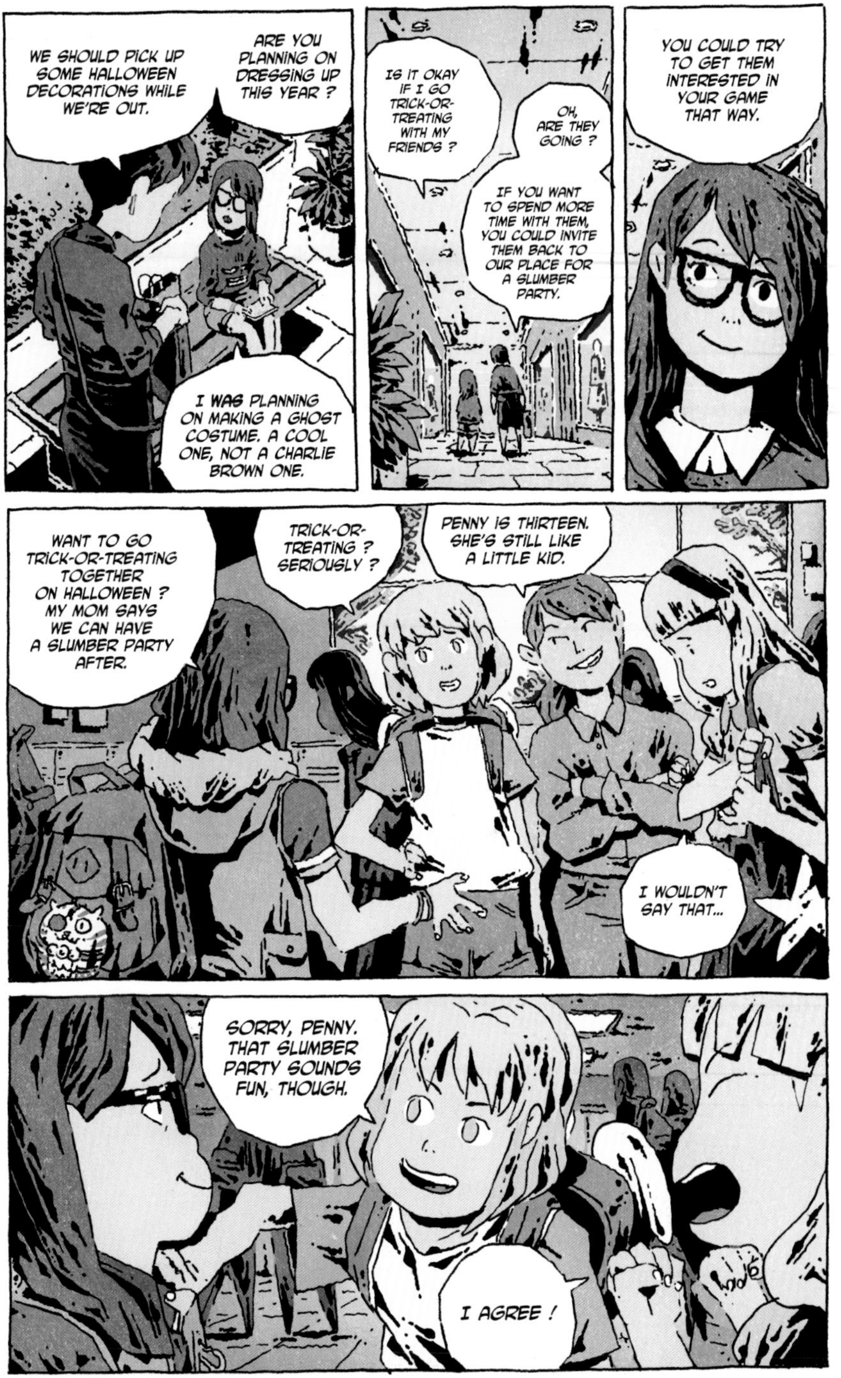
WE SHOULD PICK UP SOME HALLOWEEN DECORATIONS WHILE WE'RE OUT.
ARE YOU PLANNING ON DRESSING UP THIS YEAR ?
I WAS PLANNING ON MAKING A GHOST COSTUME. A COOL ONE, NOT A CHARLIE BROWN ONE.
IS IT OKAY IF I GO TRICK-OR-TREATING WITH MY FRIENDS ?
OH, ARE THEY GOING ?
IF YOU WANT TO SPEND MORE TIME WITH THEM, YOU COULD INVITE THEM BACK TO OUR PLACE FOR A SLUMBER PARTY.
YOU COULD TRY TO GET THEM INTERESTED IN YOUR GAME THAT WAY.
WANT TO GO TRICK-OR-TREATING TOGETHER ON HALLOWEEN ? MY MOM SAYS WE CAN HAVE A SLUMBER PARTY AFTER.
TRICK-OR-TREATING ? SERIOUSLY ?
PENNY IS THIRTEEN. SHE'S STILL LIKE A LITTLE KID.
I WOULDN'T SAY THAT...
SORRY, PENNY. THAT SLUMBER PARTY SOUNDS FUN, THOUGH.
I AGREE !

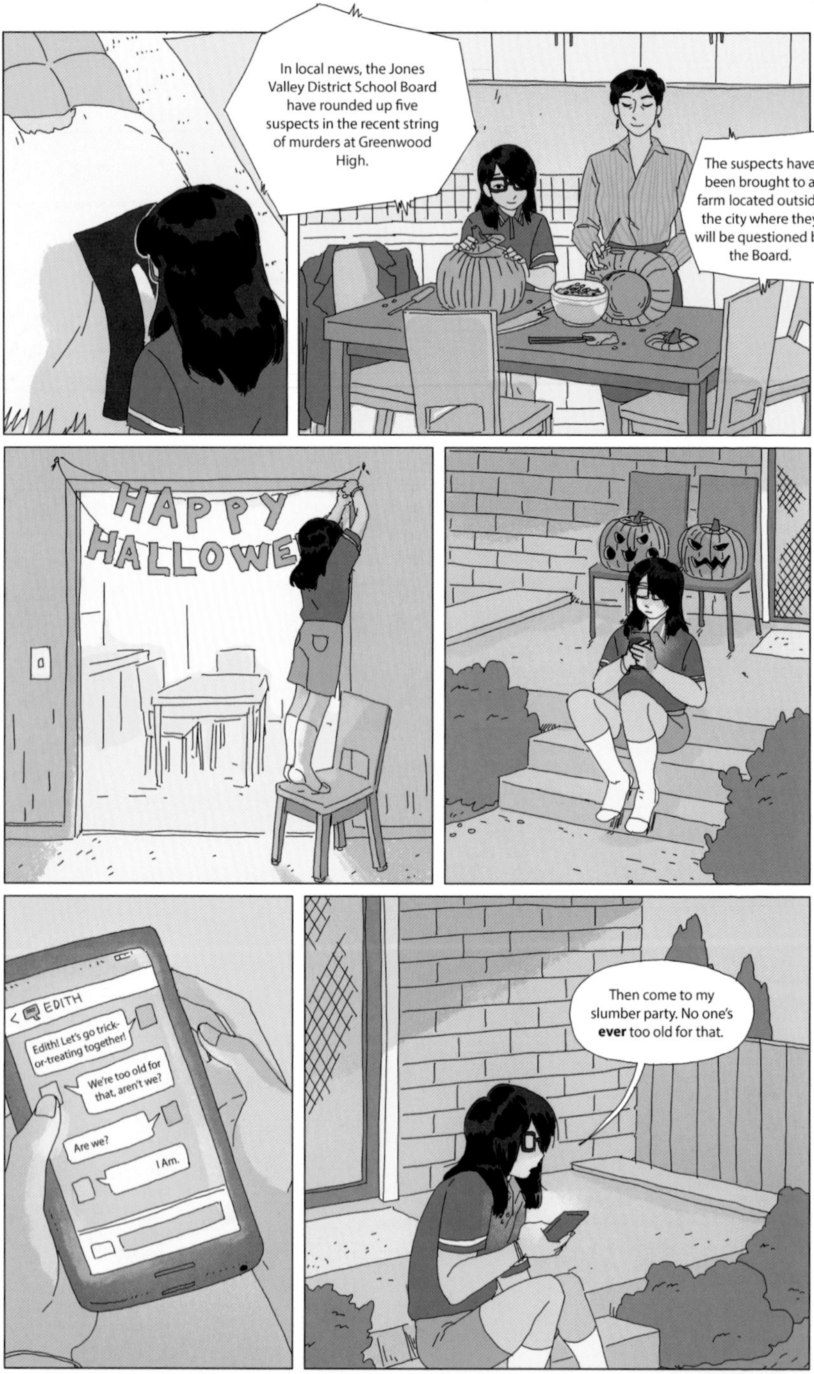
In local news, the Jones Valley District School Board have rounded up five suspects in the recent string of murders at Greenwood High.
The suspects have been brought to a farm located outside the city where they will be questioned by the Board.
HAPPY HALLOWE
EDITH
Edith! Let's go trick-or-treating together!
We're too old for that, aren't we?
Are we?
I Am.
Then come to my slumber party. No one's **ever** too old for that.

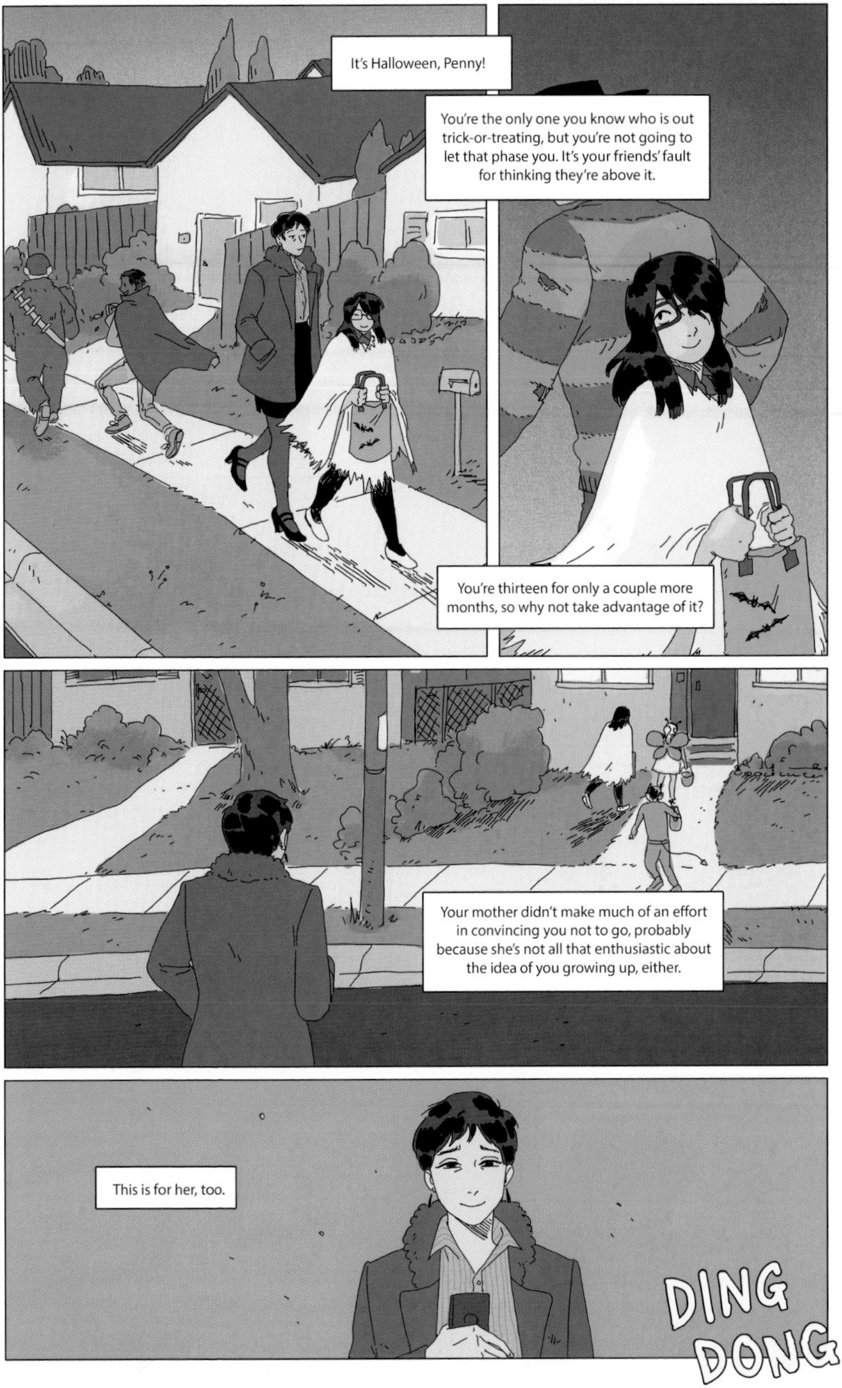
It's Halloween, Penny!
You're the only one you know who is out trick-or-treating, but you're not going to let that phase you. It's your friends' fault for thinking they're above it.
You're thirteen for only a couple more months, so why not take advantage of it?
Your mother didn't make much of an effort in convincing you not to go, probably because she's not all that enthusiastic about the idea of you growing up, either.
This is for her, too.
DING DONG

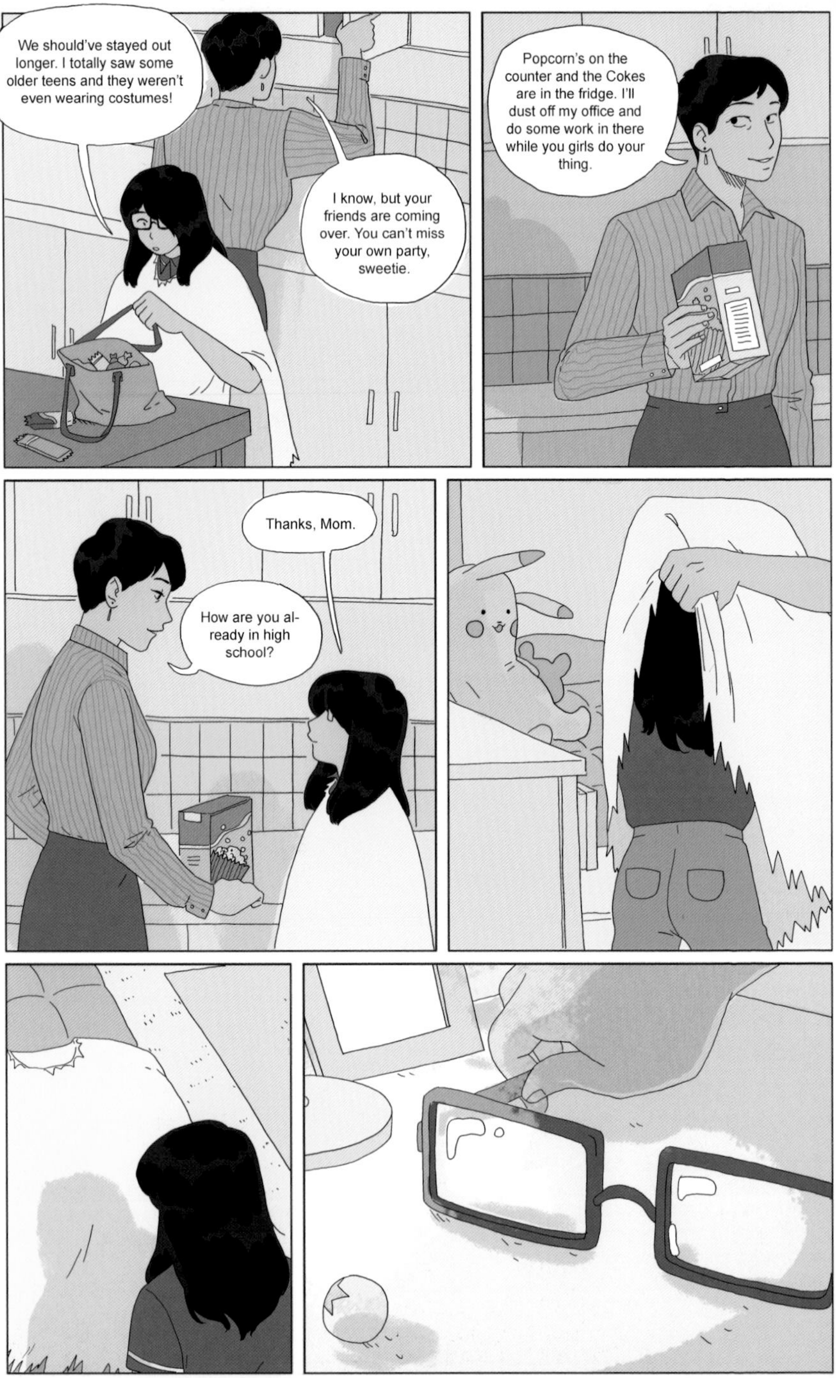
We should've stayed out longer. I totally saw some older teens and they weren't even wearing costumes!
I know, but your friends are coming over. You can't miss your own party, sweetie.
Popcorn's on the counter and the Cokes are in the fridge. I'll dust off my office and do some work in there while you girls do your thing.
Thanks, Mom.
How are you already in high school?

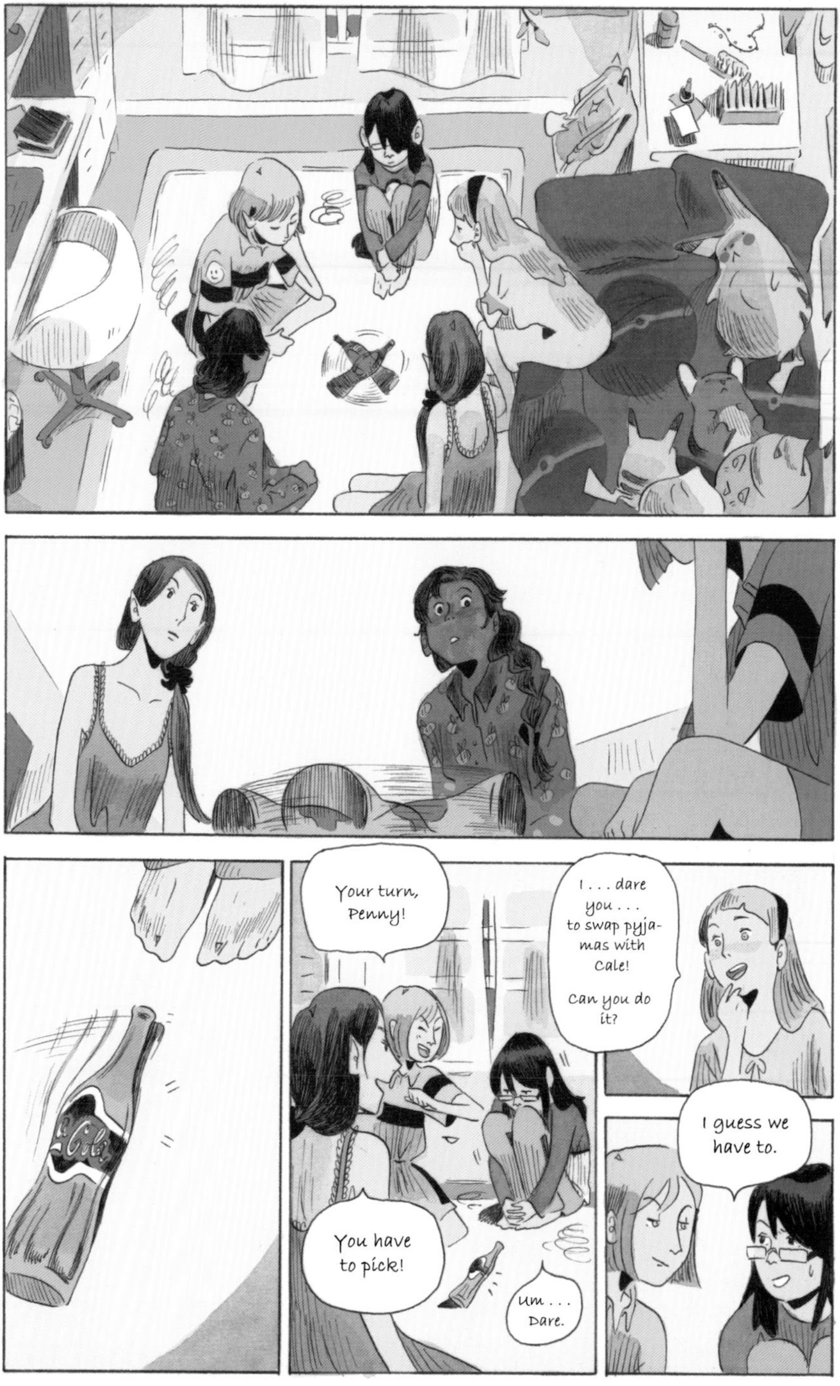
Your turn, Penny!
You have to pick!
Um . . . Dare.
I . . . dare you . . . to swap pyjamas with Cale!
Can you do it?
I guess we have to.

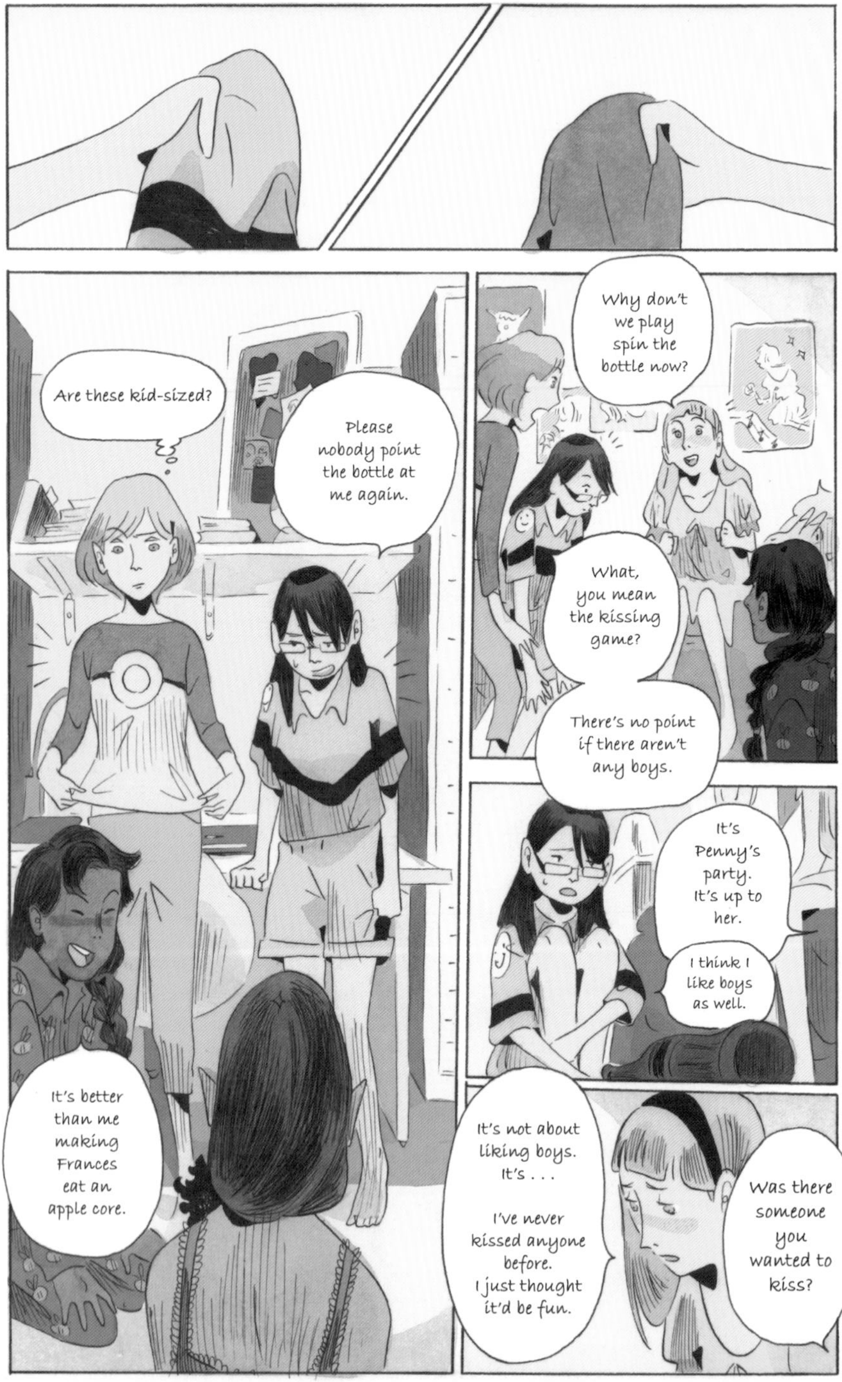
Are these kid-sized?
Please nobody point the bottle at me again.
It's better than me making Frances eat an apple core.
Why don't we play spin the bottle now?
What, you mean the kissing game?
There's no point if there aren't any boys.
It's Penny's party. It's up to her.
I think I like boys as well.
It's not about liking boys. It's . . .
I've never kissed anyone before. I just thought it'd be fun.
Was there someone you wanted to kiss?

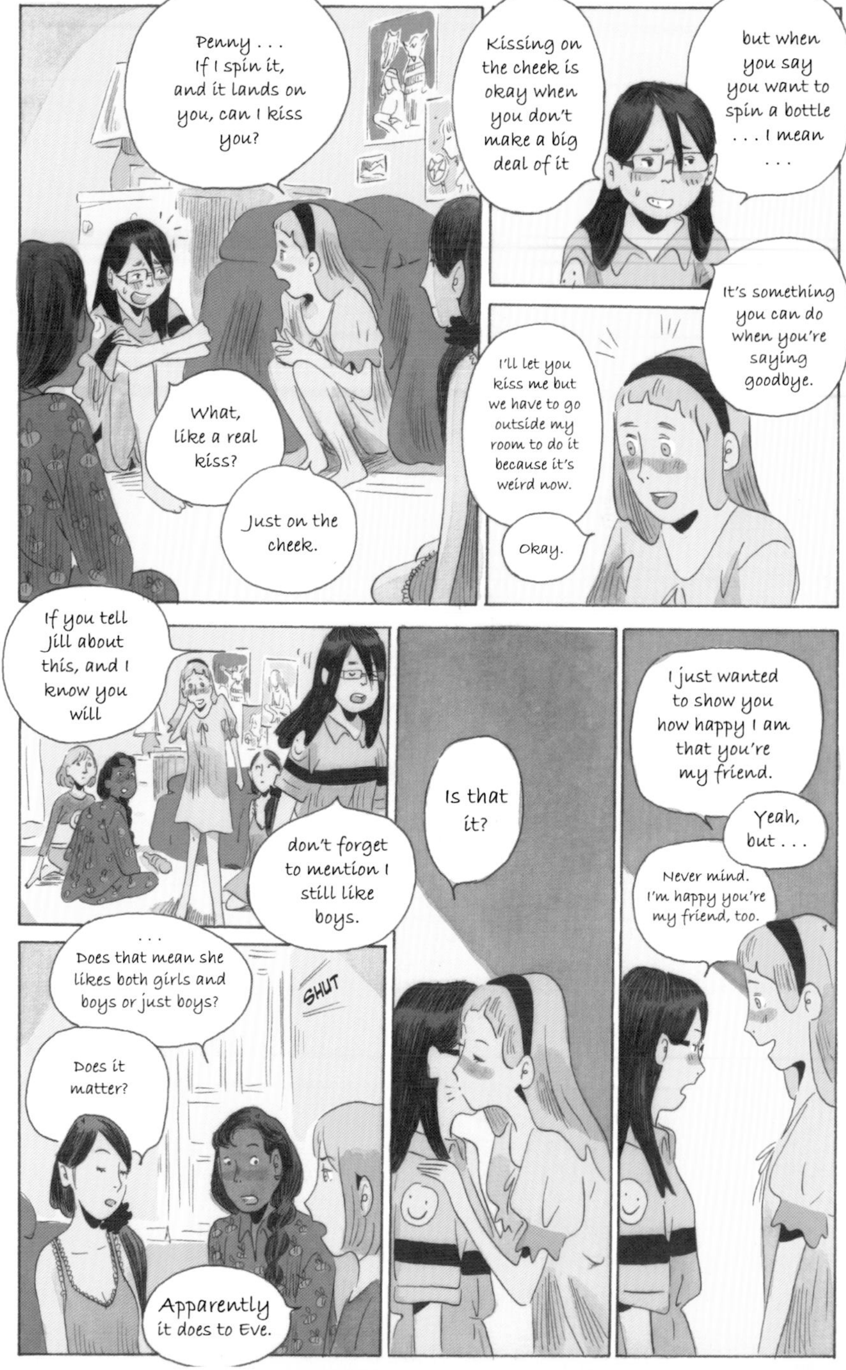
Penny . . . If I spin it, and it lands on you, can I kiss you?
What, like a real kiss?
Just on the cheek.
Kissing on the cheek is okay when you don't make a big deal of it
but when you say you want to spin a bottle . . . I mean . . .
It's something you can do when you're saying goodbye.
I'll let you kiss me but we have to go outside my room to do it because it's weird now.
Okay.
If you tell Jill about this, and I know you will
don't forget to mention I still like boys.
. . . Does that mean she likes both girls and boys or just boys?
SHUT
Does it matter?
Apparently it does to Eve.
Is that it?
I just wanted to show you how happy I am that you're my friend.
Yeah, but . . .
Never mind. I'm happy you're my friend, too.

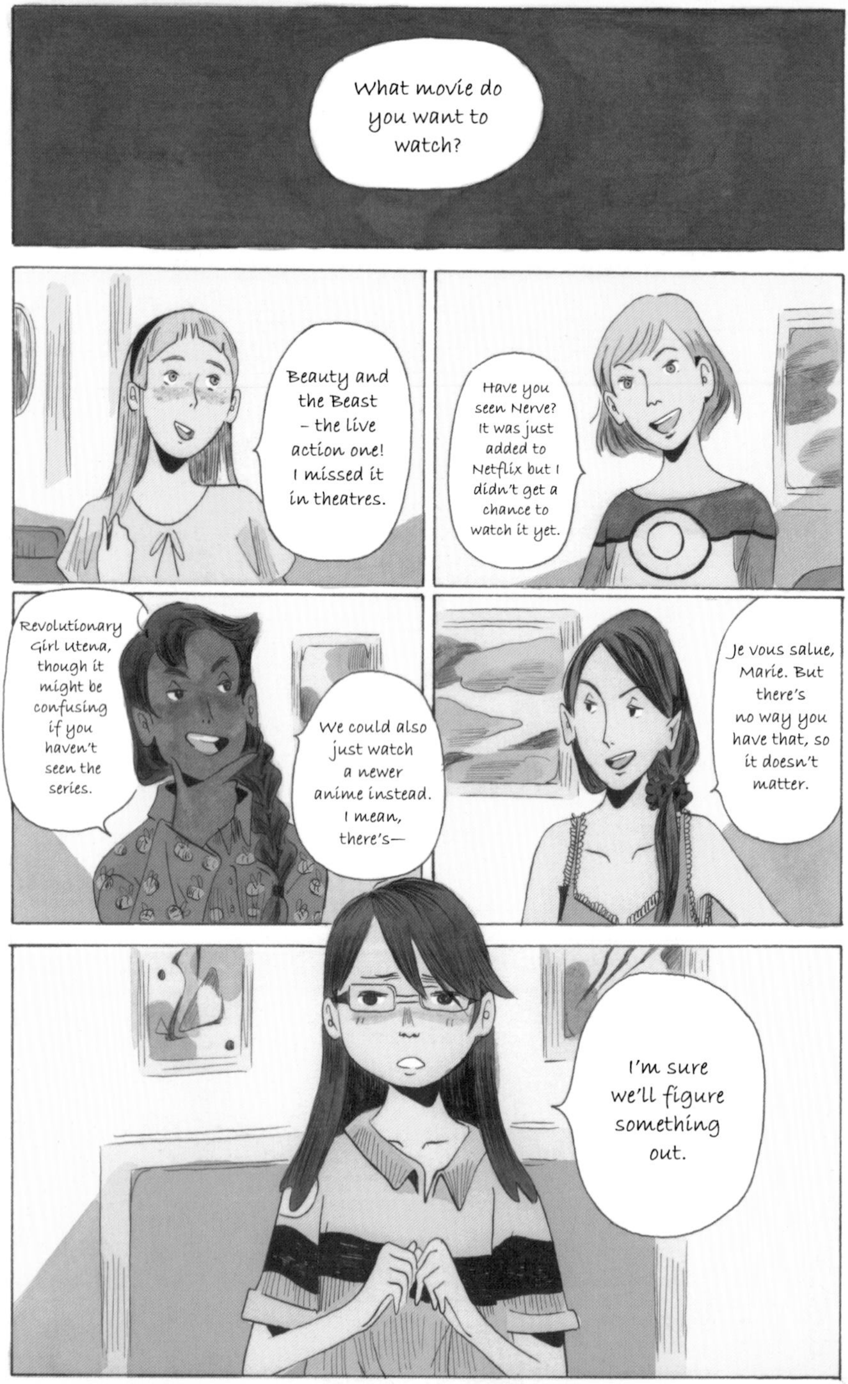

What movie do you want to watch?
Beauty and the Beast – the live action one! I missed it in theatres.
Have you seen Nerve? It was just added to Netflix but I didn't get a chance to watch it yet.
Revolutionary Girl Utena, though it might be confusing if you haven't seen the series.
We could also just watch a newer anime instead. I mean, there's—
Je vous salue, Marie. But there's no way you have that, so it doesn't matter.
I'm sure we'll figure something out.

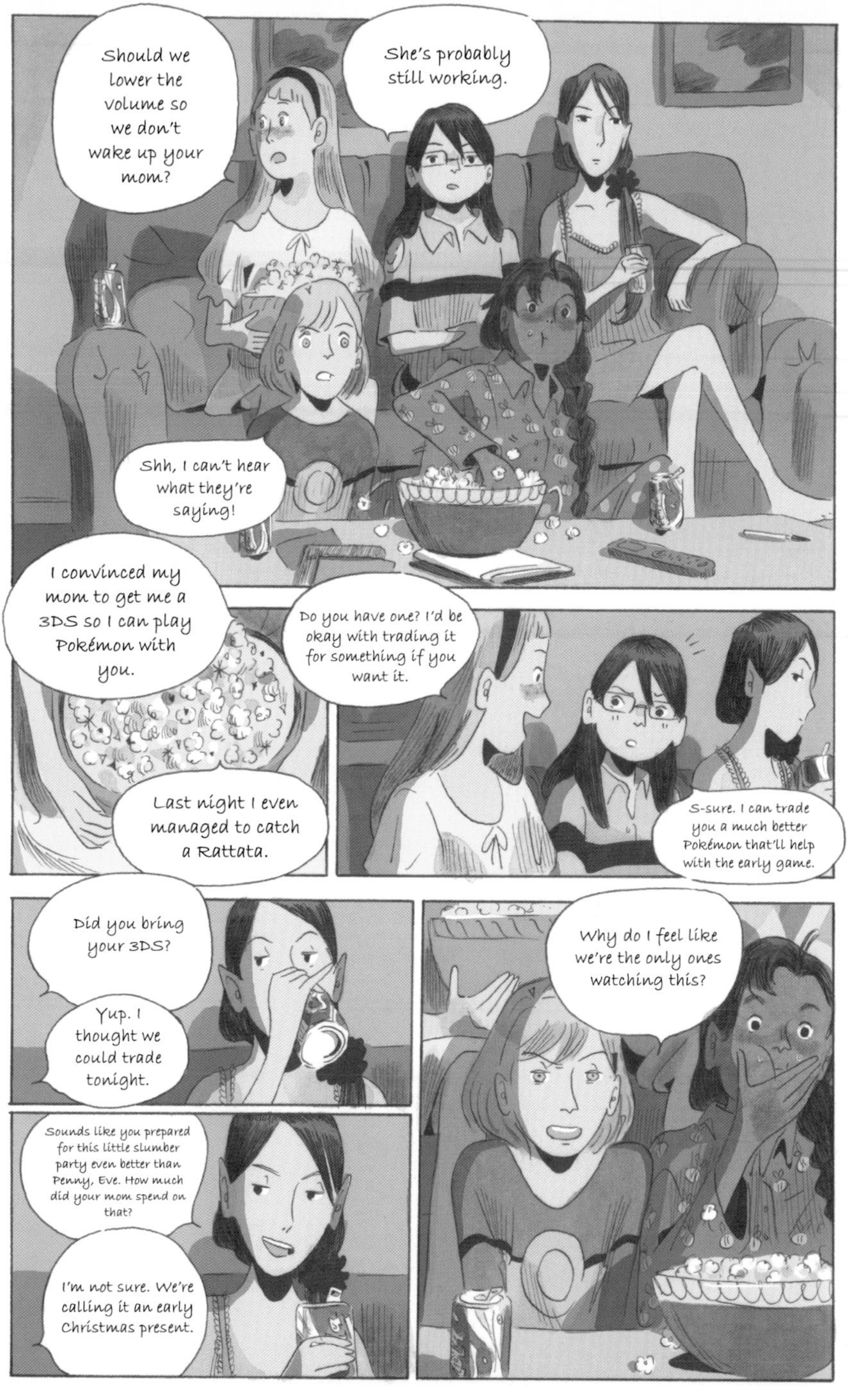

Should we lower the volume so we don't wake up your mom?
She's probably still working.
Shh, I can't hear what they're saying!
I convinced my mom to get me a 3DS so I can play Pokémon with you.
Last night I even managed to catch a Rattata.
Do you have one? I'd be okay with trading it for something if you want it.
S-sure. I can trade you a much better Pokémon that'll help with the early game.
Did you bring your 3DS?
Yup. I thought we could trade tonight.
Sounds like you prepared for this little slumber party even better than Penny, Eve. How much did your mom spend on that?
I'm not sure. We're calling it an early Christmas present.
Why do I feel like we're the only ones watching this?

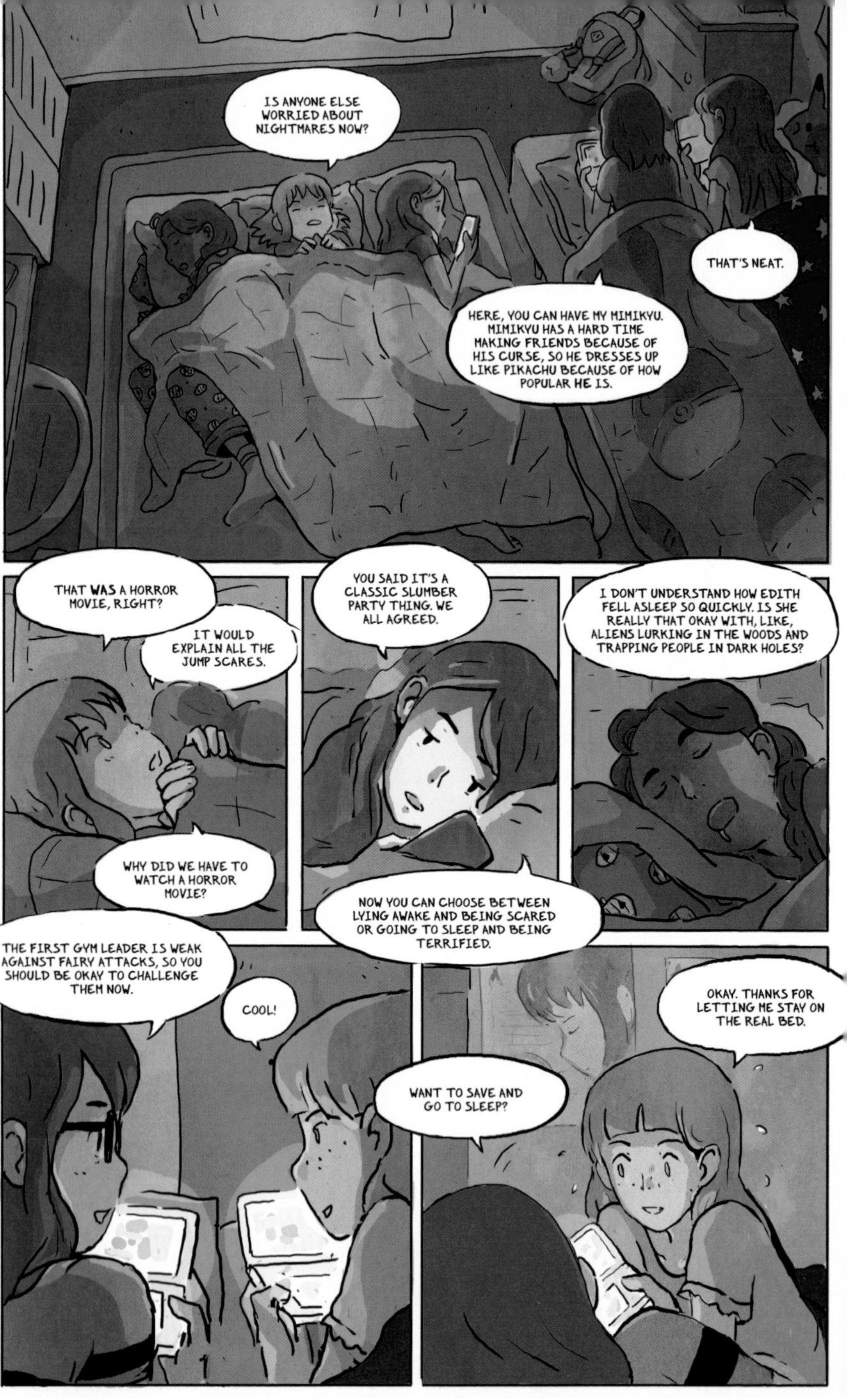
IS ANYONE ELSE WORRIED ABOUT NIGHTMARES NOW?
THAT'S NEAT.
HERE, YOU CAN HAVE MY MIMIKYU. MIMIKYU HAS A HARD TIME MAKING FRIENDS BECAUSE OF HIS CURSE, SO HE DRESSES UP LIKE PIKACHU BECAUSE OF HOW POPULAR HE IS.
THAT WAS A HORROR MOVIE, RIGHT?
IT WOULD EXPLAIN ALL THE JUMP SCARES.
WHY DID WE HAVE TO WATCH A HORROR MOVIE?
YOU SAID IT'S A CLASSIC SLUMBER PARTY THING. WE ALL AGREED.
I DON'T UNDERSTAND HOW EDITH FELL ASLEEP SO QUICKLY. IS SHE REALLY THAT OKAY WITH, LIKE, ALIENS LURKING IN THE WOODS AND TRAPPING PEOPLE IN DARK HOLES?
NOW YOU CAN CHOOSE BETWEEN LYING AWAKE AND BEING SCARED OR GOING TO SLEEP AND BEING TERRIFIED.
THE FIRST GYM LEADER IS WEAK AGAINST FAIRY ATTACKS, SO YOU SHOULD BE OKAY TO CHALLENGE THEM NOW.
COOL!
WANT TO SAVE AND GO TO SLEEP?
OKAY. THANKS FOR LETTING ME STAY ON THE REAL BED.

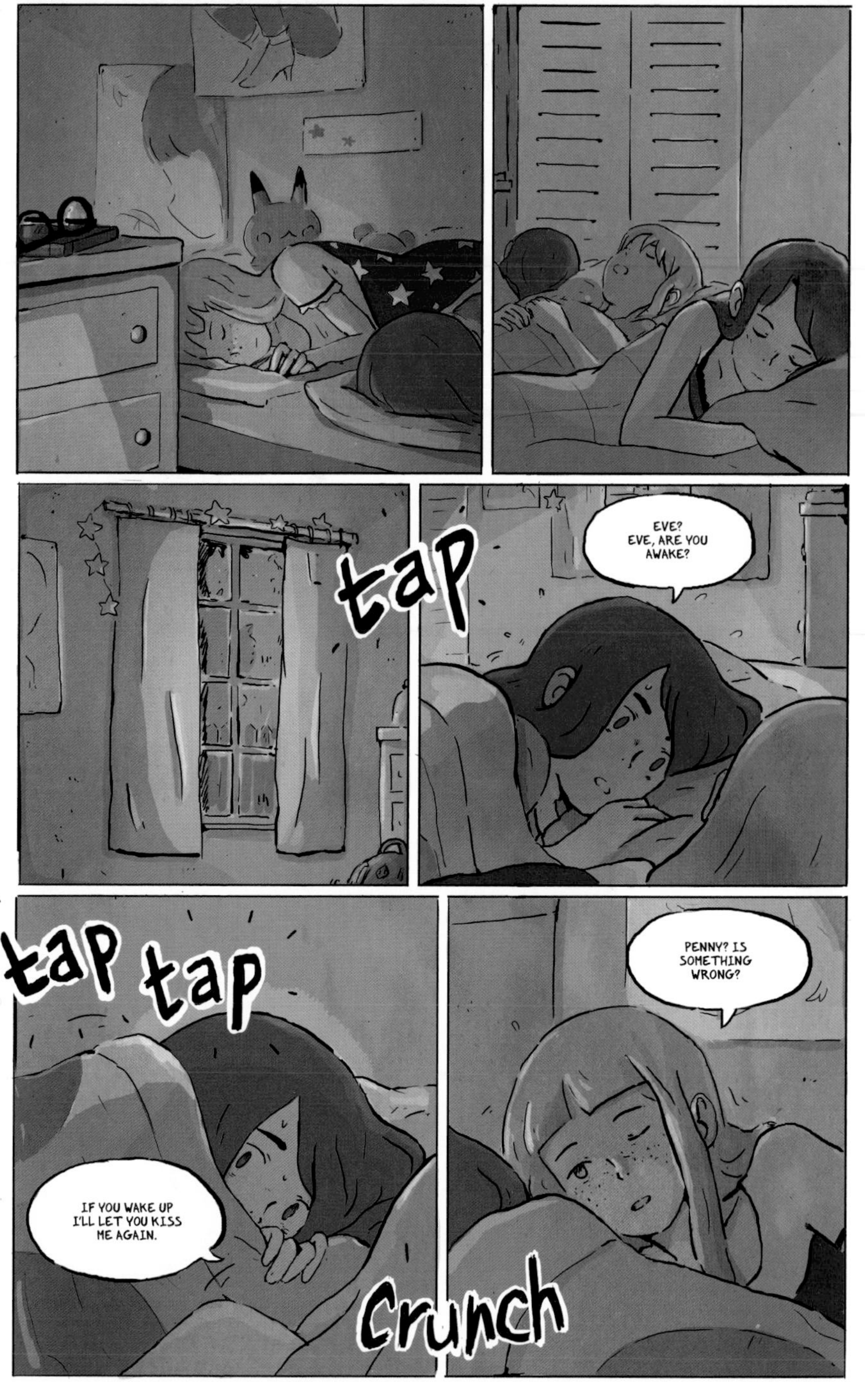

tap
EVE? EVE, ARE YOU AWAKE?
tap tap
IF YOU WAKE UP I'LL LET YOU KISS ME AGAIN.
PENNY? IS SOMETHING WRONG?
Crunch

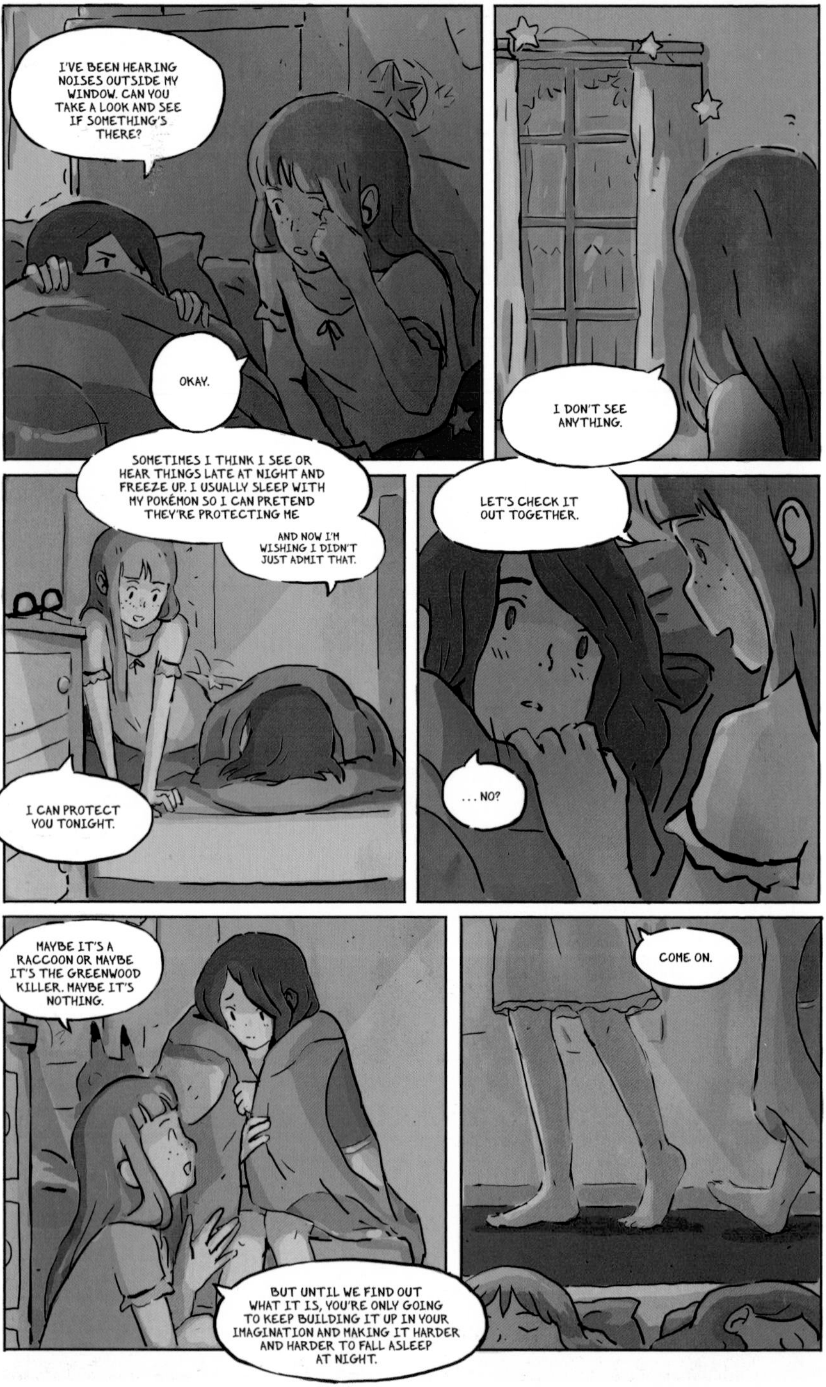
I'VE BEEN HEARING NOISES OUTSIDE MY WINDOW. CAN YOU TAKE A LOOK AND SEE IF SOMETHING'S THERE?
OKAY.
I DON'T SEE ANYTHING.
SOMETIMES I THINK I SEE OR HEAR THINGS LATE AT NIGHT AND FREEZE UP. I USUALLY SLEEP WITH MY POKÉMON SO I CAN PRETEND THEY'RE PROTECTING ME
AND NOW I'M WISHING I DIDN'T JUST ADMIT THAT.
I CAN PROTECT YOU TONIGHT.
LET'S CHECK IT OUT TOGETHER.
. . . NO?
MAYBE IT'S A RACCOON OR MAYBE IT'S THE GREENWOOD KILLER. MAYBE IT'S NOTHING.
BUT UNTIL WE FIND OUT WHAT IT IS, YOU'RE ONLY GOING TO KEEP BUILDING IT UP IN YOUR IMAGINATION AND MAKING IT HARDER AND HARDER TO FALL ASLEEP AT NIGHT.
COME ON.

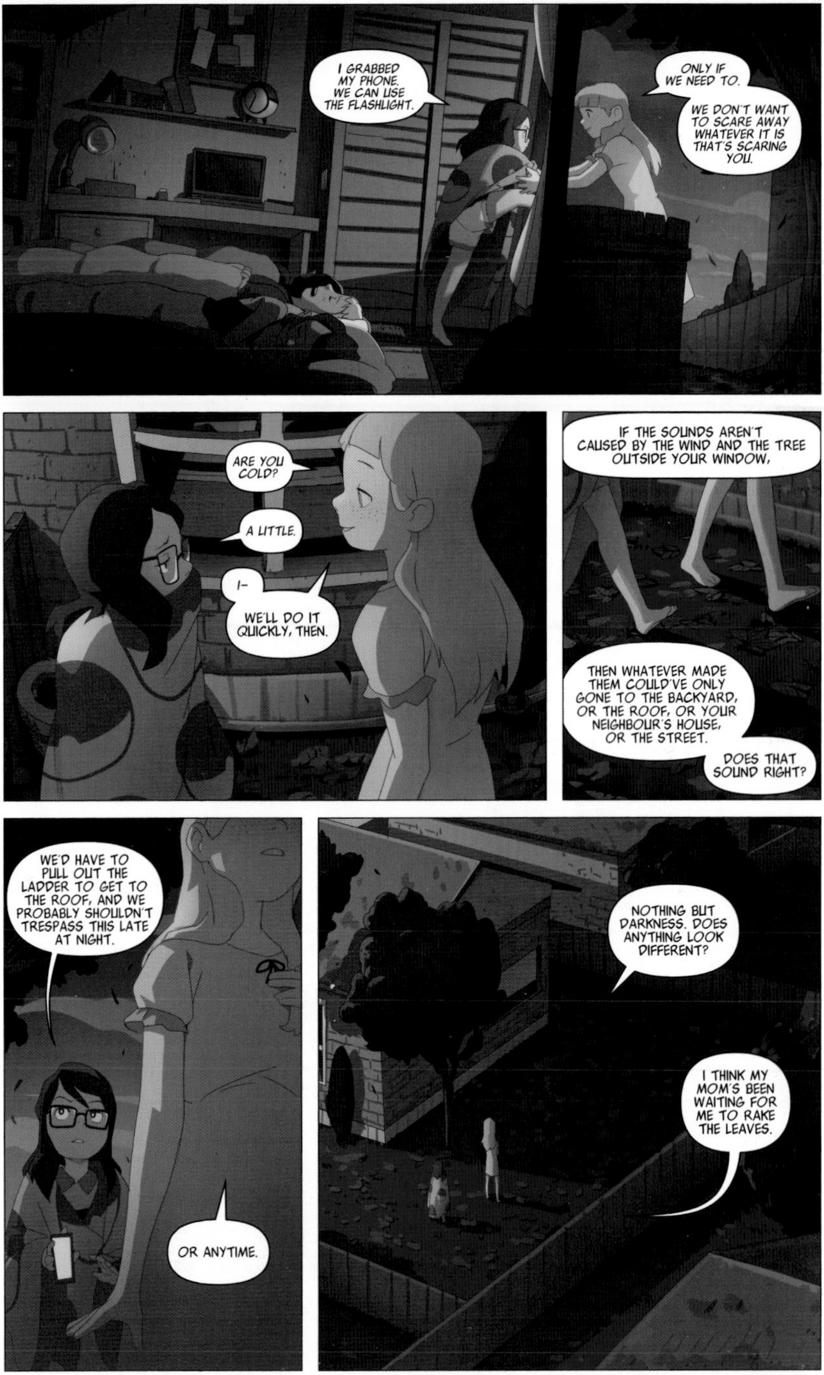
I GRABBED MY PHONE. WE CAN USE THE FLASHLIGHT.
ONLY IF WE NEED TO.
WE DON'T WANT TO SCARE AWAY WHATEVER IT IS THAT'S SCARING YOU.
ARE YOU COLD?
A LITTLE.
I–
WE'LL DO IT QUICKLY, THEN.
IF THE SOUNDS AREN'T CAUSED BY THE WIND AND THE TREE OUTSIDE YOUR WINDOW,
THEN WHATEVER MADE THEM COULD'VE ONLY GONE TO THE BACKYARD, OR THE ROOF, OR YOUR NEIGHBOUR'S HOUSE, OR THE STREET.
DOES THAT SOUND RIGHT?
WE'D HAVE TO PULL OUT THE LADDER TO GET TO THE ROOF, AND WE PROBABLY SHOULDN'T TRESPASS THIS LATE AT NIGHT.
OR ANYTIME.
NOTHING BUT DARKNESS. DOES ANYTHING LOOK DIFFERENT?
I THINK MY MOM'S BEEN WAITING FOR ME TO RAKE THE LEAVES.

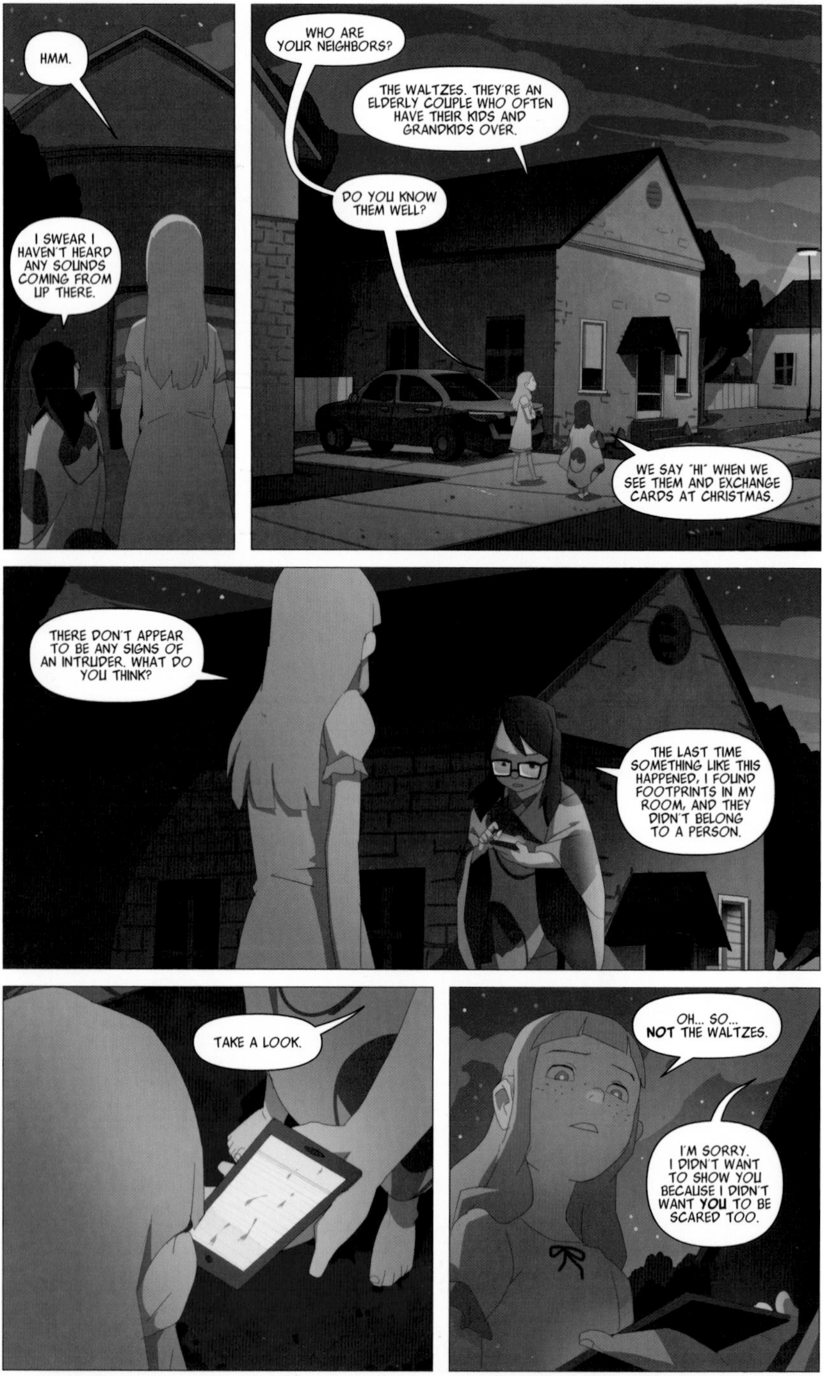
HMM.
I SWEAR I HAVEN'T HEARD ANY SOUNDS COMING FROM UP THERE.
WHO ARE YOUR NEIGHBORS?
THE WALTZES. THEY'RE AN ELDERLY COUPLE WHO OFTEN HAVE THEIR KIDS AND GRANDKIDS OVER.
DO YOU KNOW THEM WELL?
WE SAY "HI" WHEN WE SEE THEM AND EXCHANGE CARDS AT CHRISTMAS.
THERE DON'T APPEAR TO BE ANY SIGNS OF AN INTRUDER. WHAT DO YOU THINK?
THE LAST TIME SOMETHING LIKE THIS HAPPENED, I FOUND FOOTPRINTS IN MY ROOM, AND THEY DIDN'T BELONG TO A PERSON.
TAKE A LOOK.
OH... SO... **NOT** THE WALTZES.
I'M SORRY. I DIDN'T WANT TO SHOW YOU BECAUSE I DIDN'T WANT **YOU** TO BE SCARED TOO.

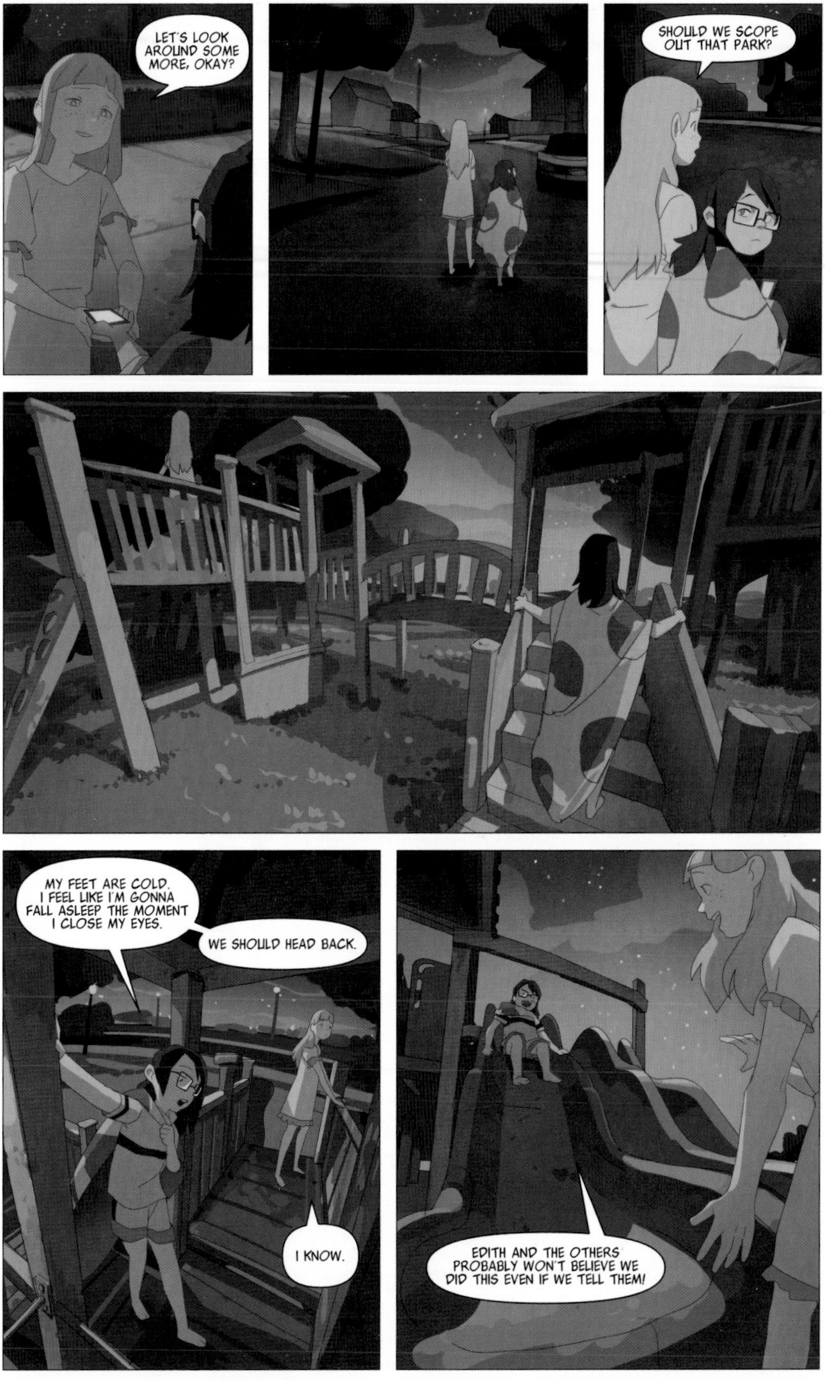
LET'S LOOK AROUND SOME MORE, OKAY?
SHOULD WE SCOPE OUT THAT PARK?
MY FEET ARE COLD. I FEEL LIKE I'M GONNA FALL ASLEEP THE MOMENT I CLOSE MY EYES.
WE SHOULD HEAD BACK.
I KNOW.
EDITH AND THE OTHERS PROBABLY WON'T BELIEVE WE DID THIS EVEN IF WE TELL THEM!

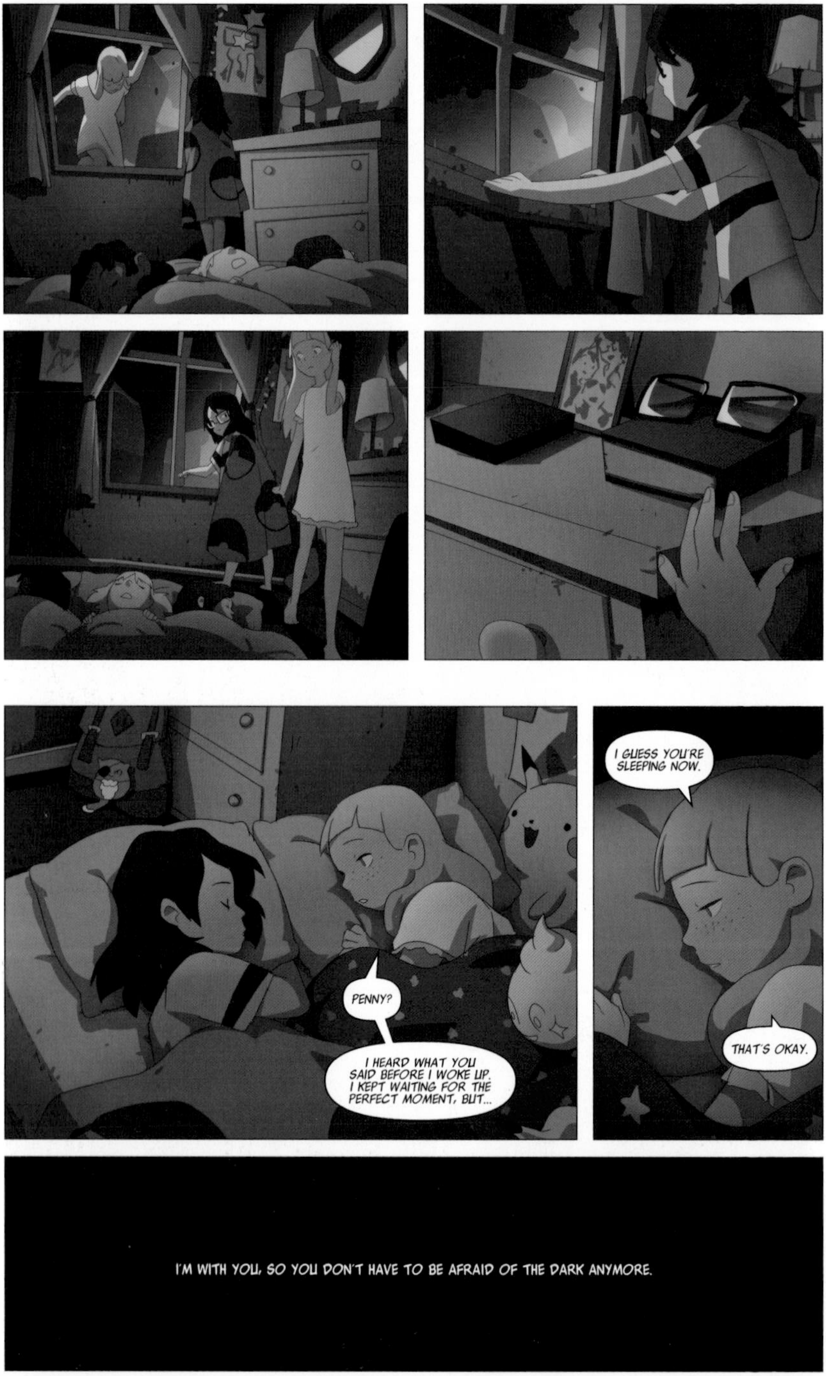
PENNY?
I HEARD WHAT YOU SAID BEFORE I WOKE UP. I KEPT WAITING FOR THE PERFECT MOMENT, BUT...
I GUESS YOU'RE SLEEPING NOW.
THAT'S OKAY.
I'M WITH YOU, SO YOU DON'T HAVE TO BE AFRAID OF THE DARK ANYMORE.

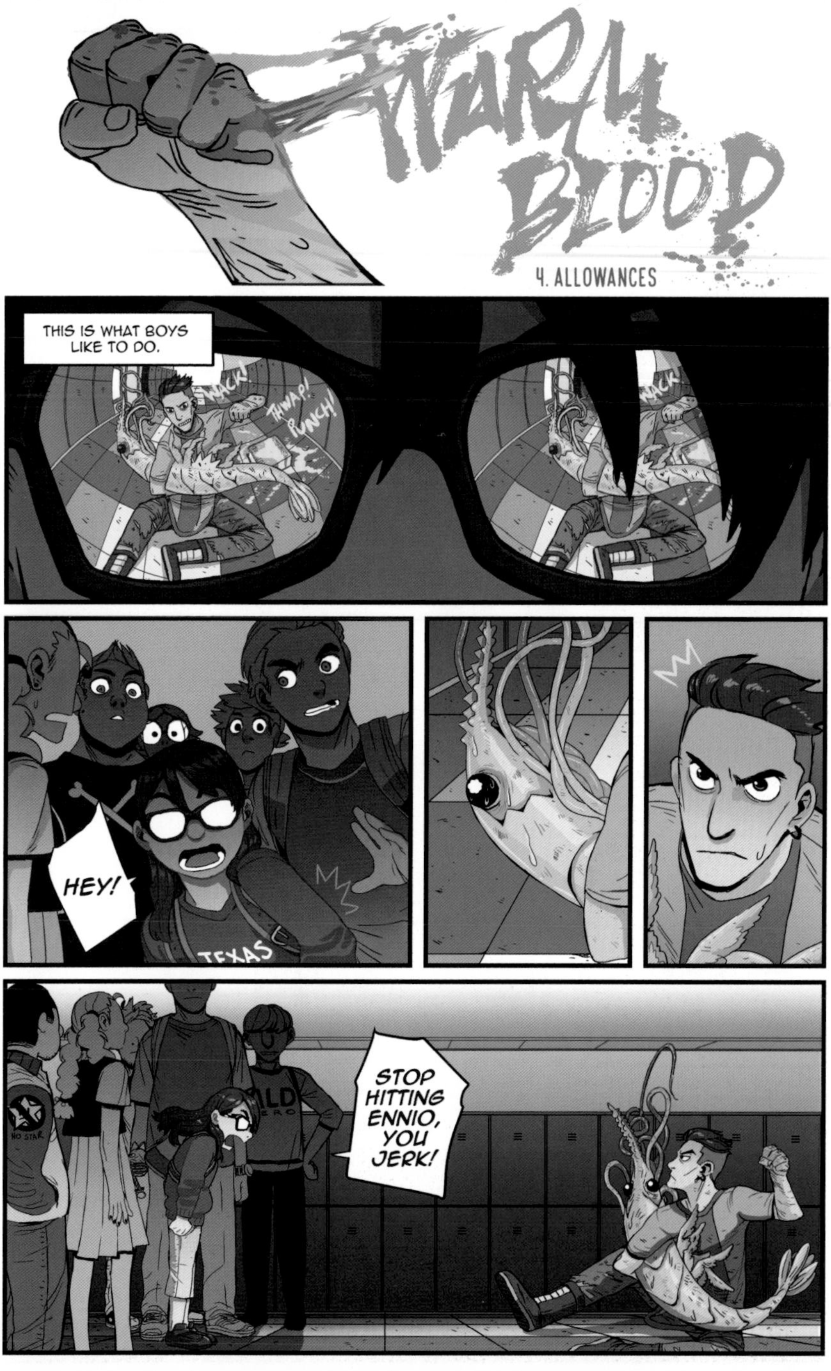
WARM BLOOD
4. ALLOWANCES
THIS IS WHAT BOYS LIKE TO DO.
WACK!
THWAP!
PUNCH!
HEY!
TEXAS
STOP HITTING ENNIO, YOU JERK!
NO STAR

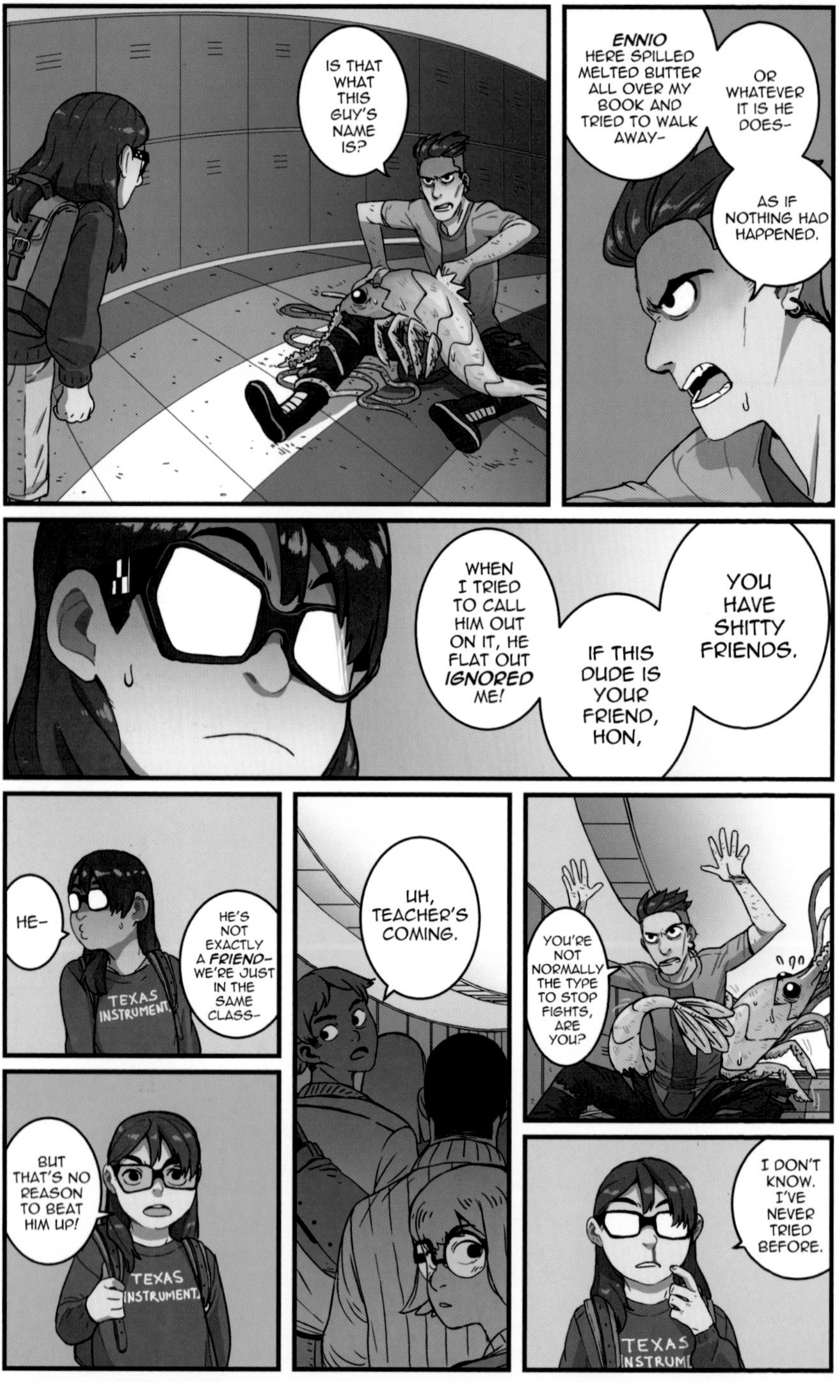
IS THAT WHAT THIS GUY'S NAME IS?
ENNIO HERE SPILLED MELTED BUTTER ALL OVER MY BOOK AND TRIED TO WALK AWAY-
OR WHATEVER IT IS HE DOES-
AS IF NOTHING HAD HAPPENED.
WHEN I TRIED TO CALL HIM OUT ON IT, HE FLAT OUT *IGNORED* ME!
IF THIS DUDE IS YOUR FRIEND, HON,
YOU HAVE SHITTY FRIENDS.
HE-
HE'S NOT EXACTLY A *FRIEND*- WE'RE JUST IN THE SAME CLASS-
TEXAS INSTRUMENTS
UH, TEACHER'S COMING.
YOU'RE NOT NORMALLY THE TYPE TO STOP FIGHTS, ARE YOU?
BUT THAT'S NO REASON TO BEAT HIM UP!
TEXAS INSTRUMENTS
I DON'T KNOW. I'VE NEVER TRIED BEFORE.
TEXAS INSTRUM

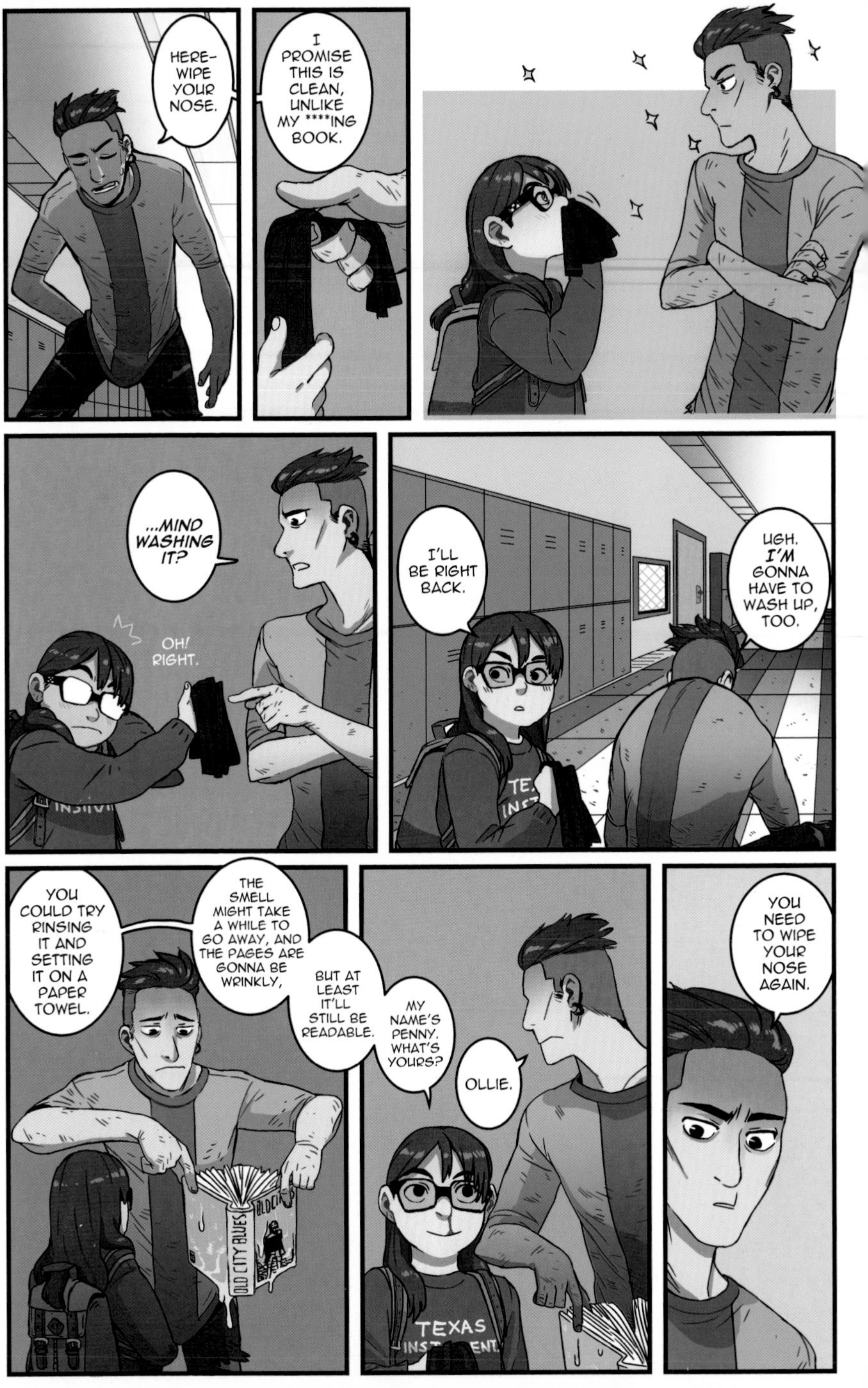
HERE- WIPE YOUR NOSE.
I PROMISE THIS IS CLEAN, UNLIKE MY ****ING BOOK.
...MIND WASHING IT?
OH! RIGHT.
I'LL BE RIGHT BACK.
UGH. I'M GONNA HAVE TO WASH UP, TOO.
YOU COULD TRY RINSING IT AND SETTING IT ON A PAPER TOWEL.
THE SMELL MIGHT TAKE A WHILE TO GO AWAY, AND THE PAGES ARE GONNA BE WRINKLY,
BUT AT LEAST IT'LL STILL BE READABLE.
OLD CITY BLUES
MY NAME'S PENNY. WHAT'S YOURS?
OLLIE.
TEXAS
YOU NEED TO WIPE YOUR NOSE AGAIN.

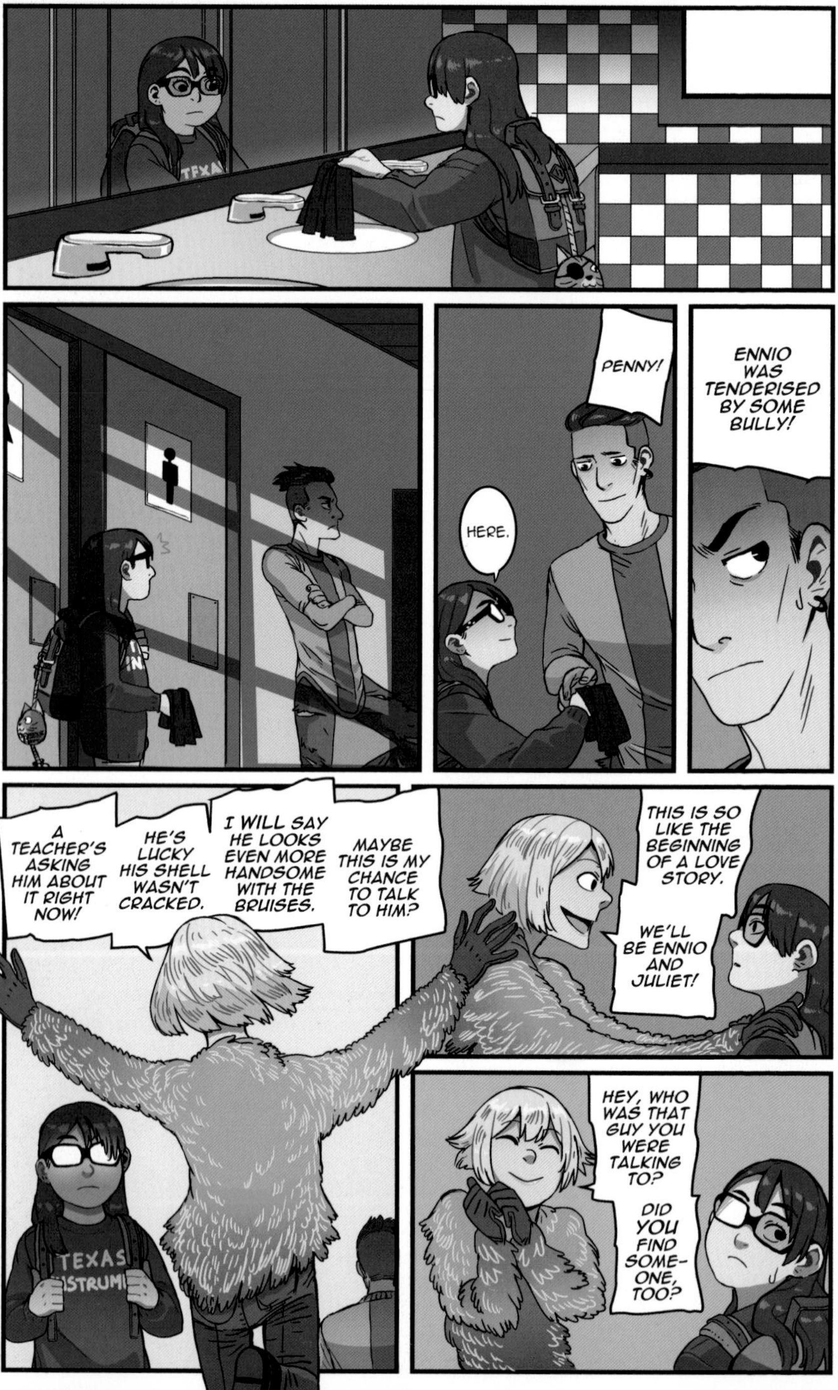
PENNY!
HERE.
ENNIO WAS TENDERISED BY SOME BULLY!
A TEACHER'S ASKING HIM ABOUT IT RIGHT NOW!
HE'S LUCKY HIS SHELL WASN'T CRACKED.
I WILL SAY HE LOOKS EVEN MORE HANDSOME WITH THE BRUISES.
MAYBE THIS IS MY CHANCE TO TALK TO HIM?
TEXAS
THIS IS SO LIKE THE BEGINNING OF A LOVE STORY.
WE'LL BE ENNIO AND JULIET!
HEY, WHO WAS THAT GUY YOU WERE TALKING TO?
DID YOU FIND SOME-ONE, TOO?

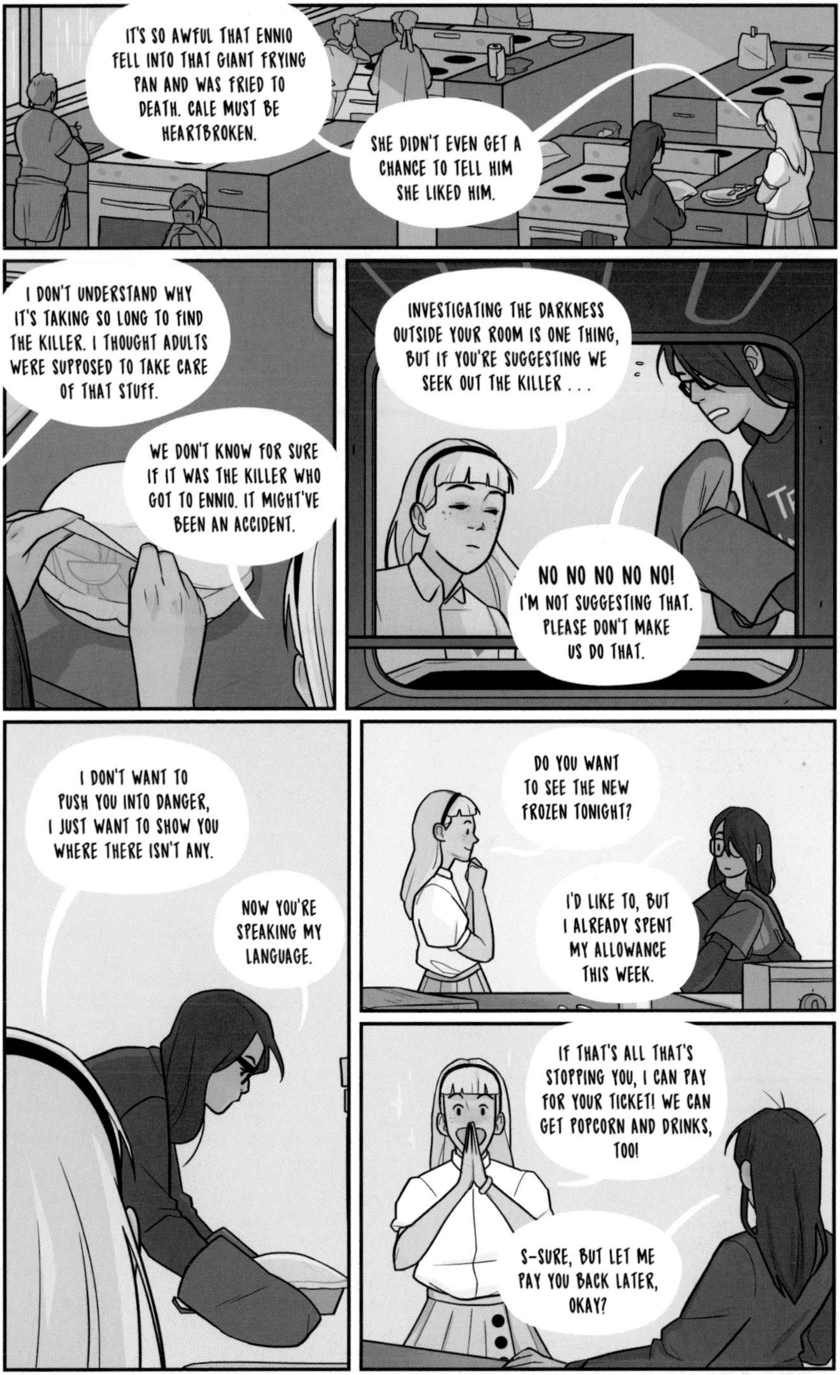
IT'S SO AWFUL THAT ENNIO FELL INTO THAT GIANT FRYING PAN AND WAS FRIED TO DEATH. CALE MUST BE HEARTBROKEN.
SHE DIDN'T EVEN GET A CHANCE TO TELL HIM SHE LIKED HIM.
I DON'T UNDERSTAND WHY IT'S TAKING SO LONG TO FIND THE KILLER. I THOUGHT ADULTS WERE SUPPOSED TO TAKE CARE OF THAT STUFF.
WE DON'T KNOW FOR SURE IF IT WAS THE KILLER WHO GOT TO ENNIO. IT MIGHT'VE BEEN AN ACCIDENT.
INVESTIGATING THE DARKNESS OUTSIDE YOUR ROOM IS ONE THING, BUT IF YOU'RE SUGGESTING WE SEEK OUT THE KILLER . . .
NO NO NO NO NO! I'M NOT SUGGESTING THAT. PLEASE DON'T MAKE US DO THAT.
I DON'T WANT TO PUSH YOU INTO DANGER, I JUST WANT TO SHOW YOU WHERE THERE ISN'T ANY.
NOW YOU'RE SPEAKING MY LANGUAGE.
DO YOU WANT TO SEE THE NEW FROZEN TONIGHT?
I'D LIKE TO, BUT I ALREADY SPENT MY ALLOWANCE THIS WEEK.
IF THAT'S ALL THAT'S STOPPING YOU, I CAN PAY FOR YOUR TICKET! WE CAN GET POPCORN AND DRINKS, TOO!
S-SURE, BUT LET ME PAY YOU BACK LATER, OKAY?

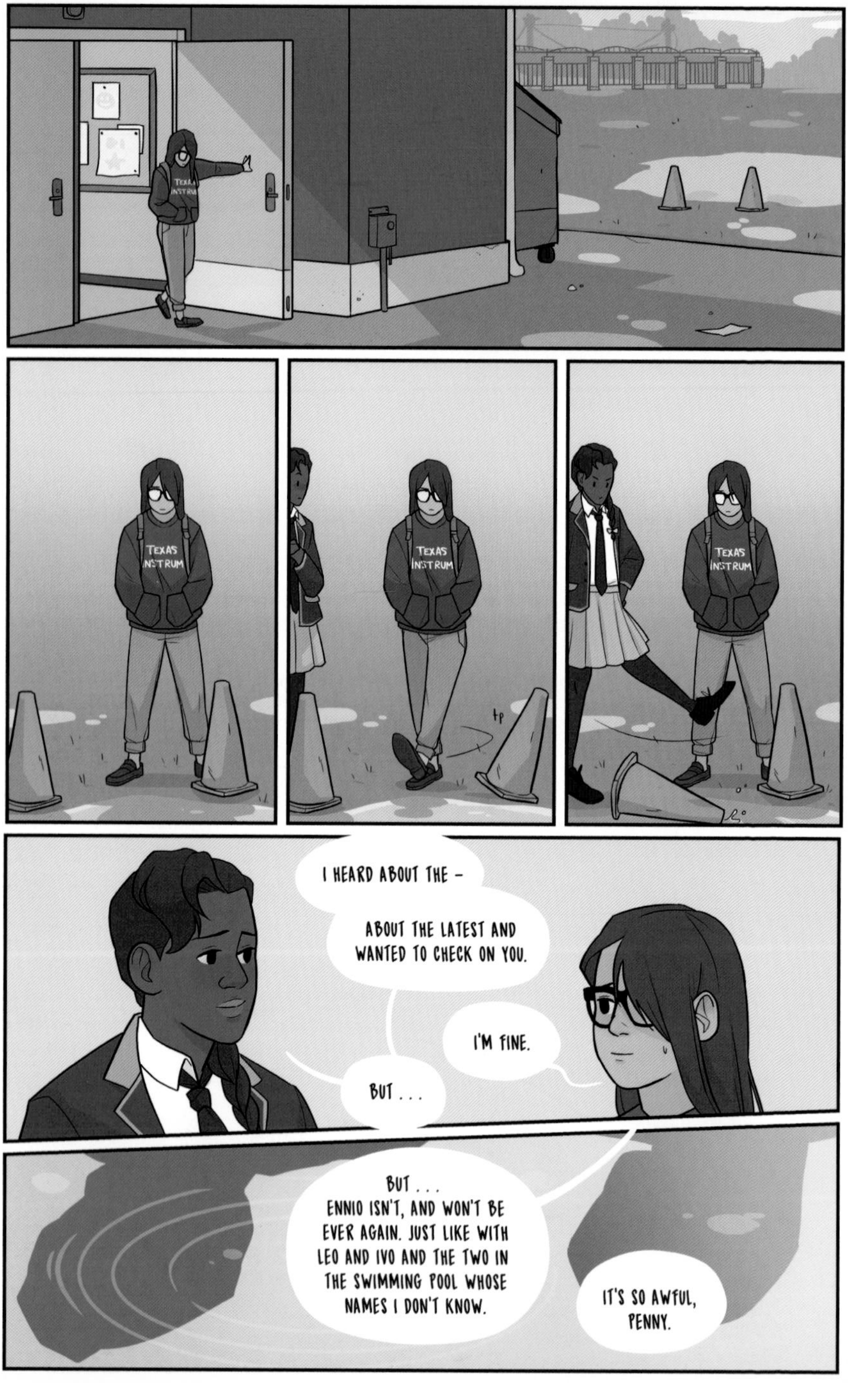
TEXAS INSTRUM
TEXAS INSTRUM
TEXAS INSTRUM
tp
TEXAS INSTRUM
I HEARD ABOUT THE –
ABOUT THE LATEST AND WANTED TO CHECK ON YOU.
I'M FINE.
BUT . . .
BUT . . . ENNIO ISN'T, AND WON'T BE EVER AGAIN. JUST LIKE WITH LEO AND IVO AND THE TWO IN THE SWIMMING POOL WHOSE NAMES I DON'T KNOW.
IT'S SO AWFUL, PENNY.

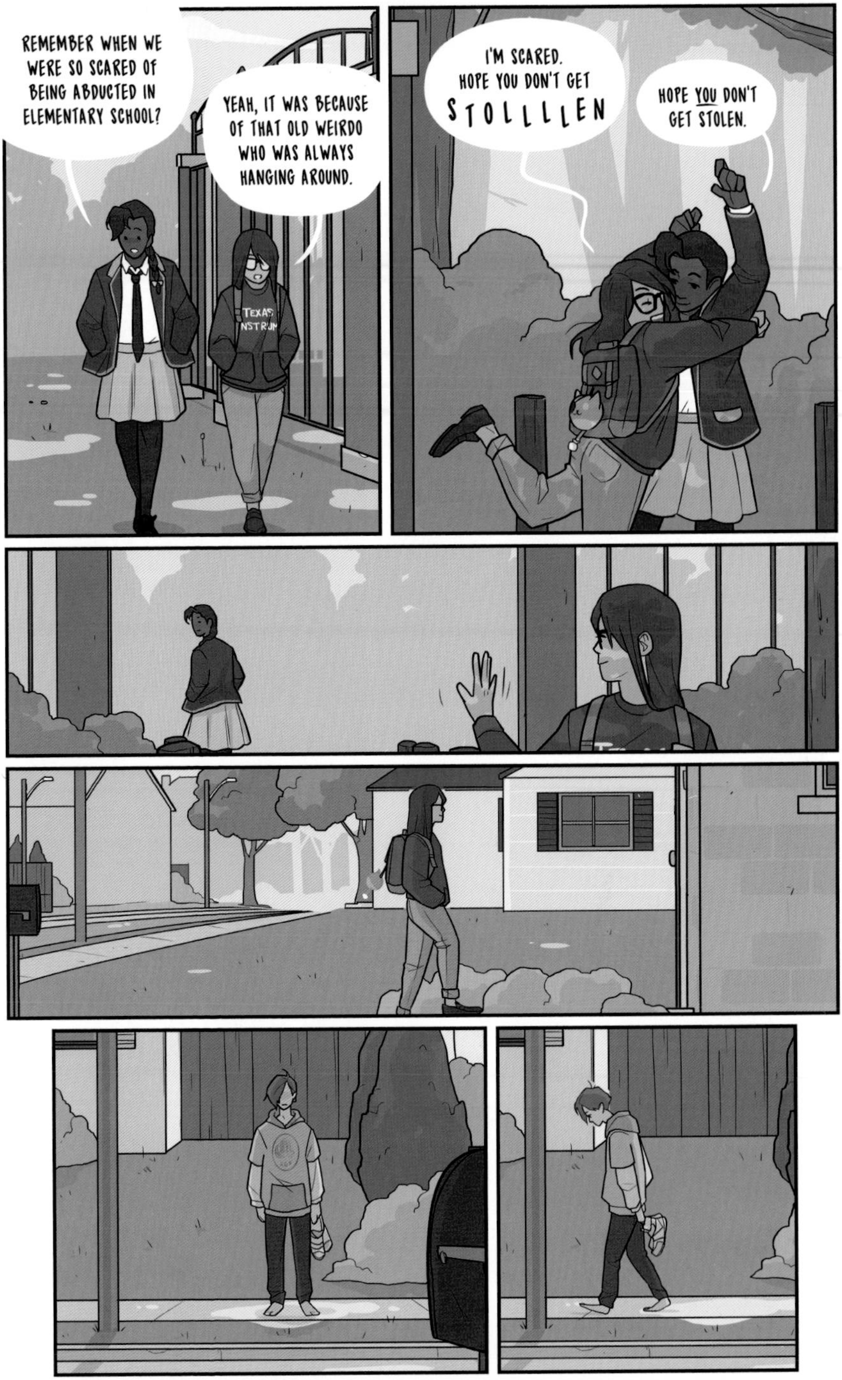
REMEMBER WHEN WE WERE SO SCARED OF BEING ABDUCTED IN ELEMENTARY SCHOOL?
YEAH, IT WAS BECAUSE OF THAT OLD WEIRDO WHO WAS ALWAYS HANGING AROUND.
TEXAS INSTRUM
I'M SCARED. HOPE YOU DON'T GET STOLLLLEN
HOPE YOU DON'T GET STOLEN.

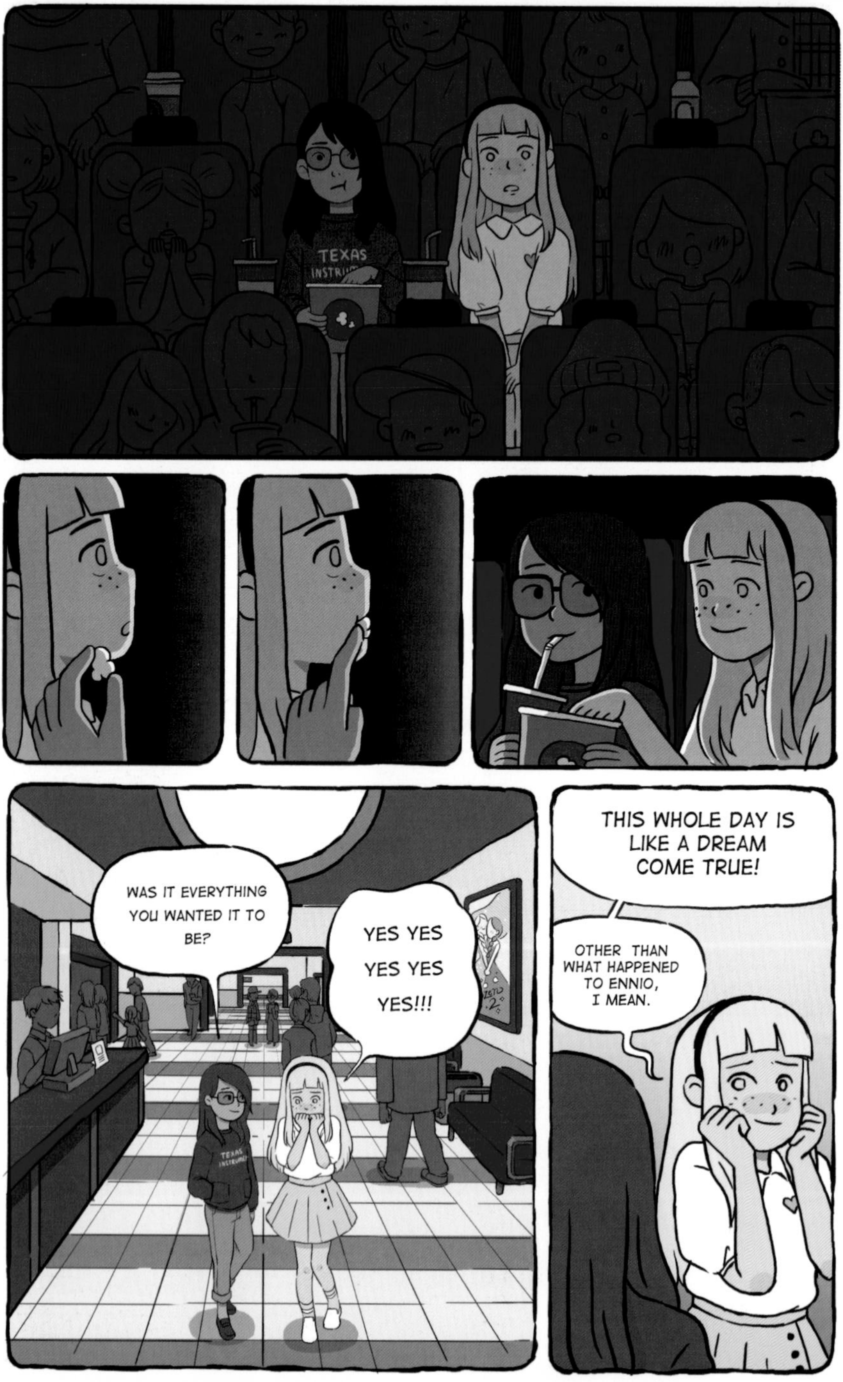
TEXAS INSTRU
WAS IT EVERYTHING YOU WANTED IT TO BE?
YES YES YES YES YES!!!
TEXAS INSTRUMEN
THIS WHOLE DAY IS LIKE A DREAM COME TRUE!
OTHER THAN WHAT HAPPENED TO ENNIO, I MEAN.

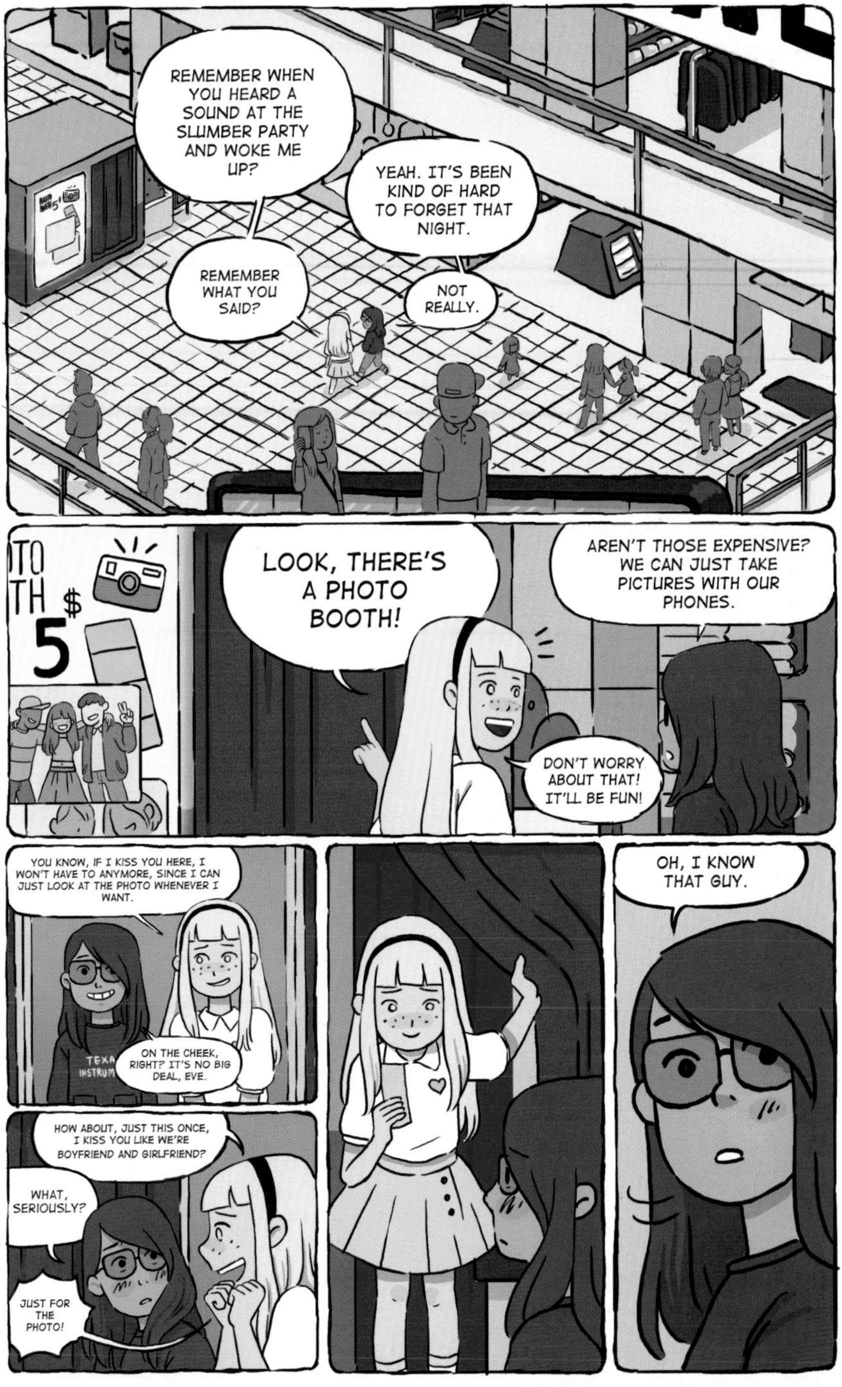
REMEMBER WHEN YOU HEARD A SOUND AT THE SLUMBER PARTY AND WOKE ME UP?
YEAH. IT'S BEEN KIND OF HARD TO FORGET THAT NIGHT.
REMEMBER WHAT YOU SAID?
NOT REALLY.
LOOK, THERE'S A PHOTO BOOTH!
AREN'T THOSE EXPENSIVE? WE CAN JUST TAKE PICTURES WITH OUR PHONES.
DON'T WORRY ABOUT THAT! IT'LL BE FUN!
YOU KNOW, IF I KISS YOU HERE, I WON'T HAVE TO ANYMORE, SINCE I CAN JUST LOOK AT THE PHOTO WHENEVER I WANT.
ON THE CHEEK, RIGHT? IT'S NO BIG DEAL, EVE.
HOW ABOUT, JUST THIS ONCE, I KISS YOU LIKE WE'RE BOYFRIEND AND GIRLFRIEND?
WHAT, SERIOUSLY?
JUST FOR THE PHOTO!
OH, I KNOW THAT GUY.

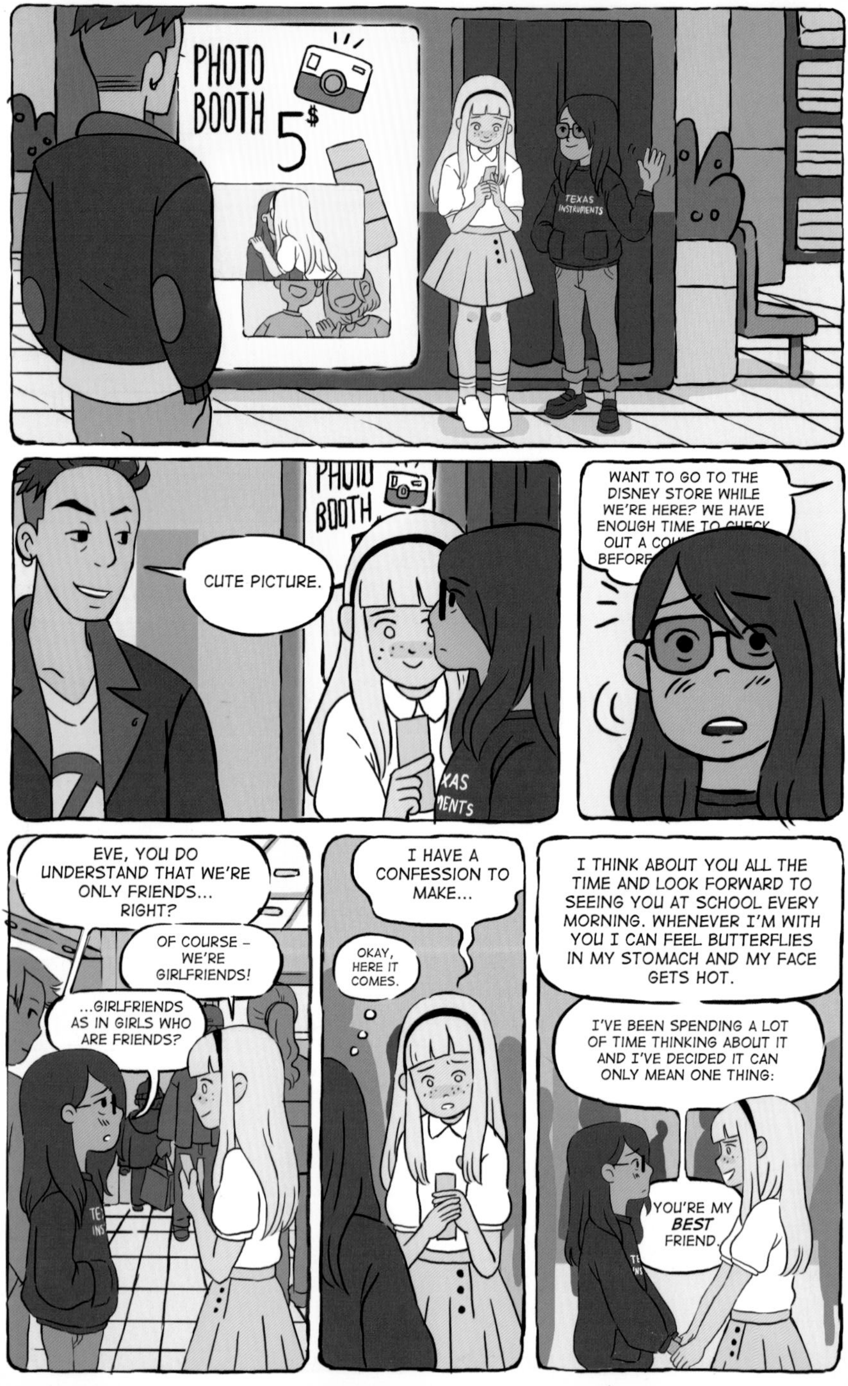
PHOTO BOOTH
5$
TEXAS INSTRUMENTS
BOOTH
CUTE PICTURE.
WANT TO GO TO THE DISNEY STORE WHILE WE'RE HERE? WE HAVE ENOUGH TIME TO
EVE, YOU DO UNDERSTAND THAT WE'RE ONLY FRIENDS... RIGHT?
OF COURSE – WE'RE GIRLFRIENDS!
...GIRLFRIENDS AS IN GIRLS WHO ARE FRIENDS?
I HAVE A CONFESSION TO MAKE...
OKAY, HERE IT COMES.
I THINK ABOUT YOU ALL THE TIME AND LOOK FORWARD TO SEEING YOU AT SCHOOL EVERY MORNING. WHENEVER I'M WITH YOU I CAN FEEL BUTTERFLIES IN MY STOMACH AND MY FACE GETS HOT.
I'VE BEEN SPENDING A LOT OF TIME THINKING ABOUT IT AND I'VE DECIDED IT CAN ONLY MEAN ONE THING:
YOU'RE MY *BEST* FRIEND.

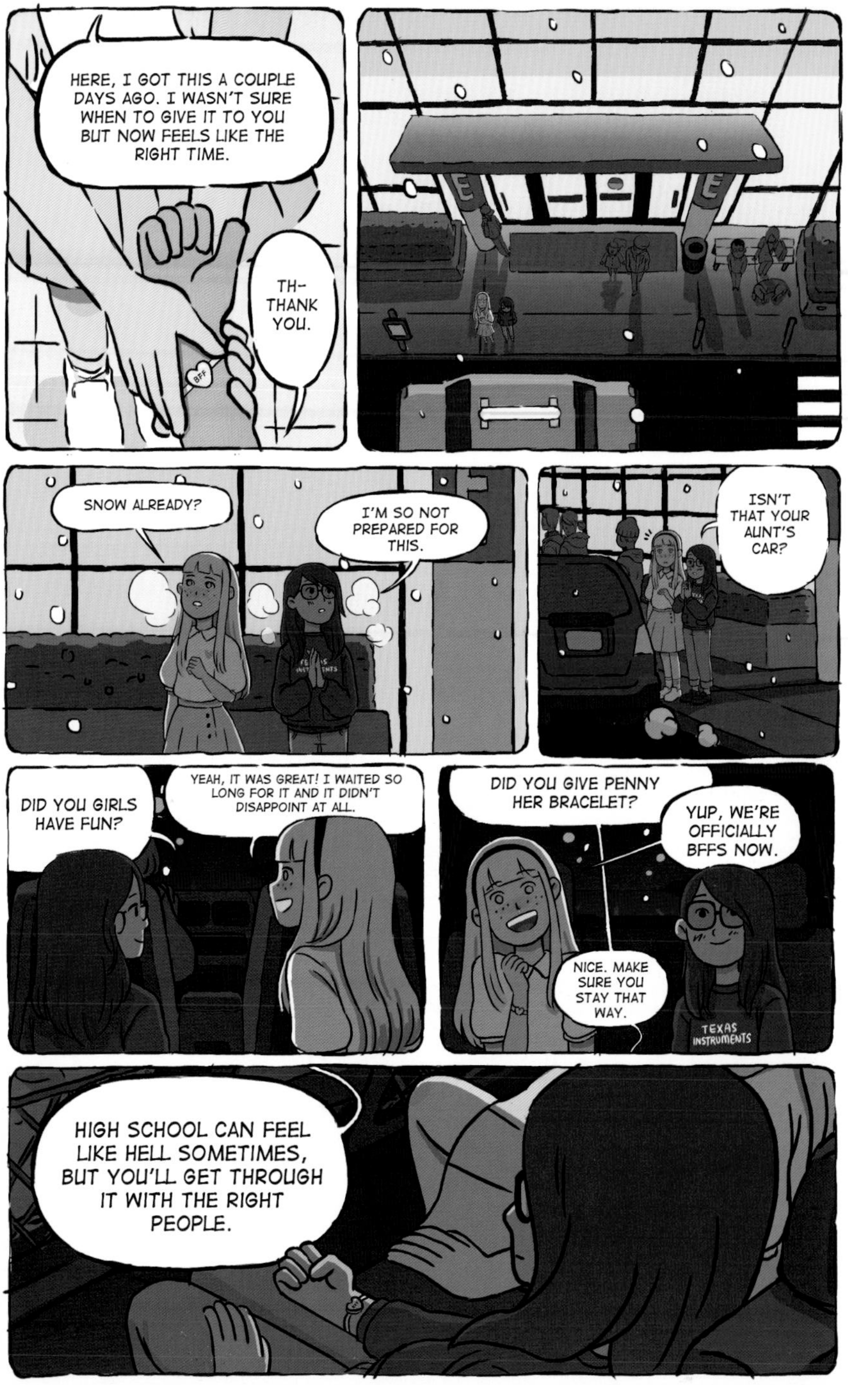
HERE, I GOT THIS A COUPLE DAYS AGO. I WASN'T SURE WHEN TO GIVE IT TO YOU BUT NOW FEELS LIKE THE RIGHT TIME.
BFF
TH-THANK YOU.
SNOW ALREADY?
I'M SO NOT PREPARED FOR THIS.
ISN'T THAT YOUR AUNT'S CAR?
DID YOU GIRLS HAVE FUN?
YEAH, IT WAS GREAT! I WAITED SO LONG FOR IT AND IT DIDN'T DISAPPOINT AT ALL.
DID YOU GIVE PENNY HER BRACELET?
YUP, WE'RE OFFICIALLY BFFS NOW.
NICE. MAKE SURE YOU STAY THAT WAY.
TEXAS INSTRUMENTS
HIGH SCHOOL CAN FEEL LIKE HELL SOMETIMES, BUT YOU'LL GET THROUGH IT WITH THE RIGHT PEOPLE.

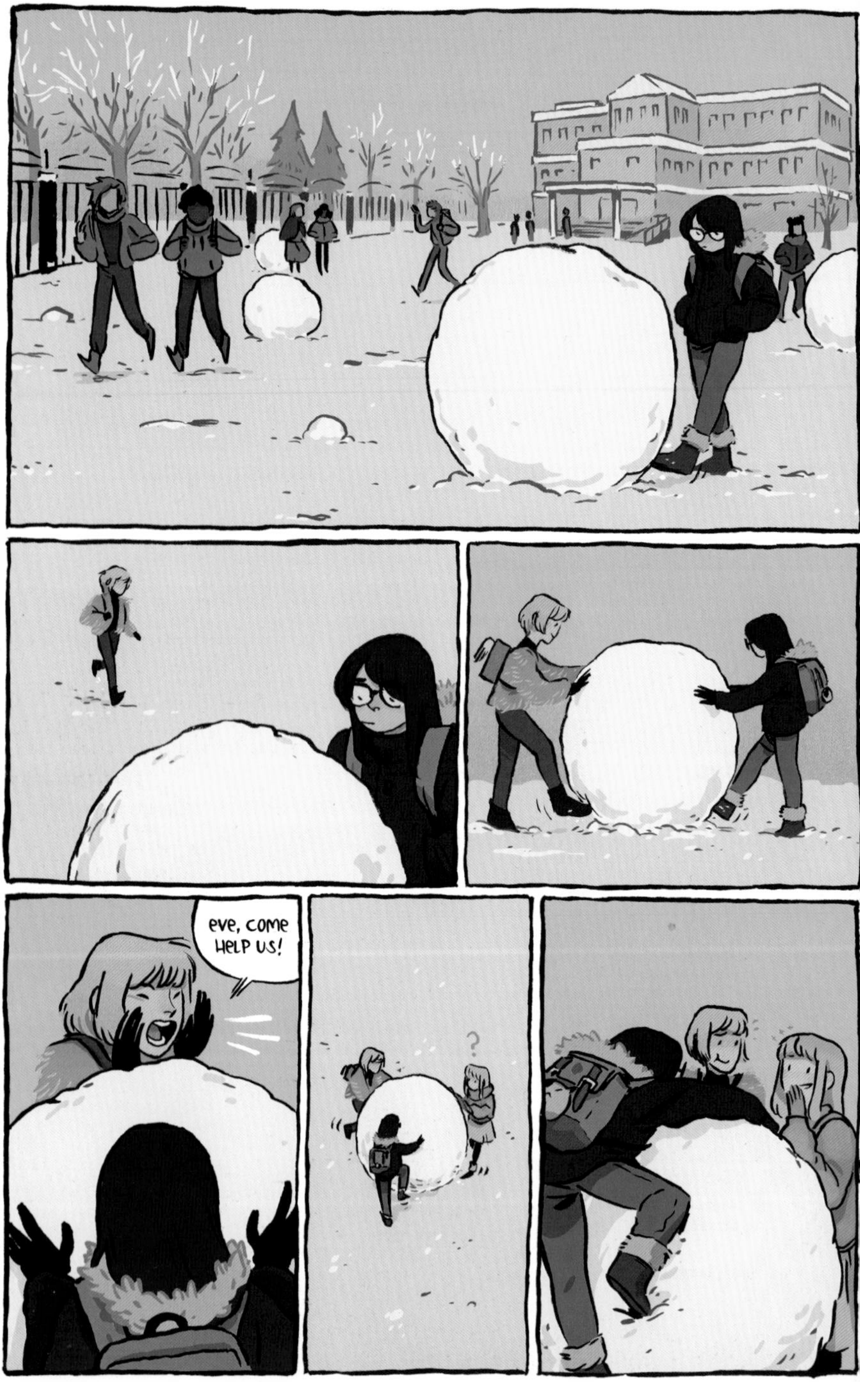
eve, come
help us!
?

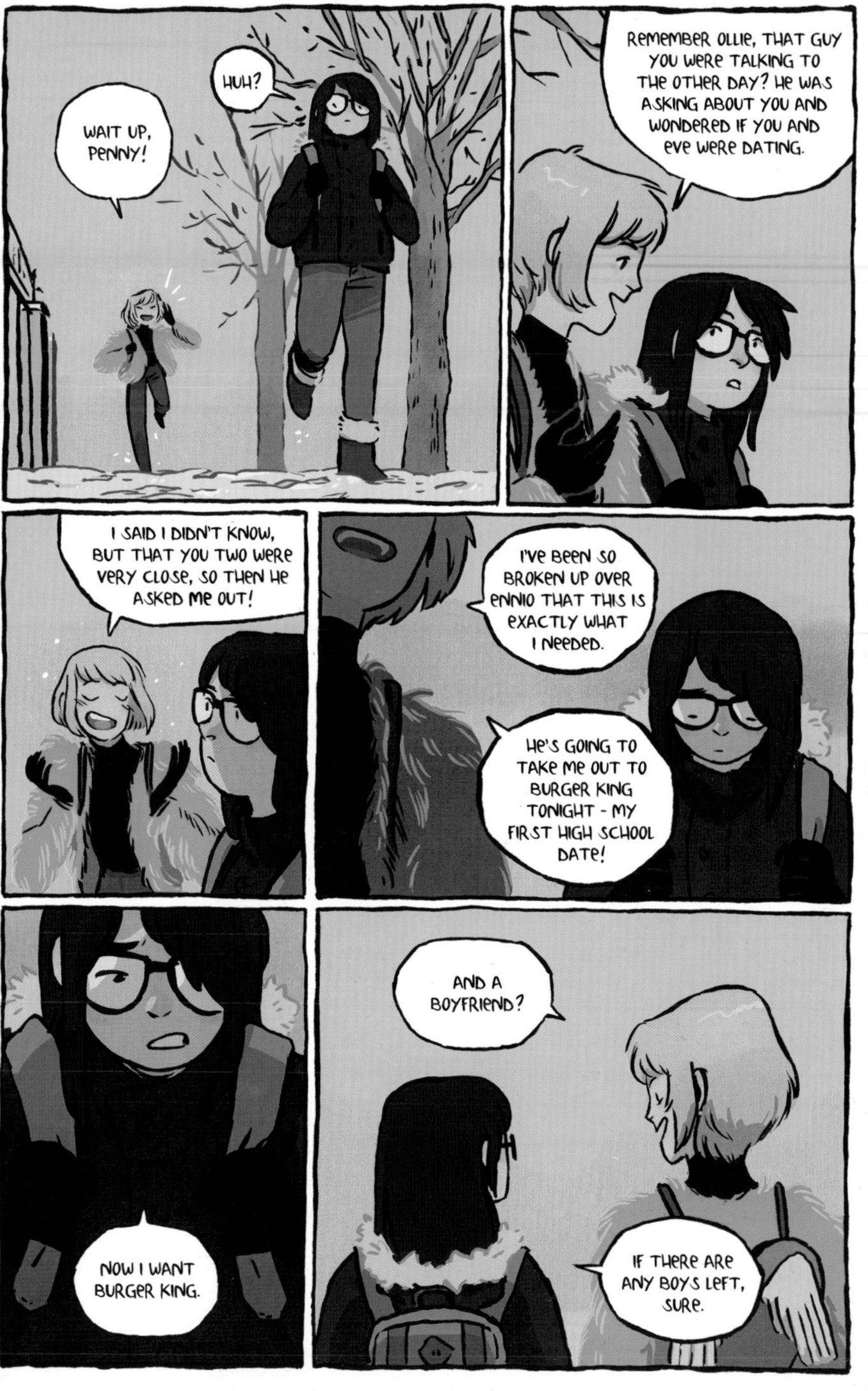
WAIT UP, PENNY!
HUH?
REMEMBER OLLIE, THAT GUY YOU WERE TALKING TO THE OTHER DAY? HE WAS ASKING ABOUT YOU AND WONDERED IF YOU AND EVE WERE DATING.
I SAID I DIDN'T KNOW, BUT THAT YOU TWO WERE VERY CLOSE, SO THEN HE ASKED ME OUT!
I'VE BEEN SO BROKEN UP OVER ENNIO THAT THIS IS EXACTLY WHAT I NEEDED.
HE'S GOING TO TAKE ME OUT TO BURGER KING TONIGHT - MY FIRST HIGH SCHOOL DATE!
NOW I WANT BURGER KING.
AND A BOYFRIEND?
IF THERE ARE ANY BOYS LEFT, SURE.

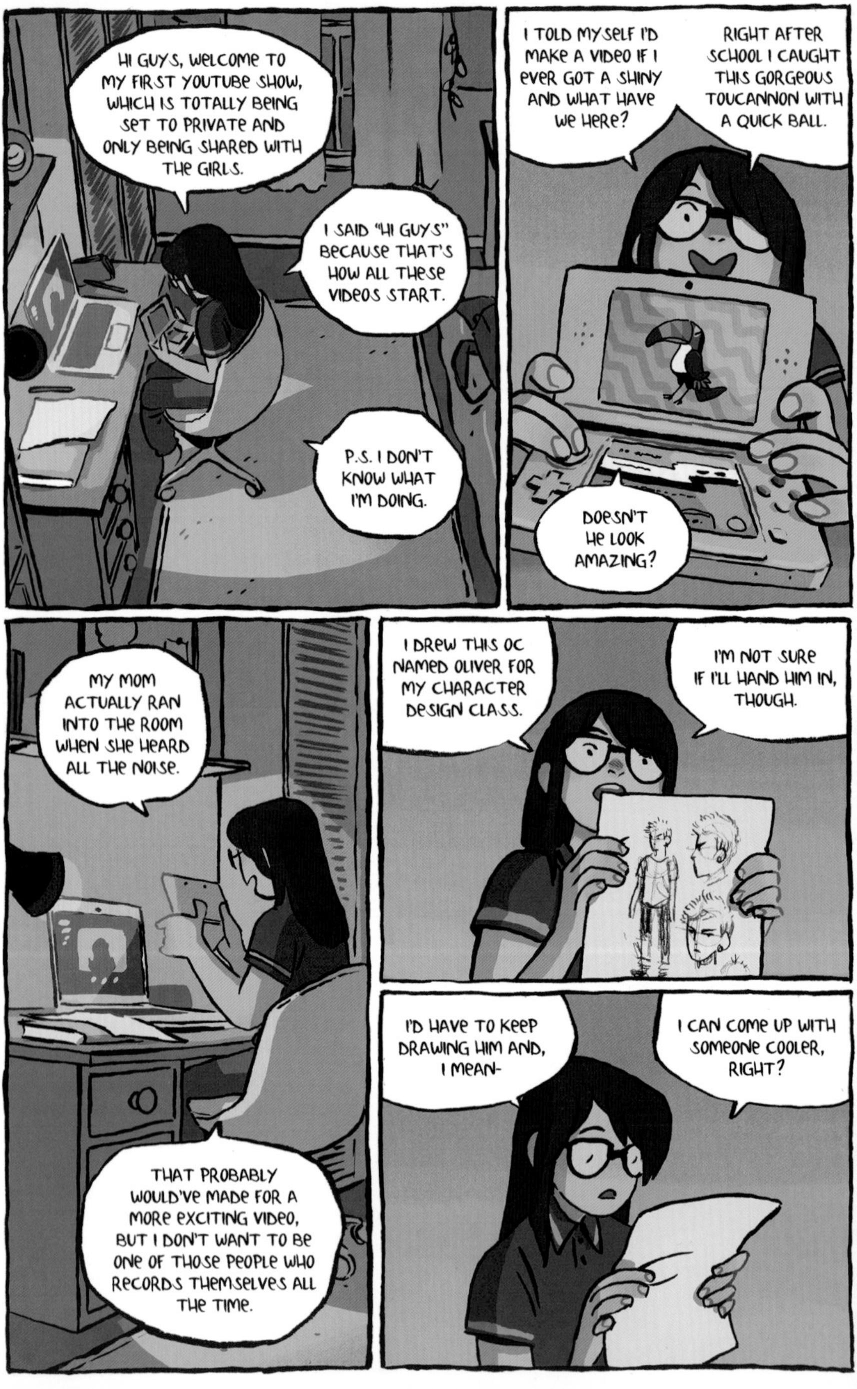
HI GUYS, WELCOME TO MY FIRST YOUTUBE SHOW, WHICH IS TOTALLY BEING SET TO PRIVATE AND ONLY BEING SHARED WITH THE GIRLS.
I SAID "HI GUYS" BECAUSE THAT'S HOW ALL THESE VIDEOS START.
P.S. I DON'T KNOW WHAT I'M DOING.
I TOLD MYSELF I'D MAKE A VIDEO IF I EVER GOT A SHINY AND WHAT HAVE WE HERE?
RIGHT AFTER SCHOOL I CAUGHT THIS GORGEOUS TOUCANNON WITH A QUICK BALL.
DOESN'T HE LOOK AMAZING?
MY MOM ACTUALLY RAN INTO THE ROOM WHEN SHE HEARD ALL THE NOISE.
THAT PROBABLY WOULD'VE MADE FOR A MORE EXCITING VIDEO, BUT I DON'T WANT TO BE ONE OF THOSE PEOPLE WHO RECORDS THEMSELVES ALL THE TIME.
I DREW THIS OC NAMED OLIVER FOR MY CHARACTER DESIGN CLASS.
I'M NOT SURE IF I'LL HAND HIM IN, THOUGH.
I'D HAVE TO KEEP DRAWING HIM AND, I MEAN-
I CAN COME UP WITH SOMEONE COOLER, RIGHT?

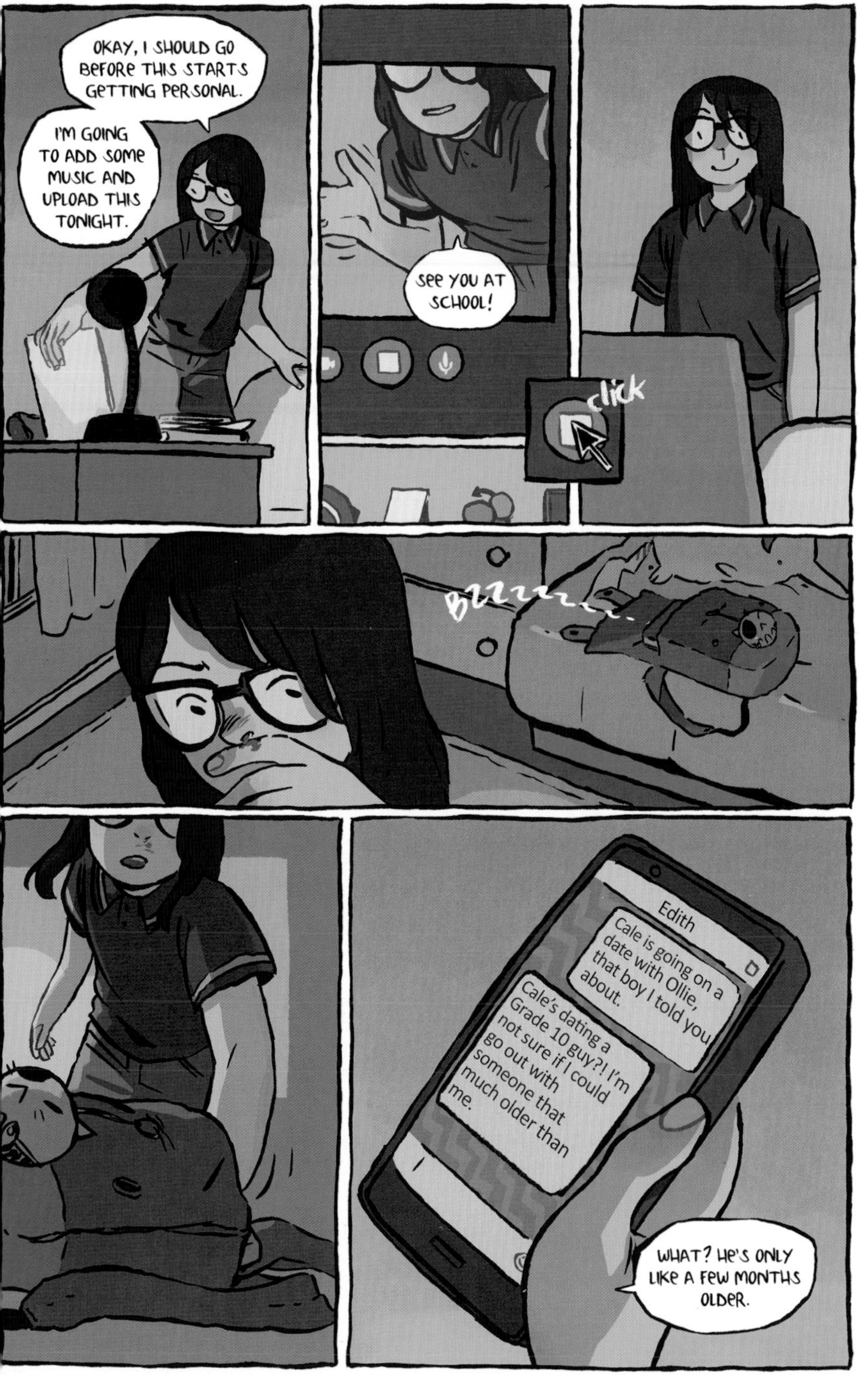
OKAY, I SHOULD GO BEFORE THIS STARTS GETTING PERSONAL.
I'M GOING TO ADD SOME MUSIC AND UPLOAD THIS TONIGHT.
SEE YOU AT SCHOOL!
click
BZZZZZ...
Edith
Cale is going on a date with Ollie, that boy I told you about.
Cale's dating a Grade 10 guy?! I'm not sure if I could go out with someone that much older than me.
WHAT? HE'S ONLY LIKE A FEW MONTHS OLDER.

I WATCHED YOUR SHOW LAST NIGHT, PENNY! CONGRATULATIONS ON YOUR SHINY POKEMON!

OH, THANKS. I CAN SHOW IT TO YOU LATER IF YOU WANT

WANT TO SHOW IT TO ME AT MY PLACE TOMORROW?

I WAS WONDERING IF YOU'D LIKE TO COME OVER FOR A SLEEPOVER.

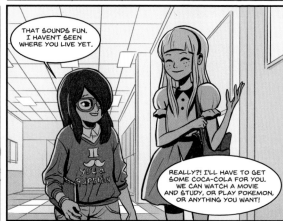

THAT SOUNDS FUN. I HAVEN'T SEEN WHERE YOU LIVE YET.

REALLY?! I'LL HAVE TO GET SOME COCA-COLA FOR YOU. WE CAN WATCH A MOVIE AND STUDY, OR PLAY POKEMON, OR ANYTHING YOU WANT!

NOW I WISH I'D PLANNED THIS BETTER. I HAVEN'T EVEN TOLD MY PARENTS I WAS GOING TO INVITE YOU.

EVE, YOU CAN BE FUNNY SOMETIMES, YOU KNOW THAT? I'M SURE IT'LL BE FINE.

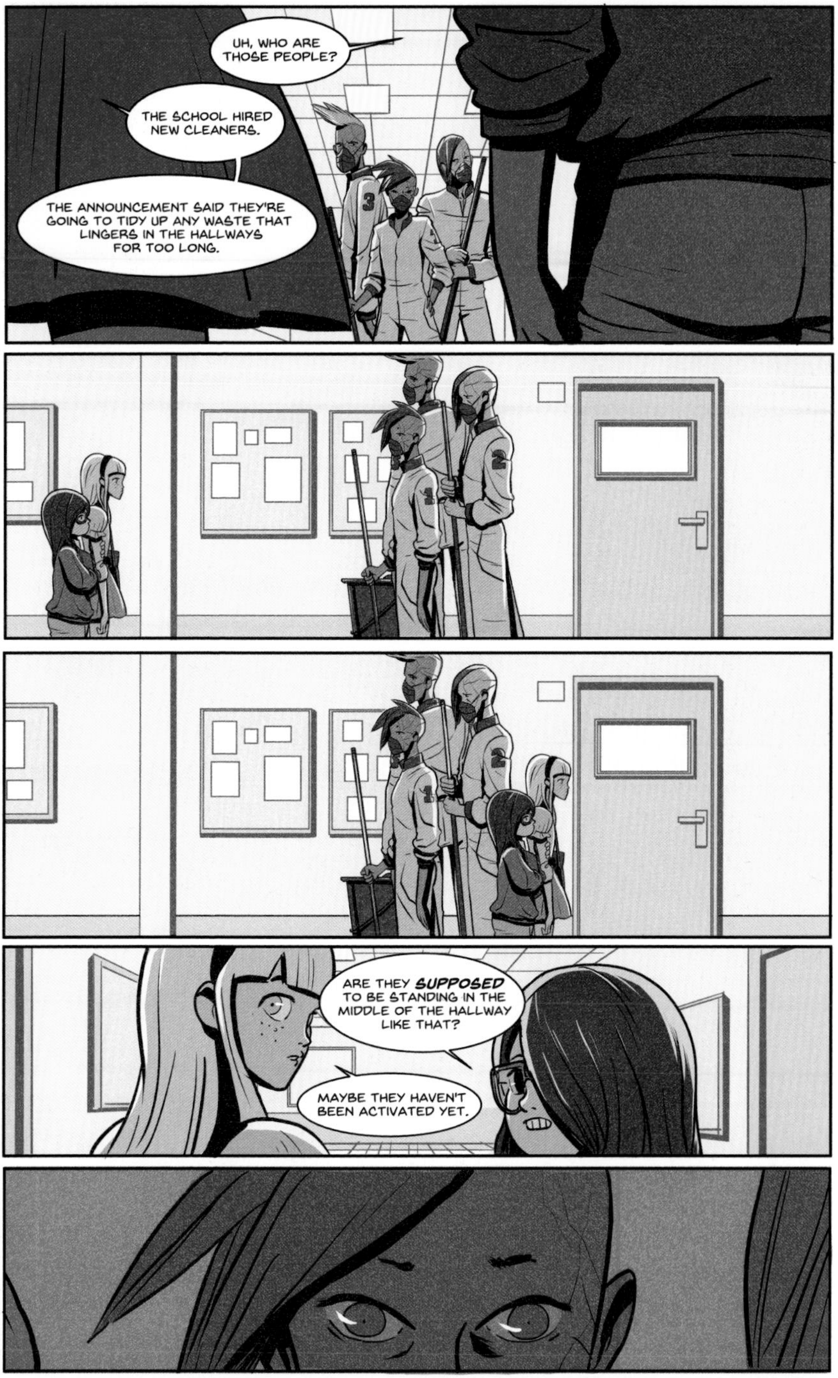
UH, WHO ARE THOSE PEOPLE?
THE SCHOOL HIRED NEW CLEANERS.
THE ANNOUNCEMENT SAID THEY'RE GOING TO TIDY UP ANY WASTE THAT LINGERS IN THE HALLWAYS FOR TOO LONG.
ARE THEY SUPPOSED TO BE STANDING IN THE MIDDLE OF THE HALLWAY LIKE THAT?
MAYBE THEY HAVEN'T BEEN ACTIVATED YET.

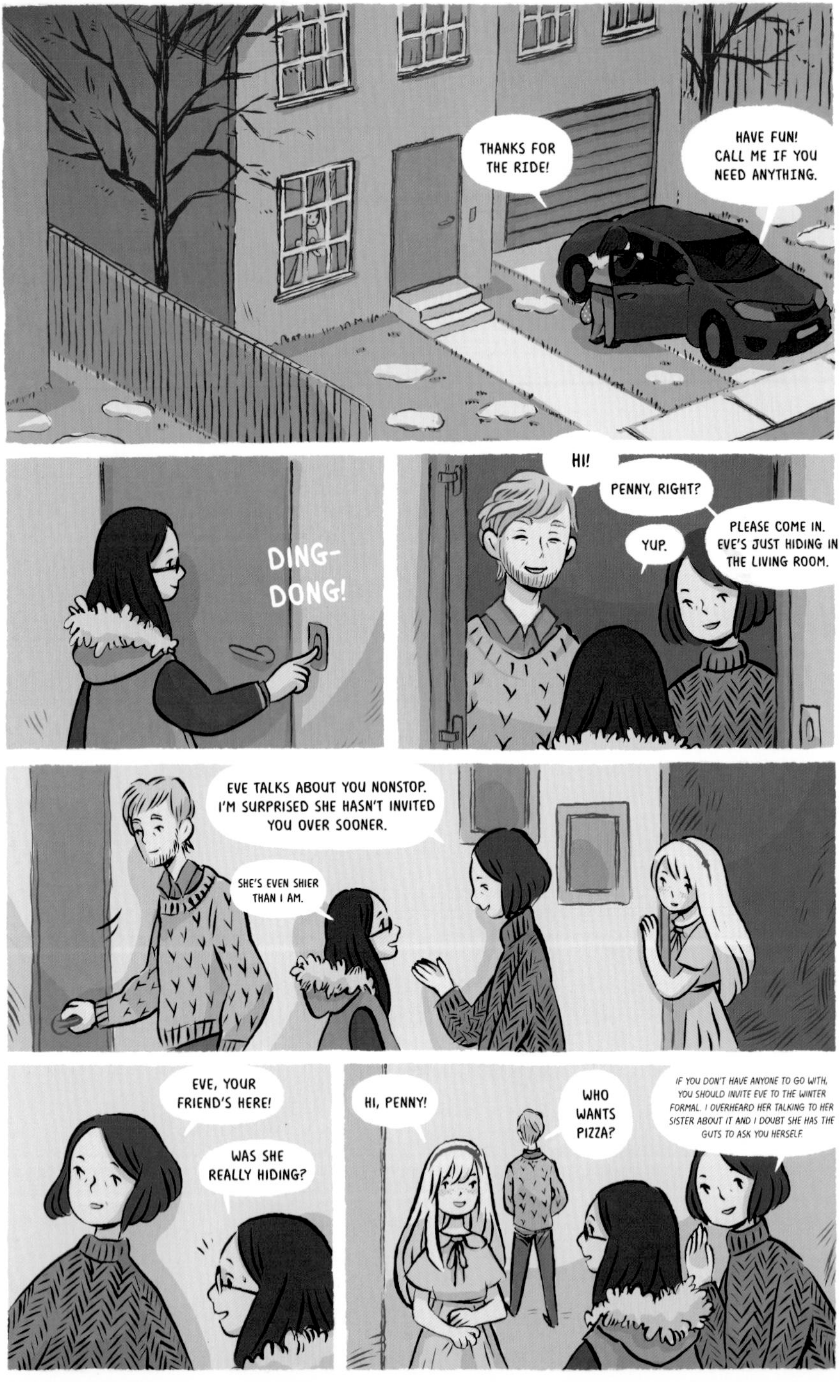
THANKS FOR THE RIDE!
HAVE FUN! CALL ME IF YOU NEED ANYTHING.
DING-DONG!
HI!
PENNY, RIGHT?
YUP.
PLEASE COME IN. EVE'S JUST HIDING IN THE LIVING ROOM.
EVE TALKS ABOUT YOU NONSTOP. I'M SURPRISED SHE HASN'T INVITED YOU OVER SOONER.
SHE'S EVEN SHIER THAN I AM.
EVE, YOUR FRIEND'S HERE!
WAS SHE REALLY HIDING?
HI, PENNY!
WHO WANTS PIZZA?
IF YOU DON'T HAVE ANYONE TO GO WITH, YOU SHOULD INVITE EVE TO THE WINTER FORMAL. I OVERHEARD HER TALKING TO HER SISTER ABOUT IT AND I DOUBT SHE HAS THE GUTS TO ASK YOU HERSELF.

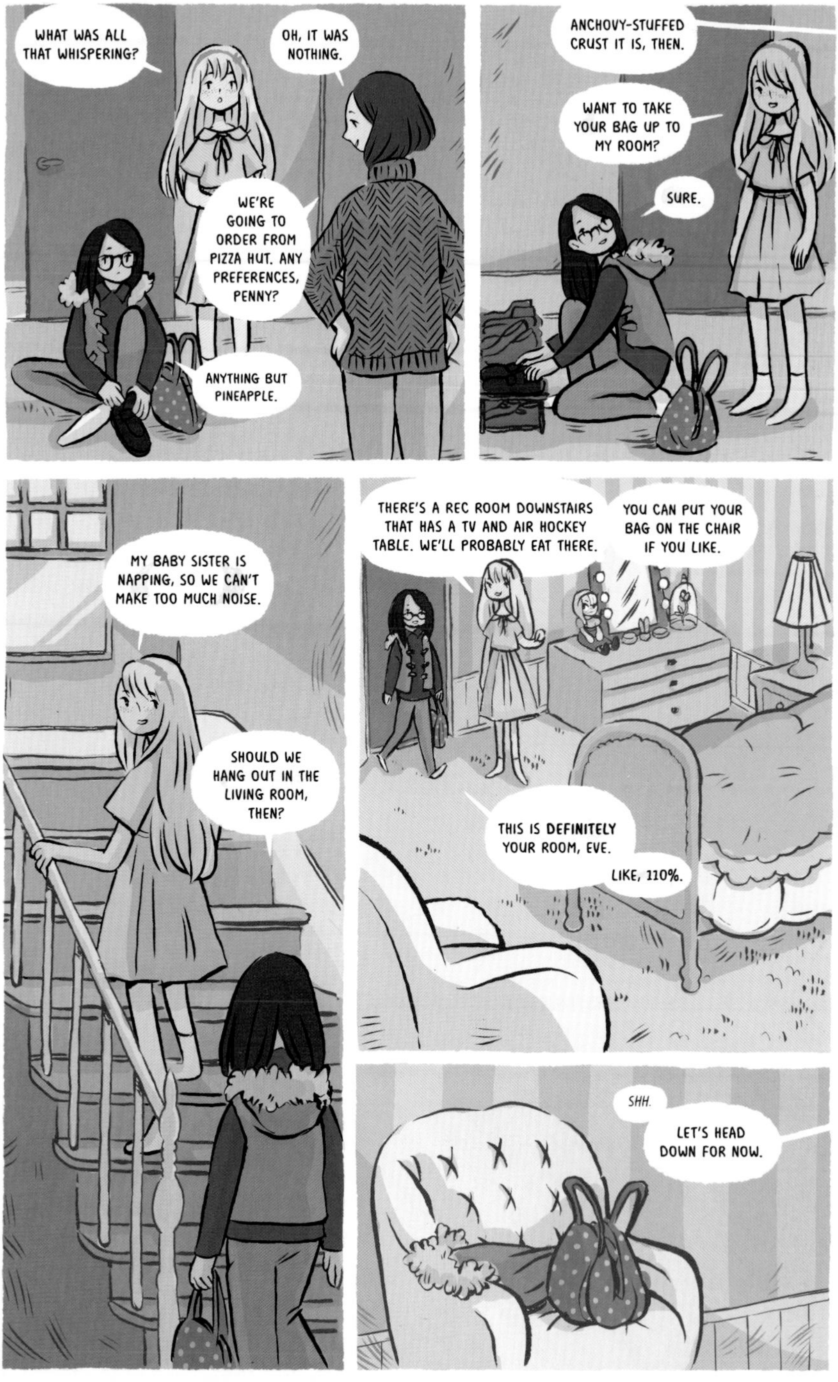
WHAT WAS ALL THAT WHISPERING?
OH, IT WAS NOTHING.
WE'RE GOING TO ORDER FROM PIZZA HUT. ANY PREFERENCES, PENNY?
ANYTHING BUT PINEAPPLE.
ANCHOVY-STUFFED CRUST IT IS, THEN.
WANT TO TAKE YOUR BAG UP TO MY ROOM?
SURE.
MY BABY SISTER IS NAPPING, SO WE CAN'T MAKE TOO MUCH NOISE.
SHOULD WE HANG OUT IN THE LIVING ROOM, THEN?
THERE'S A REC ROOM DOWNSTAIRS THAT HAS A TV AND AIR HOCKEY TABLE. WE'LL PROBABLY EAT THERE.
YOU CAN PUT YOUR BAG ON THE CHAIR IF YOU LIKE.
THIS IS DEFINITELY YOUR ROOM, EVE.
LIKE, 110%.
SHH.
LET'S HEAD DOWN FOR NOW.

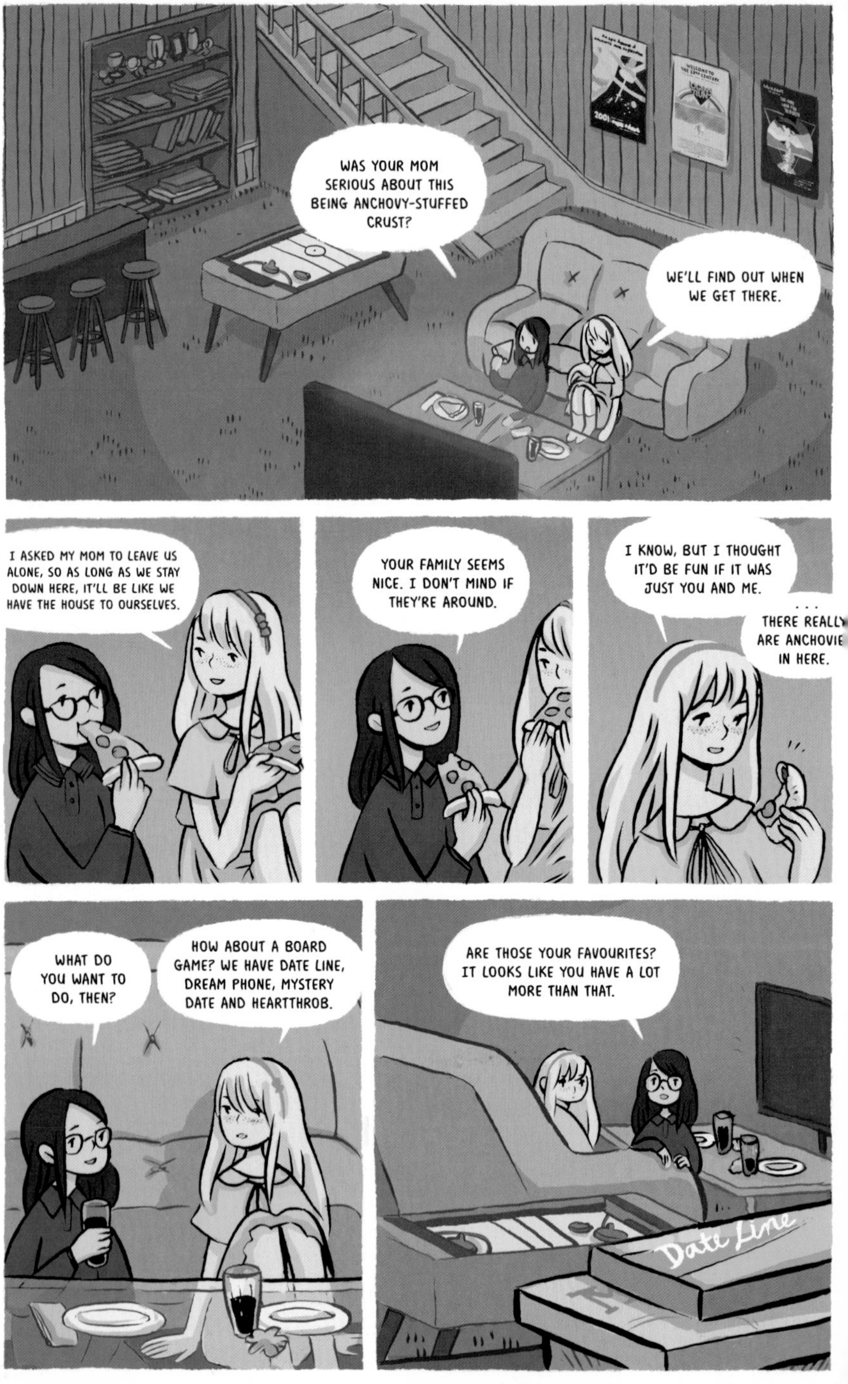
WAS YOUR MOM SERIOUS ABOUT THIS BEING ANCHOVY-STUFFED CRUST?
WE'LL FIND OUT WHEN WE GET THERE.
I ASKED MY MOM TO LEAVE US ALONE, SO AS LONG AS WE STAY DOWN HERE, IT'LL BE LIKE WE HAVE THE HOUSE TO OURSELVES.
YOUR FAMILY SEEMS NICE. I DON'T MIND IF THEY'RE AROUND.
I KNOW, BUT I THOUGHT IT'D BE FUN IF IT WAS JUST YOU AND ME.
. . . THERE REALLY ARE ANCHOVIES IN HERE.
WHAT DO YOU WANT TO DO, THEN?
HOW ABOUT A BOARD GAME? WE HAVE DATE LINE, DREAM PHONE, MYSTERY DATE AND HEARTTHROB.
ARE THOSE YOUR FAVOURITES? IT LOOKS LIKE YOU HAVE A LOT MORE THAN THAT.
Date Line

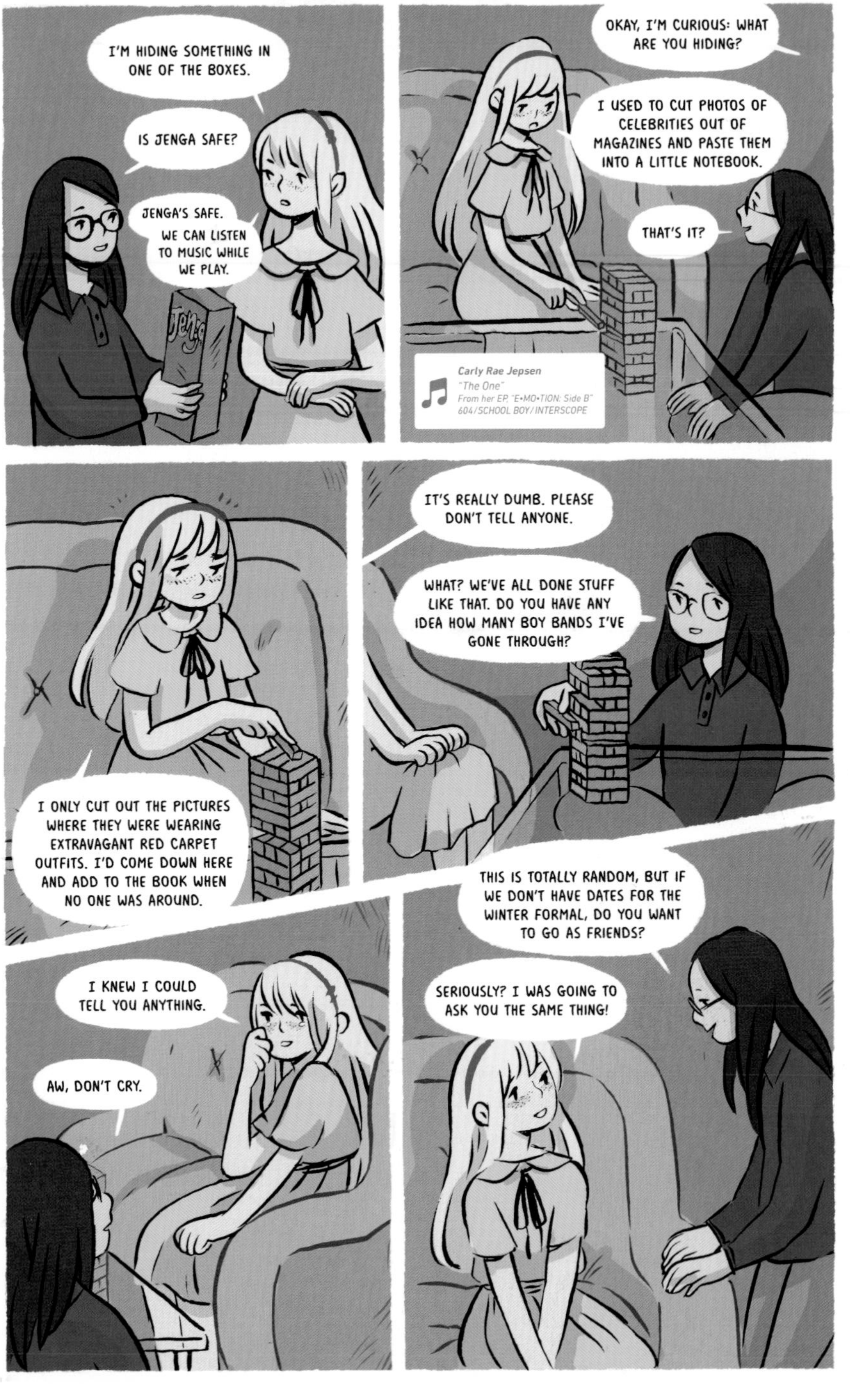
I'M HIDING SOMETHING IN ONE OF THE BOXES.
IS JENGA SAFE?
JENGA'S SAFE.
WE CAN LISTEN TO MUSIC WHILE WE PLAY.
Jenga
OKAY, I'M CURIOUS: WHAT ARE YOU HIDING?
I USED TO CUT PHOTOS OF CELEBRITIES OUT OF MAGAZINES AND PASTE THEM INTO A LITTLE NOTEBOOK.
THAT'S IT?
Carly Rae Jepsen
"The One"
From her EP, "E•MO•TION: Side B"
604/SCHOOL BOY/INTERSCOPE
I ONLY CUT OUT THE PICTURES WHERE THEY WERE WEARING EXTRAVAGANT RED CARPET OUTFITS. I'D COME DOWN HERE AND ADD TO THE BOOK WHEN NO ONE WAS AROUND.
IT'S REALLY DUMB. PLEASE DON'T TELL ANYONE.
WHAT? WE'VE ALL DONE STUFF LIKE THAT. DO YOU HAVE ANY IDEA HOW MANY BOY BANDS I'VE GONE THROUGH?
I KNEW I COULD TELL YOU ANYTHING.
AW, DON'T CRY.
THIS IS TOTALLY RANDOM, BUT IF WE DON'T HAVE DATES FOR THE WINTER FORMAL, DO YOU WANT TO GO AS FRIENDS?
SERIOUSLY? I WAS GOING TO ASK YOU THE SAME THING!

PENNY . . .

I'M SORRY . . .
I'M NOT A VERY
GOOD DANCER . . .

ARE THOSE FLOWERS
FOR ME . . . ?

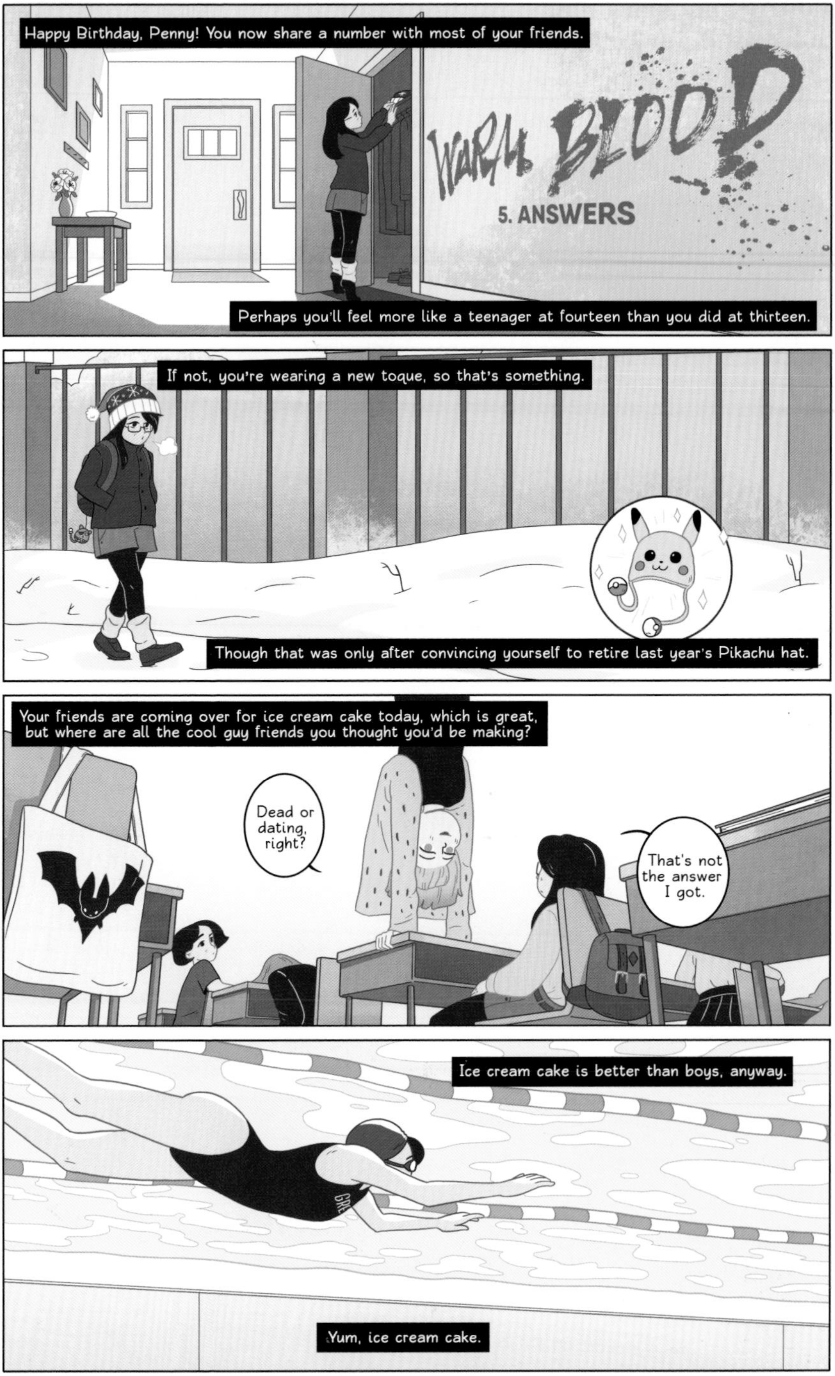
Happy Birthday, Penny! You now share a number with most of your friends.
WARM BLOOD
5. ANSWERS
Perhaps you'll feel more like a teenager at fourteen than you did at thirteen.
If not, you're wearing a new toque, so that's something.
Though that was only after convincing yourself to retire last year's Pikachu hat.
Your friends are coming over for ice cream cake today, which is great, but where are all the cool guy friends you thought you'd be making?
Dead or dating, right?
That's not the answer I got.
Ice cream cake is better than boys, anyway.
Yum, ice cream cake.

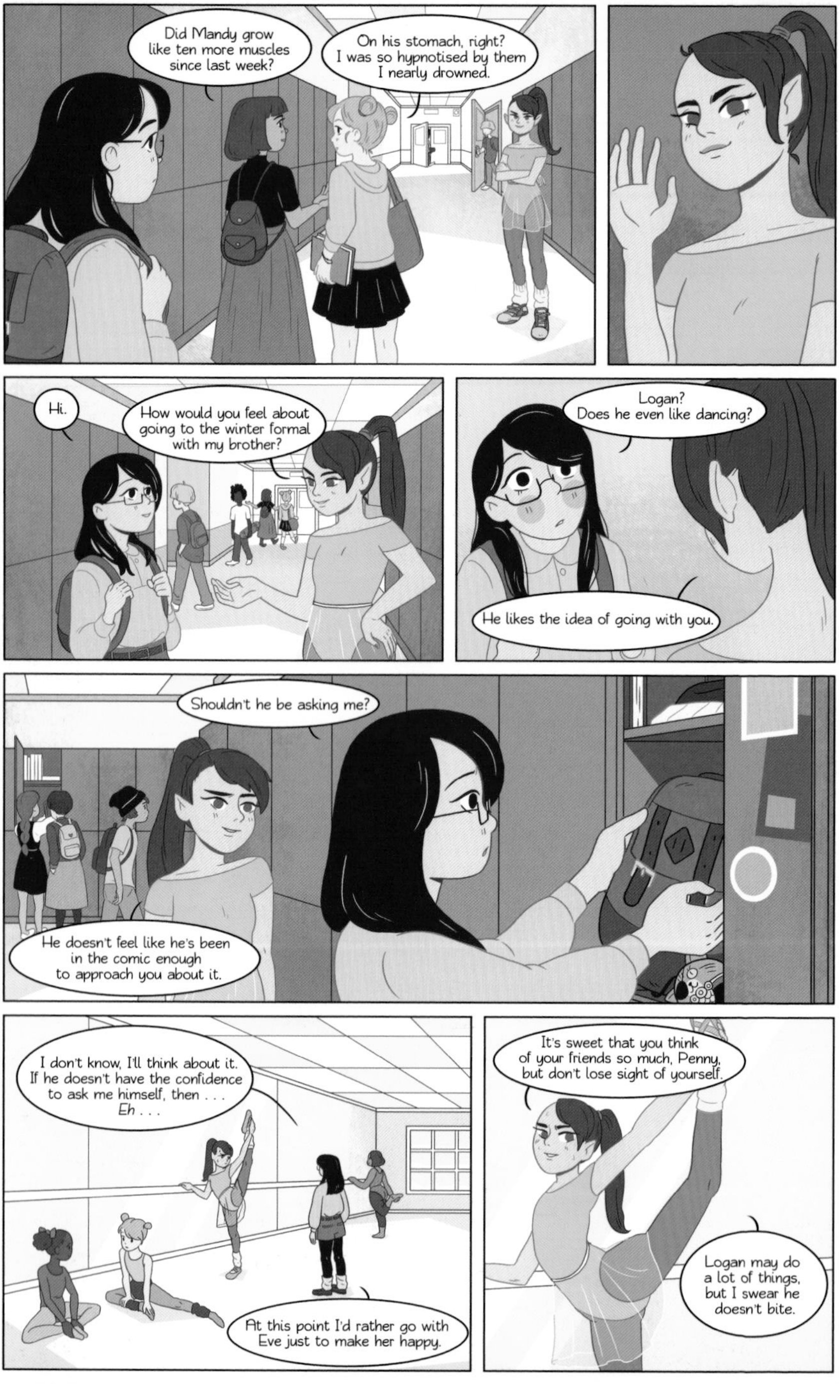

Did Mandy grow like ten more muscles since last week?
On his stomach, right? I was so hypnotised by them I nearly drowned.
Hi.
How would you feel about going to the winter formal with my brother?
Logan? Does he even like dancing?
He likes the idea of going with you.
Shouldn't he be asking me?
He doesn't feel like he's been in the comic enough to approach you about it.
I don't know, I'll think about it. If he doesn't have the confidence to ask me himself, then . . . Eh . . .
At this point I'd rather go with Eve just to make her happy.
It's sweet that you think of your friends so much, Penny, but don't lose sight of yourself.
Logan may do a lot of things, but I swear he doesn't bite.

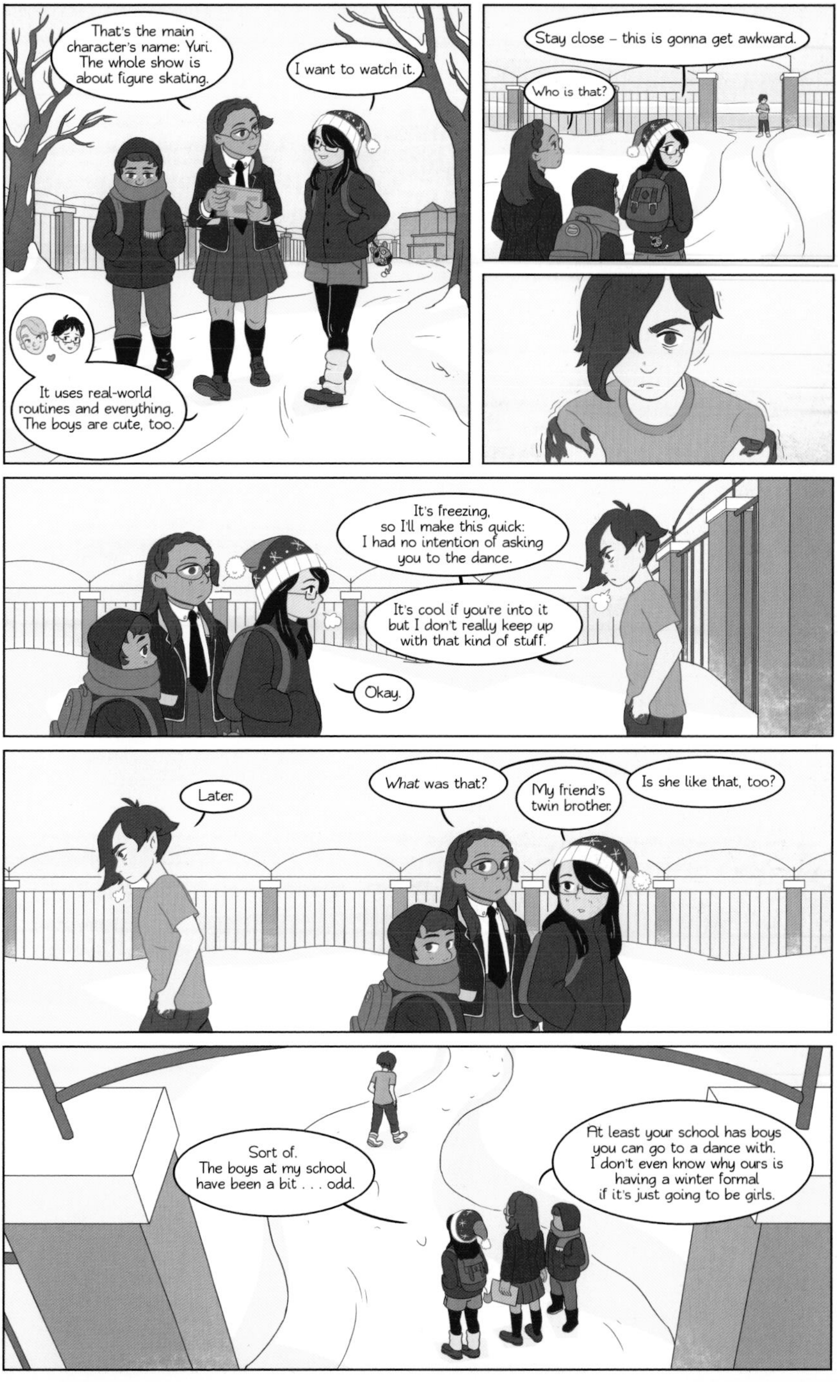
That's the main character's name: Yuri. The whole show is about figure skating.
I want to watch it.
It uses real-world routines and everything. The boys are cute, too.
Stay close – this is gonna get awkward.
Who is that?
It's freezing, so I'll make this quick: I had no intention of asking you to the dance.
It's cool if you're into it but I don't really keep up with that kind of stuff.
Okay.
Later.
What was that?
My friend's twin brother.
Is she like that, too?
Sort of. The boys at my school have been a bit . . . odd.
At least your school has boys you can go to a dance with. I don't even know why ours is having a winter formal if it's just going to be girls.

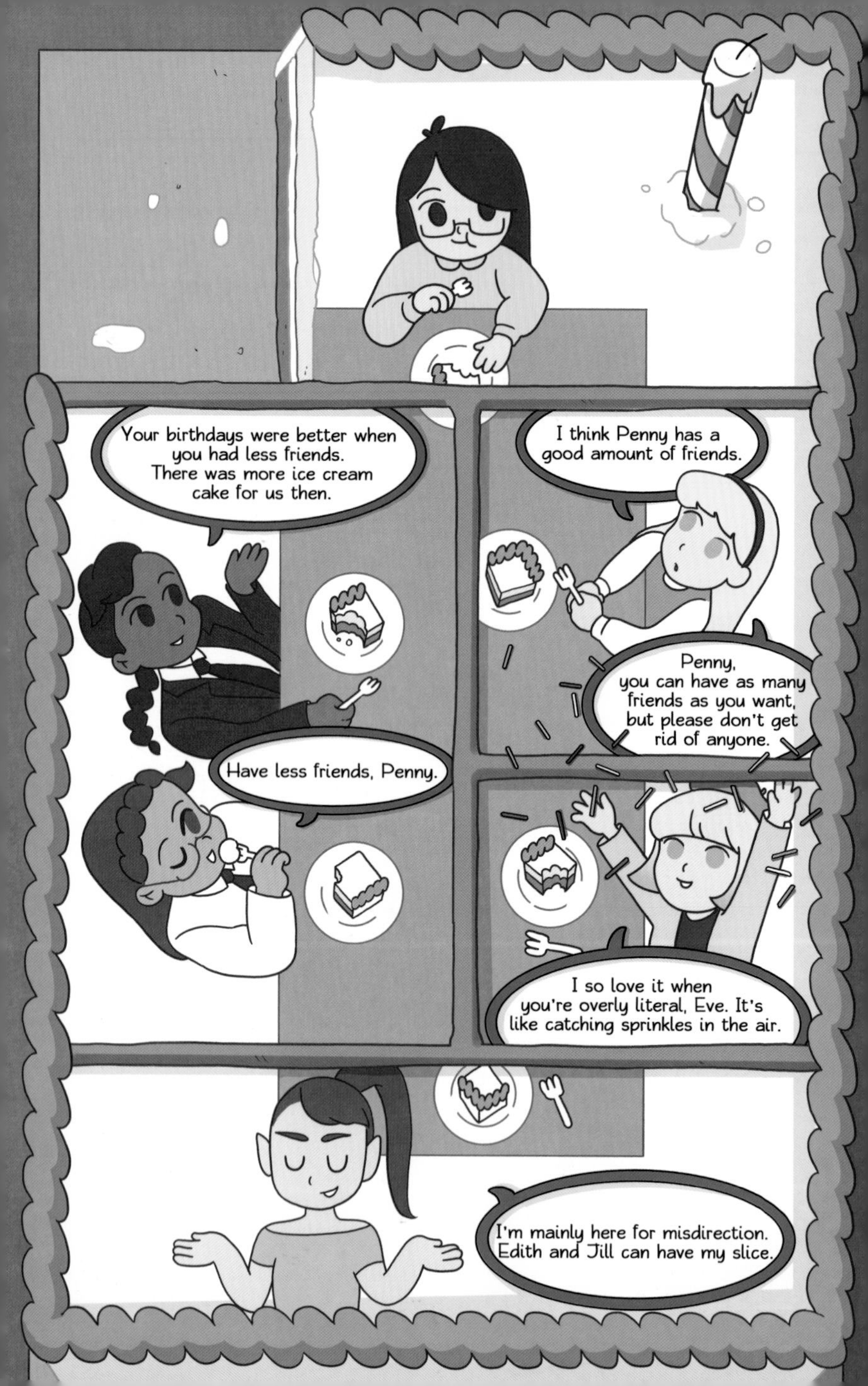
Your birthdays were better when you had less friends. There was more ice cream cake for us then.
Have less friends, Penny.
I think Penny has a good amount of friends.
Penny, you can have as many friends as you want, but please don't get rid of anyone.
I so love it when you're overly literal, Eve. It's like catching sprinkles in the air.
I'm mainly here for misdirection. Edith and Jill can have my slice.

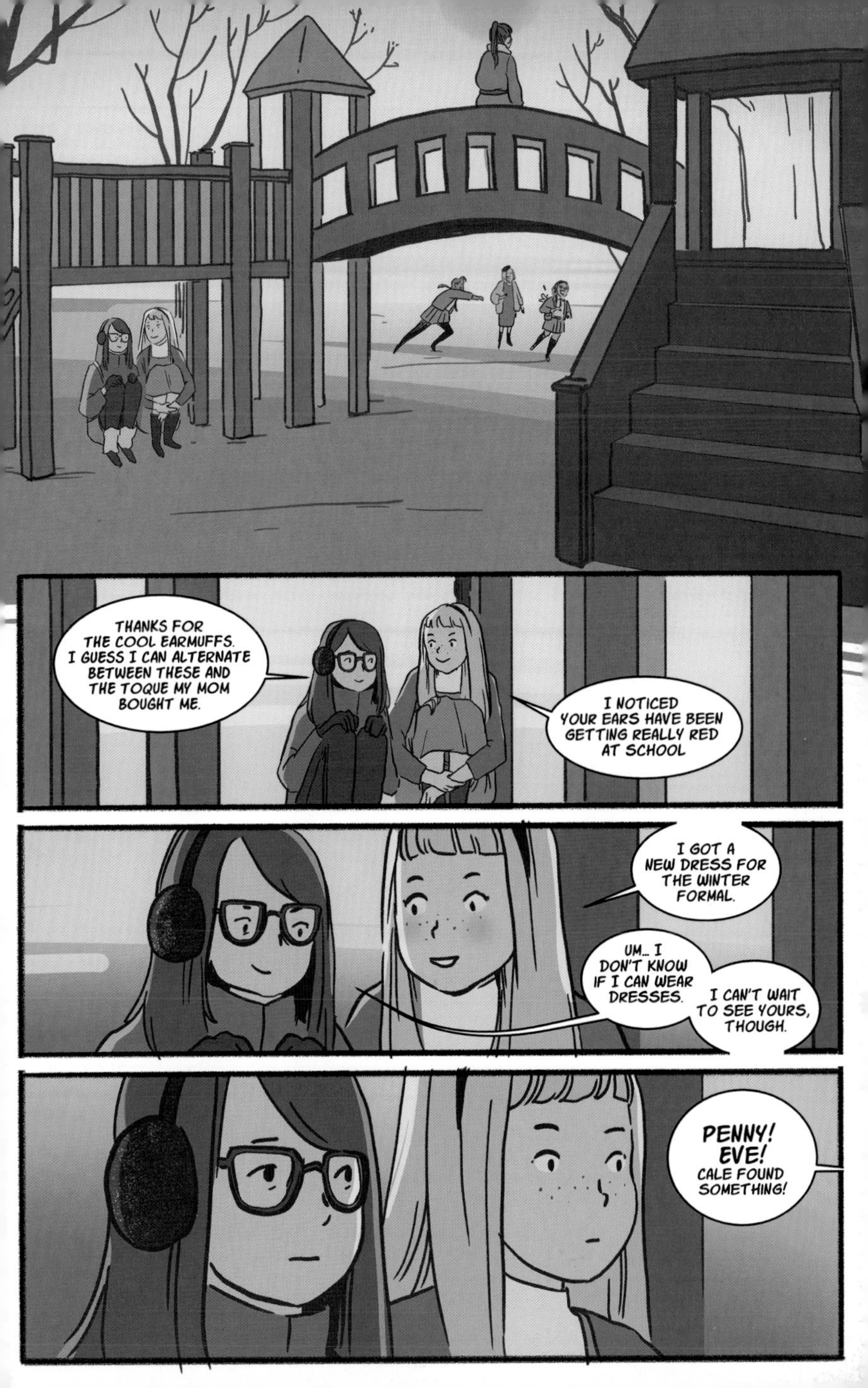
THANKS FOR THE COOL EARMUFFS. I GUESS I CAN ALTERNATE BETWEEN THESE AND THE TOQUE MY MOM BOUGHT ME.
I NOTICED YOUR EARS HAVE BEEN GETTING REALLY RED AT SCHOOL
I GOT A NEW DRESS FOR THE WINTER FORMAL.
UM... I DON'T KNOW IF I CAN WEAR DRESSES.
I CAN'T WAIT TO SEE YOURS, THOUGH.
PENNY! EVE! CALE FOUND SOMETHING!

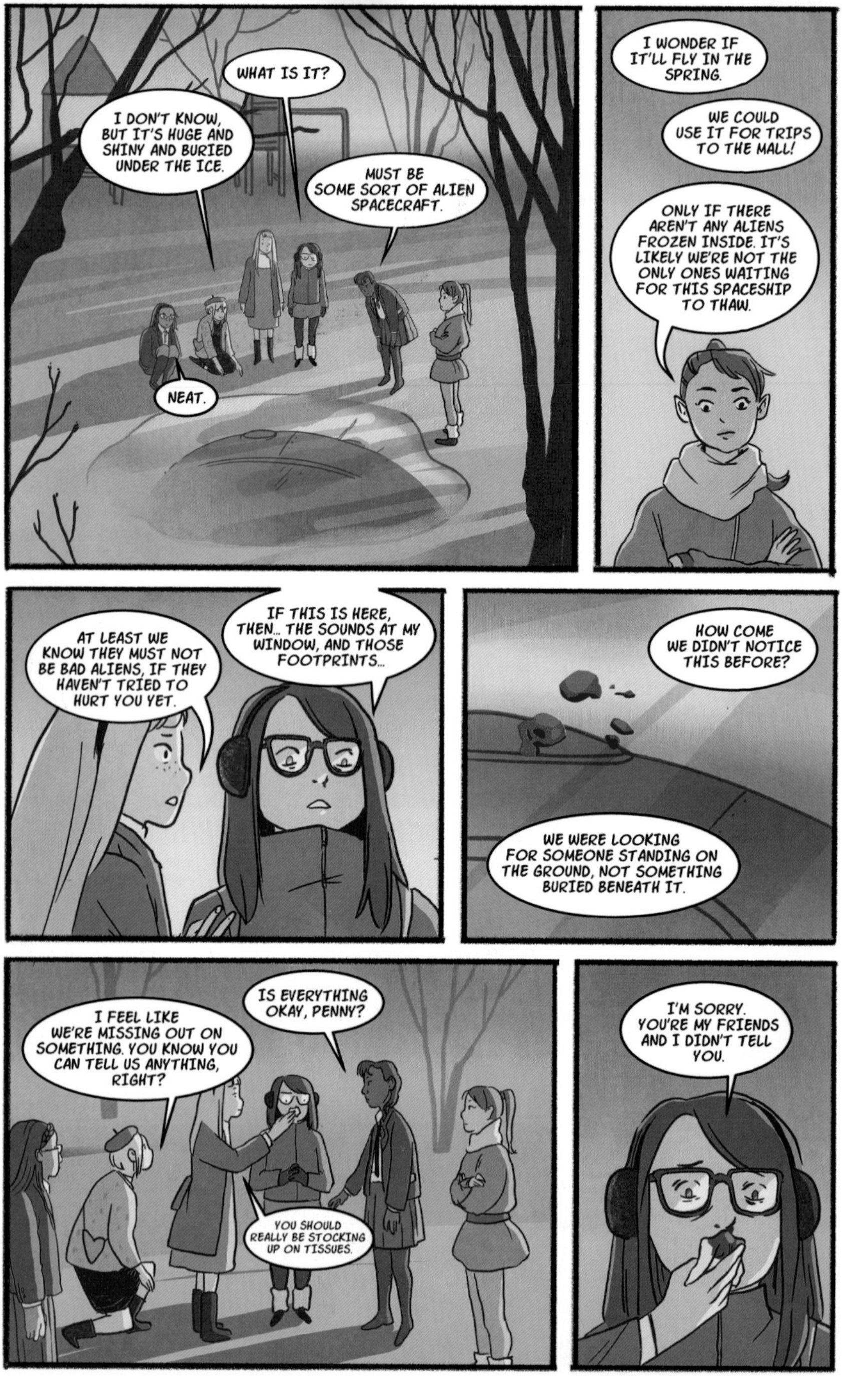
WHAT IS IT?
I DON'T KNOW, BUT IT'S HUGE AND SHINY AND BURIED UNDER THE ICE.
MUST BE SOME SORT OF ALIEN SPACECRAFT.
NEAT.
I WONDER IF IT'LL FLY IN THE SPRING.
WE COULD USE IT FOR TRIPS TO THE MALL!
ONLY IF THERE AREN'T ANY ALIENS FROZEN INSIDE. IT'S LIKELY WE'RE NOT THE ONLY ONES WAITING FOR THIS SPACESHIP TO THAW.
AT LEAST WE KNOW THEY MUST NOT BE BAD ALIENS, IF THEY HAVEN'T TRIED TO HURT YOU YET.
IF THIS IS HERE, THEN... THE SOUNDS AT MY WINDOW, AND THOSE FOOTPRINTS...
HOW COME WE DIDN'T NOTICE THIS BEFORE?
WE WERE LOOKING FOR SOMEONE STANDING ON THE GROUND, NOT SOMETHING BURIED BENEATH IT.
I FEEL LIKE WE'RE MISSING OUT ON SOMETHING. YOU KNOW YOU CAN TELL US ANYTHING, RIGHT?
IS EVERYTHING OKAY, PENNY?
YOU SHOULD REALLY BE STOCKING UP ON TISSUES.
I'M SORRY. YOU'RE MY FRIENDS AND I DIDN'T TELL YOU.

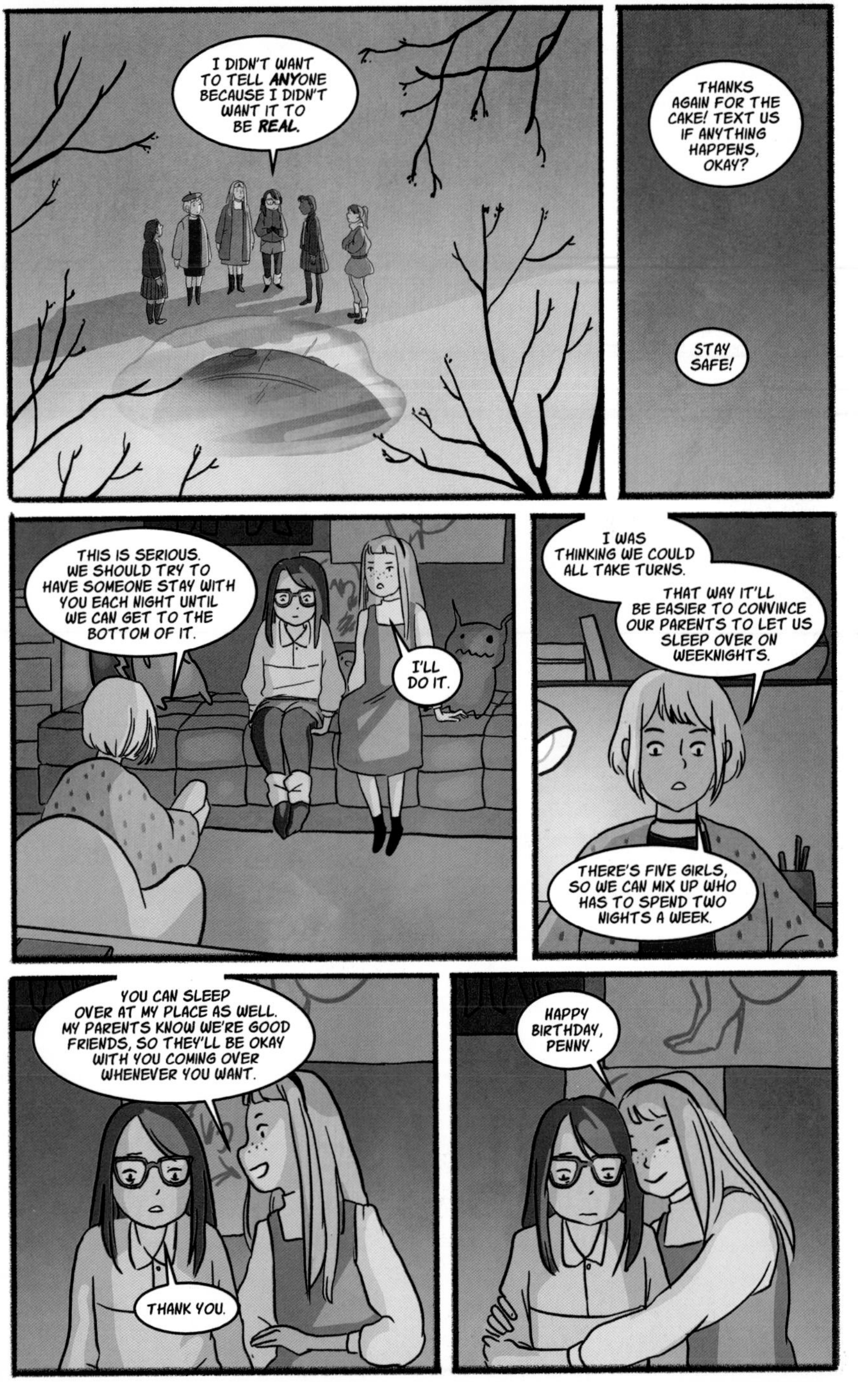
I DIDN'T WANT TO TELL ANYONE BECAUSE I DIDN'T WANT IT TO BE REAL.
THANKS AGAIN FOR THE CAKE! TEXT US IF ANYTHING HAPPENS, OKAY?
STAY SAFE!
THIS IS SERIOUS. WE SHOULD TRY TO HAVE SOMEONE STAY WITH YOU EACH NIGHT UNTIL WE CAN GET TO THE BOTTOM OF IT.
I'LL DO IT.
I WAS THINKING WE COULD ALL TAKE TURNS.
THAT WAY IT'LL BE EASIER TO CONVINCE OUR PARENTS TO LET US SLEEP OVER ON WEEKNIGHTS.
THERE'S FIVE GIRLS, SO WE CAN MIX UP WHO HAS TO SPEND TWO NIGHTS A WEEK.
YOU CAN SLEEP OVER AT MY PLACE AS WELL. MY PARENTS KNOW WE'RE GOOD FRIENDS, SO THEY'LL BE OKAY WITH YOU COMING OVER WHENEVER YOU WANT.
THANK YOU.
HAPPY BIRTHDAY, PENNY.

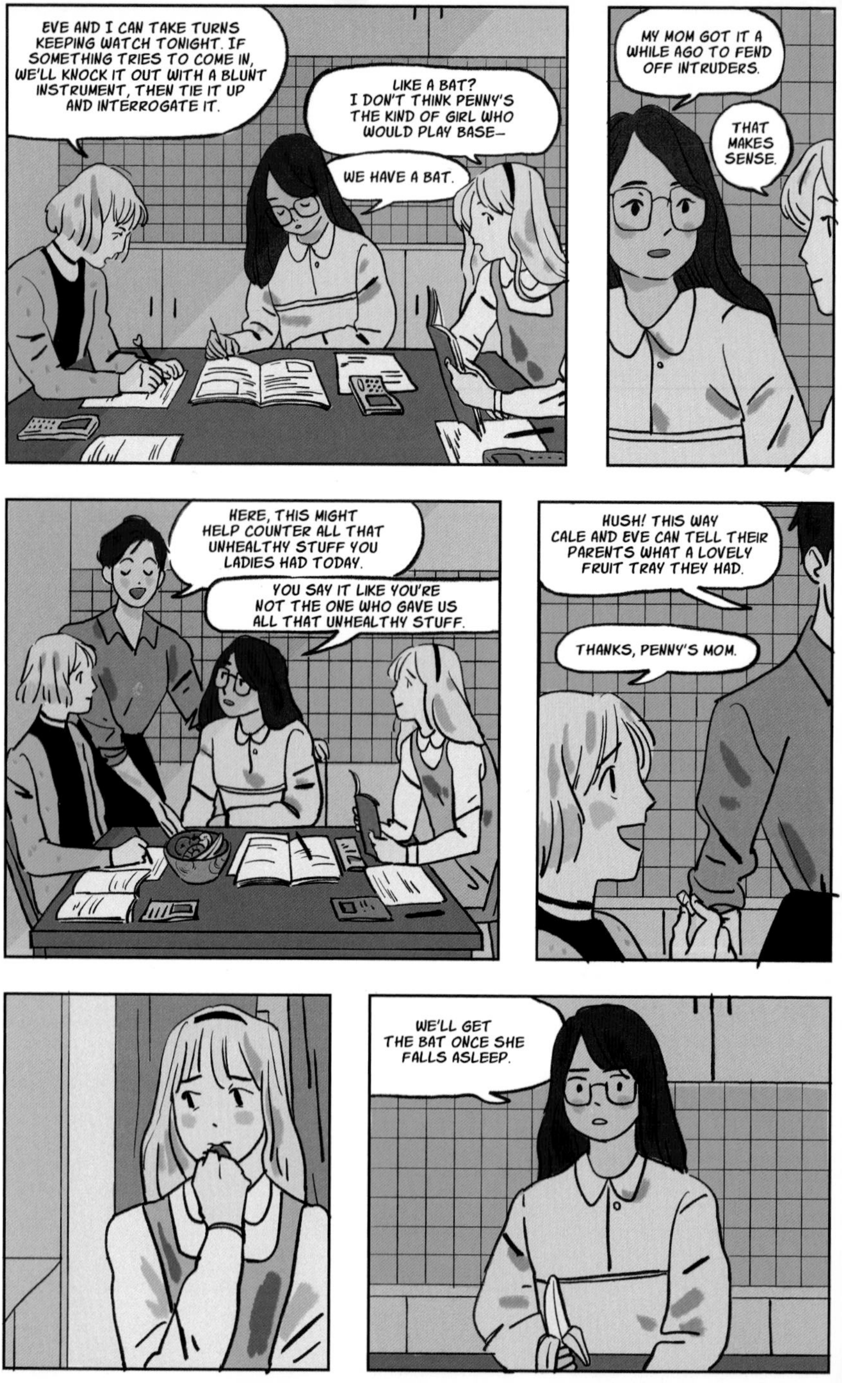
EVE AND I CAN TAKE TURNS KEEPING WATCH TONIGHT. IF SOMETHING TRIES TO COME IN, WE'LL KNOCK IT OUT WITH A BLUNT INSTRUMENT, THEN TIE IT UP AND INTERROGATE IT.
LIKE A BAT? I DON'T THINK PENNY'S THE KIND OF GIRL WHO WOULD PLAY BASE–
WE HAVE A BAT.
MY MOM GOT IT A WHILE AGO TO FEND OFF INTRUDERS.
THAT MAKES SENSE.
HERE, THIS MIGHT HELP COUNTER ALL THAT UNHEALTHY STUFF YOU LADIES HAD TODAY.
YOU SAY IT LIKE YOU'RE NOT THE ONE WHO GAVE US ALL THAT UNHEALTHY STUFF.
HUSH! THIS WAY CALE AND EVE CAN TELL THEIR PARENTS WHAT A LOVELY FRUIT TRAY THEY HAD.
THANKS, PENNY'S MOM.
WE'LL GET THE BAT ONCE SHE FALLS ASLEEP.

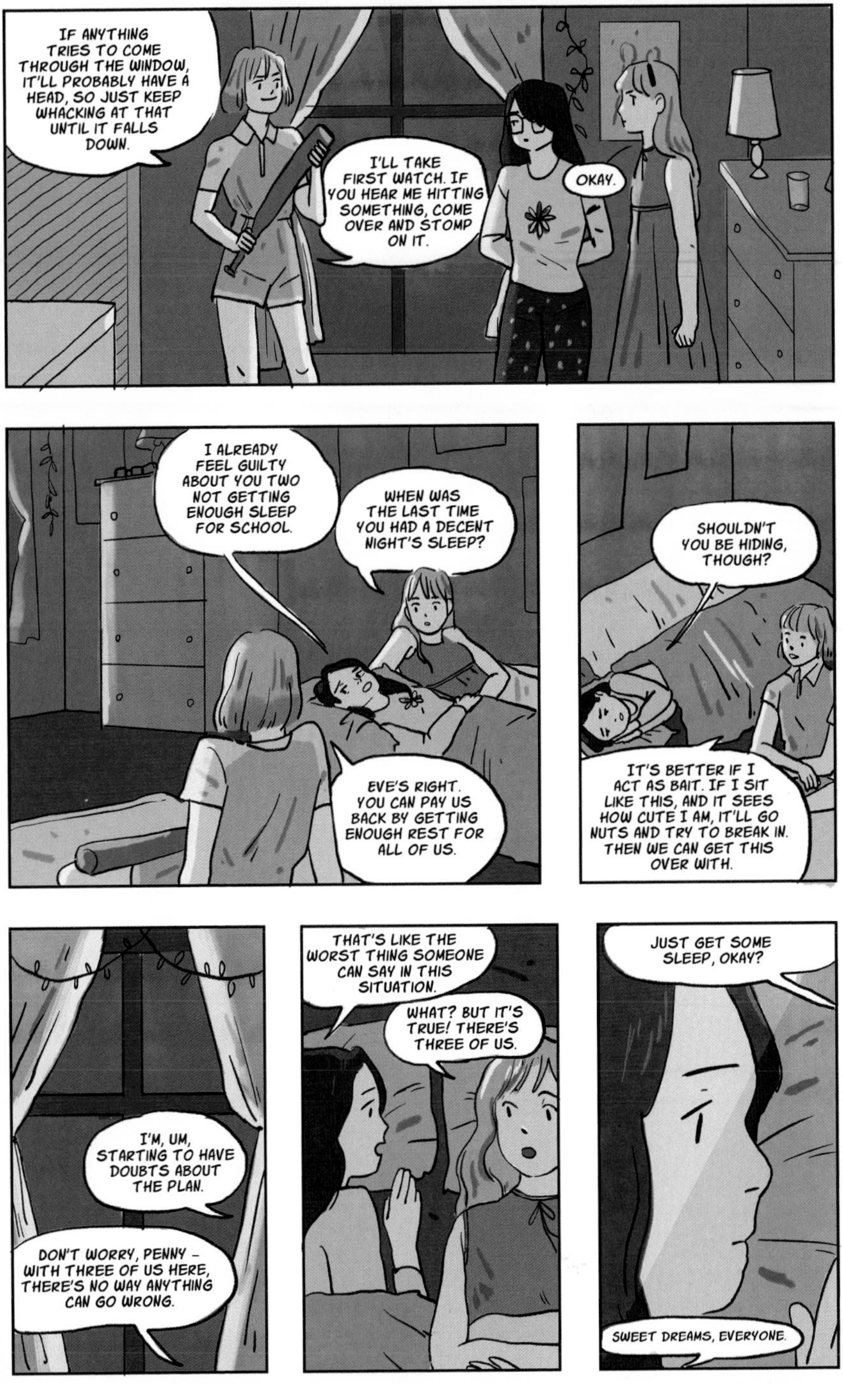
IF ANYTHING TRIES TO COME THROUGH THE WINDOW, IT'LL PROBABLY HAVE A HEAD, SO JUST KEEP WHACKING AT THAT UNTIL IT FALLS DOWN.
I'LL TAKE FIRST WATCH. IF YOU HEAR ME HITTING SOMETHING, COME OVER AND STOMP ON IT.
OKAY.
I ALREADY FEEL GUILTY ABOUT YOU TWO NOT GETTING ENOUGH SLEEP FOR SCHOOL.
WHEN WAS THE LAST TIME YOU HAD A DECENT NIGHT'S SLEEP?
EVE'S RIGHT. YOU CAN PAY US BACK BY GETTING ENOUGH REST FOR ALL OF US.
SHOULDN'T YOU BE HIDING, THOUGH?
IT'S BETTER IF I ACT AS BAIT. IF I SIT LIKE THIS, AND IT SEES HOW CUTE I AM, IT'LL GO NUTS AND TRY TO BREAK IN. THEN WE CAN GET THIS OVER WITH.
I'M, UM, STARTING TO HAVE DOUBTS ABOUT THE PLAN.
DON'T WORRY, PENNY – WITH THREE OF US HERE, THERE'S NO WAY ANYTHING CAN GO WRONG.
THAT'S LIKE THE WORST THING SOMEONE CAN SAY IN THIS SITUATION.
WHAT? BUT IT'S TRUE! THERE'S THREE OF US.
JUST GET SOME SLEEP, OKAY?
SWEET DREAMS, EVERYONE.

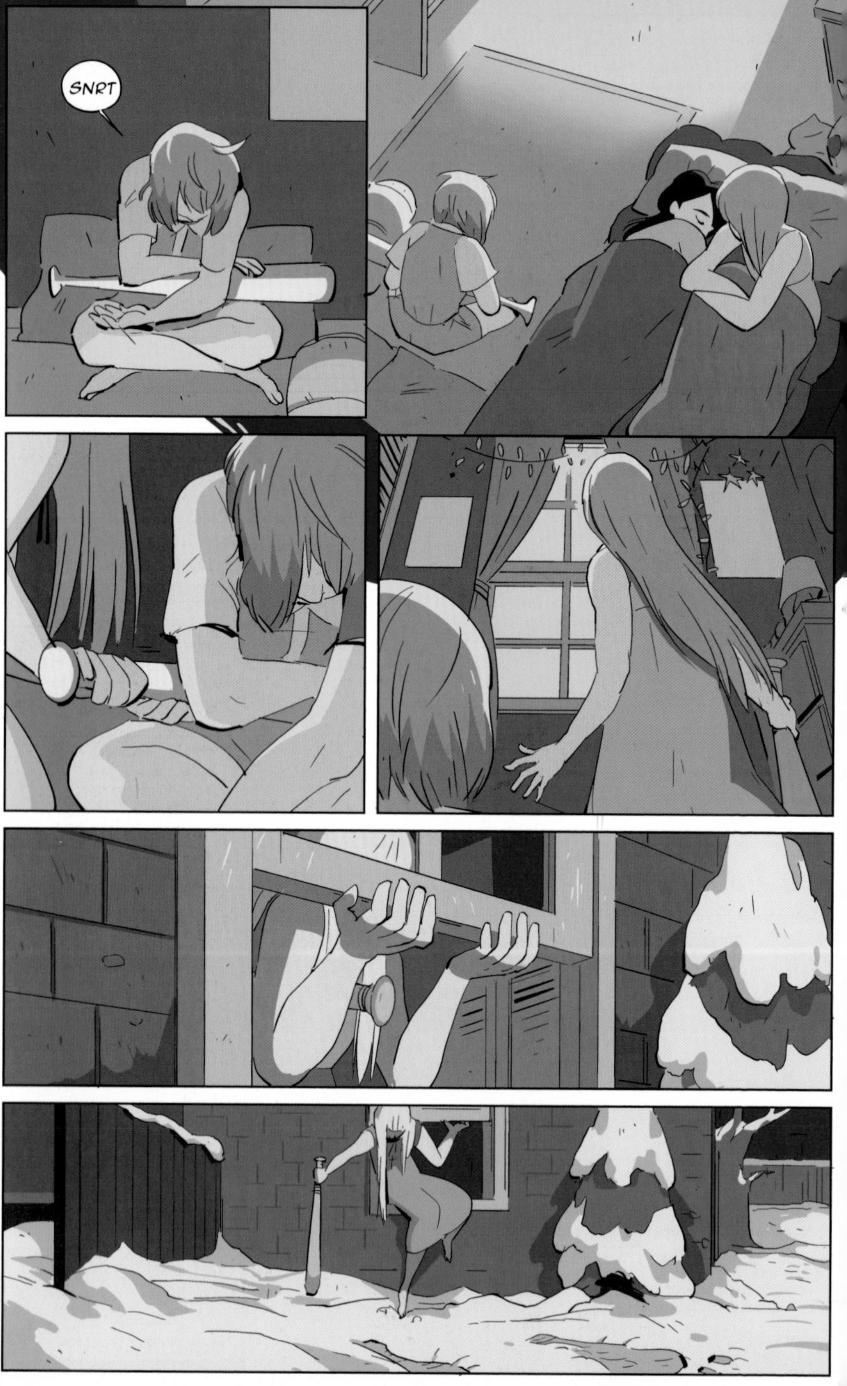
SNRT

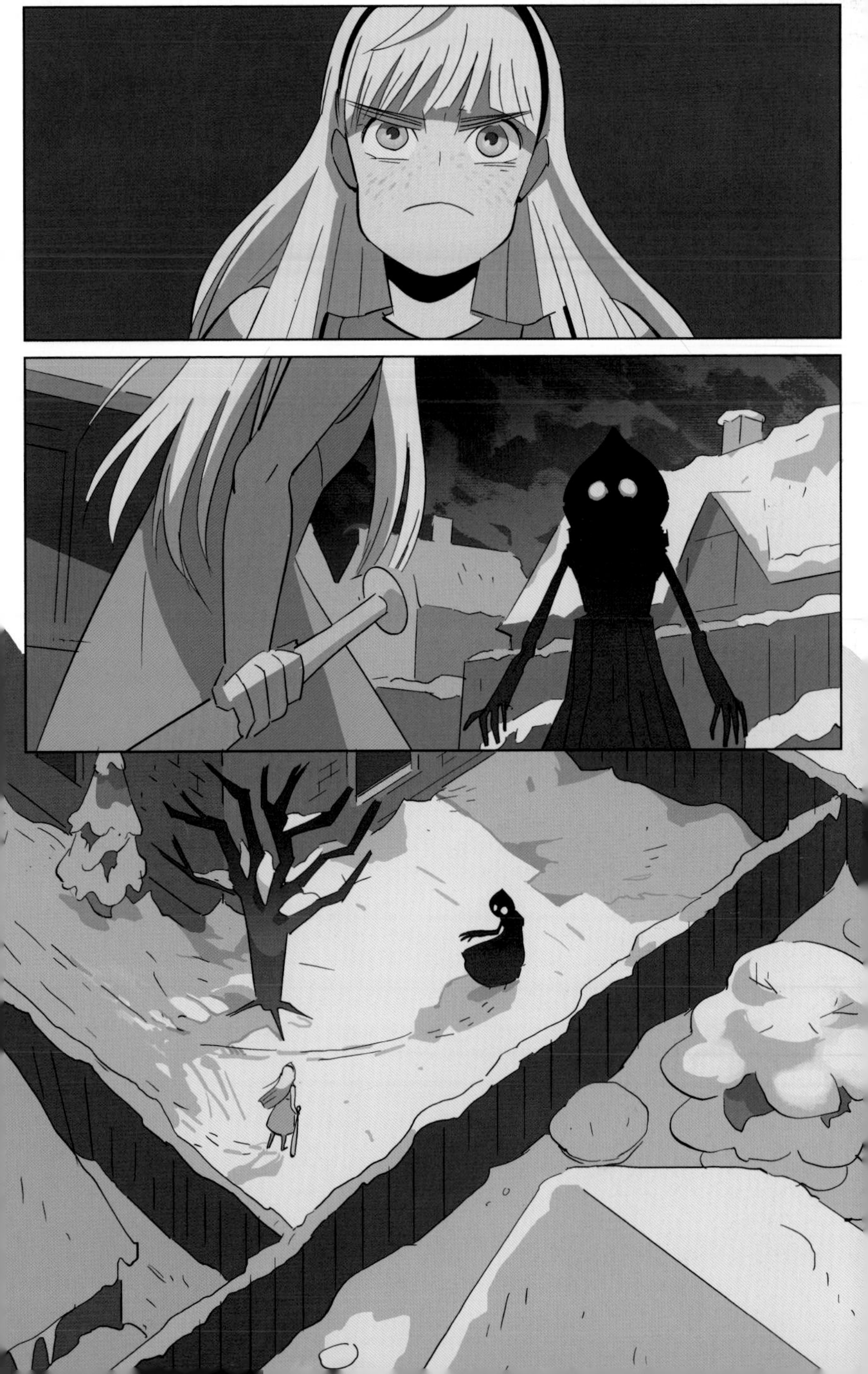

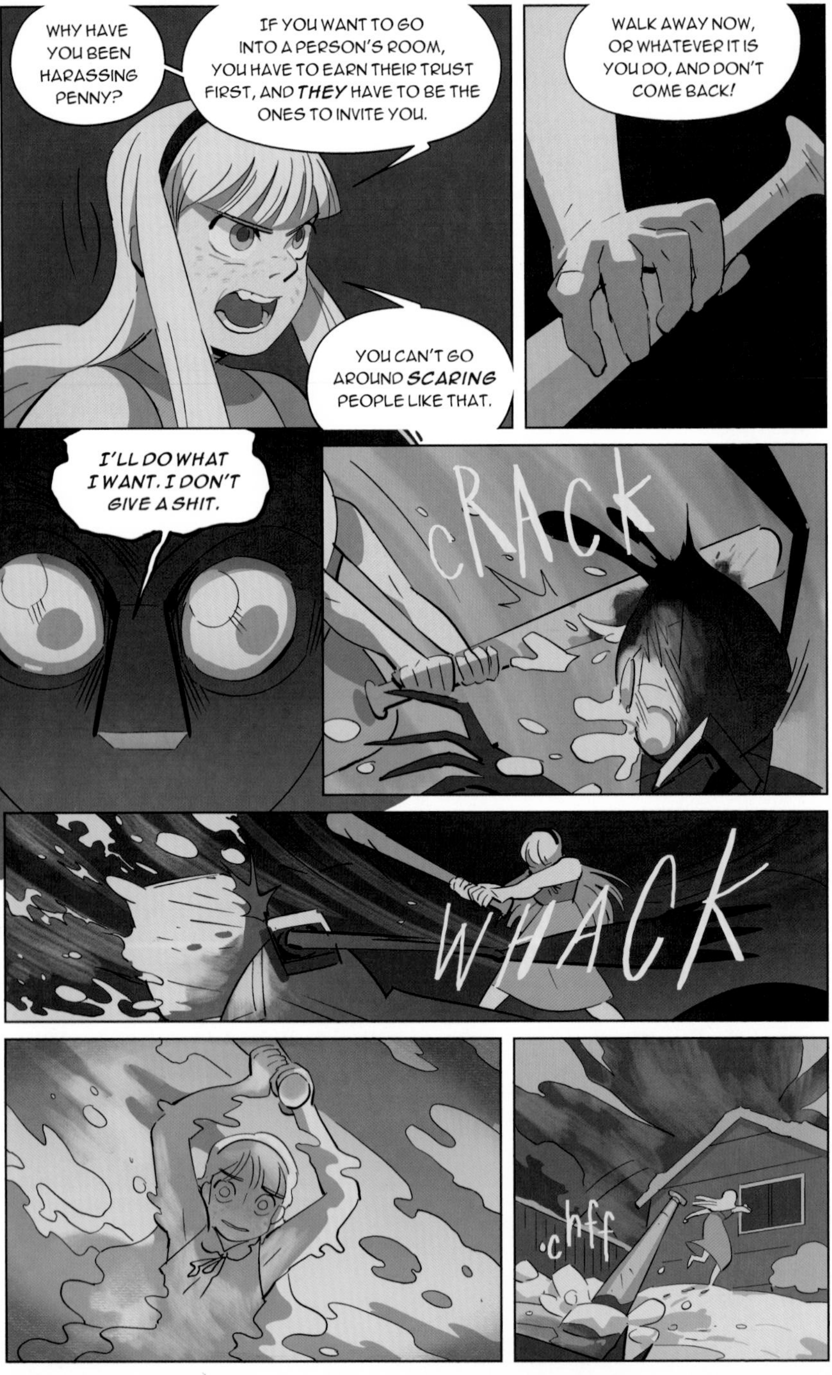
WHY HAVE YOU BEEN HARASSING PENNY?
IF YOU WANT TO GO INTO A PERSON'S ROOM, YOU HAVE TO EARN THEIR TRUST FIRST, AND *THEY* HAVE TO BE THE ONES TO INVITE YOU.
YOU CAN'T GO AROUND *SCARING* PEOPLE LIKE THAT.
WALK AWAY NOW, OR WHATEVER IT IS YOU DO, AND DON'T COME BACK!
I'LL DO WHAT I WANT. I DON'T GIVE A SHIT.
cRACK
WHACK
chff

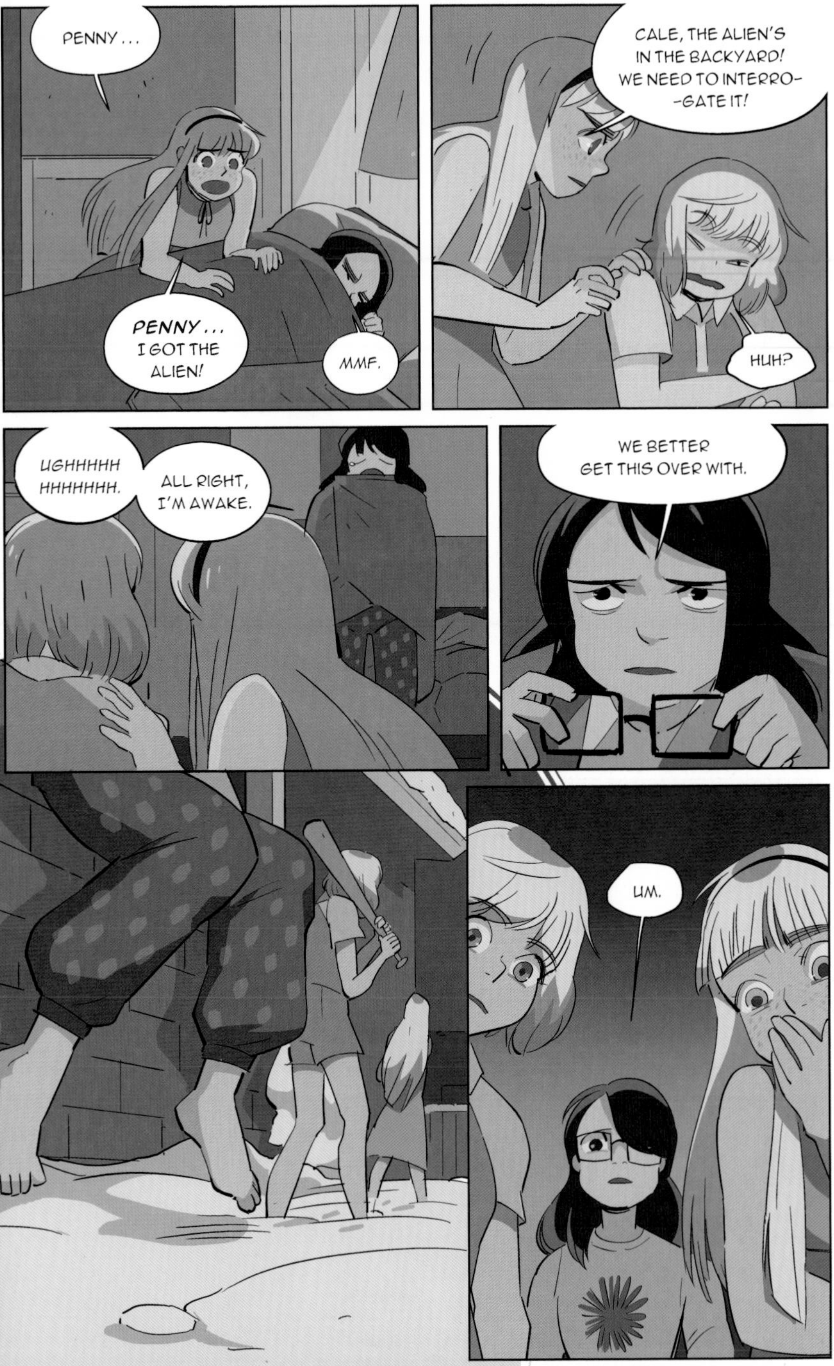
PENNY . . .
PENNY . . . I GOT THE ALIEN!
MMF.
CALE, THE ALIEN'S IN THE BACKYARD! WE NEED TO INTERRO- -GATE IT!
HUH?
UGHHHHH HHHHHHH.
ALL RIGHT, I'M AWAKE.
WE BETTER GET THIS OVER WITH.
UM.

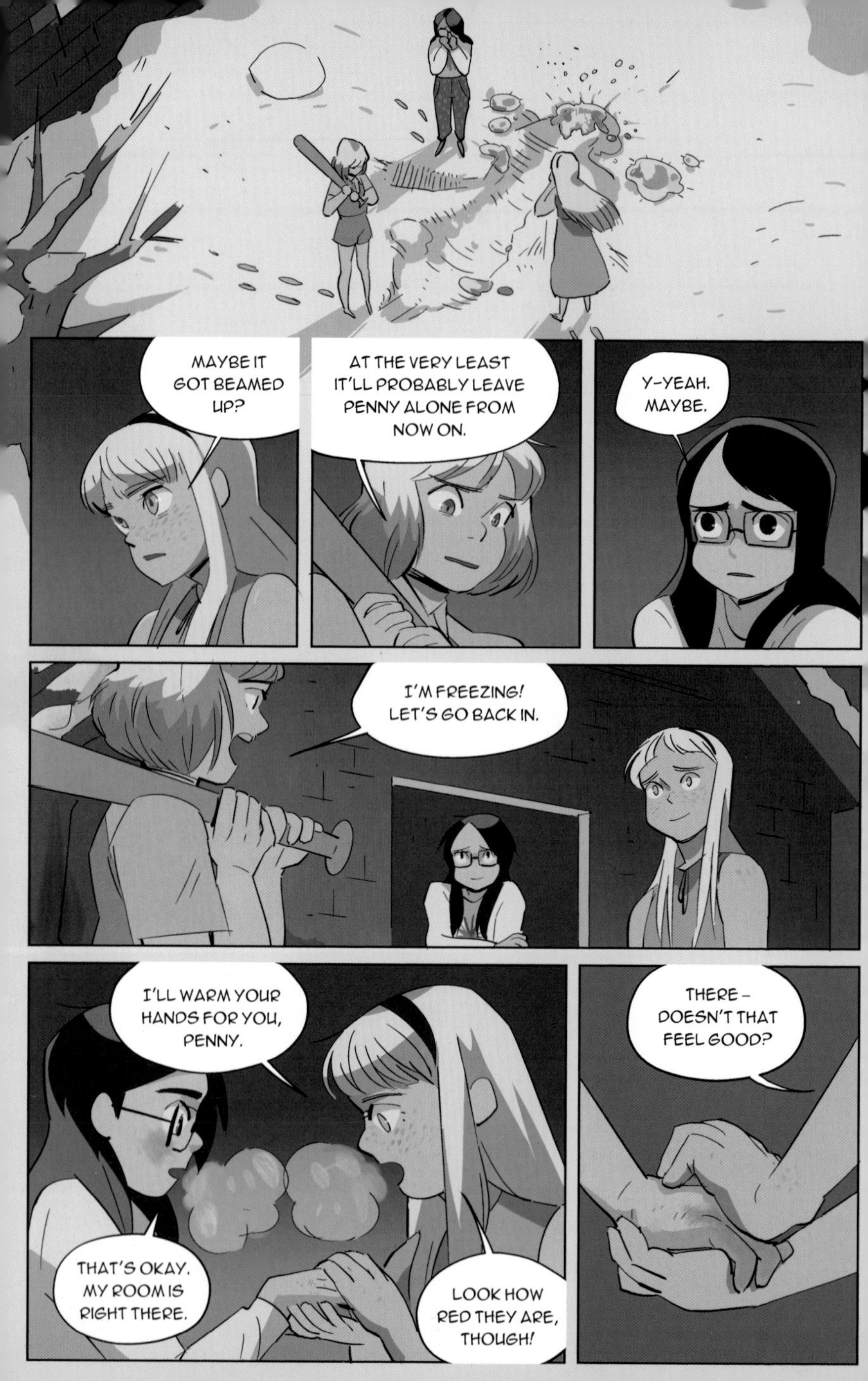
MAYBE IT GOT BEAMED UP?
AT THE VERY LEAST IT'LL PROBABLY LEAVE PENNY ALONE FROM NOW ON.
Y-YEAH. MAYBE.
I'M FREEZING! LET'S GO BACK IN.
I'LL WARM YOUR HANDS FOR YOU, PENNY.
THAT'S OKAY. MY ROOM IS RIGHT THERE.
LOOK HOW RED THEY ARE, THOUGH!
THERE – DOESN'T THAT FEEL GOOD?

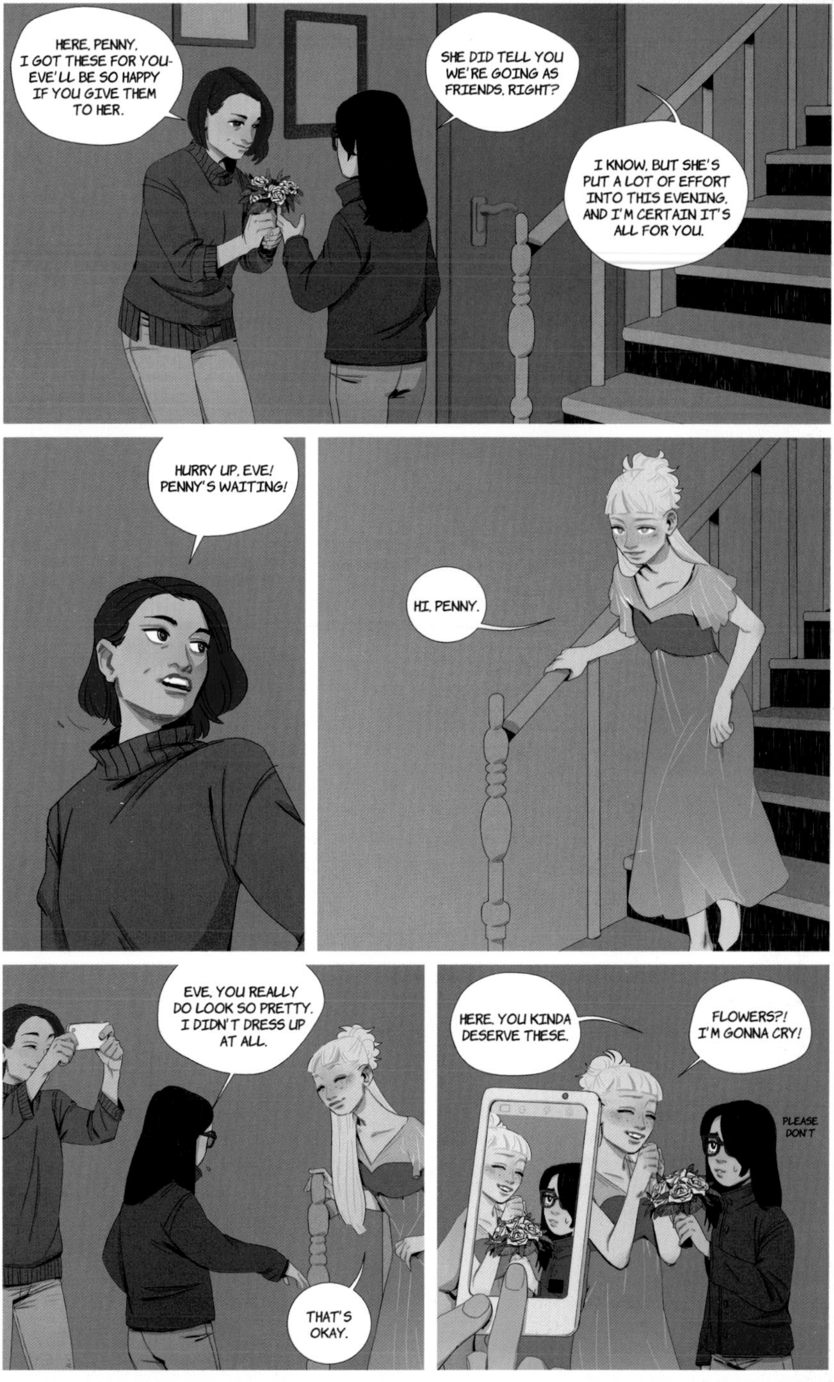
HERE, PENNY, I GOT THESE FOR YOU- EVE'LL BE SO HAPPY IF YOU GIVE THEM TO HER.
SHE DID TELL YOU WE'RE GOING AS FRIENDS, RIGHT?
I KNOW, BUT SHE'S PUT A LOT OF EFFORT INTO THIS EVENING, AND I'M CERTAIN IT'S ALL FOR YOU.
HURRY UP, EVE! PENNY'S WAITING!
HI, PENNY.
EVE, YOU REALLY DO LOOK SO PRETTY. I DIDN'T DRESS UP AT ALL.
THAT'S OKAY.
HERE. YOU KINDA DESERVE THESE.
FLOWERS?! I'M GONNA CRY!
PLEASE DON'T

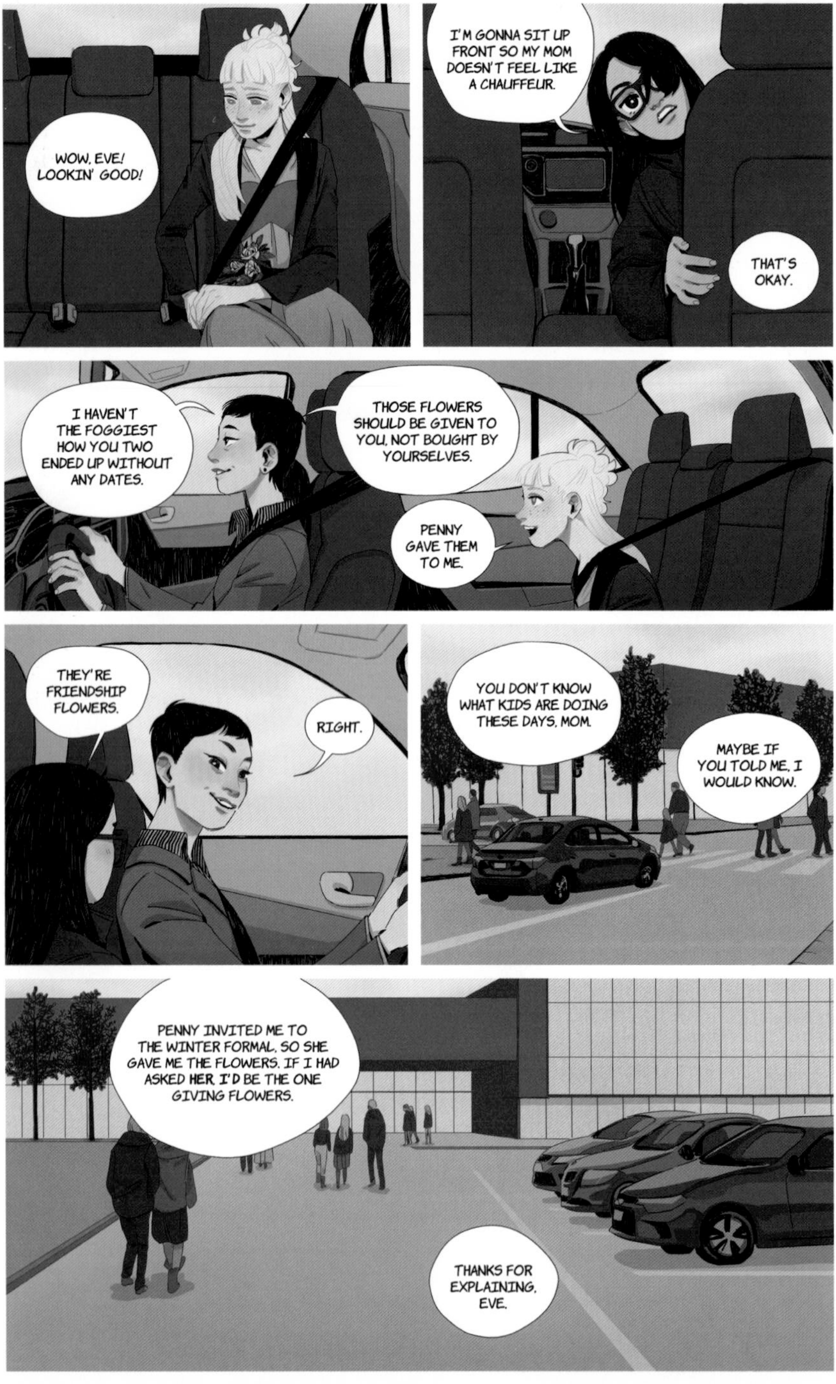
WOW, EVE! LOOKIN' GOOD!
I'M GONNA SIT UP FRONT SO MY MOM DOESN'T FEEL LIKE A CHAUFFEUR.
THAT'S OKAY.
I HAVEN'T THE FOGGIEST HOW YOU TWO ENDED UP WITHOUT ANY DATES.
THOSE FLOWERS SHOULD BE GIVEN TO YOU, NOT BOUGHT BY YOURSELVES.
PENNY GAVE THEM TO ME.
THEY'RE FRIENDSHIP FLOWERS.
RIGHT.
YOU DON'T KNOW WHAT KIDS ARE DOING THESE DAYS, MOM.
MAYBE IF YOU TOLD ME, I WOULD KNOW.
PENNY INVITED ME TO THE WINTER FORMAL, SO SHE GAVE ME THE FLOWERS. IF I HAD ASKED HER, I'D BE THE ONE GIVING FLOWERS.
THANKS FOR EXPLAINING, EVE.

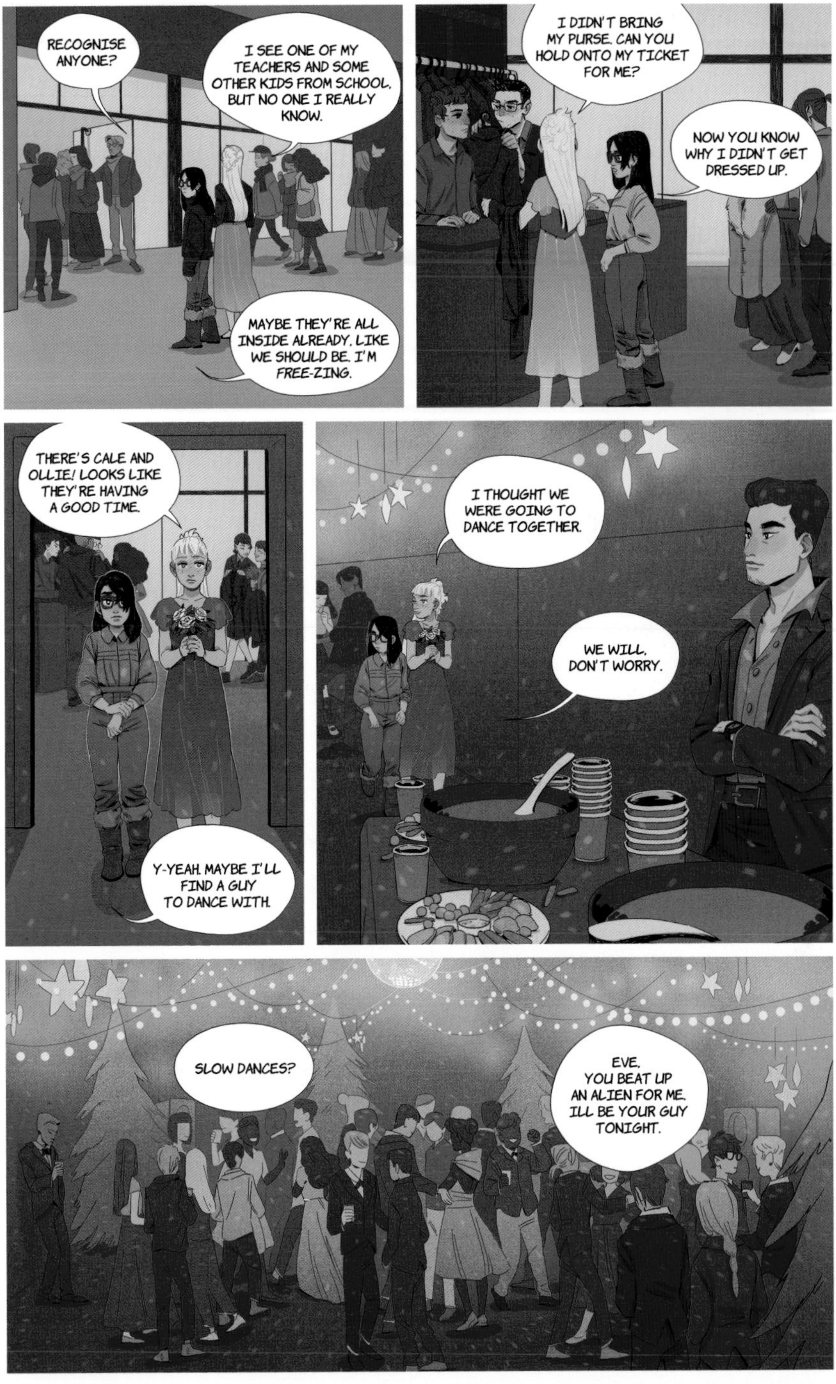
RECOGNISE ANYONE?
I SEE ONE OF MY TEACHERS AND SOME OTHER KIDS FROM SCHOOL, BUT NO ONE I REALLY KNOW.
MAYBE THEY'RE ALL INSIDE ALREADY, LIKE WE SHOULD BE. I'M FREE-ZING.
I DIDN'T BRING MY PURSE. CAN YOU HOLD ONTO MY TICKET FOR ME?
NOW YOU KNOW WHY I DIDN'T GET DRESSED UP.
THERE'S CALE AND OLLIE! LOOKS LIKE THEY'RE HAVING A GOOD TIME.
Y-YEAH. MAYBE I'LL FIND A GUY TO DANCE WITH.
I THOUGHT WE WERE GOING TO DANCE TOGETHER.
WE WILL, DON'T WORRY.
SLOW DANCES?
EVE, YOU BEAT UP AN ALIEN FOR ME. ILL BE YOUR GUY TONIGHT.

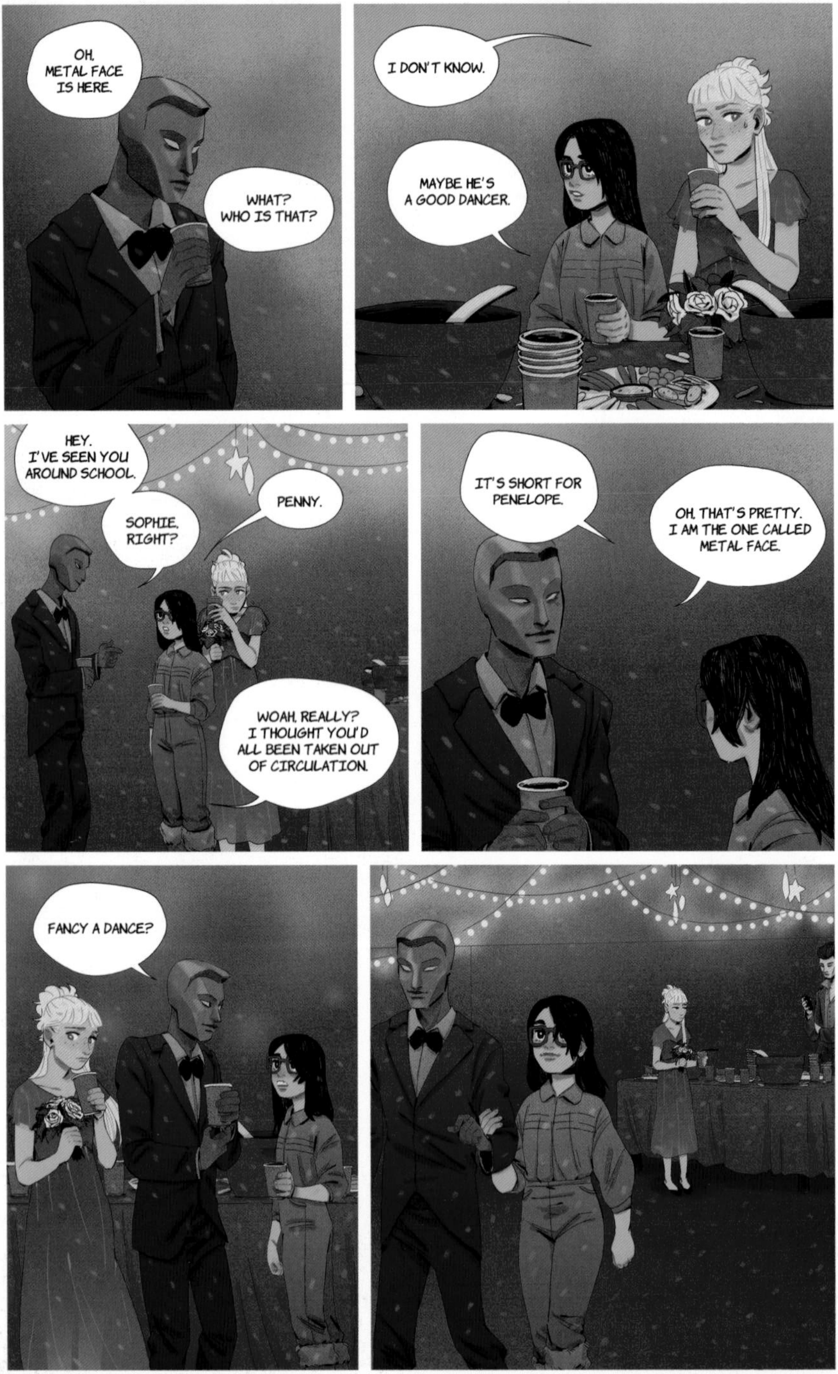
OH, METAL FACE IS HERE.
WHAT? WHO IS THAT?
I DON'T KNOW.
MAYBE HE'S A GOOD DANCER.
HEY. I'VE SEEN YOU AROUND SCHOOL.
SOPHIE, RIGHT?
PENNY.
WOAH, REALLY? I THOUGHT YOU'D ALL BEEN TAKEN OUT OF CIRCULATION.
IT'S SHORT FOR PENELOPE.
OH, THAT'S PRETTY. I AM THE ONE CALLED METAL FACE.
FANCY A DANCE?

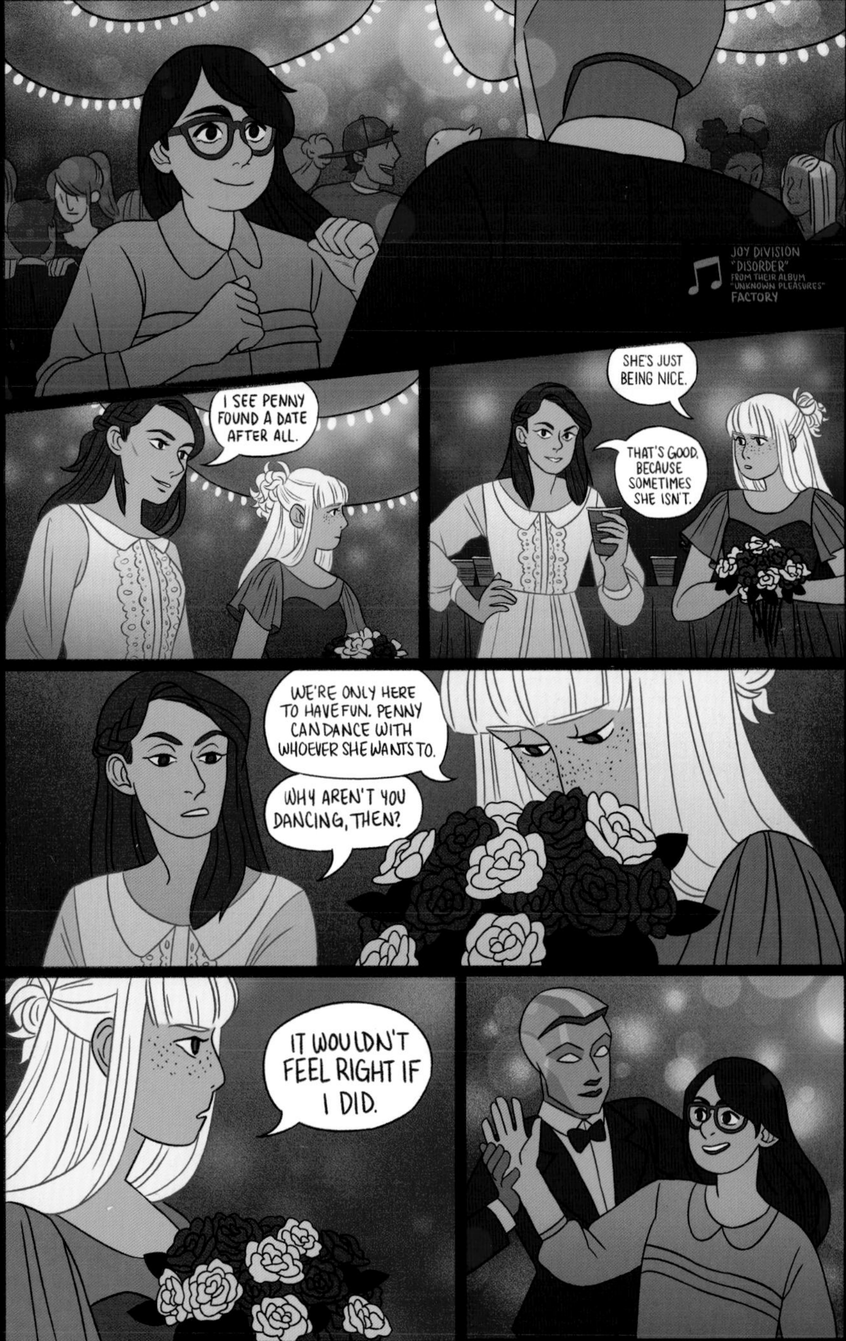
JOY DIVISION "DISORDER" FROM THEIR ALBUM "UNKNOWN PLEASURES" FACTORY
I SEE PENNY FOUND A DATE AFTER ALL.
SHE'S JUST BEING NICE.
THAT'S GOOD, BECAUSE SOMETIMES SHE ISN'T.
WE'RE ONLY HERE TO HAVE FUN. PENNY CAN DANCE WITH WHOEVER SHE WANTS TO.
WHY AREN'T YOU DANCING, THEN?
IT WOULDN'T FEEL RIGHT IF I DID.

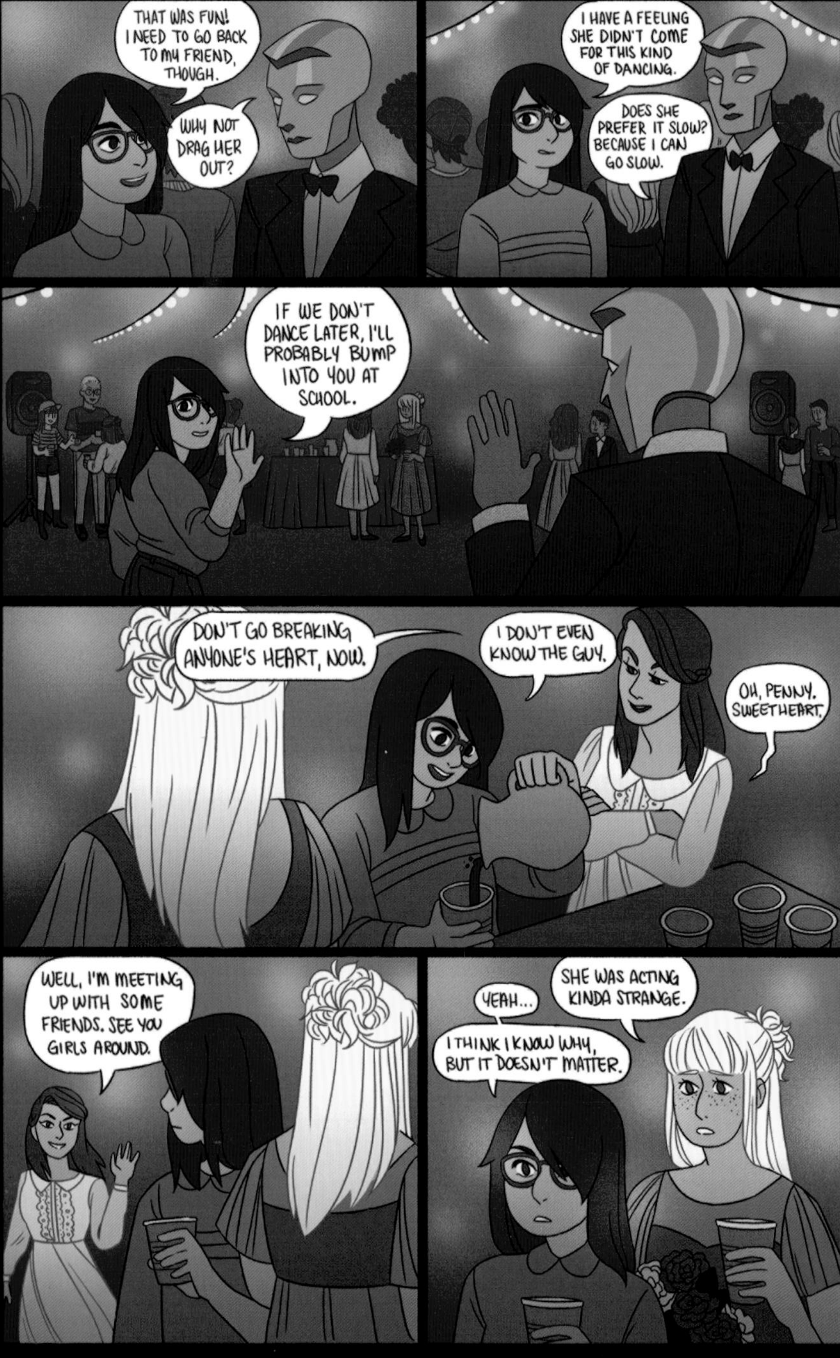
THAT WAS FUN! I NEED TO GO BACK TO MY FRIEND, THOUGH.
WHY NOT DRAG HER OUT?
I HAVE A FEELING SHE DIDN'T COME FOR THIS KIND OF DANCING.
DOES SHE PREFER IT SLOW? BECAUSE I CAN GO SLOW.
IF WE DON'T DANCE LATER, I'LL PROBABLY BUMP INTO YOU AT SCHOOL.
DON'T GO BREAKING ANYONE'S HEART, NOW.
I DON'T EVEN KNOW THE GUY.
OH, PENNY. SWEETHEART.
WELL, I'M MEETING UP WITH SOME FRIENDS. SEE YOU GIRLS AROUND.
YEAH...
SHE WAS ACTING KINDA STRANGE.
I THINK I KNOW WHY, BUT IT DOESN'T MATTER.

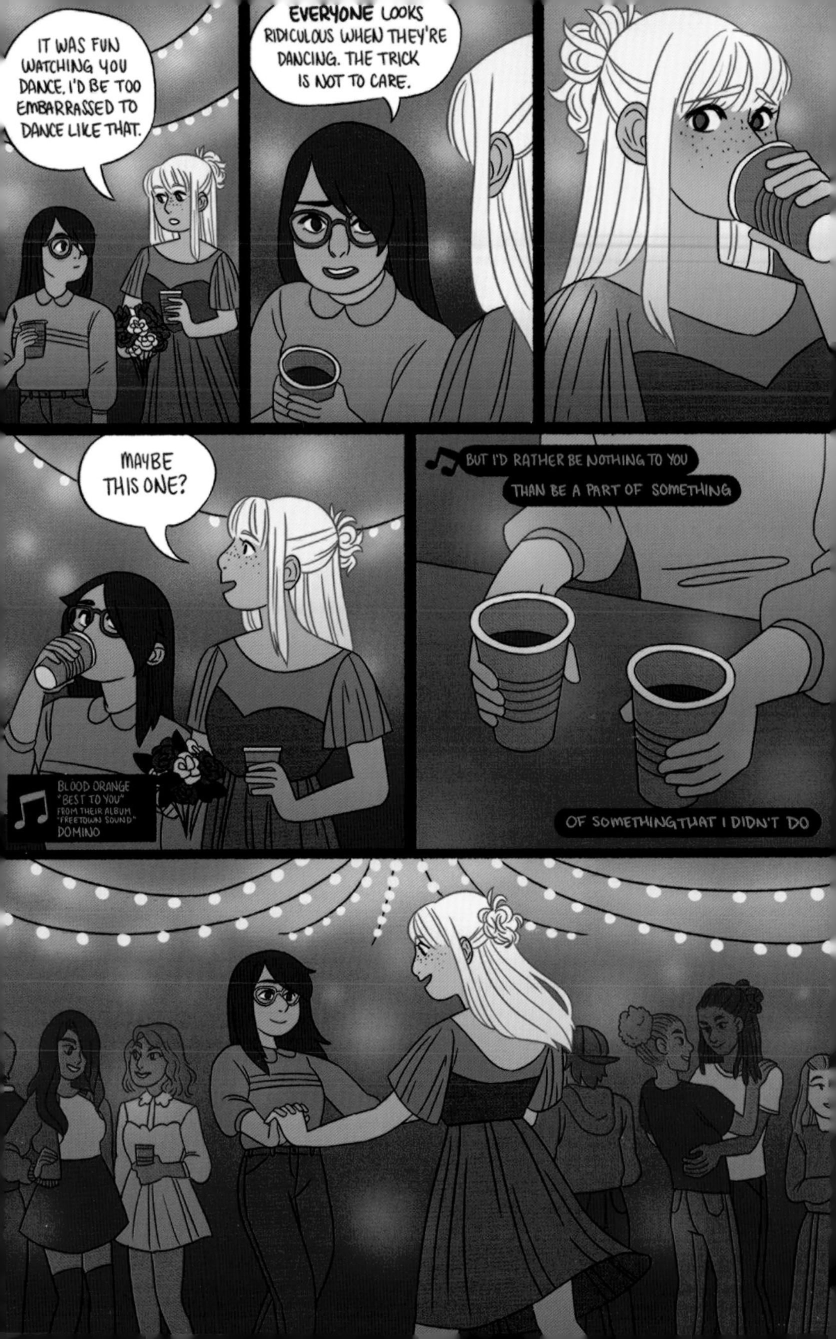
IT WAS FUN WATCHING YOU DANCE. I'D BE TOO EMBARRASSED TO DANCE LIKE THAT.
EVERYONE LOOKS RIDICULOUS WHEN THEY'RE DANCING. THE TRICK IS NOT TO CARE.
MAYBE THIS ONE?
BLOOD ORANGE "BEST TO YOU" FROM THEIR ALBUM "FREETOWN SOUND" DOMINO
BUT I'D RATHER BE NOTHING TO YOU
THAN BE A PART OF SOMETHING
OF SOMETHING THAT I DIDN'T DO

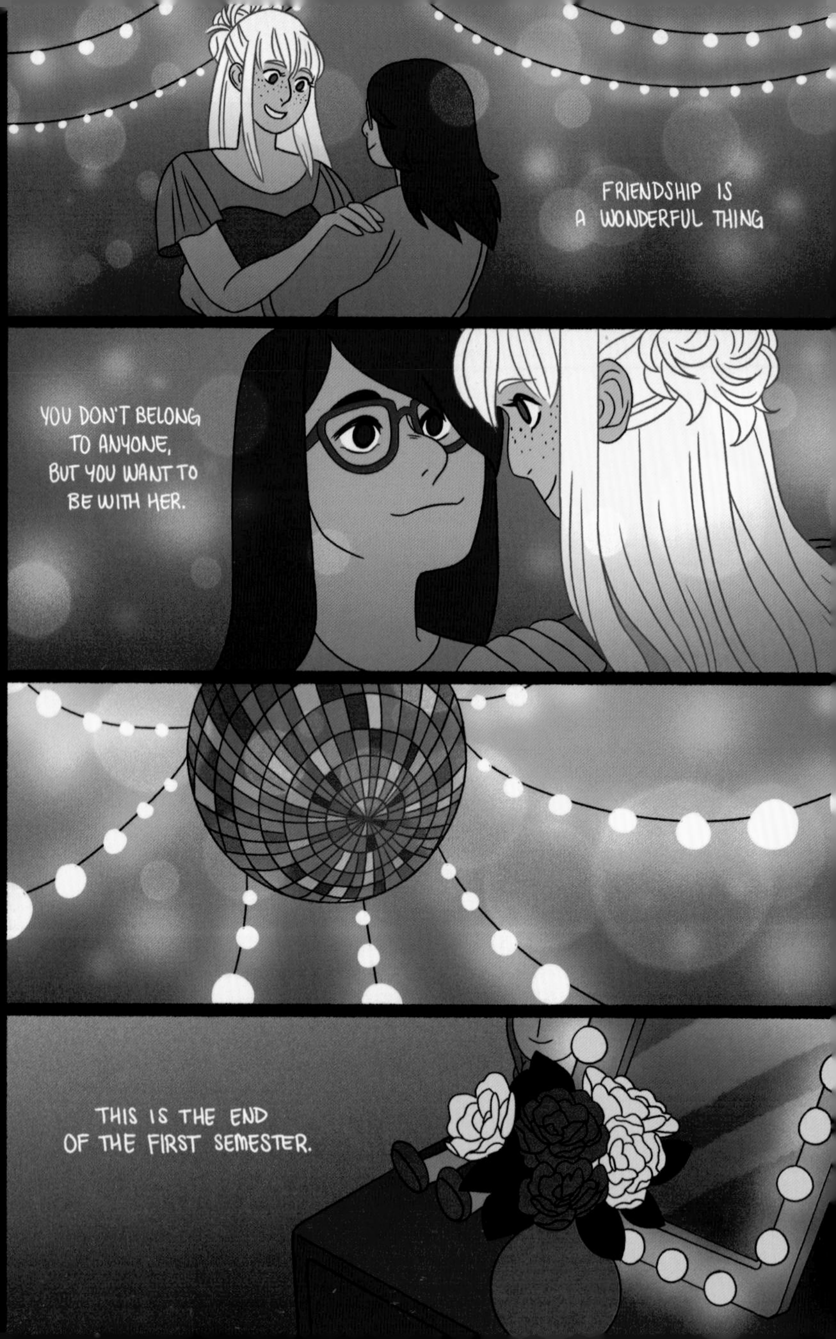
FRIENDSHIP IS A WONDERFUL THING
YOU DON'T BELONG TO ANYONE, BUT YOU WANT TO BE WITH HER.
THIS IS THE END OF THE FIRST SEMESTER.

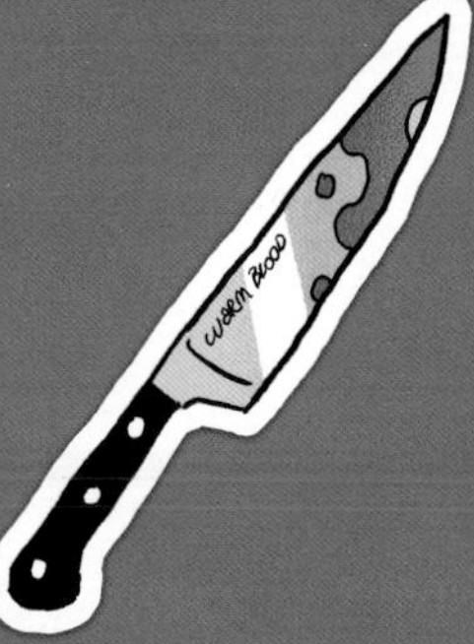
WARM BLOOD

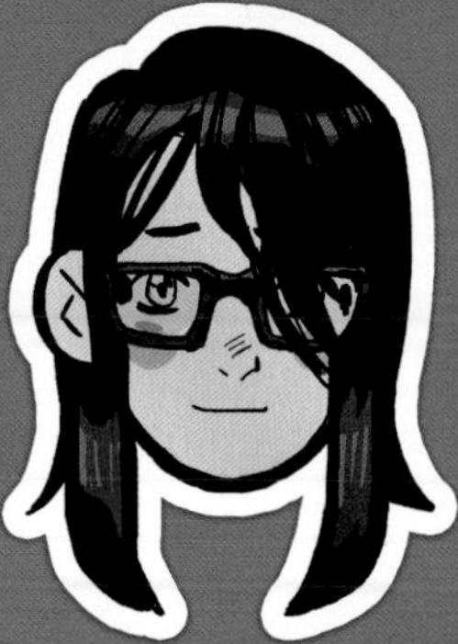

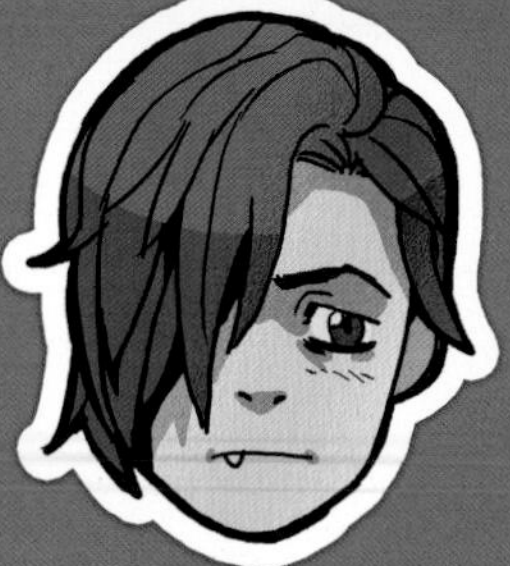

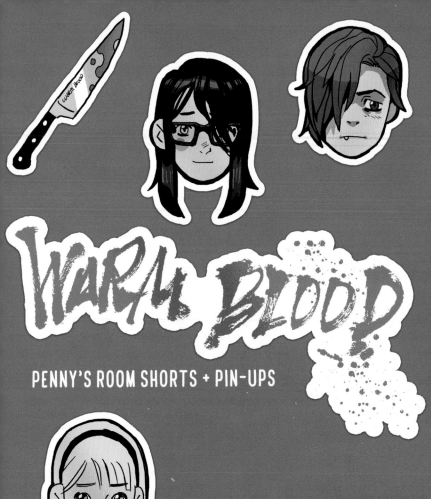

WARM BLOOD

PENNY'S ROOM SHORTS + PIN-UPS

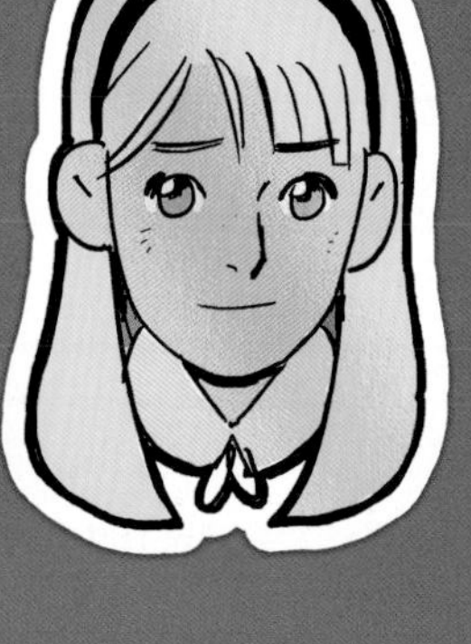

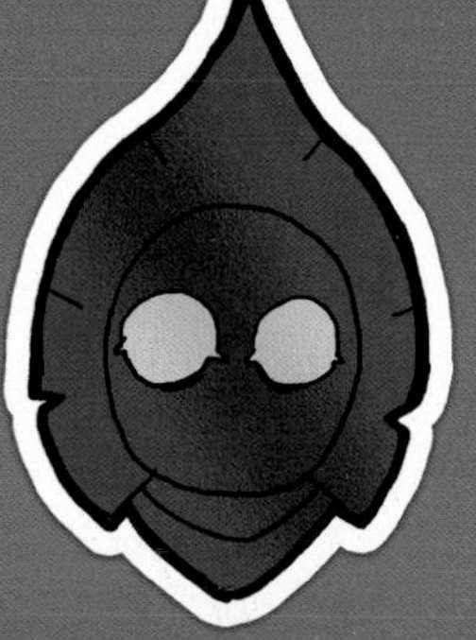

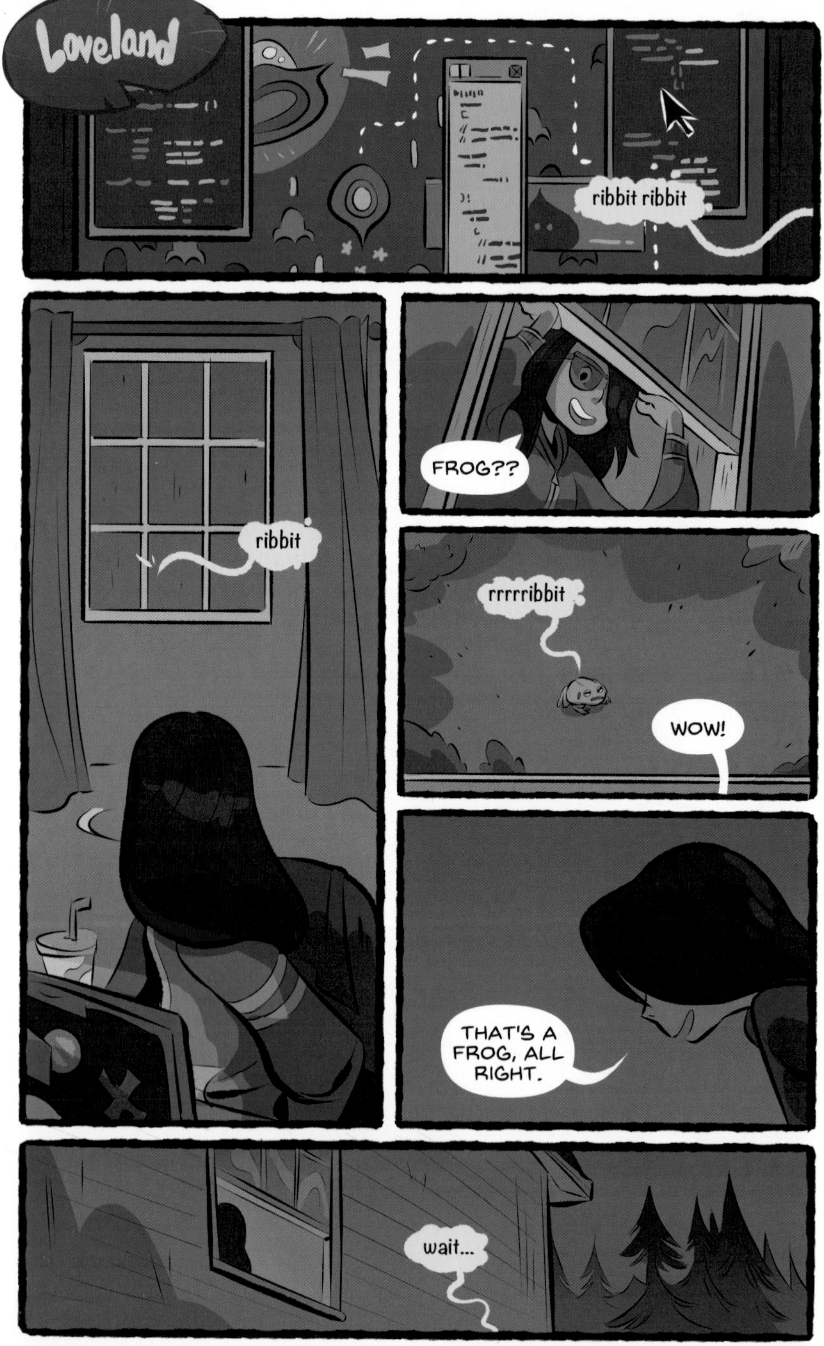
Loveland
ribbit ribbit
ribbit
FROG??
rrrrribbit
WOW!
THAT'S A FROG, ALL RIGHT.
wait...

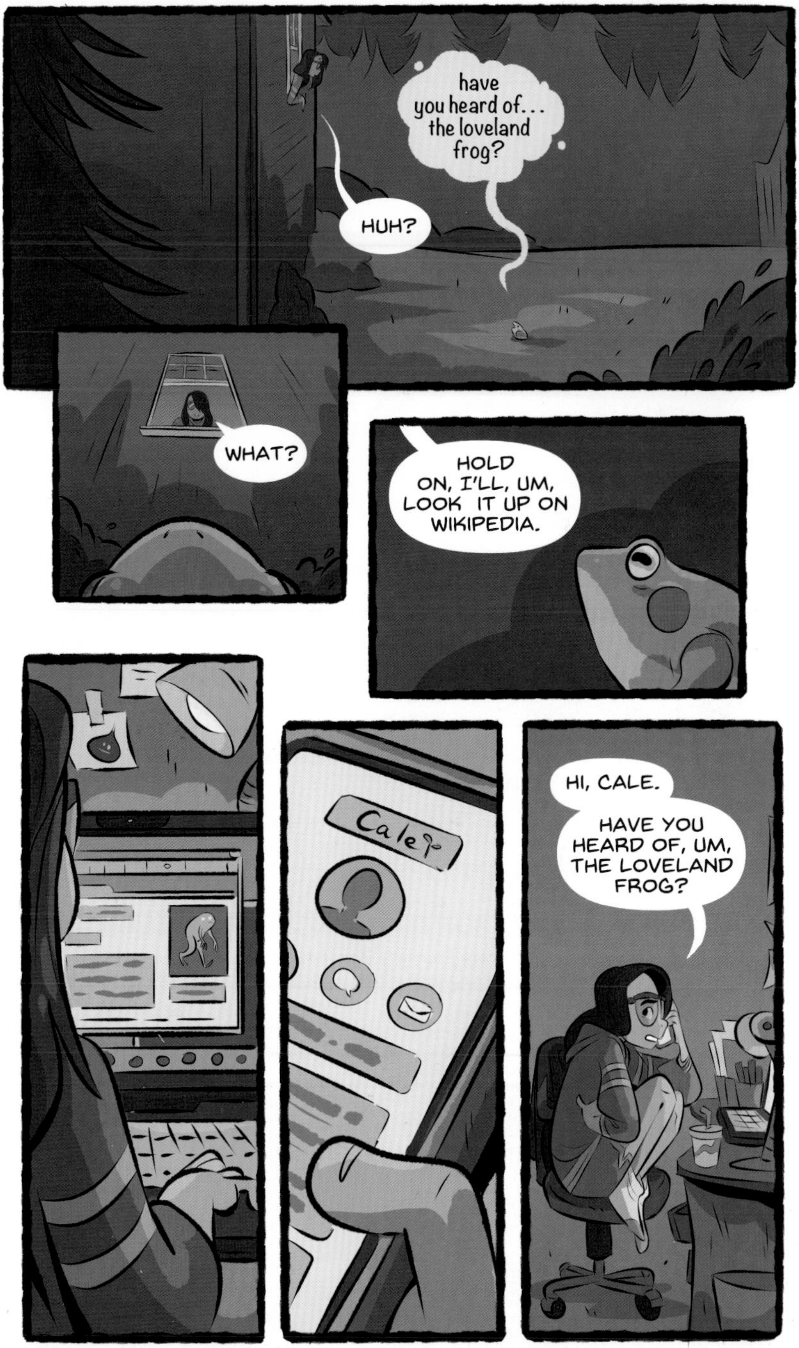
have you heard of... the loveland frog?
HUH?
WHAT?
HOLD ON, I'LL, UM, LOOK IT UP ON WIKIPEDIA.
Cale
HI, CALE.
HAVE YOU HEARD OF, UM, THE LOVELAND FROG?

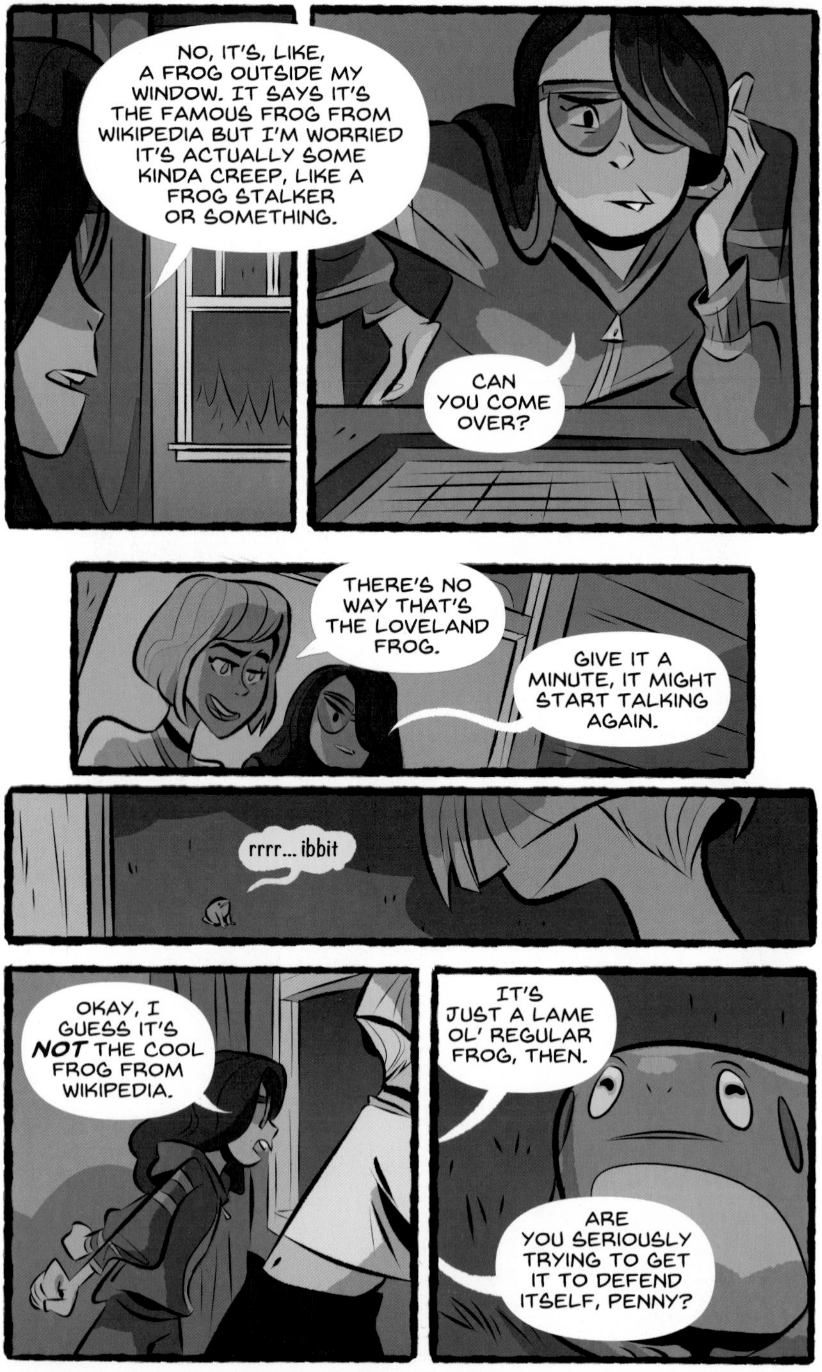
NO, IT'S, LIKE, A FROG OUTSIDE MY WINDOW. IT SAYS IT'S THE FAMOUS FROG FROM WIKIPEDIA BUT I'M WORRIED IT'S ACTUALLY SOME KINDA CREEP, LIKE A FROG STALKER OR SOMETHING.
CAN YOU COME OVER?
THERE'S NO WAY THAT'S THE LOVELAND FROG.
GIVE IT A MINUTE, IT MIGHT START TALKING AGAIN.
rrrr... ibbit
OKAY, I GUESS IT'S ***NOT*** THE COOL FROG FROM WIKIPEDIA.
IT'S JUST A LAME OL' REGULAR FROG, THEN.
ARE YOU SERIOUSLY TRYING TO GET IT TO DEFEND ITSELF, PENNY?

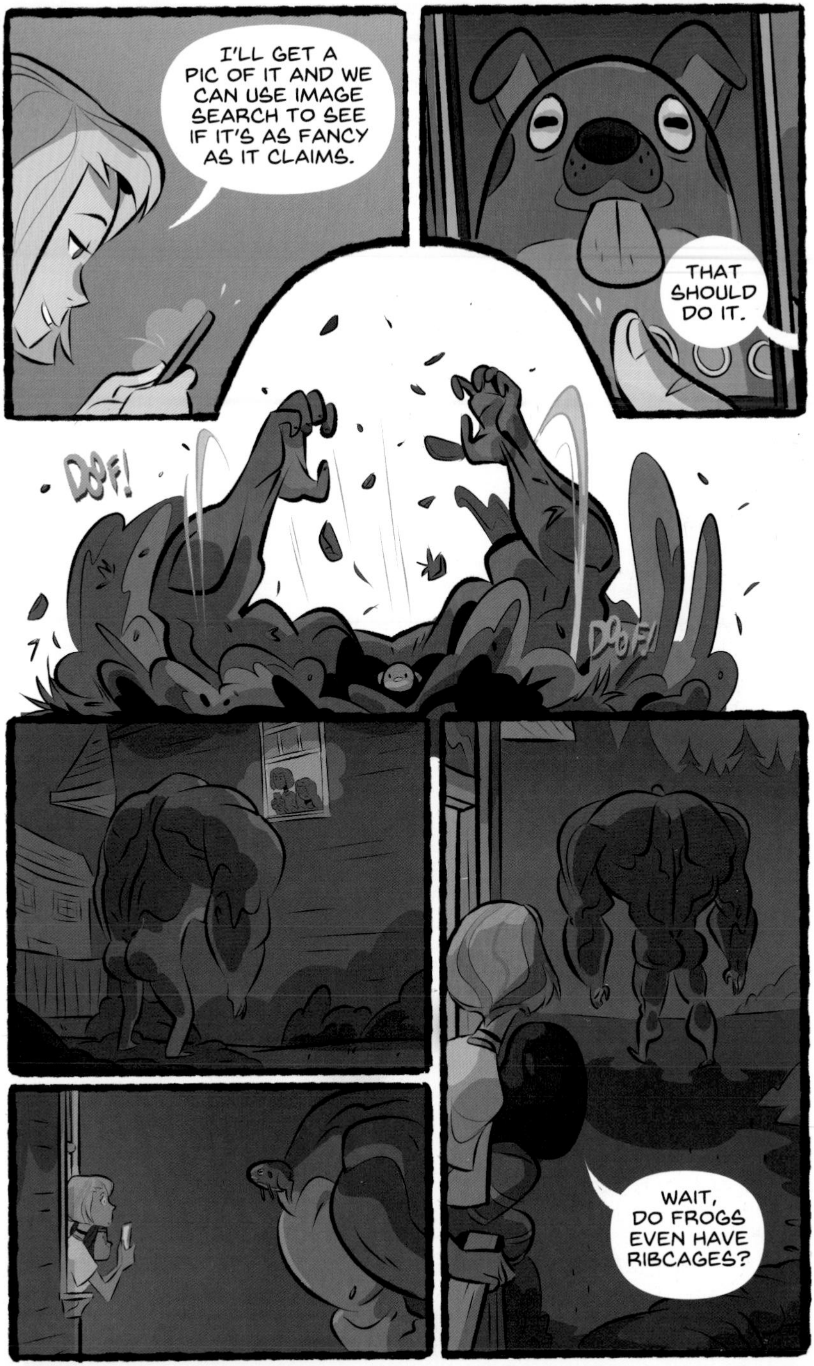
I'LL GET A PIC OF IT AND WE CAN USE IMAGE SEARCH TO SEE IF IT'S AS FANCY AS IT CLAIMS.
THAT SHOULD DO IT.
DOOF!
DOOF!
WAIT, DO FROGS EVEN HAVE RIBCAGES?

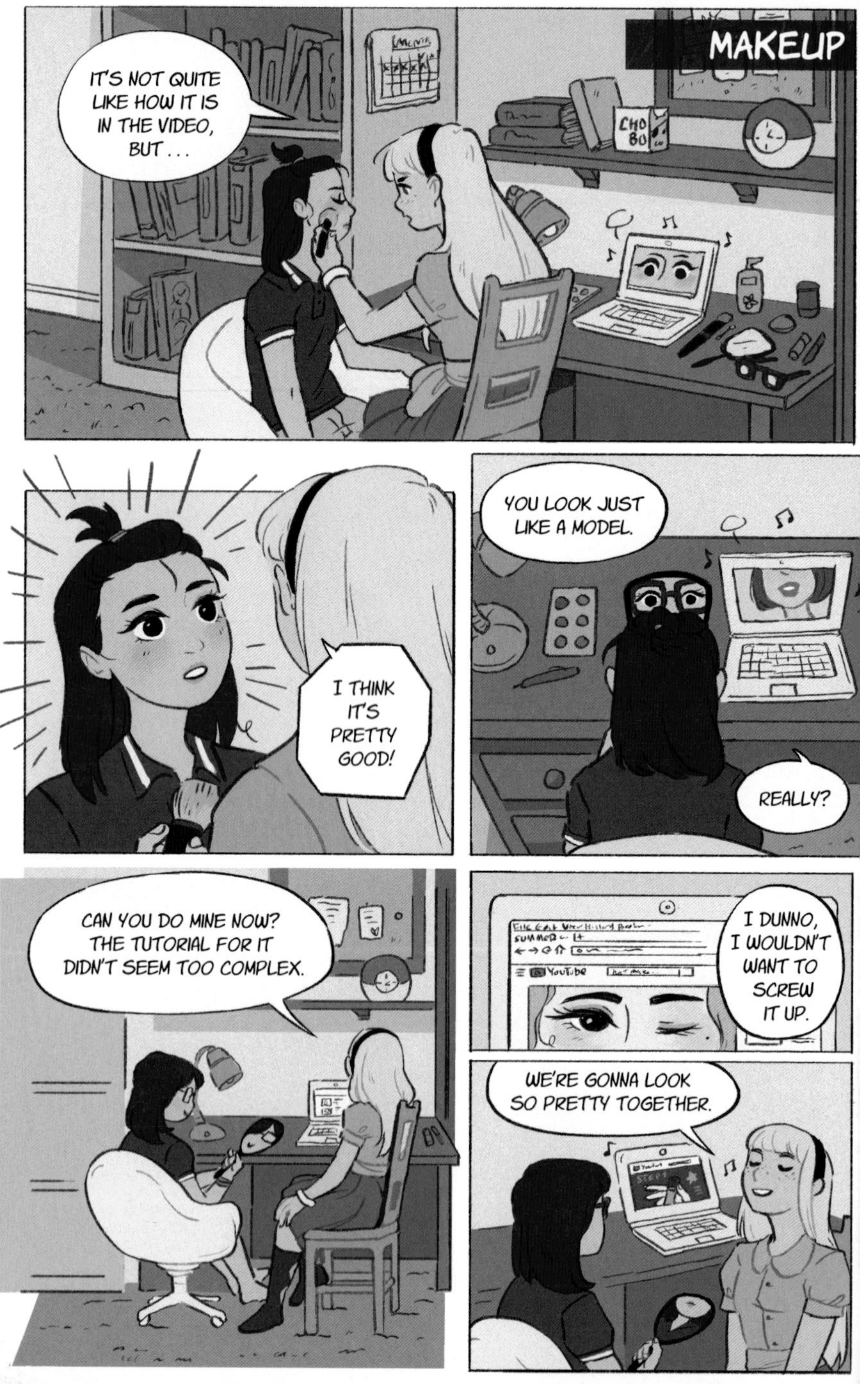
MAKEUP
IT'S NOT QUITE LIKE HOW IT IS IN THE VIDEO, BUT . . .
I THINK IT'S PRETTY GOOD!
YOU LOOK JUST LIKE A MODEL.
REALLY?
CAN YOU DO MINE NOW? THE TUTORIAL FOR IT DIDN'T SEEM TOO COMPLEX.
I DUNNO, I WOULDN'T WANT TO SCREW IT UP.
WE'RE GONNA LOOK SO PRETTY TOGETHER.

HOW IS IT?

I'M GONNA POST IT ON INSTA.

IS YOUR ACCOUNT STILL SET TO PRIVATE?

YEAH.

DON'T WORRY, NO ONE WILL SEE IT.

NEW LOOK!
Liked by cafe.cakes, judith, proudmom987, a...
keup #oot...

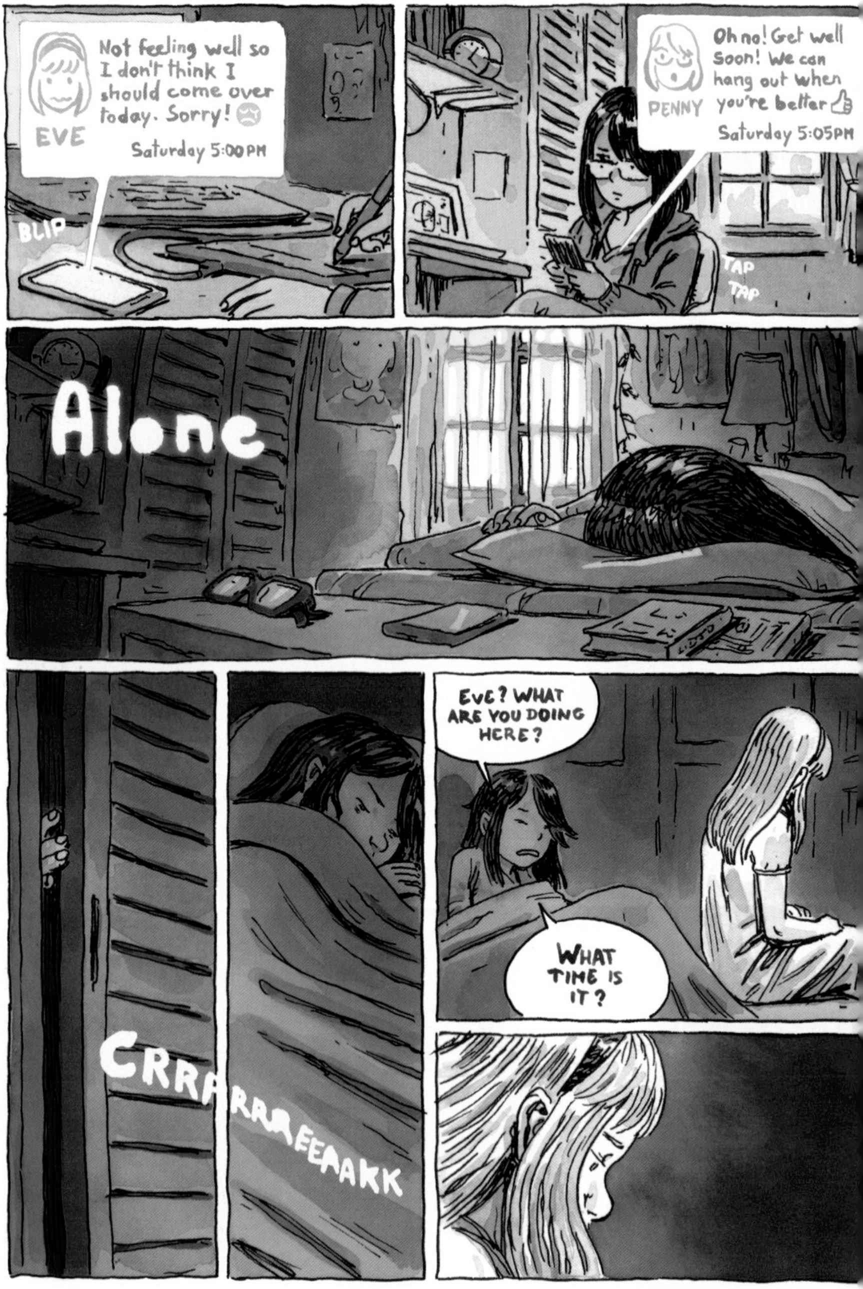
EVE
Not feeling well so I don't think I should come over today. Sorry!
Saturday 5:00PM
BLIP
PENNY
Oh no! Get well Soon! We can hang out when you're better
Saturday 5:05PM
TAP
TAP
Alone
CRRRRRRREEAAKK
EVE? WHAT ARE YOU DOING HERE?
WHAT TIME IS IT?

EVE?

FLAP

TAP
TAP

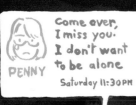

PENNY

Come over,
I miss you.
I don't want
to be alone

Saturday 11:30 PM

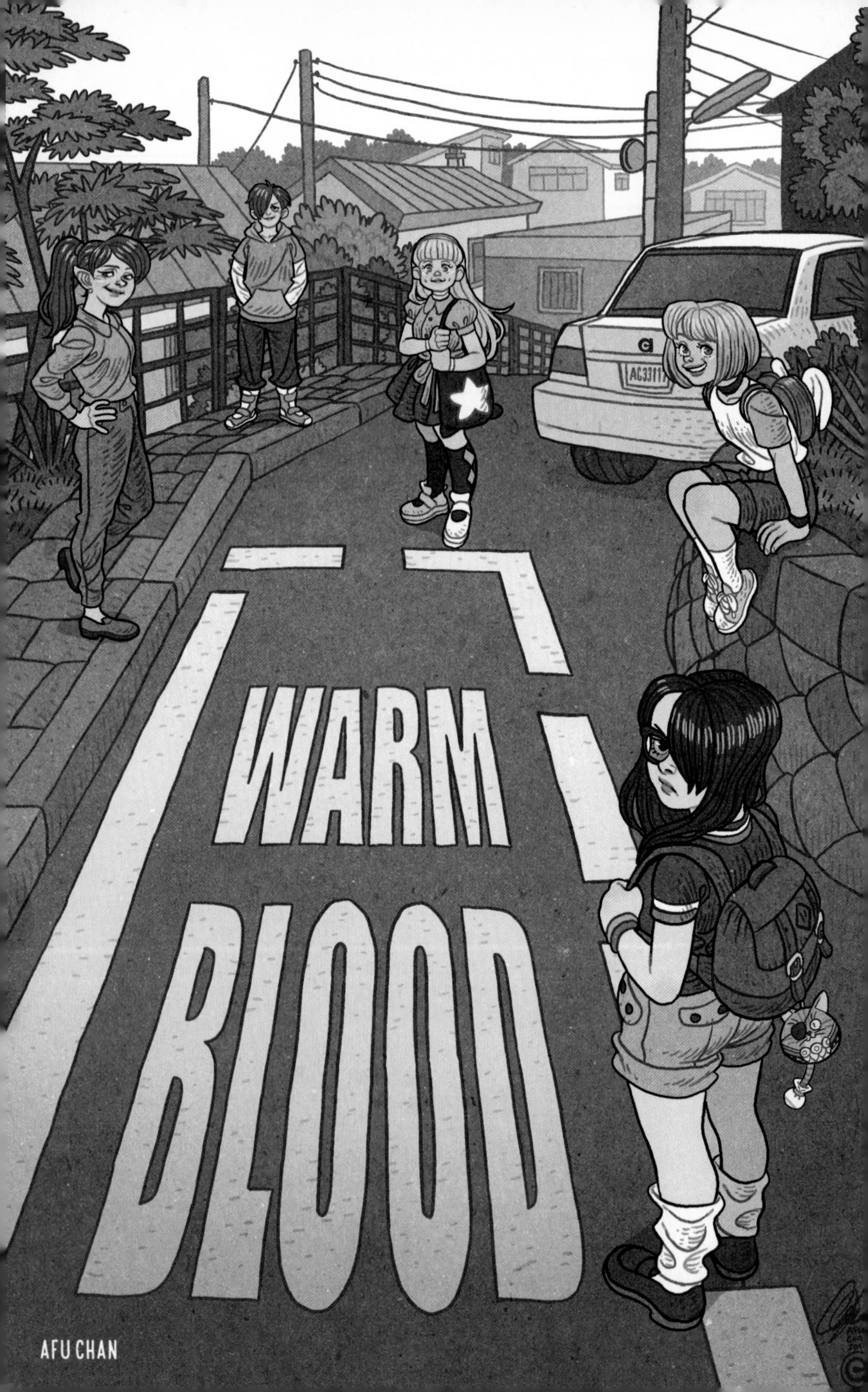
WARM
BLOOD
AFU CHAN

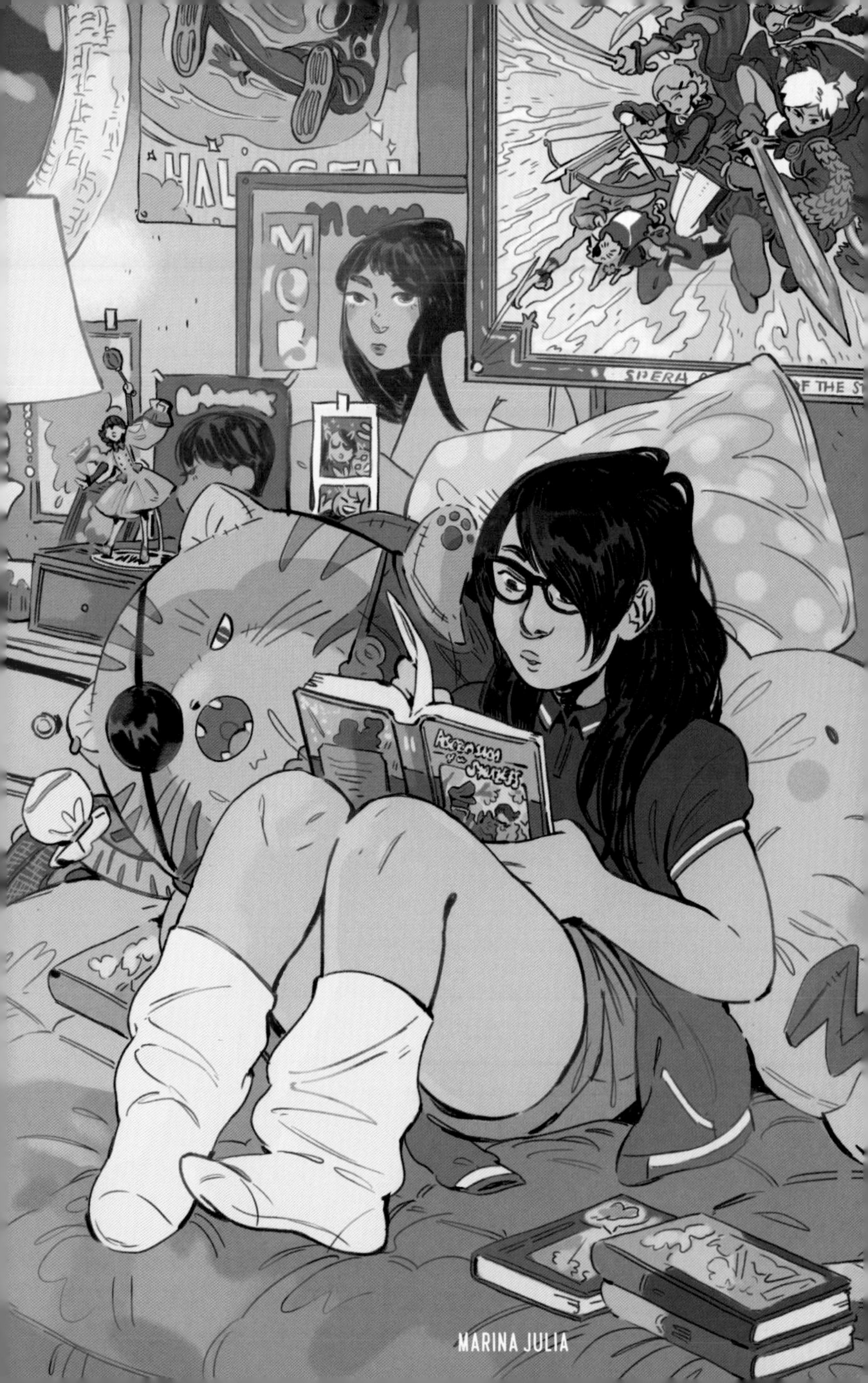
MARINA JULIA

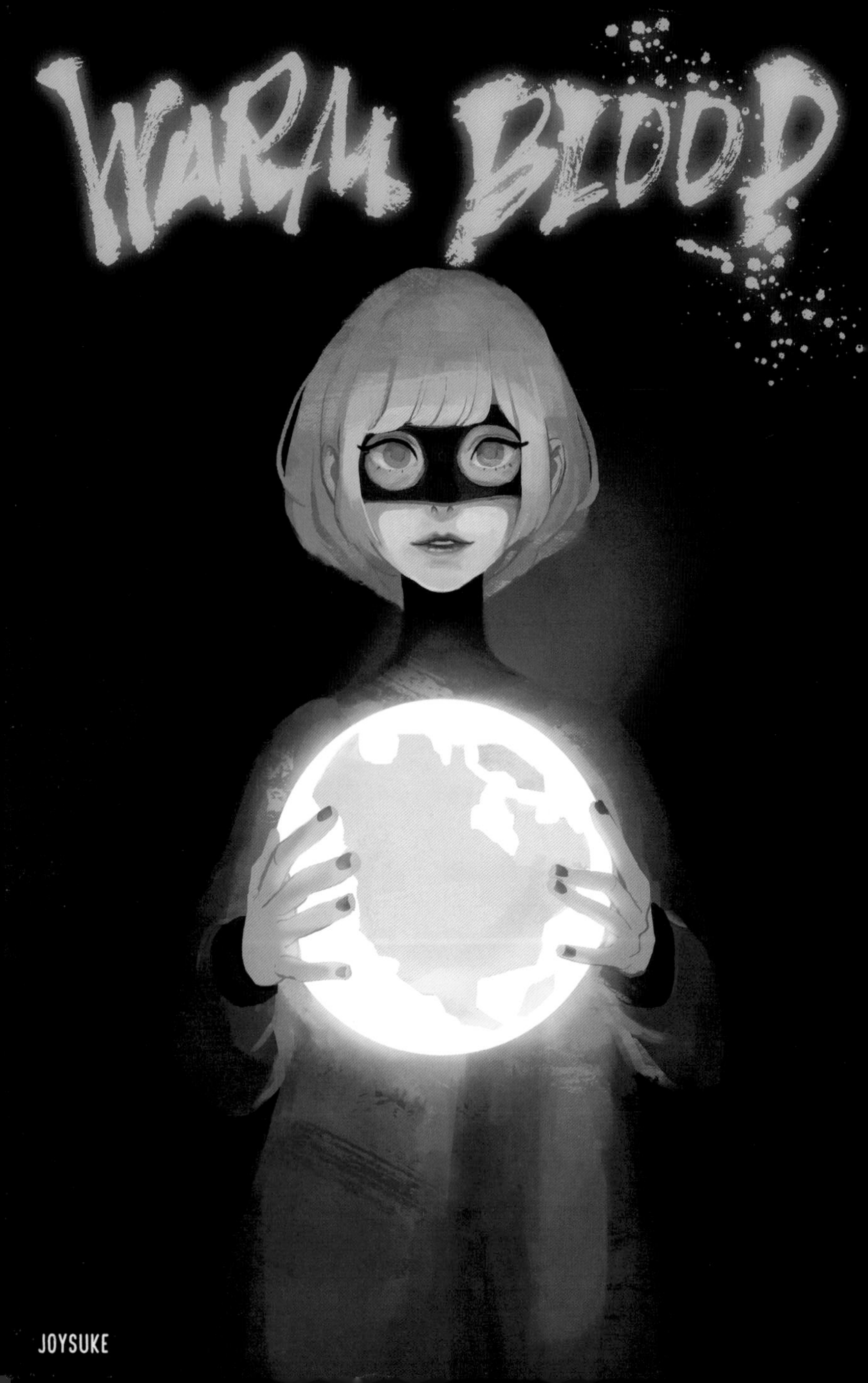
WARM BLOOD
JOYSUKE

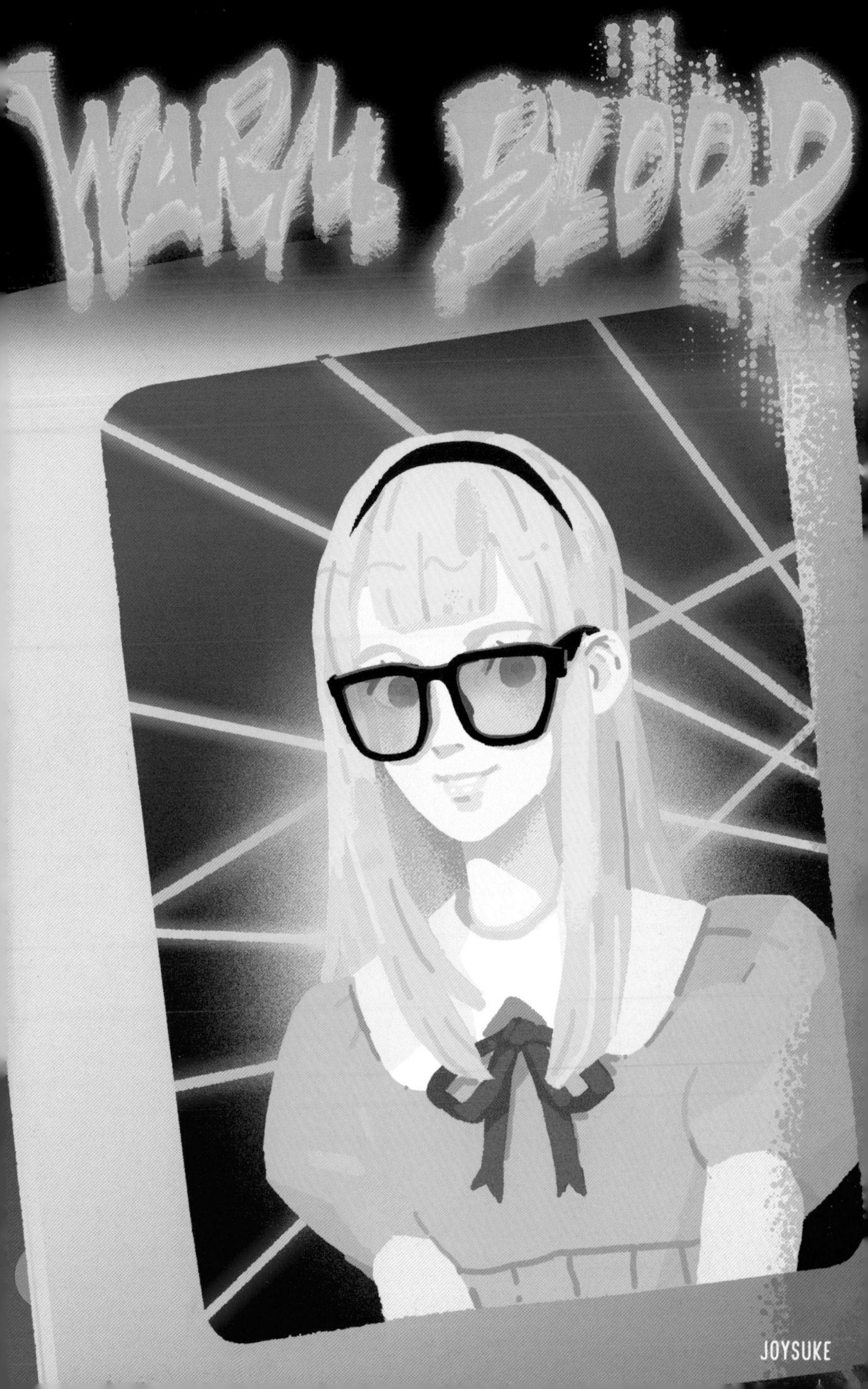
WARM BLOOD
JOYSUKE

CHARACTER GALLERY

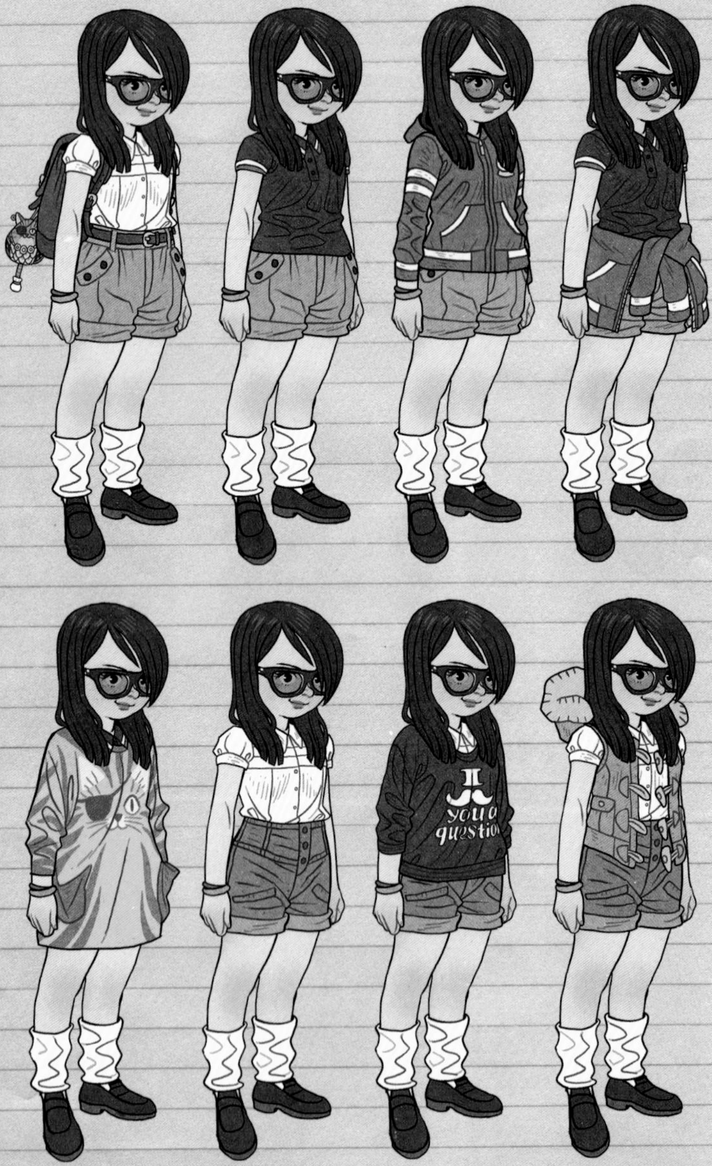

PENNY DESIGN BY AFU CHAN